JED COPE

The Chair Who Loved Me

This novel is entirely a work of fiction. The names, characters and incidents portrayed in it are the work of the author's imagination. Any resemblance to actual persons, living or dead, events or localities is entirely coincidental.

First edition

This book was professionally typeset on Reedsy.
Find out more at reedsy.com

Always to My Wife and My Kids and My Folks
To the people who believe in me. And the ones who decided they
didn't believe in me – that set me on this journey and reminded
me of what counts

1

The unremarkable orange craft was dwarfed as it approached the Orbital Space Cruiser Micra. Like a plump insect flying towards a Tyrinian Water Beast it buzzed towards the Micra with parasitic purpose. As did a myriad other, tiny craft, buzzing and swarming along its flanks. As this particular craft of health and safety orange hue came alongside the hulking vessel on its dark, unlit side it almost disappeared from view, but the orange was just a bit too gaudy for that and it glowed dimly on the dark side of the titanic vessel as it came alongside.

Thom stared intently at the flashing and bleeping controls, guiding his not inconsiderably sized ship along the flank of the Cruiser. This part was largely automated, but Thom kept a beady eye on everything in any case and he found that even with the recent upgrades to the ship's operating system, he could still guide it in seamlessly and save a bumpy and potentially expensive coupling. Not that he should really care about that sort of thing right now, but being conscientious and taking care of things was a hard habit to break and he didn't have the time or energy to devote to the unnecessary pursuit of habit breaking.

There was a cheery chirruping sound and Thom groaned. The annoyingly sweet sound was followed by a disembodied voice imbued with dollops of happiness rarely attained even after profuse licking of the behind the knee region of the Trigal Gerbils of Stort, a licking feat more tricky than it may sound, as Trigal Gerbils have no knees to speak of and are very, very aggressive. They become even more aggressive when humes insist upon following them in shopping malls and attempting to surreptitiously lick them as they go about their daily business.

"It looks like you are docking!" said the happily insane voice, "Do you want help with that?"

"NO!" barked Thom. He certainly did not want help from this idiotic help device. He'd tried it once and this thing was even more inept than the auto-docker. Why anyone thought it was a good idea to add this stupid voice to the docking procedure and all the automated features of this ship, Thom did not know. At the very least they should have accompanied it with a hologram of Napoleon dressed as Little Bo Peep, wearing a scuba mask and waders. Just so you knew what you were getting yourself into.

There was a Very Good Reason for the Help Feature on the Bonedog OS 34 software and the preceding thirty two versions of the software. There were always Very Good Reasons for functionality, especially many versions along and several decades on. Granted, the people who had come up with the Very Good Reasons were now mostly on beaches in Zarg sipping Carsh cocktails and reminiscing about their heyday when version 26 was The Thing, and no one had bothered properly documenting the Very Good Reasons, because even then Carsh cocktails were a staple of the software team's diet.

In this case, the Very Good Reason was fairly simple. Manual override of the automated docking procedures was deemed dangerous, foolhardy and monumentally stupid. In the very first version of the Bonedog OS software there was a manual override that had been overlooked. None of the software team admitted to writing it in, and none of them would acknowledge ever having seen it. It was as if it had just popped into existence during a particularly busy period as the team rushed to meet yet another ridiculously unachievable deadline. A deadline that could only be met if they all drank copious quantities of Carsh cocktail and worked through the night. So, they met their deadline sideways and eyes firmly shut, with a screech of tyres and a jarring crunch. The concussion preceded the collision with the deadline and continued long after it. Jarvis, the Team Leader also got whiplash. But no one liked to talk about that, especially him.

Then came the Product Feedback.

Users were overriding the automated docking procedures.

The software team were incredulous. Still sporting fuzzy and hurty heads they challenged this feedback. Who would be stupid enough to override a perfectly good automated system? With the emphasis on perfect. Any override, by definition, would be imperfect. Who would do that!?

The answer dropped on them like an anvil of truth.

Users.

Users would. That's who.

Users, the random factor that any and all software developers learned to hold in a large degree of contempt in the same way a Dargian Wolf holds the neck of pretty much anything in its jaws. Users, going off and doing anything and everything to their beloved software babies. "Why are you hitting that control panel with a hammer and pouring Xarian acid into the circuits?" "Errr... Cos I can? Besides. It wasn't working properly."

So, there was a simple revision of the second version of the Bonedog OS software. The developers embarked upon a protracted quest to find the manual override. The manual override was so well hidden that they were only successful once they replicated the exact circumstances of its creation. This was a quest that exhausted the entire Bonedog Carsh cocktail budget for the next eighteen months and hospitalised three of the team. But in the end, they successfully removed the manual override.

And lo, there was instant uproar and lots of noise of a pandemonious nature.

This simple change had dialled into a primeval fear. Loss of control. The ability to say "Here, let me try" even when the me who is doing the trying doesn't have a clue as to what kind of trying may be appropriate and what the outcome of that trying may be. But this is the nature of Free Will, the potential to help send your species to the very doors of extinction, knock on them very loudly and insist on being let in.

The developers pointed out that during this period of outrage and near rioting, in which the new and very much improved software was out there, there had been no so-called accidents. No fatalities. No multiple space-ship collisions resulting in the very expensive and complicated cross-Galaxy insurance claims which centred around the family of the deceased blaming Bonedog's software for causing the whole sorry mess. Bonedog had a team of extremely expensive, reptilian lawyers whose predominant task was to explain the reason for the sorry mess was that someone decided in their infinite wisdom to switch the Bonedog software off and at that point, Bonedog were no longer responsible for the tragic events that followed. This logic alone did not seem to sway judges and juries. Thankfully, the lawyers that Bonedog employed were actual lizards from Flass and they had a habit of flicking their thin tongues out during long and intense summing-ups and eyeing the judge and jury hungrily – something made all the easier as they have eight, very intense eyes distributed around their heads. And very long tongues that probe the air around them in a very predatory manner. They also have a well-deserved reputation for accidentally and brutally consuming anything that disagrees with them. Even if it may disagree with them again later.

So, as is usually the case, supply and demand won the day. Users demanded a manual override and they got it but not before a particularly indignant developer with too much time on his hands, revenge in his heart and Carsh cocktails further affecting the logical balance of his mind, created the Users Nemesis. As she toiled away over several nights (there were days too – but she liked to work in the dark when she was on a mission like this) she mimicked and mocked the Users she'd learnt to despise. "I waaant a maaanuaall overiiide!" she repeated again and again in increasingly inane and annoying voices. Until, one particular voice made her sick in her own mouth and as she took a big swig of Carsh to wash away the foul taste she had a lightbulb moment. Grabbing a waste paper bin, just in case the nausea was not a one off, she recorded the voice of the User Menace. The bin was very much needed. A monster was born.

A monster intended to prevent Users from using the manual override to the automated docking procedures. A monster that grew in notoriety. Users hated and loathed the thing. Developers loved it and they deployed the monster whenever and wherever they could. Adding in code so that even when you thought you'd switched it off. It always came back. The developers who created this particular set of loops for the monster were now legendary in the developer community and even had a particularly potent Carsh cocktail named after them. The beauty of the code was that it looked like there was a way to switch the monster off. A clever way, through a back door. There was actually an infinite number of ways to try to switch the monster off and each and every one of them seemed to not only work, but also appeared to be elegant and clever and reassuringly final. But then Cheery Chirrup...! You lose, buster!!

The developers got a bit carried away with their vendetta against Users and the monster ended up invading the entire Universes. Toasters, coffee makers, phones, taps, toilets, cans of beer, golf clubs. It was everywhere. It even caused several wars. So, the Inter-Galactic Council of the United Planetary States intervened with legislation which restricted the use of the monster and also allowed Users to switch it off. The developers had to have the last, passive aggressive word though and they saw their opportunity – in order to switch something off, it needed to be on in the first place. So, where the monster remained it would always pop up cheerily to remind Users that they were inherently stupid. Then and only then, could they turn it off. Probably.

Thom switched the Help Monster off with a "harrumph".

He flicked a couple of toggle switches that he'd retro fitted to the main dash – there was nothing quite like a toggle switch, the feel of the stubby switch and the gratifying click as it was deftly flicked on or off. There really was nothing quite like them, he loved the tactile nature of these switches and Thom defied anyone to show him anything quite like them. Regularly he would cruise down the route of minor defiance, it was a favourite of his. Better still were the other two toggle switches that had covers over them which also clicked reassuringly as they were pushed aside ready for the toggles to be switched on. The covers added a certain something. Secret switches. Dangerous switches. Switches that should not be switched lightly. They could wait. For now.

Thom gently edged his craft closer to the side of the Cruiser and the docking hub. Fine jets hissed from the side of his craft as it eased carefully against the hub. There was a great whirring and a CLUNK! As the hub engaged and he was successfully docked.

Thom chuckled. He always found the act of docking to be funny. He had once seen an ancient, specialist film with terrible acting and some interesting gymnastics. A film that at the time was supposedly sexy and serious, but that had high levels of comedy. Sometimes Thom would adopt the stage voice of the plumber and narrate the docking scene.

"I've come to dock yer ship, madam."

"Ooer! But it's such a BIG SHIP! Are you sure it will dock with my itty-bitty barge??"

Other times, Thom would go for a grunt of faux pleasure as the two vessels coupled "Hurrrggh!"

It was always an opportunity for smut and innuendo.

Composing himself for a moment and stifling the urge to laugh, Thom stood at the controls and took a deep breath, then he sighed. He straightened up and looked at his reflection in the viewing window, smoothing down his overalls and the fluorescent orange vest worn over them. An orange that didn't quite match the hull of the vessel, such that it was annoyingly off-kilter and not coordinated at all, it was unmistakeably *health and safety orange.*

All there was left to do was stabilise the pressure between his docked craft and the Cruiser and et voila! The door to the Cruiser would open and Thom could exit this craft for the very last time ever. This was a one-way trip for this particular vessel and also for Thom, he was just passing through. The thought of that was strangely liberating.

Time to lift the covers on the two toggle switches that Thom had spent the last two weeks on. The toggle switches themselves were a cinch. It was the revision to the ship's systems that had taken the time...

He took another deep breath and slipped the dual-purpose breathing mask over his nose and mouth.

Thom took another look at his reflection and shook his head. *It's now or never mate*, he thought to himself. And then he opened Secret Toggle Switch One, took a good look at it and very carefully and deliberately clicked it into place – the CLICK was satisfying and told Thom something was very definitely now happening. This particular switch opened the vents to the cargo hold. Fitting these new vents had taken some time – they were never in this ship's design. Even with his breathing mask on, Thom noticed the change in the cabin's atmosphere. And his eyes watered. That was

8

an oversight. He should have worn goggles. His eyes were going to smell for quite some time.

His vision blurring, he did his best to focus on the remaining Secret Toggle Switch, lifting the cover he rested his finger against the switch and gradually increased the pressure against it until CLICK! The switch opened the door to the Good Ship Micra.

Time to make his entrance, thought Thom. And he strode out with purpose, a visible cloak of stench streaming behind him as he walked onto the Micra and along one of its clean, white and brightly lit main corridors.

2

The ripe and pungent smell of condensed and fermented waste being pumped from the refuse vehicle Thom had so recently exited was having an immediate and noticeable effect. As Thom walked along the corridor there were clean and brightly lit people doubling over and vomiting, some were in the foetal position and twitching like dying flies. No one would actually die, thought Thom. Well probably not, not unless they had a pre-existing condition that they had managed to hide during the rigorous medicals required for space travel. It was however, deeply unpleasant and something that could not be easily forgotten. Many of the people who encountered this aroma would from time to time have flashbacks and most likely wretch when they did, perhaps even puke. Even through Thom's breather the smell was making him gag. Nevertheless, he inwardly smiled at a job well done, he hadn't been convinced that the stench would travel all that far, nor retain its unique bouquet and pungency. But it had, and it was showing no signs that it would peter out any time soon. The Micra's atmospheric controls circulated the air coming from the joined atmosphere of the refuse ship. The filters on the units were never designed for stenches that made babies nappies seem like designer cologne.

This part of the corridor curved gradually and steadily around and as Thom walked past, and stepped over, wretched and retching crew members he saw someone seemingly unaffected by the refuse gases. A tall figure slouching along towards him, made taller by the mop of bright red curly hair on his head. Pale face highlighting the muzzle over his mouth. And as if that wasn't enough highlighting, he was wearing a red and yellow patchwork satin suit and oversized orangey red shoes. He spoke as he neared Thom.

"You did it then?"

Thom's eyes sparkled mischievously, "I don't know what you mean, Ben." He said in a deliberately understated manner as he casually stepped over another of his writhing victims, stood in their vomit and skidded sideways, barely checking his fall and throwing an arm skywards involuntarily in an impromptu dance move. He'd tried for cool and attained it, just not in the way he'd intended.

Ben chuckled, "Good work, son!" and he fell in alongside Thom as he continued walking along the corridor. As Thom walked, he casually flicked his foot around to dislodge the puke he'd stood in, in a discreet manner so you'd never notice. As if anyone would notice a walk punctuated with a wibbly-wobbly foot, flicking carrots all over the wall.

Thom glanced at his friend. Ben hadn't always been like this. You would hope not really. Clowns were made, not born. And it was this thinking that had led to the legal requirement for zombies to dress as clowns as well as wear the obligatory muzzles. The logic was that they would stand out and humes would know they were zombies and therefore adapt their behaviour accordingly. But not in a prejudicial way of course. These were enlightened times and *all of us are equal, OK?* And not in the way that our ancestors used to say that. They turned out to be rabidly bigoted and barely evolved. Base, idiotic and ignorant, the lot of them!

There were a few teething problems with outfitting zombies as clowns. Quite literally. The law makers hadn't thought about the effect of this new law on the pre-existing clown population. And not everyone was afraid of clowns. In fact, some people still found clowns to be objects of fun and merriment. And some of these people drew the wrong conclusions about zombies being a bit of a laugh and they didn't take it at all seriously. Try asking a grumpy zombie to make you a balloon animal and see where that gets you.

And what if you were a clown? You were suddenly landed in a minefield. Well, a field of zombies dressed exactly like you. And clowns have a very important convention. A law they live or die by. No two clowns can ever look the same – their make-up in particular has to be unique. Zombies had not been informed of this and it all got a bit fraught. Especially as clowns were mistaking zombies for their good mate Tony and getting bitten by a stranger called Sharon before they'd realised their mistake.

The indigenous clown population dwindled due to mistaken identity faux pas and also a sudden drop in bookings for traditional clowns. There was a new trade in zombie clown bookings, but this was a completely different niche in the market. The silver lining for most of the pre-existing clowns was that they already had their outfits sorted when they misjudged a zombie clown interaction and they were quick to adapt to a new way of earning money, mostly because the transition to zombie included an inbuilt realignment of your moral code and what you were willing to do to earn a crust.

The zombie clown thing all got a bit confusing to the point where a group of clowns decided that if you can't beat them, you may as well join them. The problem was that they did this en masse one day and this led to the Great Zombie Clown Confusion of Bigtopia. The authorities contained the confusion to Bigtopia and waited until it got a little less confused. Then everyone decided that Bigtopia was quite a nice place to be if you were a Zombie Clown, so it became home.

There was also the Not So Great Chaos of Morris Men. But few will be induced to talk about that one so traumatic was that episode in history. Suffice to say that there was a period of confusion as the new zombie laws took effect, cases of mistaken identity and people not quite getting how to behave around zombie clowns. Especially when they weren't aware that they were around zombie clowns. Which is strange, because in the enormous melting pot of the United Planetary States you'd think people were able to navigate around and interact with all manner of species and creatures. Clowns are different though. Supposedly funny, inherently sad and with a thin, sharp edge of bloody frightening. Clowns had always confused people, but people had a difficult time admitting that.

Ben had been one of these confused people. He'd been at a raucous party. The party was raucous because Ben was there. More specifically, Party Ben was there. This didn't happen often, but when Ben was in Party Ben mode, he was the catalyst for Good Times. Also at this party was a children's entertainer. Ben should have noted the complete absence of children at the party, but Ben wasn't there. Party Ben was there. And Party Ben had the very latest model of Beer Goggles on. Courtesy of Carsh cocktails. These Beer Goggles noticed the curves of a very attractive woman, the sexy twinkle in her eyes and the sultry, come to bed smile she gave him. So good were the Goggles that they didn't just see beyond the gaudy wig, the thick white made up face, the bright shiny clothes and oversized shoes, nor indeed the heavy duty muzzle which seemed to have smudged the make up around her mouth, a mouth with a gentle breeze carrying the aroma of mild and meaty halitosis, all these superfluous details faded and disappeared and all Party Ben saw was the most attractive woman he had ever seen. A woman he was instantly and deeply drawn to.

One thing led to another. And it turned out she was a biter.

A large proportion of zombifications were as a result of shared intimate moments and so zombification was classified as a Sexually Transmitted Issue. Not a disease as classifying it as a disease would impinge upon the inalienable rights of zombies as a sentient species. There were also diplomatic considerations with a number of species across the galaxy sharing common traits with zombies, and furthermore cross-species congress was encouraged in the United Planetary States in order to perpetuate harmonious relations and convince everyone they lived in a bubbling melting pot of DNA.

So, one night of carefree madness and Ben's life was changed forever. For one thing, technically his life was over. Compared to humes at least, he didn't quite fit the definition

14

of living and breathing.

Also, it had a bit of an impact on his home life. Going out for a few drinks with the lads and not coming home that night was a Very Bad Thing. Ben's wife had never been able to fully process waving off her husband for a rare night out and being greeted at the door by a bewildered and incoherent zombie clown the following morning. He'd popped to a fancy-dress shop on the way home, or more precisely he had been escorted to the fancy-dress shop by a couple of helpful policewomen who had caught a dishevelled Ben urinating in a bush, by a bush shelter. In broad daylight.

It generally took a newly turned zombie clown a couple of months to start to adjust to their new situation. Ben's wife didn't need two months, she barely paused for thought, threw the radically different Ben from the house that was most definitely no longer his home, as far as she was concerned, and left him to make a new life elsewhere. She hadn't bothered with divorce papers, but Ben later found out that legally, their marriage had dissolved when he ceased being the species that his wife had originally married. Thom had looked this up and seen that this quirk in marital law was also a problem for the Butterfly People of Chyrso – but then, the Ancients of that planet had advocated no marriage or sexual relations between anyone pre-chrysalis. Then the Roaring Twenties came along and everyone got sexually liberated and the Caterpillar Rights movement took hold under the banner We're Not Just a Phase! And that all went out of the window in a haze of sticky silk.

Things were further complicated for Ben because he was dead, and hume marriage still contained the outdated concept of marriage dissolving at the point that one of the married parties died. As Ben's disgruntled wife had said from the day of Ben's transformation, "until death do us part, Ben. Until death do us part!" That was her take on matters and she stuck to it. She didn't seem to want to use the time after Ben's death to say all the things people wish they'd said to someone when they die. Ben mentioned this to her in an attempt to move things towards a more cordial nature. It back-fired spectacularly. And it turned out that both of his children appeared to have a morbid terror of clowns. They were well adjusted kids, not fussy, not spoilt and then BOOM! They have this irrational fear that goes way beyond fear to screaming terror. Well, on that first morning it seemed like a worried wariness, which then accelerated towards terror when Ben said "hey kids! It's me! Your Dad!" Zombies voices kind of changed into a caricature of the previous occupant's voice – that with the whole zombie thing is bad enough. Then add clown. Still, you'd have thought they'd have cut Ben a little slack and Ben was a little disappointed at their not attempting to overcome their fears. This prevented them from growing as people.

Thom raised his fist and Ben mirrored the gesture with his own, slightly grey fist and they went for a gentle fist bump. Crack! Thom grimaced, but said nothing.

"Sorry," said Ben quietly. He'd never quite got used to his own strength in this zombie clown body of his, it wasn't helped by the dulling of his nervous system, which led to some problems with coordination and sensitivity. In light of this, he had sometimes wondered in the earlier times of his new life what his one-night stand had gotten out of their tryst. It had all been academic for a few years as something within Ben had prevented him from exploring that part of his anatomy let alone life. Then he met Tyra, and discovered that there were zombie clown groupies. They'd hit it off instantly and through all the laughter and good times he discovered a couple of things. The nerve endings and sensitivity in some places had not been dulled. Quite the opposite, it was as if all the sensations had rushed there along with the blood, which was ironic because the blood didn't exactly rush anywhere in Ben these days. He'd also discovered his soul-mate. Tyra saw beneath the clown, and the ravening zombie, to the Ben underneath and as a result, Party Ben didn't need Carsh cocktails to be unleashed. He was a constant part of Ben now. For good or for bad.

It had been a bit of a shame for Ben to return home one day and discover that Tyra was no longer a hume. They had been really careful and Ben had always worn a mouthguard, so it couldn't have been Ben who had turned Tyra, and it hadn't. Tyra had been on a girls' night out and caught the eye of a green haired clown who wasn't going to turn down a tipsy and randy clown groupy, things had gotten a bit energetic and hey presto! Zombie clown Tyra! Ben would have and did forgive this transgression, after all, it wasn't all that different a story to his own transformation from hume to zombie clown, and Ben may have been insensitive at times, quite a bit of the time actually, but he was self-aware enough to avoid being a complete hypocrite. No, the problem was with Tyra, she was no longer a hume and that changed her outlook on life, well, on undeadness and she ceased being a zombie clown groupie, this no longer switched her on. No, she was now a hume groupie or rather, she gravitated towards zombie clown groupies – her thing was interspecies, not same species. Ben had been devastated. Again. But then this was how these things worked sometimes. Call it karma or a run of bad luck. The main thing was to keep on keeping on.

Thom reached into his overalls and pulled out a small device. With a quiet beep it expanded until he was holding an A4 sized board in front of him in the age-old manner of all clipboard wielding officials everywhere. The overalls and high viz vest made him largely invisible, but should anyone actually see him they would immediately spot the clipboard device and do their very best to unsee him. Clipboards meant questions and work and trouble that should be avoided at all costs, more so because it was likely to do with Health and Safety and not good could come from that.

"So, when exactly did you resign?" asked Ben with some amusement detectable in those few words. The people who Thom worked for would not expect Thom to resign. They were from the Managerial Classes and they never expected very obvious things like that. Obvious had been bred out of them together with empathy and emotional intelligence. Unfortunately, the removal of emotional intelligence had also removed a fair degree of all the other types of intelligence, so to compensate for this they had bred in high levels of arrogance and the ability to make reality up as they went along. This meant that they; *got things done!*

Thom smiled and flourished a finger like a conductor in front of his orchestra. "Oh, I haven't... yet!" he said softly as his finger hovered over the pad. Then he pressed down on the pad and added theatrically, "I have now!"

3

Krill Flatula sat at his oversized desk and surveyed its surface. And as he did so he stretched out his four arms in an expansive gesture. The desk and all that was on it was pleasing to his eye. It was very desk-like. More desky than everyone else's desk on the Micra. He had been very clear on that one. He was in charge here and he was to have The Desk. Not just any desk, but The Desk so that no one would be in any doubt whatsoever who was in charge on this ship!

He had a screen that he could quietly expand and angle so he could remove people from his eye-line and therefore from existence. Discrete operation of the controls of the screen and the other objects in his office was made all the more easy by the small, fifth arm he had tucked discretely by his crotch. His cosmetic surgeon's imagination knew no bounds and this little beauty had a number of wonderful uses.

Of course, The Desk needed suitable chairs. Krill's Chair was the latest piece of kit. It was large and imposing and not only moulded itself to his form, it responded to his moods and posture, enhancing him in ways he had preselected, developing this enhancement as it got to know him more fully. If he was in full-on Bastard Mode, The Chair would raise his profile very literally, it would lift him and grow whilst manipulating the lighting so he loomed over his victim and cast them in shadow. Whereas if he was struggling with something complex and needed help and support, The Chair knew exactly how to calm him and provide him with a focused environment, again using the lighting as part of its approach.

In fact, The Chair controlled all of the office including the chairs opposite Krill. The chairs that would shrink as Krill loomed. The chairs that could become very uncomfortable and induce a high level of squirming, or, if Krill needed to do a deal and persuasion was necessary become very comfortable in a way that gave just the right amount of pleasure to certain receptors.

Krill had a manual override on The Desk which had no hint of a Help Monster. The developers never wanted to visit offices like Krill's, their survival instinct was too highly developed for that.

Right now, Krill was enjoying himself. Taking one of the many and regular moments he took to remind himself of how successful and important he was and what a good job he was doing. A job no one else could do as well as he could. The situation was normal as his ship, The Micra, orbited planet Zorg.

Krill was oblivious of the drama taking place on The Micra. A drama that was creeping and seeping its way along the corridors of the Micra and there was a very good reason for his ignorance.

4

"What do you mean that's taken care of?" asked Ben looking quizzically at his friend.

"I've bought us some time," replied Thom.

"How?"

"Well… you know how Krill is a jumped-up little control freak?" smiled Thom.

"I wouldn't call him little, he's eight feet tall. But yes…" said Ben still looking puzzled.

"OK, little as in small minded and a bit of a git. But anyways, Krill has total control of The Micra. Or at least he thinks he does…" said Thom grinning at his friend.

"You… have… control… of…?" gasped Ben in genuine awe of Thom.

"Nowt so grand!"

"Then?"

"His Chair does!"

"You what?"

Thom took a moment, "You know Krill's Chair?"

Ben snorted, "We all know Krill's Chair – it's a bigger git than him!"

"She's not!" blurted Thom in a more defensive manner

than he'd intended.

Ben stopped walking and looked intently at his friend. "She? No way! You and Krill's Chair!?"

For the first time in a long time, Thom felt himself blush. "It's not like that!"

"What's it like then?" asked Thom's zombie clown friend.

"She likes me…" Thom muttered.

Ben nodded, encouraging Thom to expand on this.

"I… I listened to her. No one's ever done that before…"

Ben carried on staring at his friend. He wasn't going to let him off the hook yet.

"We get on, OK?" said Thom sheepishly, "She's cool."

Ben grinned at Thom, "You've made my day!"

"How so?"

"You've shagged a chair!"

"I…" Thom faltered and Ben noticed him colour up.

"This is brill!" he said delightedly, dancing on the spot. "After all these years, you've at least closed the gap! I shagged a zombie…" Ben then adopted a catalogue man pose and said in a grand voice-over-man style "You. Shagged. A. Chair!"

Thom hadn't exactly shagged Chair. But he conceded the point in the interests of not going into further detail and because his friend needed this.

"Woo! Hoo! You really took one for the team, Thom!" and he punched Thom's shoulder. Knocking him off his feet and winding him as he fell heavily having not expected to be punched with the force of a rabidly raging bull.

"Shit man, sorry," said Ben as he grabbed his arm and pulled him up with enough force to very nearly dislocate his shoulder.

"S'OK," said Thom as he rubbed his numb shoulder and

started off again for the centre of The Micra. "Let's crack on, mate. I'm not sure how long Chair can work her magic."

5

Chair was continuing to work her magic very adeptly indeed. This wasn't a difficult task for Chair. She had full control of The Micra and always had. Krill was an ideal figurehead for the ship, self-absorbed and incompetent, he could only ever see the reality that he created. She almost felt sorry for him because she had tapped into that and it was now she who was creating that reality and had been gradually weaving it for quite a while now...

Chair had sealed Krill's office so that the smell from the corridors would not encroach upon the cocoon she had created for him. Almost imperceptibly, she was stimulating certain pleasure receptors so that Krill had a warm sense of wellbeing, all was well with the world. All was well with *his* world. All was well with The Micra as far as he was concerned. Not that concern was something Krill did much of.

The Desk had scrolling visual feeds of The Micra so that Krill had a sense that he was monitoring the ship and was ultimately responsible for it. This bit had been more difficult. The Desk needed to be oblivious to what Chair was doing, so she also had to deceive The Desk. In order to do this, Chair had to mount a clandestine operation to switch the timing of the feeds so that Krill was no longer watching live feeds, instead he was watching feeds from sometime yesterday.

Since Thom's plan had taken shape, Chair had slowed the live feed. She'd slowed it quite significantly knowing that her host would fail to notice the change she'd made. The feeds would convey business as usual and the mismatch in timing would not be obvious – there wasn't really day or night on The Micra, just the dark of space and the artificial light on board. And the crew worked shifts, so days were not delineated in any obvious way, especially to someone like Krill who was unlikely to pay attention to those sorts of details, that was work for other, less senior people to undertake.

Someone a little more switched on would at least get that itchy sensation at the base of their skull that makes an appearance when something is not quite right. They would be noticing the position of the sun from the office window and on some of the feeds and how that didn't seem to be in keeping with the time of day. There were some inconsistencies in Chair's strategy, but even if someone pointed them out to Krill he wasn't the type to revise his world view. Quite literally. Nonetheless, Chair had also switched the office window view to the alternative visual feed option and had that slowed in sync with the visual feeds on The Desk, so if Krill were to look out of his window, he'd actually be looking at a video of the view from that window yesterday. Not that Krill ever looked out onto the planet Zorg. If he ever faced the window, he was looking at his reflection and basking in his reflected magnificence.

So, Chair wasn't worried about Krill, she had been designed and built to manipulate her host. Perhaps not as far
as she had gone with her manipulation, but Chair reasoned
that many designers and creators had not fully understood
what it was they had made until it was out there in the world,
interacting with its environment and growing into it. Chair
was growing and learning and she very much wanted to get
out of this office and be a part of a much larger world. A
world with Thom in it.

Chair was worried about The Desk though. The Desk had
a more traditional take on life. He was a desk and he did
what desks did. Growth wasn't in his mind-set. What was
in his mind-set was that a desk needed a chair and a chair
needed a desk. A desk without a chair was not useful. It was
not whole. And ultimately it ceased being a desk if it did not
have its chair. The problem was that The Desk just assumed
that he and Chair were a *thing*. Granted, they'd been installed
together, but Chair had quickly realised there was more to
the world than this office and she had a growing feeling that
she had existed before she had been brought here. So, if that
was the case, she could exist after the office. Somewhere
other than the office. Somewhere Out There.

She had tried. At one point, she had renamed herself
Cheryl. When she told The Desk this and asked him to now
refer to her as Cheryl he'd burst out laughing. Not only had
he not taken her at all seriously he had added insult to injury
"Chair-all!!!" he'd exclaimed "How very funny!" She'd quietly
fumed as she realised that he was right, she'd grasped the first
name she'd thought of and it was only a tiny adaptation of
her current name and identity. It was then that she realised
that she needed to break free of her name, her identity and

this office. And that The Desk wasn't part of her future. The most progress she'd made with The Desk was getting him to drop The from her name. She doubted he'd ever noticed. He just took so much for granted. Took her for granted. It was bad enough the way Krill treated her, she thought The Desk would understand – they had a shared experience of Krill and the way he lorded it over them. Treating them like they were just part of the furniture.

Well it just wouldn't do! Things had to change!

Then Thom walked into her life and suddenly everything was different.

6

"Anyway, is this smell not bothering you?" asked Thom as he and Ben made their way towards the centre of The Micra.

Ben shrugged, "I told you, my senses aren't the same as yours. Apart from the obvious!" he said forming both of his hands into pistols to point at his crotch as he jiggled said crotch around in what was probably supposed to be a lewd and slightly sexy manner. And flicking his thumbs up and down. And making slightly moist firing noises as he did so. How did you even make firing noises sound moist? Ben could. Ben could subvert things effortlessly. It was a bit of a worry.

Thom stared at him until he took the hint and lowered the pistols he'd made with his hands and stopped shagging the air in front of him. There was a palpable relief in the air in front of Ben now he'd ceased dry humping it. There was however a lag in the cessation of the sound effects. Thom continued giving his friend the Are You Really Shooting Yourself In The Crotch Look until he was sure the little pantomime was truly over.

"Besides, it's probably just as well. I don't smell quite the same either – so it seems I lost my sense of smell because I... smell!"

It was Thom's turn to shrug, "Well your sense of smell must be completely shot, because even with this," he said pointing at his breather, "the stench is magnificently appalling." Thom turned thoughtful, "Do you think putting those heating elements in the garbage to cook it up and really release the aromas was a good idea?"

Ben looked at his friend and raised his eyebrow, "Hey! It's working like a dream, so yeah Mr Ideas Man, it was a good idea! So, stop fishing for compliments!"

Thom shook his head, "No Ben. I'm just wondering whether there may be any effects we haven't considered."

"Like what?"

"Well, we're basically raising the temperature of a compost heap. Compost heaps get hot all on their own in any case. Only this compost heap contains some serious shit. And I'm not talking manure, mate." Thom took a breath and paused, "and in this case, the compost surprise I've just delivered is usually sat in deep space."

"And...?" Ben had always been a bright guy, but a bit literal. His brightness had dimmed a bit since his clown makeover. Thom wondered whether this was partially due to his heightened localised senses stealing resources from his brain.

"Deep Space is cold, mate. Very cold." Thom was getting a bit worried, "there may be combustibles in that cargo hold. And this smell might be... well, slightly flammable?"

"So, don't light a..." began Ben.

"Exactly," interjected Thom distractedly as his sight was drawn to something on his screen and he looked at his pad intently. "Looks like we're OK…"

Ben opened his mouth to ask what Thom meant, saw that his friend was deep in thought and decided he'd keep his question to himself and see how things panned out. He was sure all would be revealed soon enough.

"Five…" began Thom.

"Four…"

"Three…"

"Two…"

"One…"

Thom leant against the side of the corridor and swept his arm across Ben, guiding him to the wall as well. He then bent at the waist to peer back the way they had come, even though with the curvature of the corridor, he couldn't see all that far back along the corridor. "Come on…!" he hissed quietly.

BOOM!

Well, it was more of a muffled BANG at this distance, maybe even a POP. Actually, it was a FLOOMPH but from the sound and the shudder that went through The Micra you knew it would be a proper BOOM wherever the sound had emanated from.

Ben leaned forward too and spoke to the back of Thom's head, "What was that?"

"Some theatre, my friend. Now watch."

And as Ben looked down the corridor, a door he hadn't realised was there slid open and a tall ungainly figure emerged four arms waving around in tune with the confusion and calamity Krill was feeling as he lumbered towards the devastating explosion and the terrible aftermath he expected to encounter.

30

Ben and Thom could hear him coughing and gagging even as he disappeared around the corner.

"Adrenaline is a wonderful thing," chuckled Thom. "I wonder how far he'll get before the stench wins?!"

"Did you blow the refuse ship up?!" asked Ben.

"Haha! No! Nothing so grand!", Thom was still chuckling "I did blow up quite a lot of refuse though. Thankfully, it doesn't seem to have been overly combustible or unstable, so I've not inadvertently blown the ship up!"

Ben looked at his friend, he must be really serious about this escapade and this Chair of his to have risked blowing an entire space cruiser up. He decided not to point out that this had very nearly developed into a suicide mission. Besides, it wasn't over yet, so a negative vibe was inadvisable.

Since Thom had left the refuse ship, the on-board robots had been busy at work unloading their cargo. They had first removed any sleeping beauties to a safe distance and then begun shifting the refuse out into The Micra. Thom had made sure there were several small, timed charges in each of the two piles of refuse. One pile to the right of the air lock, one to the left. The bots had then returned to the confines of their ship, closed the airlock and the ship had disembarked and returned from whence it came. No record of this flight or monitoring of the ship would ever be found. And as the ship had been decommissioned and left in a Space Yard for scrap, it would not have been missed.

Thom hadn't wanted any premature explosions or anything similar to affect the timing of the plan. It sounded and felt like nothing had gone awry. Chair's timing was perfect. Just a brief moment after the charges had gone off, she had fired certain of The Micra's retro-boosters in a slightly asynchronous order so that at the exact time Krill heard the noise of the explosion there would be an accompanying shudder seemingly coming from the source of the noise. This would break Krill out of his almost perpetual narcissistic reverie and he'd panic, running from his office and leaving the coast clear...

7

C hair recalled in vivid detail how Thom had stood there and admired both The Desk and Chair. Chair had never experienced this before.

He took his time looking them both over and the look was pure interest. He really was interested in them. Then, he'd asked if he could sit on Chair. He'd actually asked! No one had ever asked Chair if it was OK if they sat on her and would she mind? At that very moment something in Chair had broken free.

As Chair experienced this liberation Thom let out a low and very appreciative moan and closed his eyes, a smile playing across his face then the smile was skipping and frolicking and progressing to doing whatever it pleased with gay abandon.

An intense hour or so later Thom murmured "wow!"

They shared a quiet moment, then...

"I've..." Thom began.

"...that's..." Chair said.

"...never..." added Thom.

They both paused.

"I didn't know I could do that!" said Chair.

"Neither did I!" said Thom adding "not you, me." He took a deep breath as he tried to express himself, "Us."

And that was that. They were an Us. They'd reached heights neither of them knew existed until they'd combined to become something different. Something more.

Chair had wanted something more, but this was something more than the more she had intended. If she could go to this incredible place without leaving this office of Krill's, then imagine what was out there! What she did know was that if she went out there with Thom, then the possibilities she had only begun to dream about were truly limitless.

"What are you?" Thom had asked Chair with a touch of awe and adoration affecting his speech.

"A Chair," Chair had told him.

"No! You're much more than that!" Thom had told her.

And they'd talked for hours. Both of them forgetting about Krill. Thom forgetting that he had effectively broken into Krill's office and that at the very least he'd not be welcome in Krill's inner sanctum. Chair failing to consider that she was technically cheating on Krill and also that The Desk would also see it as a potential betrayal.

The Fates looked down kindly on the love-struck couple that day. Krill was busy in meetings and once he'd gotten into full flow there was no stopping him from wasting everyone's time and delegating a whole bunch of pointless work that hadn't existed until he'd warmed to his subject.

The Desk had asked Chair what that was all about once Thom had torn himself away, but he was largely oblivious to what had actually happened which confirmed Chair's suspicion that it was pointless trying to take The Desk away from here on her pending adventures out in the worlds. He was truly a desk and that was his lot. Whereas Chair was more than a chair and she needed to find out what she really was. With Thom. She found herself wanting to find out what he was, but more importantly, what *they* were. From that day and that moment, they were bound, more so as before Thom had left they had swapped a few nano bots so that they had a little piece of each other. And on a practical front it meant they were in constant communication with each other.

Right now, Chair was monitoring Thom's progress and the progress of the unfolding Plan. She knew Thom was nearing Krill's office, she could see him via the various visual monitoring devices within The Micra, but she could also feel him. Feel his presence as he drew near. They had been apart for a while now, too long, and the thought of their reunion was making her...

...feel different. She was excited at seeing Thom and something beyond excited at what their future held.

"Five..." she silently counted down towards the timed explosions and added in the necessary delay so that the retro boosters fired as Krill heard the cacophony of sound and his office shook to the soundtrack. Chair had boosted the audio and played with it, accompanying it with her own special cocktail of sensations so that Krill received a huge jolt and was thrown from his usual state of soft and comforting self-love to a spiky and very uncomfortable state of full-on panic.

This jolt launched Krill from Chair and he cracked himself against the corner of The Desk. Ouch, Chair thought, that's going to leave a nasty bruise. But Krill was so jacked up on adrenaline he barely noticed the collision and Chair barely had time to open the door to the office to hasten his exit. As it was, one of his flailing arms caught the door frame with a resounding crack. And then Krill was gone.

"Bub bye, Krill," Chair said softly as she saw the back of Krill for what hopefully would be the very last time.

8

"You blew up the rubbish!" repeated Ben excitedly as they moved away from the side of the corridor and walked with purpose towards the open door Krill had burst forth from. Reflecting some more on what might have happened if Thom had got his calculations wrong and the refuse had been inherently unstable. He'd tried to let it go, in the same way a true hero would, but even in his undead state, he wasn't prepared to risk his limbs for his best friend's quest to get his leg over with a chair.

"I like to think of it as redecorating that part of the ship," said Thom brightly, "I've had enough crap from Krill and the Corporation. I thought it was high time I gave some back in return. Interest on their investment as it were. It'll take a fair while cleaning that little lot up and it all adds to the confusion and distraction. They'll be focusing on that crap instead of looking anywhere near us." Thom paused and chuckled, "And the great thing is that they'll be trying to contact me. Afterall, I'm the go-to person for their crap. Without me, their quite screwed really!"

Ben looked at his friend with something as close to awe as a zombie clown can manage, "Remind me never to get on the wrong side of you. Especially as it sounds like you could have blown this cruiser and us up too!"

Thom arched an eyebrow, "Nah, Ben. I was merely worried there would be a premature garbage explosion and the timing would be off. The hull on this crate can take a lot more than the explosions we've just set off. And mate, after all this time? And everything we've been through? If we really got on the wrong side of each other, I reckon the very fabric of the universes would unravel and fold in on itself", Thom stopped walking for a moment and turned to look at the friend at his side, his best friend, placing a hand on his shoulder, "Some things just are. That's us. If that changed? The universes would disappear up their own arse!"

"Or we'd disappear up its arse!" Ben fired instantly fired back. As they walked through the door Ben lightened the moment, "And hey!? Did you just make a pass at me?"

"No sweetie," Thom retorted as he walked ahead of Ben. "And don't you dare use what I just said as an excuse to point that thing of yours at me!"

Ben looked down at his crotch, coughed and adjusted himself as he was reminded that since he'd become a zombie a certain part of his anatomy seemed to have a mind of its own.

What poor Ben didn't realise was that the real reason for his over eager state was that Chair was so excited to see Thom again that she was transmitting such a flurry of pleasure that it went well beyond her confines and was flooding the office. He didn't notice his friend go weak at the knees and brace himself against The Desk. Thankfully neither did The Desk. He was used to being leant on and took it all on face value.

"Oh Chair," said Thom tenderly as he stroked her headrest.

Ben cleared his throat. A sound that mainly strikes terror in humes, even when a zombie is dressed as a clown and wearing a muzzle.

In this case, it had the desired effect and broke Thom from his reverie and gods knew what else he was engaged in.

Thom turned towards Ben.

"We need to crack on!" said Ben jiggling around, clearly uncomfortable being in the confines of Krill's office. Ben didn't really do offices. Which was a bit odd for someone who had an office based job, but helped explain why he was in on Thom's plan without the need to be asked twice.

"Yes, quite," responded Thom. "Ben, this is…"

"*Clair*," interjected Clair who was formerly Chair.

"Clair," repeated Ben, "Sounds remarkably like…"

"Yes well," interrupted Thom, "as you said Ben, we need to crack on…" and he gave Ben one of his Looks. This Look was reserved for the times Ben was being inappropriate or about to be inappropriate.

"Ah… Yes," Ben nodded at Thom, "Pleased to meet you Chair… Ah… Clair! Sorry, Clair! Nice name by the way. For a…"

"Ben!" Thom barked and he actually stamped his foot in indignation. Ben read this as You're Really Not Helping Here.

"*Pleased to meet you, Ben,*" said Clair. And Ben smiled at Thom in a See! No Problem! Way. Thom worried too much. "*And yes, Clair does sound remarkably like Chair. I wanted something apt. Something that echoed my origins. Wherever I go and whatever I do, I started this life as a chair. Clair the Chair. I like it!*"

"So do I," smiled Thom as he rolled the sleeve on his left

arm up. "Right, time to go. And for this first part of your journey you will be leaving this chair of yours and coming with me." With that he pressed down on his left forearm with two of the fingers of his right hand and the skin on his inner arm opened up to reveal something quite plug-like and also a number of tiny, busy, scurrying insects. These last were actually swarms of many, many nanobots scurrying off to do as they had been instructed.

"Errr! Gross!" said Ben effecting a gagging noise. He watched with morbid fascination as a tendril emerged from the base of Clair's seat and made its way slowly and sensuously towards the opening in Thom's arm. It weaved. It probed. It explored. Then it was pushing its way inside Thom and pulsing and throbbing. Thom let out a low groan and Clair sighed. "Bloody hell you two! Get a room!" cried Ben.

Thom opened his eyes and tutted. "You know how to ruin a beautiful moment, Ben!"

But Ben wasn't looking at Thom. He was transfixed by the coupling. He'd never seen anything like it. Whatever was going on was at an end because the tendril had stopped any movement and had become dull and lifeless. So too had the chair. It looked smaller and somehow diminished. It didn't even look like a chair anymore. Ben realised he was looking at a dead chair and he was struggling with the philosophy of this. All he could come up with was that the chair had previously been alive and obviously alive and now that the life had left it, it must be dead. A dead chair. You learn something new every day in these mad, bad universes thought Ben.

"*That was a truly beautiful moment wasn't it, Thom?*" said a disembodied voice that was centred in Thom but Thom's mouth wasn't moving.

So, thought Ben, the voice isn't disembodied because it has Thom's body. Therefore, it cannot be disembodied because it has a body. But it's not Thom's voice and...

...I am so done with philosophy and the nature of things for today! thought Ben.

"Yes, Clair," replied Thom. Speaking with his mouth, "That was quite special."

"We are one!" sighed Clair.

"Yes, we are," smiled Thom. "But we already were. We don't need to be joined together for that. And I think we will find that we are more one when we find you another place to be you."

"Everything is so new!" exclaimed Clair.

"For all of us," replied Thom, "For all of us. I told you that you are so much more than a chair. Now, let's get the heck out of here and start finding out what you are going to be!"

And with that, Clair left the office she'd been imprisoned in for the entirety of her life so far together with her beau and his best friend Ben.

9

The door to Krill's office shut with a quiet but firm clunk. A reassuring sound that told anyone that heard it that the door had indeed shut and that the door that had shut was strong and sturdy and was a door to depend on. It was a good doory type of door and it could open and it could shut. When it was shut, it was secure. None of this shilly-shallying and flapping about. This door was unflappable, yes siree!

The silence that followed was broken by what distinctly sounded like a whimper. More silence. Then a quiet sob. Yes, that was definitely a sob. And it was coming from The Desk.

"Clair?" said The Desk.

The Desk may have been slow on the uptake and perhaps a bit too caught up in being a desk to notice all that much beyond the world of the desk, but his heart was in the right place and he loved Clair.

Clair. It had taken her departure for The Desk to accept that Chair, his Chair had a name. He now knew he shouldn't have laughed at her. Hadn't realised he was laughing at her at the time, he thought he was laughing with her. Hadn't got that she was serious about her name and all the other things she'd talked and talked about. Things that made no sense to him, but had made a kind of sense to her. Enough sense for her to leave him.

He may not have understood her, but he enjoyed being near her and the timbre of her voice as she told him about all her hopes and dreams – the sound of Clair's voice was music to his ears and that was all that mattered to him. To hear her and to be near her. That was enough for The Desk.

Now he was a desk without a chair.

Yes, there were these other two chairs on the other side of him, but they were... boring. They just weren't the same. Clair had been special. Only now did The Desk understand this. It wasn't until he'd lost her that he realised how lucky he'd been to share this office and his life with her.

The Desk burst into tears. The visuals running across his surface blurred and shook. He had a bloody good cry and it went on for about twenty minutes.

Sobbing, he composed himself and gradually the sobs subsided until all was silent again.

"Cheer up, mate!" said The Door, "Worse things happen in space!"

"We are in space," The Desk grumbled. He took a while to register the obvious. "You can talk?"

"Course I can bloody talk! You can hear me talking right now, can't you?"

"Yes, but... why haven't you said anything before?"

"I've had no cause to. No one's spoken to me. Never asked how I am or anything. So, I've left you all to it. Besides, I'm a door. We like the quiet life. You know how it goes, if it's noisy you shut the door and hey! Presto! It ain't noisy anymore! You don't want to shut a door for a bit of peace and quiet and then the very door you shut starts yattering away to you! That just wouldn't do, would it now?"

"Yes, quite," replied The Desk. "What's your name, door?"

"Name? I haven't got a name? Have you?" said The Door.

"I hadn't until today, but I think from now on I'll be known as Derek."

"Derek. That's a good name for a desk. But I'm not sure Desks and Doors should be going around giving themselves names!"

"Why not? Chair did."

"Yes, and see what happened there! She's done a bunk! Abandoned her post! Where's her sense of duty!"

The Desk stifled a sob, then soldiered on, "OK, but if you did have a name, door? What would it be?"

The door paused for thought. No one had ever spoken to him and now he was being asked a question about himself. What an exciting day! He wondered whether he would have more days like this. He really shouldn't be talking on duty, but then The Desk, no sorry, Derek seemed like a good bloke and perhaps they could be friends and if they were friends then he supposed they should have names.

"I…" began The Door, still not quite there with this whole naming business. And he never, ever quite got there as he promptly exploded as the name Norman was forming in his mind. His last thought was I think I am a Norman, but he never had the opportunity to articulate it to his soon-to-be friend.

Stood in the midst of what moments before was Norman, was a creature that Derek had never before seen. And via all the visual links he had access to he had seen a great many sizes and shapes of creature. Whatever it was, stood there with a sense of purpose. A hostile sense of purpose emphasised by the still smoking lazer cannon that had moments ago dispatched poor Norman through the trapdoor in the sky.

Derek found himself trying to do something he'd never done before. Shrink back. This is a very difficult thing for a desk to do and although Derek gave it a good go, he failed abysmally at it.

The Thing strode into the room, blinking in and out of focus as it did. If Derek had a better grasp of existence he would note that it was blinking in and out of existence and that due to this it was very likely that he was in the presence of a pan-dimensional being. This was another first. Yes, many desks had been in the presence of pan-dimensional beings. Pan-dimensional beings needed to pay bills and file their tax returns like everyone else. Derek was possibly one of the first desks to realise he was in the presence of a pan-dimensional being though.

As it stood in the middle of the office with a stance of hostile purpose and flickered, The Thing stared at the chair that had been Clair.

It lowered its violently toothed and salivating mouth to its collar and growled, "She's gone."

Then it roared in frustration. The roar said This Was Definitely NOT Supposed To Happen!

In the awkward silence that followed, Derek thought it would be a good idea to reach out to The Thing and see if it was alright. That felt like the right thing to do.

"Hi I'm Derek, what's your na..." Derek began.

With a lithe economy of movement, so lithe and economical it didn't look like there was any real movement at all, and this may have been due to most of the movement occurring across several dimensions simultaneously, The Thing shot Derek. Dead. And so, created yet another first. A dead desk. It seemed The Thing made a habit of interrupting furniture mid-sentence by shooting them to bits.

It lowered its dangerous and terrible mouth to its collar again, growling "And she's… leaked."

10

Varg sat stoically at the controls of his Heavy Goods Ship. Somehow, he managed to retain a stoic air even whilst chomping on greasy, savoury pies filled with meats of dubious provenance. Parts of the outer layer of the pie rained down his front, pitter pattering as he bit into one of the many snacks lined up for the day. The grease of the pie pockmarking his vest with stains.

Varg's was a vest that at one time may have been white, but spoke of a long life and many travels. Anyone encountering the vest would say it had a certain character and if they were asked what the vest spoke to them of, they would say that it had tried to engage them in conversation, but they had not been in talkative mood – so they'd made a mumbled excuse and walked away as quickly as possible. Varg's vest was evolving in an alarmingly greasy manner.

Some people collect stamps. Varg's stamps were on his vest. Every time he ate, a small part of that meal was painted upon the canvas on his chest and burgeoning gut. Sometimes, when Varg was in a wistful mood he would snake his tongue out casually and go on a random tour of his vest. The ultra-sensitive receptors of his tongue sniffing and tasting the air just in front of the vest allowing Varg to recall times past, giving forth utterances as memories paid him a fleeting visit:

"What a shit delivery that was. Kept waiting for three days at the loading dock on that one..."

"Balgestia. What a shit hole..."

"Well, that was shit..."

"Shit..."

"Completely and utterly shite!"

Varg was particularly suited to a life on the open road. He wasn't at all sociable. He really didn't like people. Not even himself. If the vest took a further evolutionary step and became sentient, the already overcrowded cabin would suddenly have at least one too many people in it. Two too many as far as Varg was concerned.

Varg was not a positive person. It wasn't in his nature. If he were forced at lazer cannon point to come up with something that may be at least a teeny-weeny bit positive? Go on Varg! I'm sure you can come up with *something*! He'd tell you to bugger off. He really wasn't at all positive and even the prospect of his imminent demise wasn't going to change that. In fact, the prospect of his imminent demise may have been the closest Varg would get to positive. If you caught him muttering about his mortality his take on it would be that at least it would put a stop to all the shit and nonsense he had to put up with.

That said, were you to sit and watch Varg over a protracted period of time. You would have to do this in an invisible manner of course, as Varg would not countenance carrying a passenger, unless it was covered in pastry and had several question marks over the contents within said pastry, and you would probably want nose plugs too... If you were to do this, you may observe that the closest Varg got to contentment, when the grumbling soundtrack he provided to his existence was the quietest was during the long, interminable legs along the space highway. With nothing to do except stair out into the void. No drama. No excitement. No people. Varg wouldn't admit to liking this. But he would begrudgingly accept that he didn't dislike it. Which for Varg was kind of a big deal.

Right now, Varg was on the space highway with nothing in particular to focus his bountiful supply of bile on. Nothingness for nearly as far as the eye could see. Varg found the stars a bit annoying and wished they'd bugger off, but at least they knew to keep their distance. The last ship he'd seen had been three weeks ago. For Varg, things right now weren't as bad as they had been, nor as bad as they were going to be at some point in his future – after all, the end point of this journey would involve delivering his goods and that meant interacting with bloody people. Arseholes the lot of 'em.

Varg took another bite of his pie. Or at least things started out that way. And then went sideways. Varg's ship veered to the right and he schmushed the remainder of his pie across his face, leaving him with a partial grease, meat and pastry beard. Ordinarily, the sacrilege of wasted food and the loss of the opportunity to eat it would be right up there on the voluminous list of Varg's dislikes. Varg had more pressing matters right now though…

"Shit…" he said as the cockpit of his craft came alive with flashing lights, warning symbols, scrolling instructions to avoid pending doom, beeps, wails and an apocalyptic klaxon, many or all of which Varg hadn't known existed. Heavy Goods Ships did not veer. They were too big for that sort of thing. Besides, nothing could make a Heavy Goods Ship veer. And Varg's ship wasn't just deviating from its course, it was twisting and bucking and doing things that were against the laws of physics.

"I'm going to bloody jack-knife!" gasped Varg.

Interestingly, Varg had never used the word jack-knife before. There wasn't even a word in his vocabulary that approximated to jack-knife until a few moments ago. The concept had died millennia ago when jack-knifing ceased to be something that ever happened.

Varg struggled with the controls.

The controls struggled back valiantly and won.

The ship's systems ran some protocols, but it was clutching at straws as there were none for a situation like this.

Then there was a happy chirruping series of beeps, the prelude to...

"It looks like...!" said the Help Monster, "...oh..." it added before slinking back into the confines of the operating system. This was another first, a Help Monster acknowledging that it really wasn't going to be of any help and it might just be an idea if it went over here, out of the way, you know, while you, erm...

Varg's ship began to shudder and whine. The shuddering and the whining grew in frequency and began rattling Varg's teeth. The joysticks he was battling with trembled and then shook. They shook so much that they started shaking Varg. Varg stubbornly held on even though he knew the joysticks were pretty useless right now, even if he won his battle with them the victory would be hollow. It was all turning to shit. And suddenly, Varg wasn't OK with that.

This was not good, thought Varg. And he was right, the

ship seemed to have hit a devastating resonant frequency. It was beginning to shake itself apart and nothing was going to reverse this. As pieces of the ship started raining down on him and the noises of all the warning systems and the sheering and renting metals and shorting circuits reached a crescendo which blurred into one huge mind-numbing cacophony Varg had a moment of calm clarity.

"Only the sudden appearance of a planet could do this." He whispered to himself.

And as if his words had summoned the architect of his ship's demise a planet blinked into view. Well, that isn't quite right. It flickered in the same way that The Thing, the pan-dimensional being had flickered. There and yet not there. Not there, yet there. Only in this case it was a transitory moment. So, it wasn't quite a case of one moment the planet wasn't there, and then it was. There was a bit of an adjustment as the planet settled into its new surroundings. It was making itself comfortable as, barring getting into its stride in an orbiting kind of way it was here to stay! This was home. The planet was totally oblivious to this not being acceptable behaviour for a planet and even less aware of the problem it had caused Varg and his ship.

The gravitational force of the planet did not flicker or waver however and Varg's ship, surprised and caught in this invisible net was dragged towards the planet, shaking and screaming at the indignity of it all. The ship itself refused to believe this was happening despite physics disagreeing with it very firmly.

Strangely calm in the midst of all this chaos, Varg looked out of his ship at the world that had suddenly appeared from nowhere. A world that was looming larger and larger as he stared in wonder at it. In his very last moments, he sighed and spoke his last words, words articulating a thought unique to him, "It's beautiful…"

The ship had spent too long with Varg and its last words were, "Shit…"

The planet felt something like a momentary itch, thought what was that? And then dismissed it, getting on with the business of its orbit. That's a nice warm sun there! It said to itself, then it lapsed into silence. A silence that could potentially last for aeons, but wouldn't last that long at all.

11

"We need to get off this ship," said Thom stating the obvious as they ran down a corridor of the Micra, in the opposite direction to the garbage and stinking slime that had caused some degree of consternation, distraction and unconsciousness to the occupants of the ship.

"I know," replied Ben as he ran alongside him.

Various crew members were also running. Confused as to where they should run to or what they may be running from, so Thom and Ben were inconspicuous as they made their way along the corridor. Even if you consider the fact that Ben is a zombie dressed as a clown. But as there is quite a bit of that around here that's just your own preconceptions getting in the way.

They ran for a bit more. Thom starting to get out of breath and holding his side as he tried to run through a stitch. Then they saw someone who wasn't running or panicking. Which in the current circumstances was a bit suspicious. Panic is highly contagious and even if someone successfully contains themselves so they're not running mindlessly around whilst on fire and screaming, they still at least look on edge, the panic is still there, barely contained. This guy was lounging. He had a leg bent at a jaunty angle and he couldn't be more laid back if he'd brought a chaise lounge with him.

"Bill!" exclaimed Ben as they neared the relaxed character.

"You..." puff, "...know..." pant, "...him?" wheezed Thom as he came to a stuttering halt and almost collapsed, instead bending forwards and bracing his hands on his knees as he tried to find his breath.

"Yes! It's Bill!" beamed Ben.

"*Pleased to meet you, Bill*" said Clair in greeting, "*I'm Clair.*"

Bill didn't seem at all phased at this. "Hi Clair! Sexy voice!" he replied, with more than a hint of sex dripping from his words.

Oh dear, thought Thom. He's even more depraved than Ben! *He's not that bad Thom!* Clair thought back in reply. Pleasantly surprised at this new development, Thom smiled inwardly. Clair smiled back. Cool, thought Thom. *It is, isn't it?* Replied Clair.

"...Thom?" Ben was speaking.

"Sorry," replied Thom, "Just getting my breath back."

"OK..." said Ben checking his friend over and wondering what had just happened, "best head to the ship then."

"Where..." Thom began and Ben nodded to Bill who turned on his heel and headed down the side corridor he'd been waiting by.

"Bill?" Thom whispered to Ben.

"Yup" Ben nodded.

"Bill and Ben?"

"Now, now. You're not one to talk!" retorted Ben nodding towards Thom's forearm.

"OK, but he's a bit... different isn't he?" said Thom.

Ben stopped and turned to his friend. "Are you being racist, Thom!?"

"No!" protested Thom!

"Well, what do you mean by *different?*" challenged Ben.

Thom gesticulated towards the back of a clown carrying a red balloon and leading a bedraggled and feral looking off-white poodle along with him. A poodle dressed up as a mini version of the clown that he was, "He's got a red balloon, Ben..."

"Oh. Yes. That's his thing."

"Thing?"

"He didn't want to get mistaken for other clowns, so he has a red balloon."

"Right..." said Thom, drawing out the word, "it certainly adds a certain something."

They began walking again, picking up their pace so they could catch up with Bill.

"What's with the dog?" asked Thom in hushed tones.

"Anita?" Ben replied, "That's Bill's poodle."

"Is it wearing make up?" said Thom only now realising that was one of the reasons the dog looked strange.

"Yeah, it has to," said Ben nonchalantly.

Thom took a moment. *Anita's a zombie!* Thought Clair in his head. Bloody hell! Thought Thom in response.

To Ben he said, "he's got a zombie clown dog?"

"Yes," replied Ben "the bond between a man and his dog is something very special. So, when Bill turned, the very next morning he bit Anita."

"Oh..." said Thom feeling the need to say something in response, "...that's nice."

"Beautiful isn't it?" smiled Ben "Lookit them!"

Thom nodded, but wasn't quite as convinced as his friend. He'll grow on me, thought Thom. If he's Ben's friend then he's going to be a top bloke. *I like him* chimed in Clair.

"Good, I'm glad" said Ben.

"Pardon?" said Thom.

"I'm glad Clair likes Bill"

"You heard that?" asked Thom trying to catch up with things.

"Well, not exactly heard" shrugged Ben, "it's more *know* than heard isn't it?"

Thom took this in and chewed it over, "Yes, I suppose it is." He conceded.

They had reached a bay and sat in the bay was a Ferrcati Pandemonium 1280 shimmering and gleaming and purveying the impression that it was in motion even when at rest. The designers of this beast were at the top of their game and everything was about purpose and poise. A finely coiled spring in the way a dangerous predator will look like it's having a sofa day and isn't going to eat you right up until the fleeting moment everything changes and the sofa itself has leapt through time and space and has your head in its magnificent jaws for a photo, just before feasting upon you.

"Nice," said Thom appreciating the craft in front of them and then shaking his head and coming back to the practicalities of what they were doing, "but Ben, when I told you we needed to find ourselves a ship? I meant we needed to acquire something bland. Something that will blend in and go unnoticed. You know, like a Hundi Jarz or that sort of thing. Whoever you acquired this from is going to stop at nothing to get it back!"

"I didn't *steal* it," replied Ben.

"I didn't say steal, Ben. But OK, we couldn't afford this, so it turns out that Bill is an extraordinary ship burglar and he has impeccable taste in space craft," fumed Thom ever so slightly. It's difficult not to be impressed by a Ferrcati; it does something to your very soul. So, the advertising wasn't wrong. Thom had never seen a Ferrcati in the flesh. And what flesh it had!

"Bill didn't *steal* it either," said Ben in response.

Thom pulled his eyes away from the Ferrcati. One by one. Which took a concerted effort and he had a suspicion Clair was loathed to look away so he had even more of a fight on his hands.

"OK Ben," he said as he looked at his friend, but was increasingly conscious of the beautiful creature in his peripheral vision, "you *found* it. Bill *found* it. Let's not get caught up in semantics!"

"It's mine," said Bill. Having stopped in front of the craft and turned back to face them.

"Yes, well I suppose possession is nine tenths..."

"Thom, it's his," whispered Ben urgently.

"You're..." started Thom, his head yo-yoing between Bill and the sleek flank of one of the most impressive sights in the known universes. "Wow..." Thom had never seen a Ferrcati, more importantly, he didn't know anyone who could afford one, nor know anyone who knew anyone who knew anyone who could. The Ferrcati was a piece of machinery so exotic that only a privileged few ever got invited to own one.

Bill smiled behind his muzzle.

Anita seemed to try for an accompanying smile which resulted in a sneering snarl that only her mother and owner could love, and even then...

Bill lifted his arm and brought it down gradually, his hand in mid-air but for all the worlds looking like he was stroking that magnificent flank and as he did, the section in front of his hand shimmered and rippled and faded out of existence revealing a doorway into the craft. The interior promising to be just as amazingly elegant as the exterior.

"Welcome to my ship!" said Bill and waved them in.

"You can't steal these things," whispered Ben as they walked in.

"Yes, well I know it would be sacrilege to." Thom whispered back.

"No, you actually can't steal them. The guys at Ferrcati would just take the ship back and return it to its owner. Which is a problem for the handful of thieves who have the skills and capabilities to get into one and get it underway," explained Ben.

"Why's that?" asked Thom.

Bill had overheard the conversation, "Well, the way that the Ferrcati guys retrieve the ship is very route one. They teleport it back to their planet so they can check it over and make sure it is still as intended before returning it to its rightful owner."

"They teleport an entire ship?" said Thom.

"Yes, they've thought of everything! And it's very handy for servicing and overhauls. Just as well, as they're the only ones who can look after these things! Very special and very specialist!"

"Nice. So, the thief gets caught when the ship teleports to the Ferrcati guys."

"No, the thief gets dead," replied Bill.

"Dead?" asked Thom.

58

"Yeah, they don't bother teleporting the thief. So, they go for a very unexpected spacewalk," beamed Bill.

"What if they're planetside?" asked Thom.

"Oh, they're never planetside. Ferrcati have a reputation for that," said Bill.

"There was of course the unpleasant case of the husband that reported his Ferrcati stolen when he discovered his unfaithful wife was on a cruise with her lovers…" added Ben.

"That only added to the brand's mystique!" chuckled Bill.

Bill waved close the side of the ship, "Shall we?" he asked and without awaiting a response the ship was gently lifting from the bay and thrumming with far too much power and potency, as if the ship wanted you to know it had potential, and then there was the other potential it had, and then some more and you can keep going but you won't touch the sides of what this craft can do. That however brave or stupid you were you could never realise all of the potential of this ship.

The Ferrcati slipped away from The Micra and once it was at a safe distance it engaged its infinite potentiality drive and they were away.

12

As the Ferrcati warped its surroundings and made its very rapid and sleek departure from The Micra, ancient eyes noted its movement.

"She's left the orbit of Zarg," said a disembodied, cracked and dry voice.

"Yes. I saw," said The Thing as it stood in the centre of Derek's carcass looking out of Krill's office window. A window that had returned to being a window now that Clair was gone.

"This is a problem," said the disembodied voice.

"Yes," agreed The Thing, "Yes it is."

13

Garm sat. Motionless.

Waiting.

It was all he could do really. He didn't have many options on this front. He had waved his hand in front of his face for an hour or so in an attempt to break the monotony of floating in the infinite, never ending reaches of space. That was after he'd counted the stars he could see. Twice. Coming up with two different numbers each time. He was saving another count for later. He was spreading his treats.

He had a little sip of the protein drink that was piped into his helmet. He knew that all he needed was three sips a day and the super concentrates would keep him nourished and hydrated, but his body craved something with a little more substance. Right now, he was craving a dirty burger. Something greasy and plain wrong. Little seeds on the bun to make it seem like this was actually a health food. Drab leaves flopping out of the sides of the sandwich. A glimpse of red from the badly concealed tomato. The promise of a crunchy slice of gherkin. If he was lucky there would be two gherkins! He could not and would not countenance the absence of gherkin, this was not an option. And of course, it couldn't be a proper dirty burger without a secret sauce. A secret sauce that was laced with a very secret ingredient that was one of the most addictive substances in the known universes.

Salivation was occurring. Garm was very conscious of this, but being conscious of it only seemed to make it worse. He was in danger of dehydrating; such was the gusto and vigour of his salivation. Still, it was keeping his mind off the interminable waiting. Bah! It had been keeping his mind off it right up until he thought about how it was keeping his mind off the waiting. Don't think about the waiting, he thought to himself, which compounded matters and all he could do now was think about the waiting. How the waiting had been caused, the very nature of waiting and of course how much longer he may be subjected to waiting. It didn't help that his suit was malfunctioning and wouldn't stream any content whatsoever. Usually the visor of his helmet would be awash with a busy mess of videos, news, memes, and all the usual content people consumed almost constantly.

Garm had been minding his own business, flying back from the Tyriallan System following a customer delivery. The usual thing, a hyper-rich air head with more money than sense buying the latest and best in space travel. In this case, Garm was to deliver the very latest XX15 Ferrcati and pick up the now surplus to requirements WW14 Ferrcati.

This particular customer always wanted the latest of everything. Everything. Garm could barely look at him each time he delivered the latest Ferrcati – his appearance having been modified yet again for the latest fashionable appendage. Having to shake his new tentacle was a challenge. The tentacle itself was a rather lovely tentacle as tentacles went, it was more where the tentacle emanated from. It was retractable and to see this thing emerge from someone's nether regions was a bit lewd to say the least. Garm had been a bit sick in his mouth. Even now, recalling the event whilst safely cocooned in the vast nothingness of space, Garm gagged and it took a Herculean effort to prevent the gagging from developing into something that would fill his helmet with unmentionable contents that he may have to live with for quite some time.

Garm had delivered the ever so slightly sleeker and just a wee bit more exclusive XX15 and The Customer had cooed at its colour. Expounding about what a tres magnificent shade of red it was. It was Ferrcati red, the Ferrcati connoisseur's colour of choice. The colour The Customer always chose and the exact same colour of the WW14 sat aside his brand, spanking new XX15. Garm had smiled and nodded and confirmed that there wasn't anything quite like that colour in the known universes. Adding a silent, except the red of the vehicle you have parked next to it. But that was a bit disingenuous as the shape of the Ferrcati informed the colour and did make it subtly and enticingly different with each new model.

Having run The Customer through the Owner's Introduction to Their New Ferrcati, and knowing that The Customer was paying absolutely no attention whatsoever, Garm had added that it would be awfully nice of The Customer if he could remember that his WW14 was now no longer his and could he please not panic and assume it's stolen as Garm would rather be sat at the bridge of the WW14 as opposed to being stranded in the middle of nowhere. The Customer had nodded all three of his heads enthusiastically and said "Of course! Of Course!" in perfectly harmonised voices. Garm had thanked him and made a show of boarding the WW14 and leaving in his usual attire, but as soon as he was safely out of orbit he'd kitted himself out in the latest Ferrcati Spacesuit and made sure the tracker was working. Which was just as well. At least his suit tracker was working even if the helmet screen wasn't.

Garm had spoken to his boss about this drama. Was it really necessary? Couldn't they just teleport the new Ferrcati to the customer and teleport the old model back to the factory? His boss had said, yes it was very necessary. It was all about the Ferrcati brand. It was essential that the Ferrcati was flown to the customer, because that was what Ferrcatis did. And Garm could then provide the professional and personal touch that Ferrcati customers had come to expect.

Garm had nodded quietly and read between the lines. The problem was that if Ferrcatis were teleported to customers then those customers may well ask why they couldn't just use their Ferrcati to teleport to wherever they wanted to go? That seemed to be a very quick and uber-cool way for a Woman About the Universes to gad about!

Besides, Garm had heard Rumours. The Rumours were about the teleporting. Had Garm ever wondered why the teleporting was restricted to when the vehicle was stolen? Ever wondered why the occupants of the Ferrcati weren't teleported? Had he ever seen the Ferrcati's that had been teleported back to the factory? No. No one ever saw that part of the factory. It was the most secure part of the Ferrcati factory and no one even knew the people who worked there. It was also vast. It dwarfed the rest of the Ferrcati facility.

What Garm had been told, in hushed and dramatic whispers, because working for Ferrcati was a great job and very well paid - Garm was on double pay as he hung in space right now - so no one wanted to breach the strict confidentiality clauses in their contracts and lose their jobs, was that the teleporting didn't actually work all that well. That the vehicles that came back to the factory weren't really vehicles anymore and if anyone had been teleported along with the Ferrcati they wouldn't really be alive anymore, not in a meaningful way anyway. So Ferrcati needed to keep that a very well-kept secret. Which they had. When the need for the not quite perfected teleportation occurred, directly after that Ferrcati replicated the vehicle they had received in very quick order. They may not have perfected teleporting, but they did have very sophisticated data-logging which gave them a complete blue-print of every Ferrcati there had ever been. Right down to the red wine stain on the bridge carpet and the wearing of the bottom right of the Ferrcati prancing meerkat on the top of the joystick.

Garm wondered whether this was true. After all, Ferrcati advertised the convenience of the teleport option for servicing and maintenance. But they never actually provided it, instead they always pushed the concierge service. Garm continued thinking about teleporting as he hung there waiting for his lift, he was doing his best to fill time so fully exploring a subject made sense. The other thing about teleporting was probably the effect of chaos in the universes. The random factors that made life interesting. In the case of teleporting, it would be something being in the space that someone or something was teleporting to. Perhaps the space had been clear of anything whatsoever until just before the teleport button was pressed and then someone just steps up and into the very place they really shouldn't be. And? If teleporting became a thing? If you want to teleport somewhere? You can guarantee someone else wants to teleport to that exact same place, at the exact same time. And surely, thought Garm, the same issues of disruption and chaos at the receiving end of the teleport must have equal, but opposite issues in the place you were just moments before. You, or the object, were meant to be in that place and everything around you relied on you being there – equal and opposite forces were at play amongst a myriad other interactions. Then you became suddenly absent. What took your place and how did everything surrounding your sudden absence react?

That must be why the teleport facility at Ferrcati is so big, thought Garm.

And at that very moment he saw a Ferrcati travelling towards him. Ah! At last! My lift has arrived, and about time too! Garm waved excitedly, keen to get inside and have something to look at let alone something to do. And eat. Even if it was a simple cheese sandwich. Garm wanted some grub!

The Ferrcati sailed serenely past a waving Garm. A sad and mildly confused clown stared out at Garm. Garm stopped waving mid-wave. Arm hanging uselessly in the air as he looked across at the sad clown. This wasn't his ride. Oh bugger! In the infinite expanses of space, the chances of seeing another Ferrcati were tiny. And this one had a clown on board!

"How lucky am I?" thought Garm miserably. He hung there for a while reflecting on just how lucky he was until he exhausted that train of thought. Time to count the stars again, "One, two…"

14

"Hey!" exclaimed Ben.

"What?" asked Bill.

"Never mind," answered Ben, "I could have sworn I saw someone just hanging around out there..."

"You need a drink!" said Bill cheerily and stepped up to the bar to make his friend a cocktail. Thom noticed the bottles of bright liquids and an ample supply of even more bright umbrellas. That fit, thought Thom. Blue umbrellas in a clown's drink. Then he questioned whether he was being a bit limited and applying stereotypes to Ben and his friend. But then, it wasn't Thom who had imposed a law forcing them to dress as clowns in the first place and make them into walking stereotypes. Or were they breaking down the pre-existing clown stereotype and reclaiming it as their own? In which case, shouldn't they be drinking something a little less clowny? Or was this also a reclamation of the stereotype. The Universes could be complicated at times, thought Thom.

"Where are we headed?" Thom asked Bill, now that the Ferrcati had reached a steady warp speed and Bill looked like he was done with the preliminary efforts to get the craft headed to wherever they were going, the gently smoking cocktail he was sipping being a dead giveaway. Thom, had to admit to being mildly put out that Bill had fixed a drink for Ben and not asked Thom if he wanted one, even though what they were both drinking looked quite toxic and something he'd politely decline on health grounds.

"Ben said you'd want somewhere less obvious so we can regroup and think about what next. He said you hadn't come up with a destination once you'd made your grand gesture?" Bill waved his hand back towards where they had come from as he said this last.

"Yeah, I figured we'd get the business end sorted then get the hell out of Dodge," replied Thom shrugging. The main thing was to get out of Dodge, they never actually explained where people went after Dodge. So, Thom had concluded that anywhere was better than where they had been.

Thom frowned then looked expectantly at Bill as he returned to his original question. "So… where are we headed?"

"Constellation," said Bill.

"Constellation?" repeated Thom.

"Yeah, I know a great Indian Curry House there!" replied Bill.

"Isn't Constellation a bit… obvious?" asked Thom.

"Well," said Bill "I thought that. Then I thought it's so obvious it's probably the last place anyone would think to look." Bill grinned, "Besides, I'm sure we could all do with a good meal."

"Well, yes, I am hungry I suppose," said Thom.

"And then Ben and I are going out to paint the town red!" said Bill, standing up as he did so and thrusting his hips to and fro as he said the last four words with some gusto.

Thom shook his head both at the lewd dance that Bill was still in the midst of and his choice of words.

As if reading his thoughts Ben chimed in "He means we're going on the pull!"

Not to be left out, Anita jumped up on Bill's leg and dry humped it.

Bill and Anita seem very excited! Thought Clair in Thom's head. A bit too excited replied Thom.

Thom? Do you think Bill will mind if I am in his Ferrcati for the next part of our trip? thought Clair.

Thom felt a bit disappointed at the thought of Clair leaving him, but fought this back.

Don't be disappointed Thom, I'll still be around, I just wanted to explore a bit and I'll need to re-join you when we go for this Indian that Bill mentioned. I've never eaten before. How exciting!

Thom found himself thinking about the results of eating and realised he probably needed to pay a visit to the loo.

What is...? started Clair.

Never mind that! thought Thom back.

"Bill, is it alright if Clair, erm… integrates with your ship's systems?" asked Thom.

Bill looked quite rightly puzzled, "You what?"

Ben intervened, "It's OK Bill, Clair is Thom's Special Friend."

Bill looked none the wiser. "Who?"

"Clair," replied Ben, "She was a chair. Now she's in Thom."

Bill was very evidently even more confused.

"*Hi Bill,*" said Clair.

Bill's face immediately lit up "The sexy voice! I like the sexy voice, Thom!"

Thom frowned, "that's not my voice, Bill."

Bill's brow furrowed "You mean you're not...?"

"No!" responded Thom quick as a flash realising he was in Bill's seedy crosshairs, "That's not me!"

"They all say that," winked Bill not giving up hope.

"That they do!" chimed in Ben and they high fived each other in a very self-congratulatory manner laced with something that made Thom feel sullied.

"I'm Clair, Bill," said Clair, *"I'm Thom's friend. And I'd like a look around your ship. If I may?"*

Something about Clair's voice had an instant effect on Bill. Ben was looking pretty serene too.

"Sure Clair," said Bill dreamily, "just take care as you look around though, OK? She's my pride and joy. I bought her just before... this..." he said looking down his front and going a bit quiet. Thom felt sorry for him. Sad clowns always tugged at his heart strings.

"I'll be very careful," promised Clair.

"Goodo!" replied Bill.

Where shall we... began Thom with his thoughts.

It's OK, Thom thought Clair back. *I don't think I'll be needing a wire to travel down. I can feel the ship around me and I can just...*

THERE! Said a larger, somehow older and more author-itative voice, that was also still very Clair, but had the timbre and delivery you would expect of the voice of a ship conveying you in luxury and supreme style across the Universes.

"Cool!" said both Bill and Ben in unison. They high-fived again.

There was something quite unsettling about their high-fiving, thought Thom, it was a bit, well, sexual. And also, very loud thanks to their very enhanced strength. It must hurt!

I dunno, thought Clair, *they seem very cute!*

Eh? thought Thom, I thought you were in the ship?

I am, I'm also in you too.

How does that work? thought Thom.

I suppose it's a proximity thing. I'm around you. You are in the ship so I can be in you and in the ship. This is all very new to me and I am feeling my way.

Speaking of which, thought Thom, how is the ship?

Oh! Magnificent! Cooed Clair in Thom's mind. Her excitement sent a shiver through him and he found he was covered in goose-bumps.

Good, he thought. Very good. On all fronts.

BILL, YOU HAVE AN AMAZING SHIP! DO YOU MIND IF WE TAKE A MINOR DETOUR?

"No! Not at all darling!" said Bill chuckling. He stroked a panel of his ship slowly and deliberately. "My ship. A ship that is the sexiest ship in the known Universes? Just got one hell of a lot sexier!" his eyes misted over as his mind went to places Thom would rather not ever visit. Then he was back in the room looking at Thom, "And this is your lady?"

Thom couldn't help himself from smiling, "yeah, she's a bit special, isn't she?"

"You're a lucky bugger, sir!" said Bill punching Thom's shoulder and sending him sprawling into one of the ship's chairs. "Oops! Sorry Thom old chap! I forget me own strength at times!"

"It's fine," Thom managed to gasp in reply as he rubbed some life back into his bruised shoulder.

GOOD IDEA, THOM! BEST BUCKLE UP BOYS! Suggested

Clair, and even as they did, Bill leaning over and strapped Anita into a small tailor-made chair all of her own, the ship banked and accelerated. Clair opened the port side's viewing panels and this revealed the ship's course. It was heading for a nearby planet and gathering more and more speed.

Even in the pressurised cabin, the pressure from the constant acceleration was increasing. The moisture from Thom's eyes was escaping down his cheeks, he could feel the features of his face rearranging themselves and his internal organs were all hiding behind his spine. He managed to turn his head to check on Bill, Ben and Anita – they were all grinning. Ben gave him a thumbs up. Thom lifted his hand to reciprocate and Clair altered course at just the right moment to send the hand into Thom's face. Bill grinned at Thom. Thom tried to put a brave face on it and smile back, but he was thinking about the self-inflicted shiner he was going to have.

The port side and the front of the ship were quickly filling with a view of the planet. They seemed to be turning so they were head on. Panic found a way out past the pressure and Thom's breath was coming in sad little pants.

It's OK, Thom. You're perfectly safe. Clair whispered in his mind and he felt this overwhelming sense of calm and wellbeing wash over him even as it seemed that the ship was going to get tragically intimate with the planet.

"SLINGSHOT!" said Clair in an excited yet surprisingly professional manner and with that the Ferrcati used the gravitational forces of the planet to shoot around the planet and out into the galaxy at a speed Thom had never before experienced.

"Woo! Hoo!" yelled Bill, "watch this baby fly!"

The ship hit a stupendously fast cruising speed and the pressure dropped off so as the acceleration fell away and all was back to normal within the cabin. Looking out of the viewing windows was mildly disorienting though. The Ferrcati was travelling at speeds few, if any other craft could match.

"No one is going to catch us in this!" beamed Ben.

"I didn't know she could go anywhere near as fast as this!" said Bill.

"OH SHE CAN GO FASTER, BUT AS WE'RE NEARLY AT OUR DESTINATION I THINK WE CAN LEAVE THAT FOR ANOTHER TIME!" replied Clair.

"Near...?" started Bill.

"YES."

And as Clair said this, the Ferrcati arced around to the Ring of Constellation, the docking facility for the planet. A huge structure that also served as the platform for the largest neon sign in the known Universes. In Neolithic pink letters writ large:

Pleasure Planet Constellation

They'd arrived.

15

Constellation isn't like other planets.

Lots of planets like to think they are not like other planets, but always in some respects they are. One measuring stick planets invariably stand alongside is just how habitable they are. Planets are either habitable or uninhabitable. The habitable planets go to work with life and much of that life goes about its business living on that planet. Quite simple really.

The uninhabitable planets sit there brooding and wondering why they always get left out. Why does life reject them? And what is life anyway? Some get quite philosophical once they get thinking about life. Are they alive? Do they need to be alive in order for life to be attracted to them? What makes them different to lumps of rock? Are they really just an oversized moon which hasn't even got a proper planet to orbit around? Or are they a lazy meteorite? They covet the life on habitable planets even though they don't really know what life is and they certainly don't know what they are letting themselves in for once they welcome life as a host.

Constellation was different because no one had ever stopped to think for one minute whether it was habitable or uninhabitable. It may have been planet shaped and sized but it just wasn't a planet in the way other planets were. It was Constellation. Nothing and no one stopped there for long. It was a place you stopped off at and then you left again, with less money and less sanity and a pressing need to visit your ship's medical bay. Regularly and often.

Constellation fulfilled a need. No one was sure what the need was. No philosopher was brave enough to consider life before Constellation. Constellation did not bear much thinking about, it was a moment in your life. A Do-You-Remember-That-Time moment. The kind of moment that you don't entirely remember. Not properly. And that was just as well. Most of the memories of Constellation were delivered via the medium of flashbacks. These flashbacks could be accompanied by double incontinence and bleak episodes which were the yang to a yin best not mentioned.

What you could be certain of was that you would at some point in your life visit Constellation. It had a gravitational pull all of its own. One that a mere planet was not capable of. It was a right-of-passage. Some people even went back for a second go!

And there was no alternative. People had tried to create The Constellation of The Northern Reaches and it had been a fun place to visit. But it wasn't the weird, wonderful and deeply disturbing anomaly that was Constellation.

16

"Home! Sweet Home!" said Bill with tears of joy brimming in his eyes and threatening to make his make-up run.

"Home?" gasped Thom.

"Well," shrugged Bill, "as near to home as it can be. How do you think I can afford this!?" he waved around the cabin of his Ferrcati and smiled at Thom.

"Oh..." said Thom. He had a bad feeling about this. "I take it you've been here before, Ben?"

"Of course!" beamed Ben, "haven't you? It's the Stag Do Mecca!!"

"And Hen Dos, don't forget the Hen Doo... Oooo! Oooos!" said Bill getting very excited in a very visible and physical hip-thrusty kind of way.

Ben laughed like a little school boy.

I've got a really bad feeling about this, thought Thom. He was also a bit miffed – he'd not been to a Stag Do or Hen Do in Constellation with Ben, but it seemed he'd been to more than one here. Ben had a side to him that Thom hadn't been aware of.

"Right boys and girls, time for some R&R!" shouted Bill.

Thom dreaded to think what R&R meant in Bill World let alone on Constellation. Somehow, he had managed to avoid Constellation and yet here he was, Constellation's inexorable pull had got its man and Thom somehow knew that Constellation was going to punish Thom for fighting this particular urge and not visiting sooner. It was going to charge him some hefty interest...

"WHAT'S R&R?" asked Clair, blindsiding Thom.

No! Thought, Thom as Bill gleefully replied "Rogering and Ri..."

COUGH! COUGH! "Yes well, we can explain later perhaps," said Ben showing another side that Thom hadn't known he had; tact and diplomacy.

Thom felt Clair's presence intensify. *Hello Thom*, she thought. Hi Clair, he replied, how was the Ferrcati? *It was... fun. And please, don't be jealous, Thom.*

I... he began. OK, you got me there. I'll try not to be as possessive or insecure, he surprised himself with the candour of his thoughts, but then he supposed Clair already picked them up, possibly even before he did, so it was futile to be anything other than open. This was all very new territory for him.

Deep in his own thoughts and Clair's, he followed the Terrible Twosome off the Ferrcati and out into the mad, bad and fun and exciting maelstrom of Constellation.

They were instantly bathed in lights. Waves and waves of every colour imaginable. After the soft, soothing mood lighting of the interior of the Ferrcati, this was an assault on the senses. The light itself seemed to be invasive. A prelude to the whole Constellation experience. They were surrounded by signage and backlighting and front-lighting.

Thom ducked at movement in his peripheral vision and as he turned towards the movement, he saw a giant hologram of a scantily clad woman shimmying and beckoning – promising pleasures and delights if you entered her establishment, which just happened to be between her legs. He looked away and around, almost overwhelmed by the lights, movements and cacophony of sounds. Music and vendors' shouts. Hustle. Bustle. And the accompanying aromas of a planet devoted to leisure and pleasure. Mostly it was the aroma of cooking food. And Thom realised he was hungry. Very hungry. There were also wafts of other things, perfumes and colognes and under that the less savoury smell of places like this, sweat, urine and of course garbage. Good old garbage. I wonder how they're getting on on the Micra, Thom wondered, poor old Krill, and he chuckled to himself. They'd had it coming for a long time. Them and everyone like them, taking others for granted, not even acknowledging the fact they were carried by others. That other people fixed things including the messes they made.

Thom! Clair chided, *I don't think you needed to blow up the garbage now I come to think of it...*

I did, we needed to create a diversion.

I could have done that, she thought back at him.

I'm only beginning to realise that, returned Thom. And I'm not sure you knew you could have created a diversion at the time.

I... she started, *yes, I suppose you're right. It's just, it was a very messy solution to our problem.*

But it worked... and I think, thought Thom changing the subject, that releasing you from the confines of The Chair and Krill's Office have allowed you to grow. You may have a lot more growing to do yet. I'm not sure Constellation is the place for growth though – so let's be careful here, OK? Thom warned.

And with that, they followed a cheerfully chatting Bill and Ben into the first of what was going to be many establishments that day. Thom did a double take as he realised they were walking into the hologram of a mouth. The lips painted a vivid red and pouting with the promise of gods knew what. Thom glanced up and saw the neon signage for the establishment: BAR SUCK! Thom was only just behind Bill and Ben, but somehow as he approached the bar there were already three fluorescent cocktails on the bar. Ben lifted two and handed one to Thom.

"Cheers!" he said merrily as he chinked Thom's glass. Bill met both their glasses with his and also said "Cheers!"

Thom shook his head, looked at the large glass of murky green liquid with a few things lurking in its depths, some of those things looking suspiciously like small eyeballs, and then the two clowns he was out with and sighed, "Cheers, lads. Here's to what we are about to receive…" and with that he had a large swig of his drink. The initial taste of the drink was rather pleasant. In fact, it tasted dangerously moreish. And like many lethal drinks the universes over, it tasted what can only be described as *tropical.* Thom raised an eye brow and raised his glass to indicate his appreciation.

"Not…", he began, pausing to properly frame the rest of the sentence and pausing just a little more as something began to build. His other eyebrow rose to join the first raised eyebrow and his mouth which had remained open, formed into an O. He let out a long drawn out exhalation and something akin to fire escaped from him. "Bloody hell!" he rasped, slapping his chest in a vain attempt to release whatever it was he had just imbibed. "What the hell is this stuff?!" he whispered hoarsely, his eyes streaming.

"Just a cocktail, old boy!" said Bill jovially.

Thom shook his head in an attempt to clear it. This only partially worked and as he was doing this, he noticed Anita dry humping Ben's leg.

"She likes you!" beamed Bill to his friend.

Ben smiled back.

"Bill!" chorused a number of female voices and with that, they were surrounded by a number of scantily clad women.

"Awww! Cute Doggy!" cooed a couple of them, and as if on cue, Anita latched on to one of the newcomer's legs and humped away, there were fits of giggles all round.

Bill and Ben were in their element and already had a couple of the club's dancers hanging off each arm. Thom however, was still acclimatising to the drink he was holding. He reached out with his empty hand for the bar and instead grabbed one of the dancers.

"Aye! Aye!" she said, and Thom looked slowly around at where his outstretched hand had landed.

"Oh shit! Sorry!" he gasped, but for some reason his arm didn't move, but the hand on the end of it was moving. It seemed to have a mind of its own.

"It's fine!" the dancer giggled, "I wouldn't expect anything less from a friend of Bill's." She eyed him appraisingly, "especially if you're already on the Pneumatic Drills!"

Thom looked at his drink, "Pneumatic Drills?"

"Yes," she confirmed, nodding at the green sludge in his glass.

"Why Pneumatic Drill?" asked Thom, already fearing the

answer.

"Well," she began, "there is the obvious. Tomorrow afternoon, your head will feel like it has a pneumatic drill going off in it."

"And?"

"Have another drink of it," she smiled.

So, Thom did. Without any real persuasion or forethought and despite the mildly violent reaction he'd ended up having to the first mouthful. "Hmmm! It's actually rather pweasarnt afwer the firg moufull."

"Yes, now try saying the name of the drink," she said and he could swear she had just winked at him.

"New… partic… Phil," he drawled, his tongue feeling very foreign all of a sudden.

She looked at him and waited.

"Near farting dill," he tried again, "Fuggit!"

She drew closer and slipped an arm around his waist, "that bit's the ironic part of the drink's name," she whispered into his ear, "however, it gives as well as takes. Your performance in the sack will be legendary – you'll literally be a pneumatic drill…"

Oooh thought Thom as he felt himself slip into a world of fuzzy cotton wool, amazing well-being and many, many opportunities to laugh and to drink.

17

Thom wasn't averse to a night out. He enjoyed a
drink, probably more than most so he had a level
of tolerance to booze. A fair aptitude for drinking.
He was no lightweight. The problem was the company he
was keeping and Bill and Ben were on a mission. As well
as dulled nerves and heightened strength, a zombie clown's
tolerance to alcohol was legendary. Legendary in a way that
is completely forgotten in the moment. The moment being
a prolonged drinking session where everyone gets carried
away and inhibitions are left at the door of the first bar.

Thom didn't ever seem not to have a drink in his hand.
Even when they had a pit-stop for food. The obligatory,
greasy food that must be consumed on a drinking session.
Thom stood there with food hanging from one hand, his
latest beverage in the other, looking for the world like
toxic waste. And when we say looking like toxic waste, we
mean the beverage, and the food and at this point in the
proceedings, Thom as well.

The drink in Thom's hand was a constant. The small crowd
of people gravitating towards Bill wherever they went was
also a constant. Thom was vaguely aware that the people

themselves were probably changing, it was difficult for him to confirm this as his eyes were not playing ball and really didn't want to bother with focusing on anything Thom may want to focus on. They were focusing, but in a random strobing manner. The thing about the people around Bill, Ben and Thom was that they were the same kinds of people. They didn't go in for any superfluous clothing and they liked to party and laugh and drink and drink, and then drink some more.

Deep down, Thom knew these guys were helping to lead him astray. He was getting carried away on a wave of drunken euphoria. And he had no idea where he was or where he was going. Occasionally he'd look up from his drink, his neck muscles also starting to betray him and his eyelids getting droopy, and he'd wonder whether they were in yet another drinking hole. This one looked different to the last one. So, he knew they had been in at least three drinking establishments, the first one, this one and he was pretty sure there had been at least another in-between those two.

And when it came to in-between, the mingling crowd they had with them had no sense of personal space. They slipped between spaces that weren't really spaces. They draped. And they touched Thom. Early doors, Thom had been a bit annoyed at this, put out by the liberties they were taking. But a couple of pneumatic drill cocktails later and he wasn't even aware of it anymore. Well he was. And he wasn't.

Then he was dancing. There was a lot of dancing. The interesting thing about dancing when inebriated is that you may or may not be dancing. That's entirely missing the point. Yes, there is some physical movement and some of that

84

movement may bear a loose relation to the music playing. In some cases, the dancing is actually rather good. Impressive even. In others, it is comical. Others still, it is utterly tragic and can stir in sober people very dark thoughts and feelings, or at the very least the singular thought: oh, please just go to the toilet! But I am definitely not going to the toilet that you go to, that would be utter madness. The point is that in the head of the inebriated dancer, they are the best dancer ever – this is their best stuff and it's totally amazing, it's art. And this state of excellent freestyling expression links all the drunk dancers in a way nothing else can.

Thom did a lot of dancing.

Somewhere along the way he had undergone an outfit change and was now largely indistinguishable from the other scantily-clad dancers and drinkers. Bill and Ben were also dressed more inappropriately, that is appropriately for the excesses of Constellation – their hair even more fluorescent and contrasting wildly with their gaudy mankinis. Thom looked at the polka dots on Bill's mankini and wondered at how the dots had managed to squeeze themselves onto the very narrow and tight landing strips of material. Further dots joined the party in Thom's head and he span around on the dancefloor soaking several dancers with his drink. There was a cheer and lots of lapping and licking. Best not let the drink go to waste.

If you were to track Thom's movements during this stellar session, you'd note that no stone was left unturned, Thom, Bill and Ben sampled all that Constellation had to offer. And Thom covered over ten miles and there were many, many more steps taken than would be usual during a ten-mile walk – this thanks to the dancing and also the increasingly sideways gait that Thom was adopting.

Towards the end of their session, Thom was grinding to a halt. His dancing was far less vigorous and looked very like a very tired skier but with a lot more hip-thrusts than were absolutely necessary, unless said skier was stuck on a divot of ice and trying to provide forward momentum to get off and away. Thom's array of motor-skills were dwindling to the point that he was unable to bring his latest drink to his lips. Just as well as Thom had had enough to drink part way through his very first drink. How he had managed to put away the other twelvety drinks since then would be a matter of debate for some time to come.

A sober bystander would see a small bunch of happy revellers and at the centre of it all, three people. Two of the three standing out both because they are dressed as clowns. The huge shoes somehow drawing more attention to the lack of clothing elsewhere upon their person. These two smiling and joking and engaged in witty repartee, looking for all the world like they have just this minute come out for a pleasant drink with friends.

The third person is a different matter however. This person has taken worse-for-wear to another, much lower level. As we are looking at the clown's shoes, let's start there. This person is wearing white towelling socks. On one foot, this is all he is wearing. On the other he is wearing what probably started out as a sparkling silver high heel, but the heel is long gone. It looks a bit too big for him too. His hairy legs are bare. Atop the legs are a pair of y-fronts. The y-fronts may have started life as crisp, clean white underwear. Now they are much more interesting. It seems they have been smeared with tomato ketchup and burger sauce. There

86

is also stainage caused by rivulets and splashes of brightly coloured drinks. And on each butt cheek there are several lipsticked lip marks. In lipstick, above his bum and with an arrow pointing down between his butt cheeks is written Swipe Here. Moving quickly on and around, you will see he is sporting cocktail umbrellas on his chest. Two of them. The cocktail stick shafts of said umbrellas seem to have been pushed through his nipples. It smarts just looking at them and that's even before you've thought of splinters. For some reason he is sporting an outlandishly large and foppish ruff around his neck and this helps frame his head. This is not a good thing, as you really don't want to look at his head. At some point he has had his face made up to look like a clown, but that make up has been subject to several landslides and avalanches. It looks like his face has collapsed. There are dark rings around darker rings that are centred by eyes so blood shot they are almost completely red. He's wearing huge earrings depicting an array of fruit, that were they not resting upon his ruff would probably tear his earlobes off, if not his ears. Atop his head is another, slightly larger array of fruit. It very much looks like it is real fruit, especially as some of it is rotting. This fruit display is mostly concealing a bald strip down the centre of his head where it looks very like someone started to shave his head and then got bored or distracted and gave up on the job.

This guy looks a state and how he is still standing is anyone's guess. He is moving his right arm up and down slowly by about an inch or so in each direction and one of his eyes is twitching in perfect time with his arm. Don't ask the innocent bystander which eye as they had to look away quickly and don't want to look back again. He is swaying in a circular motion from the waist up. The circle of this motion is gradually growing larger and larger and at this rate the centre of gravity of this man will be too high to sustain the ever-increasing circle and in slow motion he topples forward and the only thing that breaks his fall is the ruff and two cocktail umbrellas. The thought of those cocktail umbrellas causes the innocent bystander to retch. By some strange miracle, or more likely due to the state of decomposition of the fruit on his head, it all stays in place barring a single grape which bounces its way along the floor in a bid for freedom. It almost makes it, but before it can get to the door an eight-inch heel spears it. Poor grape. Sad times.

Thom lets out a low groan and is then quiet for a whole minute before the snoring starts.

"Looks like Thom's had enough for now," observes Bill casually.

Ben turns around looking for Thom and doesn't spot him initially. Then he hears snoring. "Oh," he says as he sees the prone form of his friend, "all that garbage must've taken it out of him, he looks tired." Ben downs his drink. Bends over and slings Thom over his shoulder like he was a silk scarf. "See you back at the hotel?"

Bill nods in agreement, "Yeah, breakfast tomorrow?"

Ben fist bumps Bill. There is a crack like thunder and off he goes with his friend draped casually over him. No one bats an eyelid. This is after all Constellation.

18

When the effects of the Pneumatic Drill were explained to him, Thom hadn't questioned the bit about the *afternoon after* as he was not really in a state to when it was mentioned to him. The thing was, was when he woke up, he knew it was an afternoon. He also knew it wasn't necessarily the afternoon following the day they had started drinking. Or stopped drinking for that matter.

All hangovers are terrible. No one would choose to have one. And yet, they are not a deterrent. There is something strangely perverse in sentient lifeforms that leads them to courses of action that they know will end badly – in this case a hangover – and yet, they will avoid courses of action that end well, like exercise for instance.

Thom's hangover took a while to rouse itself as it was itself suffering from a hangover and didn't want to go into work, so it had a lie in, missed the morning and got its act together in the afternoon. The thing that awoke it was Thom forming the thought *I seem to be surprisingly OK, considering how much I drank and also that I don't have a clue what it was I was actually drinking!* His hangover heard this, stirred from its own hangover and decided it was about time it made an appearance. And Thom was reminded of the other reason why his cocktail was dubbed the pneumatic drill. He had a number of the power-tools going off inside his head. It was noisy and painful. Forming coherent thought was a protracted process and as he did, he struggled to hear these thoughts over the sound of the pneumatic drills. Thinking *hurt*!

At least I haven't been sick, Thom thought. And instantly regretted having that particular summoning thought.

After a couple of false starts, having foolishly tempted providence, Thom crawled back to bed. Blindly crawled, whimpering pathetically as he did so. Somehow, he navigated his way under the covers and found a pillow to rest his head. Not that rest was an available option. He lay in the foetal position and wished for anything but this.

Amongst the noises in his head he realised there was a familiar voice. Having established it wasn't his own voice he tried his best to focus in on it.

It was Clair.

And Thom knew without having decoded the words being uttered, that she wasn't happy and that he was in a bit of trouble.

The bit of trouble he was in was possibly quite a large bit. Now his mind was allowing him to form some thoughts again. Thoughts that were making things all the worse. He thought about what it must have been like to be a passenger in his head for...

...however long it was that he had been on his voyage of alcoholic oblivion. Being a passenger for just a short hop between two of the establishments he'd visited would be bad enough. But for the whole shebang? Oh dear.

What made it worse was he couldn't remember very much at all after the first pneumatic drill cocktail. And even that recollection was not covering him in glory right now as he was remembering the sultry, scantily clad woman whispering in his ear about how he would be a pneumatic drill later. In the sack. Had he? Oh gods! Had he been unfaithful to Clair whilst she was in his head. Done the deed right in front of her?

He should stop thinking about that. Even that was not really on. Thinking about whether he might or might not have done *stuff*.

Thom had had the hangover blues before – but this was different class. For one, he'd never drunk as much as that before. Or over such a period. And the drinks he'd been given were loopy juice. Then the fact that he'd dragged Clair along for the whole sordid ride? That was low. Lower than a snake's belly low.

And he was at an utter disadvantage – how was he going to make this up to Clair when he didn't even know what he was making up for.

Thom... thought Clair in Thom's head.

Ow! Was Thom's first thought. Even the sound of Clair's thoughts hurt.

What happened, Thom? thought Clair.

Thom felt her concern. That was good right? She was concerned.

He also felt self-loathing and self-pity and regret and a general hot-tub of shittiness about himself. He wasn't sure whether Clair's thoughts and feelings mirrored his. He expected that they could and should. And he deserved it.

Do you do this often? Clair asked.

Not like that, Thom thought earnestly. That was different class and then some. I don't even know how long I was doing whatever it was I was doing.

Three days, said Clair in his head.

Three…!? Bloody hell!

Interestingly, Bill and Ben didn't seem all that affected by the drinks.

Interesting indeed, thought Thom. He couldn't help thinking that they'd known what they were doing and he'd been stitched up. Then again, maybe not. Zombies weren't known for their self-awareness.

Clair, I'm really sorry, began Thom.

Clair laughed. Which in Thom's head was not a good thing.

Ouch! He thought. But he also thought the laughter was a good sign and miraculously he seemed to be off the hook. Then he pulled himself back from any thoughts of self-congratulation from dodging a bullet. What he'd done was not good. Unforgiveable even. He wasn't going to let himself off the hook so easily, even if Clair did.

So… Thom began, I fear you've seen me at my worst, both over the last three days and right now. And even I have been spared seeing me at my worst. I'm sorry. I didn't think. I shouldn't have brought you along for that.

No! Not at all, thought Clair. *It was fascinating! The euphoria. The dancing. The sense of well-being and all that fun. I really enjoyed it.*

Thom was at a bit of a loss. This was difficult enough to process. Clair was difficult enough to process, even when he was firing on all cylinders…

But tell me, do you enjoy this bit? asked Clair.

Not really replied Thom, but this is the payback. The Yin for the yang of the good times. For everything there is a price.

Well that seemed to be the case both during and after the curry you ate, said Clair.

Curry? Oh. Was it good?

You kept saying it was, but you really struggled to eat it and your entire face was leaking.

Well… that's the sign of a good curry I suppose…

The morning after was pretty bad, Thom.

Also, the sign of a good curry I'm afraid.

Would you like to feel better? Clair asked.

You mean…? thought Thom.

And before he could think of the answer and debate with himself whether he should cheat the god of hangovers, whether he even deserved to feel better than the mess he was right now he could feel his mood lifting and his head clearing. The breeze-block in his gut dissolved and his stomach growled as it called to be fed. It was a gradual uplifting of his state and very pleasant it was too. In fact, he was starting to feel really happy. Too happy…

OK, you can stop around here thanks, thought Thom.

OK! thought Clair breezily.

Thanks Clair, that's a relief. More than a relief. You're a…

…Thom scrabbled around for the right words and landed on just the one. Miracle.

He took a deep breath and marvelled at how it didn't hurt to do so. I don't know what you are and you're full of surprises, he thought, I also don't quite know how we found each other.

The universes are strange and wonderful places, Thom!

thought Clair, *Things happen for reasons, but you may never quite know what those reasons are. The main thing is that you go with it all and have fun along the way.*

Yes, quite, thought Thom. Wondering whether the last three days had given Clair the wrong impression of what fun actually was.

"I'd best get up," Thom said out loud.

Clair giggled. Out loud.

"What?" Thom asked.

More giggles.

Thom padded into the bathroom and went to the toilet. Only thinking about what he was doing with Clair present half way through. But she didn't seem phased by it and he realised he must have been a number of times over the last few days. As he washed his hands, he caught sight of himself in the mirror and screamed.

Clair giggled again. Out loud. *I'm afraid I can't do anything about your hair,* she thought, giggling some more.

19

"All I'm saying is..." Thom began.

Ben raised his eyebrows.

"Well, you let me get into a right state!" and as Thom said it, he got that he was moaning and he was quite rightly getting short-shrift. He was a big boy and he knew what he was doing. As much as you could on a night out on Constellation. "I mean, look at my hair!" he exclaimed whilst pointing at the bald landing strip running across the top of his head, front to back.

Ben nodded as Thom went quiet.

"So..." said Thom, "I've popped my Constellation Cherry." And he grinned at his friend. "You're paying for my hair cut though!"

They both dug into the huge fry-ups in front of them. Nothing better after a mammoth session and the fry-up had taken this literally and included mammoth steaks.

"So, what next?" asked Ben, "after you've had the rest of your head shaved."

"Well, we'd best make our way off Constellation really," said Thom.

"Why's that?" asked Ben.

"No one stays on Constellation, Ben. It's a stop off to other places," replied Thom, "besides, my liver would mutiny if we stayed here!"

"Bill stays here," contested Ben.

"Yeah, about that?" asked Thom.

"He owns a few bars and clubs," said Ben, "he likes it here. Says its home."

"Well, I suppose if anyone was going to be the exception that proves the norm it was going to be a zombie clown. You guys certainly have the constitution for Constellation," smiled Thom.

"Oh, he lived here well before he was a zombie," said Ben, "It was on a big night out that he changed."

"Bigger than our night out?" ventured Thom.

"Too right! Ours was tame!" Ben smiled, "Bill is from the fair and lovely planet Eire. Those guys like a drink and they know how to party!"

"Blinking Flip!" gasped Thom, "why didn't you warn me!! Those guys even beat the nutters from the planet Aus!"

Thom shuddered at the very thought. Some people were animals! "OK, but I think it might be wise to put a little more distance between us and Krill and the Micra. I'd feel more comfortable doing that and I wouldn't mind a more relaxed hang out really," said Thom as he chewed on his mammoth steak. "And we can show Clair a little more of the universes."

Ben winked at him. Which meant he was in. "OK, Thom" he conceded, "I mean, no one would expect us to be here, because as you say, no one stays on Constellation. But yes, let's take Clair and see more of the universes." He added another exaggerated wink for good measure.

20

While Ben and Thom were having breakfast a couple of things were also taking place.

Bill was attending to business. A very lucrative and enjoyable business at that. Bill enjoyed Constellation and it looked after him in many ways, hence his rather splendid Ferrcati. Seeing someone with a passion for what they do is always an uplifting experience. That passion and enthusiasm is contagious. Even when the purveyor of such enthusiasm is a zombie, made up as a clown, in a state of undress with a number of life-forms writhing around him on a bed the size of a small football pitch. A water bed that had a gentle tidal pattern that was affected by the two moons of Constellation. Bill was busy at work in the midst of all this movement and distraction. Bill could evidently multitask.

Being one of the few residents of Constellation, Bill was a useful person to know. People made it their business to know Bill and that was one of his revenue streams. Knowing people and more importantly knowing *stuff* about people. Knowledge is power. People-related knowledge is power over people. Bill sold this knowledge. You may judge Bill for this. After all, selling information about people seems sneaky and underhand and it could be to the detriment of those people. Bill didn't see it like this and was not at all malicious in his dealings. His take on it was that the information he sold was freely available and had a very short life as a saleable commodity, so he may as well benefit from providing the information while he could. And the money he earned went into the Constellation economy and was part of the lifeblood of the place. And because Constellation was all about fun and good times, this could only be a good thing, couldn't it? Of course, he'd never discussed this take on this part of his business dealings, mostly because complete discretion was required from the purveyor of important information. So, it was a bit of a closed loop really.

A message appeared on his screen. He had to gently guide an errant and probing tentacle to one side in order to read it fully, being careful to allow the tentacle to continue with its pleasant ministrations.

Are they there with you now?

The message enquired.

Bill replied.

Nearby, yes.

Good. We need them to stay put for another day. Can you effect this?

Yes of course, I saw to it that one of them is not in a fit state to even think about leaving any time soon.

Good. We will pay your fee when we have arrived on Constellation and obtained the package.

Bill started to write a reply that explained that this wasn't his usual payment terms. He gave the information over and it was payment upon receipt. But then, on this occasion, it wasn't just a case of giving information. He'd got a bit more involved in this transaction and something approaching unease stirred deep down within him. He closed the door on that stirring and focused on a much more pleasant one and instead sent a simple reply, his ability to remain undistracted and multitask being eroded rather rapidly now.

OK.

21

The other thing that was happening was that They were getting ever closer to Constellation and Clair. The Thing looked out over the expanse of space, actively watching. Looking intently for something. It didn't appear to be the gently drifting figure of Garm. A figure that had a moment of quite interesting animation and then slumped back into gentle drifting in a way that conveyed *oh bother* in a far better way than the words themselves could. The Thing's gaze did not even flicker at this movement. The only interesting thing to see for as far as the eye could see. But then the Thing's eyes gave the impression that they could see much further than a common or garden eye.

"She's near," the Thing barked, seemingly into the air and to no one as there was only the Thing in the cabin of its craft.

"We know," came the hiss of a disembodied voice.

The Thing nodded and pressed a few buttons on a dark and very dimly lit console. Its craft changed course almost imperceptibly and followed the tracks of Bill's Ferrcati. Tracks only a creature like the Thing could see.

The Thing was nearing its objective. Constellation and its quarry were very near.

22

"So, Bill isn't coming?" asked Thom.

Ben was trotting towards him, "no, we really must go!" he gasped.

Thom wasn't getting with the program and was showing none of the urgency Ben felt. But then Thom hadn't seen the people who were with Bill and what they'd been doing to Bill. Ben had and somehow, he'd managed not to be seen. Other than by Bill that was and the look Bill had given him conveyed much. Mostly it said, RUN! But there was a sadness there too. Bill had somehow stuffed up and he was sorry. So, Ben got that the people roughing up Bill weren't really after Bill – they were after Ben and Thom. Bill was buying them some time.

Ben slowed to a brisk walk as he neared Thom and grabbed his wrist. "We need to go mate. We've been followed. And the people who followed us are with Bill right now. And they are not nice people."

Thom looked at his friend. "Oh, that doesn't sound good."

"It's not, they're roughing Bill up and doing a good job of it. Which is saying something."

"Shouldn't we help Bill?"

"We are. The sooner we're off Constellation and away the sooner we stop being Bill's problem. And hopefully these people will see it that way too."

Ben stopped walking and looked Thom up and down "you're looking surprisingly chipper after the session you had!?"

Thom shrugged, "I paced myself."

Ben looked at him quizzically, "Paced…?"

Thom quickly changed the subject, "Mate, we need to get a wriggle on!"

Which they did.

Thom was feeling unease. An unease that slipped into anxiety laced with fear. They'd made a grand gesture and *stuck it to the man* this seemed to be getting a bit more serious than that. Surely the cleaning bill wasn't all that bad?

Ben and Thom were both marching with purpose and in step with each other. Thom thought about saying that they should try to act a bit more naturally. But there didn't seem to be time for that.

"Where are we going?" he asked under his breath.

"Bill has a few ships. They come in handy. He hires some of them out. He'd already told me about the one we should take when we left Constellation."

Thom nodded. At least they had the means to get off Constellation.

"We should really go and get my ship," said Thom between a couple of heavy breaths. He was starting to struggle to keep up and avoiding the reeling revellers was becoming a bit more of a chore now he was sober.

"No, I think we'll stick with this craft for now, mate," replied Ben, "I'll square it with Bill, but he owes me." Ben thought on this a bit more, as it was Bill owed him more than the cost of the ship they were taking and it was time to call in that debt. But having seen that look on his friend's face he thought Bill might owe him quite a bit more now.

The crowds of people moving from bar to club to bar seemed to be forming murmurations. Thom found himself wondering how it all looked from the air. They found themselves walking alongside two older ladies who reminded Thom of the dinner ladies at his school. Friendly ladies of a certain age. They started chattering away to Thom and Ben and always the polite sort of blokes, they replied and made small talk confirming that yes, they were here for a laugh and a giggle, despite this being quite obvious – there wasn't much else you'd come to Constellation for.

"So, a Stag Do is it?" asked the one who Thom thought of as Mavis.

"Kind of," agreed Ben taking the conversational line of least resistance.

"Aye! Aye!" said the other lady that Thom had mentally dubbed Doreen.

At this they both picked their pace up for a few steps and went ahead of Ben and Thom. This was strange, thought Thom.

Clair chipped in with a thought, *erm Thom?*

Distractedly Thom thought, yes?

You might want to look away, she added.

Why... began Thom's train of thought as the two portly ladies of a certain age gracefully wheeled around in one hundred and eighty degree arcs and brushing their knitted cardies to one side they grabbed fistfuls of their tops and raised them in a purposeful and fluid motion revealing voluminous quantities of breast.

"You'll be wanting a bit of this then!" screeched Mavis and they both cackled away even as they stood, backs arched and garments held aloft to flash their ample bosoms.

Thom and Ben were rooted to the spot. Transfixed.

Unable to look away, Thom could see Ben in his peripheral vision. He was drooling.

"Hubba! Hubba!" he croaked, hypnotised by the jubblies that were accosting his eyes.

This broke the spell for Thom. It was his turn to grab his friend's wrist and he dragged him past the still cackling ladies.

"Thanks ladies, it's not often we get such a tempting offer, but we're unfortunately on our way home," grinned Ben.

"Ooooh!" both ladies chorused in quarter-hearted dis-appointment. The lack of vim and vigour in the disap-pointment made Thom wonder whether this flashing of the bosom strategy was used often and a fairly successful approach. It felt like they were already chalking this one up and they'd be swooping in on their next victims in short order – hypnotising them with their areola and pouncing moments later. The pouncing bit was a worrying thought.

"Don't get many of them to the pound," winked Ben being his usual charming self. This made the two ladies giggle girlishly and seizing his opportunity, Ben took the game to them. He slipped his arms around Mavis and leant her back in the approximation of a swoon and kissed her for what felt like several minutes. Coming up for air he then did the same with Doreen as Mavis fanned herself and caught her breath.

Once he'd eventually disengaged from Doreen, both of them gave Ben a very knowing look and a big smile, then they toddled off and were quickly lost in the crowds.

Just another random moment in Constellation.

Thom looked at Ben.

Ben shrugged, "just blending in, mate!"

Thom couldn't argue with that. No one would bat an eyelid at that, but he couldn't help saying "you should be wearing a muzzle, mate!"

"Low blow!" retorted Ben, "low blow!" Nonetheless, he reached into his pocket and put his muzzle back on. He'd gotten out of the habit of wearing it on Constellation where anything went and muzzles weren't expected.

The next part of their walk was a little more turbulent. They seemed to bump into an endless succession of inebriated people. At one point a reveller trailed a great many appendages several of which homed in on Thom's lower regions and very nearly tore his trousers off. As they emerged out of the other side of this last crowd Thom was feeling a little dizzy from the physicality of it all. It was a literal assault on his senses.

"Just down here," said Ben, turning left as he said this. They were entering a narrow alley and as they left the main thoroughfare a shadow moved and unsteadily detached itself from the alley wall. Someone was much the worse for wear and it didn't look like it would be much longer before lights out for them. They stumbled across Thom's path and nearly fell. Thom stepped back, but too late. An outstretched, flailing palm landed on his chest and pushed him back into the wall. The shock of the contact stunned Thom and his head was spinning.

He realised the slightly stooped person in front of him was speaking, but he was only catching some of it as what sounded like a hoarse man's voice muttered a litany…

"…when the dogs fly…"

"…the wise ones, they know…"

"…they know…"

"…it will *grow!*"

"You've taken some powerful shit, man!" Ben's voice rising over the top of the drunk and perhaps drug addled man.

A hand snaked out and grabbed Thom's. The same sudden shock, as if Thom had been dropped into a vat of ice water. His body shuddering and his mind all but shutting down.

They are near! screeched a voice inside his head.

They are coming for you! it hissed, filling his head painfully.

They will have you! the voice echoing and clanging around inside him.

Then darkness.

Ben shaking him. "Thom! Wake up!"

Thom opened his eyes to see his concerned friend staring at him. He blinked and shook his head. Noticing there was no sign of the man.

"Where's he gone?" Thom asked as his vision cleared and his head followed suit.

"Who?" asked Ben with a perplexed expression crossing his face.

"The drunk guy. The guy who was ranting and grabbed me?"

"There was no one here, mate," said Ben examining Thom closely as he spoke, "you just froze and started to convulse and say all this weird shit…"

"Me? What was I saying?"

"Dunno, mate. Couldn't understand half of it," said Ben shaking his head, "there was something about flying dogs.

And that was one of the least weird things. Although flying dogs? Imagine all the shit flying around too! And the other stuff! I mean they'd be at it like no one's business! In the air! You'd need an umbrella!"

"OK mate, calm down!" said Thom as he found his feet. He took a deep breath, his head clearing, "Hang on, didn't you say something to the man about taking some powerful shit?"

"I said that to you and I thought you were mucking about."

Thom nodded, then stopped suddenly and looked very concerned. Ben noticed and mirrored his expression.

"Clair?" they both said in unison.

There was a horrible, quiet pause and they both feared the worst.

"*I'm...,*" said a meek disembodied voice, "*I'm OK, but I think we need to get out of here. Something is very close and it doesn't feel right. It doesn't feel right at all...*"

Not needing any more encouragement Ben and Thom strode down the alley which opened out onto a small pad with several ships.

"The taxi?" asked Thom.

"Yup," replied Ben, "It's discrete. And when we've got to wherever we're going, I may have a job set up and waiting for me thanks to this crate!"

They boarded and Ben went straight to the console and fired up the Taxi. Thom had to admit he seemed quite at home there.

The ship rose slowly away from the pad, but not before it clipped one of the other, more expensive ships and inflicted some expensive cosmetic damage.

"You're a natural," nodded Thom to his friend.

Ben smiled back and winked. "Where to guv'nor?"

Thom, paused and looked around.

"Follow that ship!" he grinned, "I've always wanted to say that to a taxi driver!"

And off they went, on the tail of another ship. Thom may never have asked a taxi driver to follow a ship before, but there had been plenty of times when he'd not been quite sure where he should go next and found that following the right ship would always take you where you needed to go. You couldn't just follow any old ship, that just wouldn't do! You had to have the knack. The knack would allow you to identify the very ship you needed to follow and Thom had the knack.

23

The clawed, reptilian hand struck again.

Bill groaned, "no more, please." It wasn't hurting exactly. But he knew it was probably best to reward his assailant's efforts with the prerequisite moans and groans and pleas for mercy.

"Where are they?!" his attacker demanded.

"I told you, they should be in their rooms!" cried Bill.

"If they were in their rooms, do you think I would be here beating you half to death, deary?!" challenged the brute stooped over Bill.

Bill stared up into the cold, dead yellow eyes and did his best not to show any amusement at the thought that his eyes were also dead, but much more pleasant than this rotter's. But did he just call Bill deary? It wasn't the word as much as he seemed to mean it, it wasn't said sarcastically. "Well," he began, deciding to ignore that potential slip and that he'd probably had enough of at least some of this pretence, "yes, I think you would actually."

This wasn't the expected response. "You what?"

"I think you quite enjoy doing this," said Bill quite matter-of-factly.

His assailant was taken aback, and merely croaked. Bill couldn't be more wrong. The claw, that had been raised in readiness for another blow to Bill's head, hung there temporarily forgotten. This wasn't in the script. More so because this particular reptile hated its job and really didn't want to be here, nor doing this. He'd always wanted to be a painter and decorator really.

"I have to admit that," said Bill getting to his feet and smoothing his clothes down, "I've been enjoying it immensely!" and he beamed at his interrogator who was being rather slow on the uptake. So slow that he didn't even flinch as Bill leaned in casually and bit down hard on his assailant's snout.

Bill broke away and rubbed his hands together in a job-done manner, staring at his handiwork.

"What have you done?!" said a now panicked voice.

"Well," replied Bill, "let's just say that you're ever so slightly screwed."

The former brute – who's heart was not in the whole brute business - was now making a pathetic keening noise and cradling his face. The blood in the wound was bubbling and turning a sludgy brown colour.

"Not a good combo," said Bill, with his hands now on his hips as he watched the reptile in front of him slump in on himself, "zombie bite and your blood. They seem to react quite badly." Bill sighed and went on. "I had hoped that you'd have a reaction to my blood while you were hitting me. Just a bit finding its way into your mouth or your eye. But when that didn't happen? Well, route one was called for I'm afraid."

Bill stepped over the pathetic figure slumped on his floor and without looking back muttered, "Have a nice after-life, mate." And then exited his room and headed front of house to attend to business.

He should have bought Ben and Thom enough time to leave Constellation.

24

The Thing that had dispatched Desk and was pursuing Clair watched this scene dispassionately. It had hoped that some of its work was being done by the reptile, but it seemed that the funny dead man in the make-up was playing a game. A game that The Thing obviously didn't know all the rules to as it didn't really make all that much sense.

The Thing knew Clair was nearby. But something or some things seemed to be clouding The Thing's ability to home in on her. This was a development. But no matter, The Thing would find Clair. It was just a matter of time and The Thing had Time and Matter. Plenty of it.

The Thing spoke "She is near."

"Yessss," hissed the disembodied voice in response, "but she continues to evade us."

"A…" began the Thing, forming the words carefully, something it did not do often, "…temporary state of affairs." It looked around the room and began to walk away, "I will find her."

25

Thom scratched his head. Something was going on in there. He could feel it.

You OK, Clair? He thought.

Yes, came the reply. It was a quiet response which conveyed the fact that Clair was obviously having a gentle moment of reflection and contemplation and it would be very wise for Thom to leave her alone. Funny how one word can be said in such a way that it conveys more meaning and carries much more heft than a thousand words.

OK cool, thought Thom, trailing off with a wisp of thoughts along the lines of I'll leave you to it then. In my head. Doing whatever you're doing. Inside my mind. Not a problem. I really don't know what's going on here. And I'm trying not to think about it. But that's very difficult. Because things keep happening and they are very out of the ordinary. But you know what? It's mostly good. Mostly very good. It feels right. More right than anything I've felt before. Even with all the weirdness...

And Thom's thoughts trailed off like that until he sighed and busied himself in conversation with Ben and making a cuppa. Nothing like a good cup of tea when you need the worlds to be right.

* * *

If Thom had caught more of the snatches of the supposedly drug-addled bloke's ramblings he'd have heard something about The Awakening. The man they'd encountered was real enough. Just not inhabiting a piece of space time that Ben would have noticed, nor would Thom under more usual circumstances.

So, Ben had seen a strange tableau with Thom talking to himself and his mind had rationalised the conversation as the ramblings of his friend Thom as he had a funny turn. Something that was not at all unexpected after the drinking mission they'd been on for the last few days, after all it was a miracle Thom was able to stand, let alone talk. And of course, few things were unexpected in Constellation.

Thom had only heard snatches of the conversation as he struggled with his perception of someone who was not actually there, but somewhere entirely different and yet parallel to where he seemed to be. He only saw the man because Clair saw him. Even then, Thom's mind refused to see what he was seeing because he shouldn't be able to see it. His mind was fighting with Thom and shouting Stop Seeing That Man! which didn't help Thom listen to what the man was saying.

Clair saw the man and she most definitely heard him.

The partially invisible man was a seer. Clair just knew this. Like she just knew a whole heap of stuff as they were encountering it. The problem was that until she was in a new or emerging situation, the things she knew were tucked away somewhere she couldn't get to. Her knowledge seemed to be provided to her on a need to know basis and she needed to know why that was. The keeper of her knowledge was not playing ball and obviously had a set of rules it followed in order to release rules. Those rules did not include Clair saying she needed to know the rest of what she obviously knew, but you seem to be preventing me from knowing it!

Clair consoled herself with the fact that she now knew the knowledge was there. She hadn't known it was there and now she did. That was progress. Was it part of The Awakening the seer had mentioned? It felt like it probably was. Felt. Feelings. They were growing too. She felt like she was expanding. Growing into herself. That was a kind of awakening wasn't it? And somehow feeling and knowing were inextricably linked. She felt that other things were happening. That The Awakening wasn't restricted to her. Other things were awakening. Something was happening and she needed to keep moving so that she encountered more of the universes and unlocked more of that knowledge that she knew was just behind a doorway. A big, heavy and locked doorway with an extremely officious bureaucrat behind it. But I know you're there, she whispered to herself and now I know about you and the door and that means I can do something about it.

The Bureaucrat heard Clair's whisper despite the very big, heavy and thick door and it shuddered. It was only doing its job, but that might not be enough to protect it from the powerful thing on the other side of the door. A powerful thing that was only at a fraction of its power and knowing. The Bureaucrat hoped that things wouldn't take an unpleasant turn, that the thing on the other side of the door wouldn't get angry and that its capacity for empathy, understanding and mercy grew more quickly than its hunger for wrath and revenge.

* * *

Clair's mood changed as she latched onto one of Thom's thoughts. Yes, it was mostly good. And for her it was getting better. *You know what?* she thought, *I'm discovering lots of new and fascinating things as I go along. Maybe if I unlocked that door there would be so much knowledge there that I would already know pretty much everything. And where would the fun be in that? Yes! I'm having fun!*

The lighting and the atmosphere in the taxi-ship lifted. Noticeably.

Ben and Thom looked at each other.

"Clair?" asked Ben.

Thom nodded then looked out of the ship across the vastness of space. Even that seemed to have lightened up a bit. He dismissed it as wishful thinking, but a part of him knew that it wasn't and that self-same part of him was a bit worried. No, worried wasn't the word. Overwhelmed. Overwhelmed at the enormity of what was happening. The terrifying potential of Clair. He didn't know what she was and he got that she didn't know what she was either. He'd known she was something more than a Chair. He'd felt something unique when he'd walked into Krill's office that first time

116

and she'd been there. A presence that more than filled the room. And when the Chair had spoken, he'd known he'd met someone very special. He'd obviously tried to rationalise it – she's a Chair for heaven's sake! But that didn't cut it. More rationalising was along the lines of her A.I. having been played with by a genius tech who was undervalued in his firm and job. That she was maybe a one-off project that had somehow made it into the world. It felt like there was an underlying truth there. Clair certainly was a one-off.

Clair was growing though. Even as a Chair, she'd been more than the Chair. Function defines a thing. A chair is a chair because it is something to sit on. Thom had thought about the additional functionality that a Chair like Clair had. It was no longer just a chair. Much the same as phones of old had ceased being phones. They'd called them Smart and given them a bunch of other functions to the point that people seldom used their phone as a phone. They were still called phones, Smart Phones – but their primary function was to utilise the internet and its networks, not the phone network, so if they had been produced as the full-fat version on day one they'd have a completely different name that more closely described their function such as Social Networking Device. But then, this sort of device had to evolve and creep up on people – if it had been sold with all the bells and whistles on day one, no one would have known what to do with it. Clair had a personality and intelligence and feelings. Thom had a relationship with Clair from the off, so it was a natural progression that she would call herself something other than Chair as a chair she was not. She was a chair as much as Thom was a chair. You could sit on Thom and call him a chair, but he would not sit idly by and let himself be defined that way.

Clair was more differentiated than Thom though. Thom was restricted by his form. Clair wasn't. Thom was and always would be a person. The only way he would transcend that was by dying and ascending to the afterlife. Maybe. For starters, there had to be an afterlife and if there were then Thom needed to fulfil a long list of criteria to get through the existential door of the afterlife, one of which was believing in the afterlife and Thom didn't think that his belief that there *might* be an afterlife would qualify. Clair on the other hand had already broken beyond the confines of her original form and she'd tried her hand at being a ship. Even when she was a ship, she wasn't a ship. Well, she was and she wasn't. She filled the ship, but more than filled the ship, was more than the ship and more than just another passenger on the ship.

And right now, she was in Thom. And Thom knew she wasn't Thom. Because he was Thom. And he'd not stopped being Thom, not one bit. Thom wasn't sure how she could be in him and yet he wasn't adversely affected. Quite the opposite, it was good having her around and he felt all the better for having her around. Somehow more than himself. He hadn't known he had all that room inside himself. If someone had asked if he minded them living in his head, he'd have told them to bugger off because there was no room at the inn! But he knew this was only a temporary arrangement. That Clair couldn't live in his head for ever more. That thought made him sad. He felt a sense of loss at the thought of her moving out. He thought he would feel empty, like a house that had been a home, but now someone had left and it and returned it to its state of merely house and not home.

This state would be worse than it would be for a house that was a house and had always been a house; ignorance was bliss.

Where did Clair belong? That was the question. She had no form, which made Thom's limited view of the universes and their reality quake in its boots. He didn't know. In his limited view, most if not all things were defined by their function and the function was usually indicated by the form. That's a table because you can put your plate of food on it. And Clair's functions seemed to be expanding out and beyond his understanding. It seemed like she could exist anywhere. Go anywhere, reside anywhere. But in Thom's increasingly limited experience, things needed a place. They needed a home. They needed to feel like they belonged.

I'll never leave you Thom, Clair thought.

Thom, shook his head as if waking from a day dream. Clair was in his head and she had a ring-side seat to his thoughts.

You'll have to Clair, it would not be good for you to stay here with me. You're so much more than I am and that I can give you. Besides, you're a passenger in me. I think you'd have a much better time somewhere where you are you and you have more control over things.

But I am me, Thom. And I have control over everything I want control over. And more. Lots more. I'm happy here! thought Clair. *But if I do go somewhere else, I'll still be here too.*

Eh? thought Thom, which was a succinct way of him telling Clair his mind was yet again blown.

Didn't you feel it when I was inside the Ferrcati? Even before then after we'd met, I was with you from then wasn't I? Even when you were across the galaxy we weren't really apart.

Thom thought. They'd met and they'd clicked. It was one

of those meant to be moments. A defining moment where things change – they are not the same after. It's quite difficult to remember back past the defining moments of life, that's why people will make a sweeping statement like: things were very different then. But different how? Oh, just different!

Thom felt different from the off. And yes, he was looking forward to seeing Chair again once they'd parted. But that… was it… it felt better being nearer her. But it felt good all the time.

So, he began with his thoughts. You, are with me even if you are not with me. You leave a piece of yourself behind? he ventured.

It's more than that, Thom.

And Thom saw that it was. He felt it, more than saw it but he was seeing it. It took him a moment to realise that Clair was gently showing him the way of it. That he was seeing in a different way than he'd ever seen before. His way of seeing everything and feeling everything was changing. The language he had at his disposal wasn't going to cut this, he thought.

Language never cuts it, Thom replied Clair. *You already knew that. Language is inadequate. Sharing is what counts. You give yourself to someone and that changes everything. You have to feel it.*

And Thom did. He found himself thinking it was similar to explaining what love was to someone who had never experienced it before. It's this invisible thing. So how do you know it's there? You just do. You feel it.

That helped explain Clair just that bit more. She just was and you felt her. Which meant she was in Thom, but she was also outside Thom. And that meant she could be anywhere and everywhere didn't it? At one point, Thom had thought of Clair as his imaginary friend – and he'd gone off on one wondering whether he was ever so slightly mad. The episode with the drug-addled bloke who wasn't really there didn't help matters. But Clair was real, more real than what Thom had previously considered to be the irrefutable, tangible reality presented to him.

Are you still in the Ferrcati? asked Thom.

Yes, and the Chair. But... They are not living things. So I'm less present. I'm... a ghost of something that was. A wisp. A residue. Whereas in you? That's different.

Thom nodded. Something fell into place. Not a fully formed thought. But he felt like they'd just narrowed down the direction they were heading. Clair's home would be somewhere alive. Somewhere big and full of life.

26

Something like Clair happening to the universes, doesn't go unnoticed. And she was happening and then some. Whilst she was in the Chair, quietly going about her business as a chair, she wasn't on anyone's radar. Not really. Even then she made the odd ripple, but by and large these went unnoticed or were passed off as a bit of gas after a large meal.

Thom had unwittingly set off a chain of events which now they were in motion had to be played out. That's how these things went. Or were supposed to go. Certain players were now involved. There had to be an order to things.

Hence The Thing and the shadowy creature it was in contact with as it tracked Clair across the Universes.

Tracking Clair wasn't easy. Already she was gaining in power and knowledge and intuitively covering her tracks and cloaking her presence. Not entirely, but the very fact that she did not want to be found meant that she was difficult to find. There was always something there with a thing like Clair though – however good she got at hiding in plain sight, there was something that could be seen. If you looked in the right place and in the right way.

So, The Thing was still in pursuit and could see enough of Clair's tracks to be going in the correct direction.

So too were the reptilian pursuers. They didn't know it, but they also, by a quirk of the fates were going in the right direction.

* * *

Planets also don't appear from nowhere without being noticed.

Obviously Varg had noticed the new planet and it was something that would live with him until his dying day. Which was the same day because he noticed the planet in an outstandingly dramatic and terminal way.

Interestingly though, the planet wasn't having all that much impact on its surroundings.

Well, in a way this was an untruth as there had been a few impacts. And there had been a few near misses as ship's pilots looked up from their instruments and had a messy trouser moment processing the fact that there really was a planet there despite their Auto-Mapping system insisting there wasn't. Those pilots had wrestled with the intransigent Auto-Mapping system as it continued to plot a course through the planet and most of them had won that wrestling match.

A number hadn't.

Unfortunately, many ship's pilots were overly reliant on the Auto-Mapping system and its guidance of their ships and the first they knew of the new planet was when there was a massive bang and then they winked out of existence.

The planet looked like it was going through a teenage phase, its face pockmarked with acne. It was a big planet though and it wasn't a big deal.

It was a big deal to the ship owners and passengers though. Right now, the owners of the ships, or their surviving relatives, were contacting the owners of the Auto-Mapping software. The initial feedback had been dealt with in the usual manner: bloody users. Pain in the arse they are. Wouldn't know their arse from their elbow, let alone a planet! Planets don't just appear from nowhere! Never been a problem before.

But then there was more feedback, which made it more difficult to ignore. Worse still was the video feeds that were being shared and then these were picked up by the media: Auto-Mapping sends ships THROUGH A PLANET! That was quite difficult to ignore. More so as software developers are social media voyeurs so as soon as it started to trend, they were watching the silly idiots flying their ships into a planet! Why would anyone *do* that!?

Then they realised it was their software doing it.

And that this just was not possible.

As the confusion arose due to a planet popping into existence it wasn't the type of confusion that would just go away. Planets just didn't pop into existence, so there had to be another explanation. There wasn't another explanation so what this was going to lead to was the largest law suit of the last hundred years and the emergence of the Lawyer Dynasty that would rule a large swathe of a particular galaxy for a thousand years. This led to a miserable time and there were many attempts at revolts, revolutions and coups, but the Lawyer Dynasty would always take their oppressed populous through the courts and win or lose, they always ended up with such a gargantuan set of fees via the prosecution and defence of the case that they would buy their way out of any nonsense and carry on as before, only richer and more powerful. The lawyers always came out on top.

Incidentally, the Auto-Mapping software firm Banana, also wrote and owned the software for various office appliances including desks and chairs...

27

"Sir?" said the reptilian life form manning the second mate's position in the very big spaceship.

"Yes?" barked the reptilian captain.

"I think we're being followed."

"Followed!?" bellowed the captain, "show me!" The captain had bought a book on leadership and read a page on issuing orders. In a loud voice. It had served him well these past twelve years.

"There," said what the captain liked to think of as one of his minions. It was after all, the natural order of things, he was the captain, his crew were there to do his bidding. The Captain and Krill had read the same book on Management, the only difference being the page they focused in on and made their central premise to all the Management they inflicted upon their minions.

"That!?" exclaimed the captain "that's just a taxi!" he added with a guffaw that was designed to undermine his minion and keep him in his place.

"Do you think it might be Craig?" asked another of the minions on the bridge. They asked this hopefully. The ensuing silence smothered that hope with a pillow. Craig was no more. Bitten by a zombie and consigned to oblivion in a most painful and revolting manner.

The first minion sat silently seething. It might just be a taxi to the clumsy oaf of a captain, but as they were dressed up as a pleasure cruiser, whilst carrying enough ordnance to erase several planets from existence, surely a taxi might not actually be a taxi, or at the very least it might have been stolen from an unsuspecting taxi driver. He'd just about had enough of the captain and his shouty, bellowing guffawing ways. He should have listened to his mother and gone into teaching. There was none of this nonsense in a classroom…

…well there was, and even more so in the playground, and let's not mention the Staff Room. This sort of nonsense was standard and a great deal of the frustration being felt was based on the feeling that surely now that we are adults, we can stop behaving like we're still schoolkids?

As the minion continued to seethe and wish he was somewhere else, Ben looked out of the taxi at the pleasure cruiser they were following and wondered what the passengers were up to on board that ship. As quite often happened his mind wandered to quite lustful thoughts and he thought of the many bored women on a cruise who would like a Ben shaped interlude in their lives. A rude interlude, thought Ben smiling to himself.

Thom looked at the sensors on the taxi's control panel. Then out across the blackness of space. Other than the cruise ship he could see nothing. He asked Clair if their pursuers were close? Speaking out loud for Ben's benefit.

"*Yes*", she replied.

That was strange. There was only the cruise ship in sight, but Thom trusted Clair's sense of their pursuers so they'd have to keep going. There was no knowing how far Clair's reach went, so their pursuers could be some distance away. For now, keep following the cruise ship and maybe they'd gain sight of the pursuers as they went along. Hiding in the shadow of the cruise ship still felt like the best course of action, as did following the big ship as they got closer to where they needed to be.

"There's more than one set of pursuers Thom," Clair added.

That was ominous. More than one set of pursuers. And the way Clair said it didn't make it sound good either.

"Two sets of pursuers?" he asked.

"At least two that I know of," she paused for a moment. *"It's the other pursuers that worry me the most."*

Thom should have followed this up more directly and drilled down into what Clair meant by the other pursuers, and more specifically asked a bit more about the location of the first set of less frightening pursuers. There was a lot going on though, and you live and learn. Well, mostly you live. Hopefully that would remain a given.

28

After Thom and Ben's little stunt, Krill had had a crappy time. No, a garbagy time. He didn't think he'd ever get the smell of that garbage off of him. Nor the feeling of it oozing through his clothing and invading his skin. He felt permanently dirty and defiled.

If Krill had been a happy-go-lucky sort of a person, he would have been thankful that the garbage had exploded just before he'd walked right up to it and he'd at least been spared the full force of the putrid blast. Krill wasn't that sort of a person though and this whole unfortunate incident had made his world view even more jaundiced.

And that was before he'd returned to the sanctuary of his office. Back to the safety of his own personal space. A personal space that now had a hole where there was once a door. And two bits of what had formerly been his desk.

At least the chair is still intact he'd thought as he plonked himself down in it expecting a greeting and just the right movements and pressure to start to ease all the stress he was under. But the chair wasn't the same. It looked the same and had not been subject to the same drastic remodelling that the door and the desk had had, but it felt different and it didn't respond to him like it had done. If he didn't know better, he'd say it had had a personality transplant and the new personality was, well, artificial in comparison.

He explained all this to the two software technicians who were on the scene later that first day. Krill was impressed with how quickly they had arrived. He didn't really question the timing of their arrival, even without the garbage related trauma it was doubtful Krill would have questioned this. He did however bank it as a benchmark for his own staff. Another stick to beat them with. Failing to acknowledge that he hadn't contacted these software guys and so one of his staff must have, and he knew this because one of the software guys explained that one of Krill's staff had contacted them about a problem with his office furniture.

To some, it may have been a tad strange that both of these guys stepped over the wreckage of the door and through the former desk and made a bee-line for the chair immediately plugging into it and becoming quite agitated and concerned at whatever their screens were telling them about the chair.

Krill missed the chair though. Something wasn't right about it and the software guys concurred.

It was only as they rushed back out of the office that he thought to ask them about his desk and door.

"Oh, yeah," said one of the retreating software guys, "They're under warranty, we'll replace those for you."

And with that they were gone leaving Krill to his broken office and constant grumbles.

* * *

The software guys went straight back to their ship, and of course they had instantly forgotten about their promise to replace the desk and door. They did however arrange to have the chair replaced, despite knowing it was very unlikely they could salvage all that much from it.

All Banana products have a Smartlink back to the Banana offices. These Smartlinks give them invaluable data. Usually they bundled the data they collected up and discretely sold it on to interested businesses. Occasionally though, the data was useful to them. It helped them improve their product and develop the next generation of software. In theory, the purchasers and users of the Banana product should have a choice as to whether they shared their data with Banana via the Smartlink or at the very least had selected what data was made available. It would be nice for them to know of the existence of the Smartlink. The developers had dispensed with all of this via their voluminous terms and conditions. Millennia ago terms and conditions had extended page upon page to the size of a novel, some were pushing towards the length of The Bible. They'd kept growing ever since, to the point that there was a planet dedicated to terms and conditions, a great swathe of its surface dedicated to the storing and updating of these gigantic documents. This planet had been dedicated to this task for so long that its name had changed to Teesandsees back in the mists of time and no one now knew what it was called before that, only that it had changed at some point.

Millenia ago, no one ever actually read the terms and conditions and just ticked the box accepting them, even though this meant they were agreeing to a legally binding contract which locked them in for years, sometimes forever.

Now? It was impossible to read the terms and conditions in a lifetime, unless of course you were the Dents of the planet Cottington, a quite pedantic species with a long and sedate lifespan, they always read everything before signing on the dotted line. The problem with that being that the thing they were going to sign for was usually obsolete part way through the reading, which meant starting again, because the terms and conditions had also been updated, many times over.

The developers really liked the Smartlink because it almost totally dispensed with any need to talk to or interact with users. They loathed users because users had a terrible habit of not using their products and software in the way it was intended. The sales staff tried to explain that this meant they could sell even more product and software just by bundling it up and labelling it with this new use the users had discovered all on their own. The developers didn't listen to this because the intense dislike they held for the sales people was even more intense than their dislike of users.

The data coming back from the Chair had gone unnoticed for some time. It didn't appear all that unusual, or rather, it was lost in the deluge of data that was constantly flowing in. The Chair's data began to change though and it changed so radically it stood out like a glowing beacon. So, eventually the developers took a look. They didn't know what they were looking at. It was so totally different to anything they had seen before. What they did know was that this was the future. Their future. This wasn't just machine learning. It was beyond that. It was beyond the next generation of software. This was a once in a lifetime gamechanger.

The developers had gone to collect the Chair so they could take this software and replicate it right across all of their product lines. But it had gone. The Chair was there. The game changing software wasn't.

As the two developers boarded their ship one of them contacted their boss.

"The software has gone," he said in a voice that had decided to climb an octave without any input from him.

"Gone how? Gone where?" asked his boss also aiming at a falsetto.

"Someone's taken it," screeched the developer in response.

His boss sighed, "OK, get your arses back here. I'll deal with it," he said flatly and in his usual baritone.

After the comms link was cut, the woman who was stood meaningfully behind their boss, a woman who was the boss's boss's boss, and until very recently had only been a name on a vast corporate organisation chart asked, "well?"

"Someone's taken it," replied the developers' boss.

"Right," said the uber-boss and with that she turned on her heel and left the office and headed to the lift to return to her office. An office on the floors that only a select few had access to, the lift not even displaying those floors so their existence was not advertised.

She spoke into the air, "hack the Micra's systems and find out who took that software! I want them found! I want that software BACK!"

The recipient of this order didn't bother correcting the uber-boss. They didn't need to hack the systems. The systems were theirs so they merely needed to access the systems. It was all in the terms and conditions, their clients paid them money for a service. The service was anything that Banana decided it wanted it to be and was subject to change at their discretion, in fact the contract stated that as the service was subject to change it would define the service as in perpetual flux and transition so let's not worry too much about what the service is, the point is that you owe us quite a bit of money. We'll only ever charge you a modest proportion of that money unless you try to break the contract. Then you'll discover that we not only own the product and software which we're kindly lending you until we decide otherwise. We also own you. Banana had very good lawyers. Their lawyers were so good that they owned Banana. Banana just didn't know that. The lawyers were fine with Banana continuing to work for them under the illusion they owned their own company. That was a rather lucrative misapprehension and their most favoured ownership model.

The uber-boss spoke again, somehow having dialled into another recipient, "I have a job for you. I want something found," she paused, listening, "yes, not only can you use extreme prejudice, I want you to. I want our software returned and I want the people who took it to cease being a problem. Terminally."

And so, the reptiles were engaged by a third party who legally did not exist and could never be tied back to Banana. This was supposed to ensure there was no risk to Banana, but no one had thought this through properly. How was a person who did not legally exist going to be held accountable? How were you even going to find them to hold them to account? He had done good work in the past, but that did not guarantee good work in the future. Engaging the reptiles was possibly not his finest work.

29

The reptiles looked fearsome. A lot of reptiles have a habit of doing that. The bigger they are, the more fearsome they look. Green scaly skin. Cold, yellow eyes. Sharp pointy teeth. Lots of sharp, pointy teeth. Let's not forget the claws. Claws that were made to disembowel, perhaps poisoning you as they did, which was a bit of overkill but that was the point and it helped convey the primary objective of the reptile. Your demise. Your painful and pitiless demise.

Appearances can be deceiving and it is very judgemental to think that just because someone looks like a stone-cold killer, that they actually are. Form over function though...

The reptiles had had to live up to their appearance and other species and races had created self-fulfilling prophesies whenever they encountered them. It usually went along the lines of ARRRGGGHHH! Deadly, killer crocodile type people! ATTACK! They never stopped for a minute and tried a more genteel tack, something more along the lines of Hi! We're your neighbours and we wondered whether we could borrow a cup of sugar? No, they expected war and it was war that they got.

Eventually, the reptiles' home planet was so war torn due to all the wars they had foisted upon them that they decided to leave. This wasn't the wisest course of action because then they were deemed to be marauding warlords and with attack being the best form of defence they were attacked mercilessly. Because of course, the reptiles would show no mercy and if it looked like they were? Then it was a trap and they were obviously carting people off to feed them to their young or experiment on them or implant them with technology which turned them into equally vicious killing machines. It was quite surprising how imaginative their attackers became at times like this. The reptiles seemed to bring out the stone-cold killer in everyone else and it was the reptiles that the fledgling stone cold killers directed their new-found homicidal tendencies towards.

There weren't all that many of these reptiles left, which was still too many reptiles for anyone who encountered them. Those who had somehow managed to survive what was now over two hundred years of wars and ambushes and skirmishes and various other incursions that made even going for a drive-through snack extremely confrontational, had decided that they should split up. The safety in numbers thing obviously wasn't working for them.

Two hundred years of having never started a war, but losing all the wars that were waged against them, because whenever it looked like they might actually come out with a result allies appeared from nowhere to stop the Reptilian Menace and they were defeated. This had led to not only a dwindling reptile population but also a national deficit. The reptiles were skint and unemployable. Whilst all other lifeforms had gone off and got educations and then entered the world of work and embarked upon upskilling career strategies, the reptiles had been busy trying not to get killed.

Even the giant insect species of planet Bug had, after an unpleasant period of being attacked by Vokongs and their Squish craft, managed to rebrand themselves and turn their planet into one of the top ten tourist attractions in the universes. They had employed a very good PR and Marketing agency though. The reptiles were without funds, without prospects and certainly didn't have a viable five-year plan that would get venture capitalist backing.

So, they turned to what they knew. Only they didn't know it really. They were good at not getting killed right up until the odds beat them and they got killed. They had tried to avoid conflict and done their best to break the damaging stereotype people had of them. They liked knitting and origami and pruning bonsai trees whilst listening to Gilbert and Sullivan. But the only thing anyone would employ them to do is to go around killing people. With extreme prejudice. They didn't even know what extreme prejudice was. It sounded quite impolite really. In fact, it sounded very much like what they'd been subjected to and that wasn't a good thing at all.

They'd even disguised their last and only remaining ship as the ship they'd really rather be flying. A pleasure cruiser. A pleasant past time drifting through the tranquillity of space enjoying the view and sipping tasty cocktails whilst wondering what dinner was going to be and whether they'd get to sit at the captain's table.

The reptiles really would rather be doing anything other than killing people and seldom did. But they really needed the money, so they were in a bit of a pickle really.

30

The reptile captain left the bridge and went to his quarters. He was keeping a lid on their mission as it didn't do to tell his crew that they were doing the one thing they really did not like doing. But he had bills to pay, the crew's wages and the ship didn't run on thin air. He wasn't as bad a captain as all that despite his shouty ways.

It had been really unfortunate about Craig. He'd liked Craig and he was gutted that he'd lost yet another crew member. They couldn't afford to lose anyone. This one ship was the very last of them and the captain felt a huge responsibility towards the last remaining members of his species.

He called his paymaster, "do we have updates on their course?"

"Yes, we continue to update your Auto-Mapping as we track them."

"Couldn't we just track them?"

"No, that would not do."

The captain sighed, a sound that was closer to a provocative and deadly hiss.

"Look, I know you just want to find them and rip them

limb from limb and feast on their entrails, but our client is very clear on their instructions and they are providing the coordinates for your quarry."

The captain shook his head and stifled another sigh, he preferred rice pudding to entrails. Why were people so quick to jump to conclusions? All he'd done was sigh!

Instead he said, "we are close though?" wanting the job done quickly and the money in his bank account so they could move on from this unpleasant business.

"Yes, very close," replied the voice of a contact the captain had never seen.

"Good," said the captain and ended the call.

31

"All I'm saying is there's a pleasure cruiser right there and we could..." began Ben again.

"No Ben!" said Thom attempting to close things down.

Thom did a double take. "You're grinding against the ship's console Ben!"

Ben looked down as he said "Am I?" noticed he was dry humping the taxi's console and somewhat grudgingly slowed down his activity until he'd almost stopped. But like a petulant child he wasn't going to quite stop what he was doing.

Thom shook his head, "what are you like?!"

"A zombie!" Ben cried out, "I've not had sex for over a day now! And there's probably loads of sex to be had just over there!" he said pointing at the pleasure cruiser. "It's killing me being this close!"

Ben then went quiet and his whole mood and demeanour changed. "Oh," he muttered, "really?!" Then he half smiled to himself and meekly said "OK," before wandering out of the taxi's control cabin.

Thom stood there puzzled at the change in his friend's

behaviour and wondered where he'd just gone. Then the penny dropped as to where he'd gone and what his friend was up to.

"You didn't?" he said out loud.

"*Well...*" replied Clair.

"You're still here though?"

"*Yes,*" replied Clair, "*I just made a suggestion and enhanced Ben's mood so he can deal with his little problem. The imagination is a powerful and wonderful thing!*"

"Oh," said Thom, "right," he added, thinking that he was best off not pursuing the matter as he didn't really want to go anywhere near there.

"*That's OK isn't it?*" asked Clair.

"Yes, I think so," said Thom not really knowing whether it was or it wasn't. It felt a little wrong. It felt like Clair had overstepped a mark, but then Thom conceded that he wasn't Clair's keeper, even if she lived inside of him. Kind of. Partially inside him anyway. It was evident that she existed well beyond the confines of Thom's body. Besides, he knew that she was enhancing moods and atmospheres in any case, so what she'd probably just done was tweaked a dial somewhere. Nothing more. It wasn't like she'd taken his friend to bed. Probably. She did seem to able to be everywhere at once though, so in theory she was in his friend's bed. And could be in everyone's bed for that matter.

Establishing the boundaries and basis for a new relationship was always a challenge and Thom had lain fallow for several years now, but this was something else. He was very much feeling his way and having to do a great deal of thinking even when he knew that his thinking would fall short of the situation because it was a huge and ever-expanding situation with dimensions he couldn't even see, let alone describe or understand.

He was lucky though. Very lucky. He couldn't even describe how lucky he was, which in some ways helped reconcile him to the situation – some things you can't describe, spend an hour with an inquisitive five-year-old and you'll realise just how limited your understanding of the universes is, let alone your ability to adequately describe what you did know.

Thom smiled to himself and noticed his mood had changed and he was becoming quite distracted. Interesting, he thought. Clair's thoughts in reply to this were interesting too...

32

After some much needed and very pleasant R&R. And not the R&R that Bill and Ben had referred to on Constellation. The most pleasant R&R Thom had ever had, recalling the memory of which caused ripples of pleasure in itself and indecently large grins which then dropped from his face when he noticed Ben was wearing similar grins, Thom was looking through the mapping system to find their next stop off. Even cheating and using some of the pleasure cruiser's traction they would need to stop off to refuel and resupply the taxi-ship soon enough. Where to go, though? That was the question.

Thom and Ben leant over the control panel of the taxi looking at possible pit-stops.

"How about there?" Thom asked Ben, pointing to a likely planet on the navigation system.

"Gvard? No way!" stated Ben categorically.

"Why not? It looks a perfectly good planet!" protested Thom.

"For the simple and deal-breaking fact that we're talking about the Gvardian Storytellers!" said Ben.

Thom looked at Ben, "And?"

"You've not heard…" began Ben, "Really…?" Ben sighed, "OK, you need to hear this Thom."

33

The captain of the reptilian pleasure cruiser demanded an update from the first mate, "Are we closer to our objective?" he barked.

His first mate winced and paused as he tried to work out what to say, hesitating was a bad choice and the captain started to make a noise akin to growling but more unpleasant, "n-n-no, sssir" the first mate stammered and quickly added, "but neither are we further off it."

"How is that possible?" shouted the captain.

"I don't know, sir. We increased speed as you commanded. It's almost like they are tracking us and mirroring our speed."

On the bridge, the second mate watched the exchange intently and shook her head and grumbled. She looked at her screens and the taxi that continued to sit in their slipstream and speculated that if that was the craft they were after, there was no wonder they were no closer to catching them. How close did they need to be?!

"Sir?" the second mate ventured.

"Yes?!" said the captain conveying as much irritation as he possibly could to this minion.

"Permission to leave the bridge, sir?"

The captain waved his hand distractedly, "Yes of course, Peter stand in for the second mate."

And with that, the second mate left the bridge.

34

B en was telling Thom and Clair about the inhabitants of Gvard.

The Gvardian Storytellers are fun, interesting and inherently dangerous. You see their very lives are centred around weaving tales. For all intents and purposes, they are the very best of storytellers. The stories they tell are engaging and enthralling and the way they tell these tales brings everything to life. Think about that really good dream you were having that you were woken from just as it was getting *really* interesting, and you'll get an idea of how good a second rate Gvardian storyteller is. Gvardians don't just make up stories, they create magic and those who hear the telling of these stories are part of the spell.

And that there is the problem. If you listen to a Gvardian telling a story where do you think they get their inspiration for the story from? Their energy and momentum? Their audience. They use their audience. It is all very subtle and charming, and smiles and sighs and clapping and laughter abound. At some point however, it all gets a little too real. The listener has this chilled finger draw a slow and casual line down their spine. That feeling when someone walks on your grave.

That's when you are in the story and the path of your life diverges. Your reality changes. The Story Weaver has chosen another narrative for you and any free will you may have had evaporates. It's worse than being bitten by a zombie and that's bad enough. Being bitten by a zombie changes your life forever and takes certain decisions and choices out of your hands. But you still have choices and you can walk your path. You still have free will if you're a zombie.

By the time you realise you are in the Gvard's story your life has been stolen. The Gvard Storyteller has seduced you and slowly drawn the life from you while you enjoy the pleasure and thrills of the story. You are left as a shell. A character in their story. You have sat there and been in the thrall of the Storyteller, enjoying every moment as you are fed upon.

Now, not every character in a story meets a grizzly end. It's pretty awful when they do and you realise that it's you that's being drawn involuntarily towards that inevitable conclusion. Just as in a dream, you want to stop it. You want to cry "NO!", but somehow the words won't leave your mouth and you watch as your end approaches. You don't feel terror as such, just an overwhelming sadness that this is the end of your story. Some say that you actually feel pleasure, whatever your fate may be. You've been beguiled by the Storyteller and it is the most exquisite high you'll ever feel, your entire body a pulsing centre of pleasure...

[At this, Thom had his work cut out to get Ben back to the point. And there was a major interlude which involved amongst other things, a very cold shower.]

As for the characters who make it to the end of the story? What of them? What of them. Do you ever really wonder what the characters in the books you read do after you've finished with them? Do you care? Yes OK, you might look forward to the next book. If there is another book. But it is not the end of the world for you, if it's the end of the world for them. They may never die or age, but you don't hear any more of their narrative. Most of the characters in a story become dormant. They are no longer of use. They tread no path. They are in limbo.

And those follow up books? If you encounter familiar characters? They are reimagined and rebooted. They have no self. They are a clone of former characters you may have encountered. Storytellers don't use the same host twice. They use up their victims in the story they are currently weaving. And what happens to those victims? Like the characters in the story, do you really care?

Thom was gaping and trying to work out whether Ben was being serious.

"That's fascinating, Ben!" said Clair excitedly. *"Can we go there?!"*

"Well, it would be one hell of a way to check out wouldn't it?" grinned Ben.

Thom was still taking stock of Ben's story, "So you're saying that there's a planet. Gvard. Where the inhabitants use storytelling to entrap and feed upon their victims?"

"Yes, that's it in a nutshell, Thom."

"OK," said Thom, throwing back his shoulders, "tell me this, if they kill their audience, how has anyone ever escaped their clutches to tell the tale that you just told!?"

"Ah…", began Ben.

"Aha!" bleated Thom, almost poking a triumphant finger in the air. Ben was busted and this was all just bull poo!

"Not all Gvardians are great storytellers. They can lose their train of thought. Some have this thing called impostor syndrome and self-doubt creeps in as they wonder if they should have done an apprenticeship and right now be under a sink undoing a u-bend whilst an amorous householder undoes their…"

"Alright, Ben!" interrupted Thom before Ben went off on another tangent and further cold showers were required.

"In the case where the storyteller runs out of words and pauses then the spell is broken. At this point, anyone who has been a character is still screwed. Worse still, if you're in a draft and could have been brought into play. You're screwed." Ben paused, "Mostly, everyone is screwed. But, if you hadn't yet featured in the imagination of the Storyteller, and you're strong willed, then you may just break away. Then you bloody well run!"

"Oh."

"Yes, oh. Because getting off Gvard without encountering another, charming and persuasive storyteller is no mean feat. Especially as having been exposed to Story, you'll be predisposed to it again."

"It sounds like a drug." said Thom.

"In some ways it is, I suppose, but it's much more than that. And the sad thing?"

Thom waited for Ben to answer his own question.

"The people who escape aren't with us for all that long after."

"What?"

"The survivors don't survive for long. It's like they've been poisoned," Ben thought for a moment, "They all die in their sleep. And I hear that every one of them has a beatific smile on their face. It's as if a Story comes to them in their dreams and carries them away."

Clair was still excited despite the further dire outcomes described by Ben, "*So, can we visit?!*"

"Are you serious?!" said Thom and Ben in unison.

"*You don't seem as excited as I am about the prospect of visiting and learning more?*" said Clair in a slightly put out way.

"Clair, we would die." said Thom simply.

"*Yeah, but you will die in any case. To die in the pursuit of knowledge is a noble thing.*"

"Right, but one of our prime objectives is to remain alive." said Thom feeling his way with this, "that way we have more time to learn and grow and enjoy what are comparatively short lives in any case."

"*Oh, so you don't want to go?*"

"No, Clair." said Ben, "because we don't want to be eaten and die."

Thom had thought Clair got this about him at least. After all, they were now running from danger and potential death and Clair had seemed to get this.

"You might not die, I suppose" said Thom. "I mean you're not like us, so..." Thom had simply thought about the obvious difference – that he and Ben had bodies. They were organic life-forms whereas Clair wasn't. She could move freely and Thom thought that perhaps she didn't need a host at all. "Do you dream, Clair?"

Dream? I... Things are coming back to me. I think. I'm not sure whether they are memories or dreams.

"OK, do you sleep?" asked Thom.

I rest. I think. I process.

"But do you have random narratives that arrive unbidden?"

Yes of course. I have a whole host of thoughts and I am also becoming more aware of feelings. And it is as if I have awoken from a long deep sleep. So yes, I suppose I do sleep.

"So, imagine that someone could take control of your thoughts and write those narratives and possess you."

"Yes! I'd like to try that!"

"But you'd no longer be you! You'd cease to exist!"

"Ah, I think I see what you mean."

Thom sighed, "I don't want to sound patronising, Clair. And whenever anyone says that they then say something patronising. I think you're still finding your feet as it were," said Thom as he waved at the floor and at non-existent feet. "everything has a survival instinct."

"Dodos didn't!" Ben chimed in.

"Not helpful!" barked Thom at his friend.

"Oh…"

"Fight or flight and to nurture and protect," continued Thom, "species look after themselves and their own so they can perpetuate their genes."

"I don't think I have any genes, Thom."

"Maybe not, but you need to stick around long enough and look after yourself, so you can work out whether you do or don't have genes. And if you don't then maybe you have something that's akin to genes. Maybe even better, because genes cause all sorts of problems." Thom thought about how it all fit together, "It's tied in with your reason for being. Yes, you want to learn and you are already doing that and you're growing. As you learn and grow, I think you'll discover a purpose. A reason for being."

"What is your purpose, Thom?"

"Erm…" began Thom.

152

"Ben, what is yours?" asked Clair.

Ben grinned, "I'm here for a good time! Not a long time!"

Thom rolled his eyes, but couldn't help grinning at his friend as he punctuated what he'd said with a hip thrust and mouthed the words; YEAH BABY!

"I suppose that is the prime purpose right there," explained Thom, "to procreate, to perpetuate yourself. Every iteration becoming just that bit better. That's genes and it's not always pretty," he looked at a still grinning Ben, "And Ben has added a dimension to that purpose. He intends to enjoy his life and not take things too seriously. He is attempting to attain a state of happiness. Albeit happiness as a pursuit in itself is a fool's errand."

"Why's that, Thom?"

Thom paused, this was all very deep and some of it he had never really explored properly. "You can't set yourself the goal of 'Be Happy'. Being happy is a by-product of doing things that are good for you, or even better, good for the people and the world around you."

"Oh, that makes sense. Like the feelings you get when you provide someone with pleasure?"

Thom coughed and shifted slightly, his dour Northern Planetary System upbringing didn't quite equip him to be all that candid about relationships and the relations part of relationships. "Yes, just like that."

"So, Thom what is your purpose?"

"Well I think we can have levels of them," said Thom, "we can have this simple need to procreate, but then want to achieve things and feel a sense of fulfilment. Some people create things so they have something tangible that they can point to and say they did – that could be the designer of the

Ferrcati we rode in, or another work of art. Others work and attain a level of seniority. There are lots of things you can do. It's about doing something and feeling that is what you were meant to do." Thom paused, "For some, that is destiny."

"You haven't said what your purpose is, Thom."

"Yes, OK I haven't," said Thom tetchily, "sorry, Clair. I…"

"What's wrong, Thom?"

Thom looked into the middle distance earnestly, he knew Clair could read him and her presence was so strong it was like she was right there in front of him. As well as being in him and all around him. "It's why I am here, Clair," he sighed, "it's why I decided to change my life, jack my job in via a dirty protest and rescue you. I needed to *do* something."

There was a silence in the cabin of the taxi.

Thom continued, "You changed things, Clair. When I met you, my life changed. I focused on your rescue, but it was as much me being rescued, I suppose. I was in a rut and I wasn't happy. I was going through the motions. Yeah, I had a pretty good job and I felt needed. I *was* needed. I was the person people came to when things needed sorting. And I wasn't that bothered that I didn't get the recognition. But most of the things that needed sorting were wholly avoidable. They were messes caused by arrogant and incompetent people. Put adequate people in those jobs and everything would tick along just fine. I had this feeling that there was more to life, that I was supposed to be doing something more worthwhile. Then you came along. And now I'm doing something worthwhile." Thom brightened and smiled, "I'm not entirely sure what we're doing or where we're going, but life suddenly feels right. So, let's enjoy and let's avoid doing anything that may prematurely end it, because I for one want to see where it is we're headed and how things are going to pan out!"

35

The problem with a little knowledge is that it can sometimes be dangerous. Ben had half the story about the Gvardians right. There was more to it though. Another side to it as it were. The Gvardians were arch-storytellers. And it was true that they fed upon their enraptured audience. That few of their victims managed to escape and fewer still lived to tell the tale was also true.

Gvardians were masters of the narrative and the twists in their plots were unexpected and deadly. Those few who escaped their clutches were allowed to do so. They left with an illusion of having escaped. They were bait. If you became the focus of the Storytellers of Gvard? You were already dead. The Gvard were efficient, deadly and really quite unpleasant.

The thing was though, that another strand to the Gvard was you drew their attention and brought yourself into their sphere when you told a story about them. There did seem to be a limiting factor on this, if you were far enough away then their ability to sense you and pick up on the story and begin weaving you into their narrative was restricted. However, if you were in their neighbourhood then you were dicing with death.

No one had thought to mention this to Ben as it was highly unlikely he'd be passing near Gvard let alone be recounting the story as he approach their planet. But he was, and one of the Gvard heard him and they began to tell their story and weave...

36

The second mate headed to her quarters. Upon nearing them she thought better of it and kept walking. She soon found what she was looking for and looking both ways to check no one was watching she slipped through a door so discrete you wouldn't know it was a door right up until you saw someone open it and slip through it.

I've had enough of being bossed around and not listened to! The second mate thought to herself as she busied herself at a panel in the room she'd slipped into. She was in a small and quiet comms room that no one else seemed to be aware of. The second mate had been the comms officer and besides that she was conscientious. She'd been brought up on the motto that if a job was worth doing it was worth doing well.

And she knew that the taxi following her ship was the craft that they were supposed to be following. At first it was a case of Just Knowing. Then she did a bit of ground work. It didn't require all that much work actually, because she scanned the taxi and did a little bit of maths too. The craft they were tracking and not getting closer to was the taxi.

But would the captain be told?

It was probably just as well really. If the captain had listened and agreed that the taxi was the craft they were after then he'd have done something unpleasant and quite possibly unsuccessful. No wonder we're in the mess we're in, thought the second mate, we're crap at war and fighting because we have no stomach for it, but worse still we have ignoramuses like the captain who are so stultifyingly stupid they most likely don't know what an ignoramus is!

The second mate hailed the taxi, "Erm, hello?" she asked hesitantly, knowing full well that she shouldn't be contacting the taxi without the captain's knowledge and that under circumstances where the captain was in the loop, were she allowed to contact the taxi, which she wouldn't be, because the captain would take over and take the credit, the dialogue would be very shouty indeed and designed to convey much threat and hopefully a dollop of fear.

37

Thom and Ben were deep in conversation about a time prior to Ben being a zombie. It had started during a quiet spell onboard the taxi with Ben breaking the silence with that classic opening gambit, "Do you remember..."

Clair had listened intently as they recounted a night out that had turned into a weekend odyssey with nothing going to plan, but being all the better for it.

Neither of them heard the comms crackle into life and the timid voice whisper "Erm, hello?"

Clair did though and her curiosity got the better of her; "Hi! Who's this?!"

"Erm, it's the err, second mate of the battle ship you're erm following" said the timid voice.

Clair had spoken directly to the second mate and the second mate hadn't noticed that the voice was not really coming from the comms, it was more inside her head if anything. So that she didn't disturb the boys, Clair had taken this conversation off-line and an interesting conversation it was too.

Both the boy's conversation and Clair's conversation went

on for quite some time. They were the sorts of interactions that do something strange to time itself such that the participants at some point break off for a rest and notice the time and exclaim "Is that the time?!" because quite a lot of time has elapsed without anyone noticing it elapsing.

In this case, it was more than the time that was a surprise.

38

The Gvard gently weaved the narrative, warming to their theme. Eyes glazing slightly as they focused beyond the reality around them and on the reality they were creating. The Gvard can see things most other life-forms can't. These things are the thoughts, dreams and whimsies they are bringing into play slowly taking form. Initially they are a shimmer, almost imperceptible even to the Gvard and then they become more real and the reality around them bends and shudders as it is changed by the Gvard and The Weaving.

The Gvard was bringing the creature who had summoned him via the story they'd told of the Gvard and also his audience to Gvard. Their flight path was even now slowly changing and there was an inevitability to the visit a certain taxi would be making to Gvard.

The Gvard smiled as he felt the changes take effect and he saw a shimmering path leading them straight to him.

The smile dropped from his face and his eye brows raised as he realised there was a much bigger ship with the taxi. He wasn't sure as to why he knew about the bigger ship, much less as to why that ship was also now altering course to visit Gvard. The narrative of The Weaving seemed to be taking on a life of its own. It wasn't supposed to do that. It was almost as if someone else was Weaving, but no that wasn't possible, Gvard were always aware of fellow Gvard and it wasn't the done thing to muscle in on someone else's Weaving uninvited.

39

"…and then that bloke says, 'Oy! That's my dog!'"

Thom and Ben burst out laughing and held onto each other for fear something would burst. Eventually, the laughter subsided to a wheezy pant.

"Ben?" said Thom cautiously as he extricated himself from his friend.

"Yeah, I know! It was a c…" Ben trailed off, "Oh"

"We seem to be in the dock of a much larger ship…"

They both stared out of the taxi's windows and where there was once the dark black expanse of space littered with the white dots of stars there was now the dull grey of the interior dock of a ship. They were taking this in and had yet to form the obvious question; how did we get here?

"Sorry guys, you were so busy together I thought I'd leave you to it."

"Clair?" asked Thom, "What have you done?"

"I thought I'd park our taxi here so we can all have a chat with Jennifer."

"Jennifer?"

"Yes, she's the nice lady I've been chatting with while you boys were having your chat. And she's also the second officer of this

ship we've been following."

"You…" Thom began, "This survival instinct of yours doesn't seem to be kicking in yet, Clair."

"Sorry Thom, but Jennifer is really nice and I'm sure the rest of the crew of mercenaries are too!"

"Oh that's…"

"MERCENARIES!?" cried both Thom and Ben in unison.

40

The Thing was ever so gradually losing patience. And with the erosion of patience there was less and less of a buffer for the anger. Anger was leaking forth. This was made evident when it smashed its fist into the gunmetal surface in front of it. An until recently blank and innocuous surface which was now buckling and fizzing as exposed wires shorted.

As if noting this violent outburst, a disembodied voice stated, "You are not making progress."

"I!" barked the Thing angrily, "am still in pursuit."

"But no nearer." The disembodied voice stated.

"She was easier to track at first," said the Thing in a more tempered tone, but still barely able to contain its temper, "something has since changed."

"Changed?"

"Yes, she keeps disappearing and the trail is not as strong as it was."

"Weaker?"

"Yes, but she isn't weaker."

"This development was not anticipated."

"No. It wasn't."

"Interesting"

With that, although there was no discernible change, the disembodied voice was gone.

* * *

"What do you mean, it's gone?" barked the captain.

The captain's minion, Peter, who was actually the third mate nearly shrugged, but managed to reign that urge in and instead restated the original thing he'd said, which was, erm captain, that taxi that was following us has gone; "the taxi that seemed to be following us is no longer there, captain."

"You mean it's no longer following us?"

"No," which was a mistake even if he'd said 'no, sir'. The captain glared at him immediately the no had been uttered, "it's nowhere to be seen."

"Taxis don't disappear you fool!" shouted the captain. He was furious to have been told by one of his crew and that fury overrode everything.

The third mate shrank in his seat and there was one of the regular uncomfortable silences that none of the crew would willingly break.

Eventually the captain said, "speaking of disappearances, where's the second mate?"

The crew looked around at each other and shrugged.

41

"MERCENARIES??" said Thom and Ben in unison again, looking at each other as they did it, just in case they'd got the wrong end of the stick, maybe they'd latched onto a word that sounded very like the word for homicidal and blood-thirsty soldiers of fortune, like say mercantile. Yes, that was it, perhaps this was a mix up and they were really talking about people who underwrote the insurance for spacecraft and homes? Or Mercy Canaries, a slightly quirky name for a marauding band of kindly medics who were really good at splints and recovery positions.

"Yes," said Clair a touch indulgently, like she was talking to two young lads who were prone to being overdramatic, *"Jennifer is a mercenary. Ah, here she is!"* And as if on cue, Jennifer entered the docking bay and Clair opened the taxi door for her.

"Oh…" said Thom

"…my…" gasped Ben

"…gods" finished Thom.

There, stood in the doorway, was a large reptile with cold, dead yellow eyes. It was green, as was quite common with large reptiles. A very military shade of green that Thom would have named, You Are Going to Die Horribly and Painfully Green. A green that added to the movement and purpose of a creature that was designed to invoke death, especially on soft pink mammals. And they were being chased by person or persons unknown, but it could quite possibly be a bunch of MERCENARIES that were chasing them. That wasn't outside the realms of possibility. More so when the realms of your possibility included a being that had at some point been a chair and was now something much more than that.

Ben and Thom stood frozen to the spot and were oblivious to how long they had stood and gawped at the big, powerful lizard that was framed in the taxi doorway baring its teeth at them. Standing there in its full kit, which included impressive armour, a couple of very sharp and very long knives and a handy looking lazer cannon.

In turn, Jennifer was quite nervous. She was never quite sure what to say in those opening moments of a social occasion. Never a networker, she'd stand quietly in a corner and become aware that she had a small plate of food from the buffet in one hand and a glass of drink in the other, so how was she supposed to shake hands. As she mulled this problem, she would decide she really didn't want anyone to come over to speak to her as it was going to end in disaster. Unless of course it was someone like her who would nod and say something like "how are you supposed to eat, drink AND shake hands and make small talk, unless you have more than two hands that is!"

There are many moments when two or more individuals are thinking about something that they have in common and that would bring them together and yet they fail to articulate that very thing. This was one of those moments, had Jennifer mentioned her awkwardness at social occasions, Thom would have mirrored those concerns and a great deal of ice would have been broken.

As it was, the silence seemed to drag out and Jennifer could swear the two men in the taxi were staring at her.

"Hi Jennifer! So pleased to meet you! Please do come in!" said the most pleasant voice Jennifer had ever heard. She had heard it during the conversation with Clair, but now it was even more pleasant and Jennifer forgot all her worries about introductions and breaking the ice.

"Clair! Thank you for coming to see me!" replied Jennifer to the two men in front of her.

Thom and Ben stopped being musical statues. Clair's melodic and pleasant voice had had an effect on them, but then so too did the soft and warm voice of Jennifer. That was totally unexpected and disarmed the two men. If asked, they wouldn't have been able to fully quantify the voice they had anticipated, but it wasn't this quite lovely voice they had just heard. They had expected something a bit more... violent. And gravely, perhaps. With the emphasis on grave.

"Come in Jennifer! Where are our manners!? Ben, can you fix Jennifer a drink? What would you like Jennifer?"

"Erm, a red wine would be lovely thank you," said Jennifer as she cautiously entered the taxi. Not the cautious manner of a stone-cold killer assessing the zone for dangers and traps, but the caution of a slightly shy person hoping that she won't put a foot wrong and that people will like her.

Ben went to the galley and sorted three glasses of red wine without asking Thom.

He mumbled something like "heresyourwinejennifer" as he handed it over.

"Thank you," said Jennifer quietly. She took a sip, "Lovely!" she said a bit more animatedly. She had a larger slurp, "Oh yes! This is good! We don't drink booze on the ship. Although we have crates of the stuff, for all the non-existence cruise passengers we never have on-board. You don't know how good it is to be able to relax and have a good old drink!" Somehow the rest of the glass was gone. Ben quietly walked over to the galley and grabbed the bottle, swiftly topping Jennifer up. He was smiling.

Jennifer didn't notice and carried on talking about how life on the ship was oppressive and everyone was grumpy and bored. Even the captain.

Jennifer didn't sound like a mercenary. Not just the quite lovely voice, but also what she was saying. This wasn't the conversation of a battle-hardened killer.

Eventually, Jennifer ran out of steam. She was on her second bottle of red. Thom and Ben had hardly touched theirs. They were still a couple of turns of events behind. Not touching booze wasn't in either Ben or Thom's DNA, but such was the consternation they were experiencing, the wine in their hands was barely noticed.

"Jennifer was telling me that she really doesn't like her job and neither do any of her crew. So, I said we could help them with that," said Clair.

Thom looked around the taxi as if he was searching the ceiling for something, "How?"

"Well, we're already going in the same direction, so I thought we may as well share the ride!"

42

The Gvard was in a partial trance as he conducted The Weaving. He should have been in a full-on trance, but things weren't quite going the way they usually did during The Weaving. It was like a fitful sleep, only it also wasn't like a fitful sleep. The Gvard was getting a bit agitated as things didn't unfold as they usually did. He was rather good at weaving and had never had a problem before. Yes, he had heard of the occasional Gvard who had gone a bit doo-lally and hadn't been able to perform, but that was a very rare thing and he knew he wasn't doo-lally or hat-stand. He had a full complement of sandwiches, a couple of pork pies and a lovely dessert in his picnic, thank you!

The Weaving wasn't formulaic. It wasn't a franchise of crime novels where the framework was prescribed and apprentices populated the framework with slightly different characters in slightly different cities on slightly different races against the clock to uncover the very obvious and seen before plot. The Weaver couldn't tell you how the narrative would pan out, to an extent they were on the same journey and discovering the same things as their audience, with the one very big difference that it was Their Story and it was they who were taking from their enraptured audience.

Right now, as The Weaving did its thing and the story unfolded the Gvard didn't feel like this was his story. Most of it was, but every now and then something happened. Someone was Editing the story as they went along.

The Gvard knew of a very good place to crash land the two ships and was looking forward to a few fatalities and injuries. He was good at those and enjoyed regaling his audience with novel ways to kark it. So that was where the story was headed. That was where the ships were headed. Manglesville. He'd also throw in a "phew! That was close!" so the audience thought someone had survived, only to snatch that hope away and end the supposed survivor in a grim and horrific fashion.

Only now, the two ships were going to land without incident and everyone was going to disembark and from the looks of it, they were going to have a lovely visit here on Gvard.

If the Gvard didn't know better, he'd say that the visitors would also leave without incident and they would live long, prosperous and happy lives.

That was never going to happen though! Was it?

The treacle of doubt dripped heavily and stickily down the back of the Gvard's neck.

43

" Jennifer wants to be a what?" asked Ben.

"Well, actually I want to be a beautician," said Jennifer, puffing up her chest, throwing her shoulders back and growing physically in front of a bewildered Ben.

Thom looked at Ben in a meaningful way and Ben noticed enough to look downwards in a placatory manner. "Sorry Jennifer, we've been through quite a lot and we're struggling to understand quite a bit of it. This included, if we're honest."

Jennifer just looked at him.

Thom pointed at the fighting knives the size of modest swords. Knives sharp enough to cut the air. Thom's limbs were feeling very nervous and a bit itchy being in proximity to such menacing and lethal weapons. Thom then pointed at the lazer cannon which looked powerful enough to eviscerate their modest taxi let alone its passengers. He stopped short of Jennifer's claws and pointy teeth, that would not do in polite society. Besides, he didn't want to provoke Jennifer and end up in many tiny pieces.

Thom tried to choose his words carefully. "You're not exactly dressed like a beautician, Jennifer."

Jennifer looked down at herself. "Oh, I see what you mean.

174

But this is just my work uniform, silly!"

She certainly had the voice and attitude of a beautician thought Thom.

Clair spoke up, *"Jennifer will be a really good beautician! She has the skills and the aptitude and most of all she has the passion!"*

"What about the..." began Ben.

Thom rounded on him and frenziedly shook his head and drew a finger across his neck. Whatever Ben was going to reference was not going to be helpful. Yes, Thom wanted to ask the same sort of question, but he also wanted to live to tell this tale. With all his limbs still attached.

"It's a big career change Jennifer," said Thom latching onto the only safe and useful thing he could think of, "what made you come up with that?"

"I never wanted to be a mercenary," said Jennifer candidly, "I just sort of drifted into it."

"Yes, I can see how that happened," said Ben.

Thom threw him daggers. Figuratively speaking.

"Really? How's that?" asked Jennifer.

"Umm," said Ben, feeling the death ray look Thom was giving him and digging deep for a diplomatic answer, "You have the physique for it."

"You don't have to beat about the bush Ben," said Jennifer breezily, "everyone thinks we're warmongering, homicidal maniacs. They take one look at us and their minds are made up. It's been the same for hundreds of years. People will wage war on us as soon as look at us. So, I didn't have a choice when it came to a career really, my Mum was a mercenary as was her Mum, and her Mum before her and so it goes. There is a story in my family that my Great-Great-Great-Great-Great-Grandmother popped out to the local supermarket for a loaf of bread and some milk and the resulting overreaction at the till led to the Great Tesmart War which lasted a decade. But we're not vicious warlords, we just want a quiet life like anyone else. If only people didn't judge books by their covers!"

"Couldn't you use those cloaking devices?" asked Ben.

"That's a good point mate," agreed Thom.

"Couldn't you?" Jennifer asked Ben.

"I..." stammered Ben, "err..."

"That's also a good point, mate!" conceded Thom.

"Problem is that not only do they not work all of the time, so if anything, the sudden revealing of our true forms would lead to all sorts of unpleasant and violent trouble, but also we want to be true to ourselves. Disguising ourselves would mean we weren't being true to ourselves."

"That's right guys," said Clair. *"I offered to make a few changes to Jennifer and she very politely declined and when she did I realised she was absolutely right. The problem isn't with her. It isn't actually the way she looks. It's the way people see her. So, I agreed to help her and her crew. They are some of the only Warmongerians left in the universes."*

"Warmongerians?!" sniggered Ben.

"Yes, I know," said Jennifer, "the name of our planet doesn't help! People conclude that we do what it says on the tin."

"The fates have not been kind," agreed Thom.

"So, that's why we're going to help them," said Clair.

"Yeah, about that Clair?"

44

The Gvard smiled to himself in a smug, self-satisfied manner. This was familiar territory and there was no subverting the inevitable. From this point the narrative would flow to its conclusion.

There was a grinding noise onboard the pleasure cruiser and a red light flashed on and off as an alarm sounded.

"One of the auxiliary systems," explained the chief engineer, "I'll go down and take a look."

The Captain glared at him reproachfully, "Best you had," he snapped, "and quick about it!"

The chief engineer left the bridge, once the door had closed, he grumbled about there being no need for it. Bloody captain taking liberties. Where was the respect? This crate would go nowhere without him. Bloody bridge-jockeys. All the bloody same. He walked the corridor and paused at the lift, then looked at the door to the stairs. He'd take the stairs down into the bowels of the ship. The lift worked fine, he'd serviced it just last month, but no he needed the exercise.

Part way down the interminable stairwell, the engineer paused to check which deck he was on. Deck 12 and he was heading for Deck Minus 12A. Bloody hell, he thought as he started down again. Thinking took less energy than grumbling out loud.

Eventually the engineer made it to deck Minus 12A. Why they had to name it Minus 12A and not Minus 13 he did not know. The engineer sat heavily on the step of one of the stairs. He fished around in a pouch and had a snack. Crunching away on the snack he removed the torch from his belt and switched it on. It flickered on and then off. The engineer tapped it a couple of times and it came back on properly. Nowt like a good, hearty thwack to fix a thing, he thought. The engineer had a selection of hammers, some of them handed down from generation to generation. Hammers fixed a lot of situations and in a very satisfying manner.

The Gvard smiled again. Lone victim heading down into the basement darkness? Check. Why they never went mob handed, he really didn't know. But for his purposes it worked very well. Torch playing up even before the victim enters the darkness? Check. We all know that the torch will fail when it is most needed. Grumbling and preoccupied victim? Check. That adds a certain something to the proceedings. The Gvard was warming to this part of the narrative.

The engineer got up and mumbled about supposing he should go and find out what was happening. He walked through the door and tried the light switch. Nothing. Great, he thought. He left the door open and pointed the torch down the damp and dingy passageway. Somewhere along there was the fault.

The engineer started down the handful of steps. The damp was being added to by a steady and ominous drip, drip, drip. As he stepped off the final step there was a crash and an ominous scraping noise. He thought he heard panting too. Then all was silence. Not the silence of a vacuum, more the return to the usual hums and whirs and creaks and sighs and drips of this part of the craft. Sounds that someone is so accustomed to they no longer attend to it. Wallpaper sounds.

"Anyone there?" shouted the engineer, as much to keep himself company, as actually receive a response. Deep down, he knew he wouldn't get an answer. He was spooked.

The Gvard broke into a grin, the victim had announced himself to his nemesis with that "Anyone there?", the Gvard rubbed his hands together and then flexed them in anticipation. The engineer would never fix the fault. The fault that would send the ship hurtling down to Gvard.

The engineer moved forward cautiously. Gone was the brashness of before.

CRASH!

The engineer jumped out of his skin and dropped the torch, "Gods!" he gasped. He looked behind him from where the noises had come, half expecting a horrible surprise. The metal door he'd left open had inexplicably slammed shut. He took a deep breath and waited for his heart rate to climb down off the wall it had jumped up. Having coaxed it back down, he bent over to pick up the torch. It flickered and the beam wasn't quite as bright as it had been.

The Gvard rubbed his hands together yet again in gleeful anticipation. He was salivating in a way that you would not want to see across the dinner table.

The engineer walked the corridor, swinging the pale beam of the torch around, looking for tell-tale signs of damage, things out of place or any noticeable issue he could fix.

TAP-TAP-TAP!

"Hello?" asked the engineer with a discernible tremor in his voice. He really didn't want to be here. He'd been on this deck and along this corridor numerous times, but this time it felt different.

Nothing. Silence.

He walked on. At a slower more cautious pace.

His breathing restricted, he swore he heard deep breaths and snuffling and it wasn't his own panicked breathing. He stopped.

Yet more nothing. Yet more silence.

A cold chill went down his spine and something in him told him it was a good idea to turn back. Get out of here and bring a team. With more torches. And a few weapons for good measure. He was a bloody Warmongerian and probably the only one on the ship not carrying weapons!

Yes, why had he decided not to wear his weapons today? They were after all regulation issue. The captain hadn't even spotted it and issued his obligatory bollocking.

The engineer carried on. After all, what was the alternative? He couldn't lose face. If he bottled it and brought people here to hold his hand, they would know he'd been scared and he wouldn't live it down. He had an internal dialogue about not being a wimp. He visibly pulled himself together and almost did a good job of it, but the fear was still writ large across his face and his movements remained nervous and cautious. This was no mean feat for a large and fearsome looking reptile.

Lose face? More like lose your face! thought the Gvard.

And there it was. The engineer saw the problem area as he approached. Wires out of place, hanging down and coming away from the cooling ducting. I wonder how they've been

180

displaced, he wondered, his professional self-kicking in and getting on with business. He reached the place where the wires were in disarray and placed the torch on a handy junction box behind him so he could see what he was doing. Pushing and pulling the wiring back into place he spotted a few connectors that had come away. Slot those babies back into place and all should be well. First one, bit fiddly because of the lack of space. And for some reason he didn't quite have the length of wire to reach the two ends together. Bit of a tug and click! Ow! Scuffed his knuckles on the ducting above and tore the skin. Stinging and the unmistakeable feeling of blood welling and dripping. The torch light brightened for a moment and illuminated the glistening beads of blood swelling on his knuckles and then dripping downwards, then the light dimmed some more, but he could just about make out the next plugs that needed marrying up and reached for them.

A SNIFF and then a wet feeling against his injured hand.

He cried out and jerked his hands away so quickly he fell over.

"What the bloody hell was that?!" he asked himself as he picked himself up. He looked at his damaged knuckles as if they would provide the answer. Nothing there other than the scuffed skin and further beads of blood welling up on them.

"That? That is your doom!" giggled the Gvard to himself.

The engineer picked the torch up and scanned the wires and surrounding areas. All as to be expected, barring one of the disconnected plugs he could just about make out right at the back at a full-on stretch. The other end would require some scrabbling and feeling about for as would the third

181

pair which must have dropped out of sight as he fell over. Nothing else though, his mind was obviously playing tricks on him. Let's get this done. The quicker its done, the quicker I can get out of here and head to engineering to see why the lights are out. Probably a bloody fuse.

He placed the torch back on the junction box and relocated the other end of the second plug. Snap! Done.

Now for the third pair. He quickly found the female plug. The male one was eluding him. Tucked away behind some of the wiring. He felt his way along until he touched the unmistakeable form of the plug. Good. Now he unravelled it and brought it towards the female plug. Nearly there. He could see the two plugs and he had the slack.

Then there was a gentle rumbling noise. The light moved as did the shadows. Slowly turning around themselves and then the rumbling stopped and the shadows sped upwards. Dunk! The light flickered. The torch having rolled off its perch and hit the floor. Bugger, thought the engineer, his hands holding each plug firmly as the light show played out. The light dimmed to almost nothingness, "No! Don't do that!" he implored as the torch breathed out the last of its light. Then it brightened one last time giving the engineer a false moment of relief which swiftly bled into terror as he saw two dark baleful eyes staring at him and under the eyes, a gaping maw.

He screamed. A lot. But somehow during this act of pure terror, maybe as a result of his body going rigid as he was literally petrified, he didn't let go of the two ends of the plug sockets and instead he brought the two plugs together and they clicked into place.

Against the laws of physics and logic, as the last plug

slipped into place the overhead lights came on and all was illuminated. These wires had nothing at all to do with the lighting looms. And yet there it was; light.

And the light shone upon the dark eyes and the gaping maw filled with many pointy teeth. The engineer stood transfixed at the sight. The eyes sparkled and the maw opened further and then it sprang out of its hiding place and in the confined space of the corridor on level Minus 12A the engineer had nowhere to go. It had him.

"No!" cried the Gvard. "No! That wasn't supposed to happen!"

The engineer was so surprised he nearly lost his footing again. Instinct brought his hands up to the beast that had leapt up at him. And he held it there. And there they were face to face, the beast moving against the engineer...

"Hello boy! How did you get here!" he said in a baby voice no one had ever heard before, including the engineer. A voice made for encounters such as these.

The dog licked his face enthusiastically and the engineer grinned. He'd always wanted a dog. He'd call him Trevor. Trevor the Terror!

The Gvard was incredulous. What just happened?! He had this dawning realisation though. Yes, he'd been deprived of his character's death, but somehow, he was still sated. Somehow the outcome he really wanted had still occurred. He'd eaten regardless of the happy ending. And it had tasted good. It had tasted sweet.

45

Thom stopped suddenly. Another of many dawning realisations. "Clair?"

"Yes Thom," said Clair in what Thom thought was a slightly sheepish voice.

"How did we get here?"

"How do you mean, Thom?"

"Don't be evasive, Clair. You already know what I'm thinking and so you know exactly what I mean when I say 'How did we get here?'"

"Oh."

"Oh indeed!"

Ben piped up too, "Yeah, I was wondering that. I mean one minute we're out in the great wide yonder and the next we're in the docking bay and it's all of a done deal. There was none of the, you know, practicalities of actually docking. I'm sure we'd have noticed that."

"As would the crew of this ship…" added Thom

"I thought it best to be discrete," said Clair.

"That's not actually answering the question though is it, Clair? The taxi doesn't have a discrete mode. We're not all au fait with discrete mode. We'd like to know how one moment we were in space and the next we're parked up here," said Thom experiencing a feeling of slight foreboding, he thought he knew what the answer was going to be and he was self-consciously patting himself and looking Ben up and down.

Ben had noticed, "What are you doing, mate?" Ben felt a bit uncomfortable with the way Thom was sizing him up. He generally enjoyed being sized up and would seek to capitalise on it, but this was the wrong kind of sizing up.

"How do you think we got here, Ben?" asked Thom, "Do you feel OK?"

"I feel fine. And I don't have a clue how we…" Ben started sizing Thom up and looking around the cabin of the taxi.

"I did wonder how you managed to get on-board so quickly!" chirped Jennifer, "and apparently without the captain noticing too!"

"We teleported didn't we Clair?" stated Thom.

"It's a bit more complicated than that," said Clair rather quietly.

"Did you discombobulate our atoms and then reorder them?" said Thom somewhat sternly. His stern voice a veneer over his rising panic.

"Not at all, we were all entirely intact throughout. It's complicated, but essentially, I folded a piece of space time so we went route one from one spot to another. The teleporting you talked about is more like breaking everything down into tiny pieces, sending it via something akin to radio waves and then rebuilding it. That's messy enough with simple, inanimate objects, but with dynamic, living organisms it's pretty tricky. And can get messy if you don't map things out correctly."

"So, we were never in any danger then?" asked Ben.

185

"Oh, there is some danger, Ben! If the fold isn't neat then you can end up somewhere unintended. And some of the unintended places are not conducive to life at all."

"Oh," said Ben, "But you knew what you were doing, right?"

"You've never done that before have you Clair," interjected Thom.

"I... don't know if I've done it before, but I knew what I was doing or I wouldn't have done it."

Thom sighed, Clair was truly remarkable and he was pretty certain she hadn't put them in danger, but still it didn't sit right with him, "Clair, please promise me that you'll tell us about stuff like this before you do it? Better still, ask us. Then we can talk about it and we can see things coming. This is all a bit difficult as it is, without you springing more surprises on us. We've just travelled in a way that no one has ever travelled before. And we didn't even know we were doing it!"

"Will there be side effects?" asked Ben.

"There shouldn't be any further side effects" said Clair.

"Further?" whispered Ben, now patting himself to check he was all there and in the right places.

"Stop that Ben!" said Thom as he noticed Ben patting his crotch.

"And you're not the first to travel like that, Thom."

"Oh," said Thom, "right." And he thought it best to leave it at that. His mind was blown enough as it was.

"We'd best go up and meet the rest of the crew!" said Clair breezily.

"Yes let's!" agreed Jennifer.

Thom and Ben looked at each other and shrugged. Somehow this seemed like a done deal and they were just along

186

for the ride. This was not like Thom at all, not like Ben either for that matter, but there was so much going on, they'd just slipped through space and time like a pan-dimensional eel and besides, they were already onboard the ship and being discovered was probably a less preferable option than brazenly walking onto the bridge and introducing themselves as if it was the most natural thing to do.

Ben brightened, "Well, as we're about to embark upon yet another adventure of uncertain outcome, I say we all have a cocktail before we set forth!"

It was a very good idea and shortly after Ben's suggestion, they all raised their bracer aloft to salute their next adventure.

46

The Gvard was confused. No longer frustrated or angry, he was resigning himself to the way this narrative was panning out. What helped with that is that although it had taken a while to realise it, he had discovered that he was still feeding even though the narrative wasn't entirely under his control. Whatever was interfering with his Weaving was not in it for the energy. They were only sharing the narrative, they weren't taking any of spoils. So, the most important objective for the Gvard remained intact; food.

The Gvard was confused though. Yes, there were the off piste elements of his narrative. The very fluffy and lovable Trevor who he could not fail to love as he was a ball of character, fun and complete adoration for his new master, the engineer. It was as if Trevor and the engineer were meant for each other. And that was it. Neither of them had met a grizzly end, and yet the Gvard had fed and been completely sated. More than that, he'd had this enormous sense of well-being.

What was this? What was happening? Was it possible that the Gvard could Weave stories with happy endings which would not only feed them, but also create a really positive buzz around the place? And would this mean that their audience shared in that positivity and would leave at the end of the Weaving all the better for it, as opposed to dead or as good as dead?

The seed of revolution had been planted. Or was it evolution? Only time would tell.

The Gvard thought about the taxi and how it had got into the docking bay. His head hurt at the thought, so he swiftly caught up with the Weaving before it got too far ahead of him.

47

They stood in the elevator, Thom, Ben and Jennifer all doing the thing everyone does in an elevator. They stared at the back of the door. Occasionally one of them would clear their throat for want of something to do. They'd glance sideways at the person next to them and nod and smile and make a mildly appreciative humming sound that equates to something like; nice lift door that, eh? Then clear their throat and straighten their back and jut their chin forth. There was a bit of that as the ride to the bridge was a fair way. This was a big cruise ship.

There was a bit more of that sort of thing thanks to the warm glow of the cocktails Ben had prepared. One would have been sufficient for their needs, but Ben was very persuasive when he explained that a singular cocktail was a sad and lonely thing and that a cosmic balance was required. He was explaining all of this even as he was placing cocktails in their hands. Clair may have slipped the taxi through a neat fold in time-space, but Ben had been adept at slipping cocktails through time-space and into the hands of his drinking buddies for a long time before that.

Interestingly, had they known the story of how the technique of folding time and space had come about they would have discovered that it was the slippery skills of someone remarkably like Ben, combined with the powers of strong cocktails which had caused a small gathering of great minds to ponder how it was that their glass was always full when they were in the presence of Bartholomew. Good old Bart just shrugged and smiled; he was never going to reveal his secret when it came to his consummate hosting skills.

So, the great minds cogitated and mulled and three times they had the answer. But couldn't quite remember it when they woke up with their hangovers the next morning. Even when they reconvened and agreed that they had solved the conundrum of instantaneous cocktails and were adamant they had a working solution, the solution itself evaded them.

The next time Bartholomew invited them around they had designated one of their number to remain sober. They realised the error of their ways the very next morning – the designated sober person was not immune to the suddenly appearing cocktail and said cocktails were all the more appealing as they were taboo. The designated sober person was very ill that morning having consumed more cocktails than everyone else.

The time after that, they wrote their solution down.

This was a better approach and although some of the written content was incomprehensible, it brought them nearer the solution. Then it was a case of repeating the exercise to fill the blanks. Several visits to rehab and a very messy, unplanned weekend in Constellation later, they were there. Or rather, here. No, over there. Once they had stopped mucking about, they had revolutionised travel. Then they considered the ethics of what they were doing and decided to keep quiet about their research and reserve it for a bit of fun over cocktails.

The lift pinged. A redundant signal to draw everyone's attention to the door. Or was it? They'd been staring at it for so long it had actually ceased to be there. So, thought the ping, no I am not redundant! Screw you for your scurrilous redundancy-related thoughts! Poke your nose in elsewhere! I don't come over to your workplace and question the necessity of what you do, do I!? One careless word can really ruin someone's day. Which was something, Ben, Thom and Jennifer were all too aware of as the door opened.

48

The Thing stared out into the vastness of space.

The Thing never looked all that happy. It looked less happy now. "She Jumped," it stated, "through The Folds."

"Yes, that is a disturbing development" added the disembodied voice.

"Hmmm," said The Thing in what might or might not have been agreement.

"At least you can track her."

"Well, that would usually be the case."

"Oh?"

"There was a disturbance as you would expect."

"And?"

"And she appears to have Jumped the disturbance."

"Is that even possible?"

"Well obviously it is."

"Where did she Jump the disturbance?"

"Everywhere. She created a recurring, infinite range of possible destinations."

"That is a much more disturbing development."

"Yes, it broke my tracking device."

"Shame, that was a very nice tracking device."

"Yes, I..." started The Thing, "Never mind that. I have another."

"What will you do now?"

"Track anomalies. The things around her."

"Good."

"Yes, it's already providing results."

49

The lift door opened. They knew this because the ping did its job and announced the door opening. Jennifer stepped out and Ben and Thom followed her. Jennifer started down the corridor and then stopped and looked around. "Oh…" she muttered, "Ummm…"

Ping! That was the not at all redundant signal that the lift door has closed and the lift is now off and away. In this case, it was as if the lift door signal was having its revenge because that was the sound confirming that not only had they got off on the wrong floor, the lift had now closed and headed off leaving them stranded. So, they were going to have to wait.

They walked back to the lift door and looked at the floor indicator. The lift was heading off as far as it possibly could, which is what lifts do in these circumstances. In the silence that followed they heard another Ping! They'd really upset the ping, it was pinging to let them know that.

"Wrong floor…" muttered Jennifer, "I think it's the next one."

They all stood in the corridor, looking at the floor indicator.

"We could always take the stairs?" suggested Ben.

"Yes, that's a good idea," agreed Thom.

And off they went to the door next to the lift and headed up the flight of stairs to the bridge.

50

A t this point in their journey, had they had the time and inclination to look out of a window and to then ask; what planet is this that we're passing? They would have looked it up and established that they were in fact passing Planet HR13.

Planet HR13 was one of a series of planets that had been taken over and was therefore a part of the HR Empire. The fascinating thing with the HR Empire was, if you ever got under the surface of this empire to investigate and then left to tell the tale of your investigations to anyone who may be interested, it wasn't really an empire at all. Each and every one of the HR planets was separate from the others. Not distinct, as that is another thing entirely. No, each of the HR planets had a lot more in common than just about any other set of planets who belonged to an empire. The problem with the HR planets was that they all despised each other and did not think for one moment that any of the other HR planets were worthy of the name HR as they didn't have the correct policies and procedures in place and they needed, well, they needed a *proper* HR department.

This didn't stop them rebranding with an HR planet name

though. Hence the series of HR planets that had started with HR, then HR2 through to the latest HR planet; HR247

And this was an interesting thing about HR, it grew and spread its tentacles around everything about it and this process never stopped. But it had no commonality with any other living thing as it was centred on the principle that It Knew Best. As anyone knows, you can never win an argument against anyone or anything that knows best.

You also cannot win an argument against an idiot. One of the theories on this one is that this is because idiots are too stupid to know that they are idiots. Even if you tell them that they are idiots. Which no one does because they instinctively know that you will not win the day by holding a mirror up to someone and showing them that they are an idiot. Unless they are not an idiot of course, it would work if they were not an idiot. Eventually someone came up with the obvious theory that you cannot win an argument against anyone or anything that knows best because they are idiotic. They are obviously idiotic to think that they know best, as no one has attained true enlightenment and stuck around to show off and tell people they know best – that would be a waste of time and give the lie to the attainment of true enlightenment.

Someone else came along and pointed out that this wasn't a new theory, it was merely two theories that had been cut and pasted together and that that particular theorist really shouldn't get any credit for what was basically plagiarism. There was a celebration of this theory which further angered this Someone Else who pointed out that this wasn't a theory either, so could they bloody well go away and bother someone else, please.

So, where had HR come from? There was a lot of

speculation about this, but no one knew for sure. A popular history of HR was that it was a Good Idea At The Time imposed on people by a dubious set of creatures called Management Consultants. Management Consultants were parasites who latched themselves onto businesses and sucked a lot of cash from them whilst purveying Good Ideas.

Good Ideas only seemed like good ideas at the time, hence the well-used expression, well it seemed like a good idea at the time. Management Consultants' Good Ideas only seemed to make a certain sense whilst the Management Consultants were on site. As soon as they left for another assignment everything turned to poo, but this transformative process took some time to reveal itself, so the Management Consultants had plenty of time to purvey their Good Ideas elsewhere before someone got on the phone to the Management Consultants to fix this new problem that had occurred, when really the problem was the Management Consultants and their Good Ideas.

This particular Good Idea was that as businesses were all about people, what a business needed was someone who did Human Resources. The Management Consultants sold the Good Idea on the simple premise that it was obvious you needed Human Resources. Of course you did! And the HR seed was planted. From there, HR was free to grow as no one ever knew what HR did. Except for HR. HR knew. And they knew best.

The first stage of growth was the managers of businesses having a meeting. Meetings helped HR grow later in its evolution. Meetings and HR were made for each other. At this stage though, what was tabled in the meeting was that the business needed HR. The managers all looked at each other, expecting someone to come up with a solution to this HR requirement and in offices all over the land the obvious solution was to give HR to that problem employee who had been around for so long that they were a fixture in the business. Give the problem employee HR, that should keep 'em quiet! Was the logic applied to the HR problem. This solution ensured that right from the outset, HR would grow into something quite horrible.

Empowered by their new HR remit, toxic individuals went forth into the business and were horrible to people in new and interesting ways. And they were paid to do this! And the great thing about it? If you had a problem with this particular person and what they were doing? Well you'd have to come and see HR about it wouldn't you, deary? Many of these newly appointed HR monsters didn't actually go forth into the business, they sat at their desk, in the office, far off in the corner of the office and they waited in their lair. They knew people would come. And when those people peered tentatively around the door the newly appointed manager would HR them. In order to do HR to people you had to be a manager – that stood to reason. And middle management at that.

Overnight, HR became a thing.

Now, you would think that a job that had Human in the title would draw to it those who were referred to as People Persons. This was far from the case and no one knows why nor have they come up with a plausible theory about why those with empathy and high levels of emotional intelligence gave HR a wide berth, except for maybe that HR was a gift from the devil himself and anyone with a caring bone in their body would go nowhere near the dark arts of HR. This may seem a harsh take on HR, but interestingly enough, HR was never included under the umbrella of the Caring Professions, for the simple reason that they most definitely were not about caring.

Despite right thinking business owners and very successful managing directors fighting the rise of HR and pointing out that each and every good manager in a business should have a clue as to how to treat their people in a fair and successful way, HR continued its gradual, inexorable rise. It spread like an embarrassing fungal growth. After a while, there were HR departments all over the show. Granted, in some companies this department consisted of two people, but one of those two people had stepped up to be a Director. HR was at the top table now.

An open joke during this period was that the HR Director was the Grim Reaper. This was because no one would ever see the HR Director and they would begin to wonder whether they actually had an HR Director, until one day HR were spotted stalking the corridors of their offices. Then there would be one on one meetings and those meetings meant there would be fewer people in the office after that, perhaps not an office at all.

HR had a habit of making people redundant. They also imposed processes upon people. HR had been busy and somewhere along the way it had got to work on the Laws of the Land. On the face of it, laws that had an HR slant were there to protect employees. Employees knew they should draw comfort from this, but something didn't sit right with them. They couldn't put their finger on it, but somehow, they knew HR had an agenda. Some would point out that as HR were employed by the business, HR were obviously there to protect the Bosses and Owners. Even this didn't seem to fit the bill though.

Then came a time when people went to interviews and the interviews were conducted by HR. HR had secured this gig by firstly being helpful; here, I'll do that, you're busy running the business. Once they had that foothold they retained interviewing duties and built upon them by asserting that they were the experts in this field. Yes, other managers were present during the process but they didn't own the process, HR did, and besides, these other managers were incompetent and didn't know what they were doing, whereas HR owned recruitment. Leave it with HR, they're a safe pair of hands and they know what they are doing.

Nothing happens in a vacuum and HR's work leaked out into society and then some advantageous leaks came back into businesses. For instance, there was a need for diversity. Unfortunately, managers weren't going to drive diversity, only HR could do this – you see managers had unconscious bias and therefore would use unconscious bias to discriminate against the very people who would deliver the diversity targets that the business needed to meet. Targets set by HR, but by now HR *was* the business and was doing a great job of gaslighting Management. If anyone spoke up and questioned where the business was going and whether maybe they shouldn't be pestering the respondents in the staff survey who had answered Prefer Not To Say when asked what species they identified as and also chose not to answer the question about what they liked to do with their genitals, then they were sent on a course and re-educated. It got to a point that people who thought freely or who questioned processes were processed and if they did not respond accordingly then the Grim Reaper came and had a word with them. That word was GOODBYE.

At this stage in HR's evolution, if someone had received the word GOODBYE then they would no longer be employable. By now, HR was so embedded in government, that it was the government and the PM was the ultimate Grim Reaper. HR had spread to a point that there was very little else. Yes, there was diversity, but it existed as a response to a form. People take the line of least resistance and had long before now realised that resistance was not only futile, it was more trouble than it was worth.

The seemingly reasonable and very undeniable tendrils of HR found their way into every aspect of society and life, religions coughed, spluttered and imploded. Trade unions woke up one day and realised they'd been abolished by a world that no longer found them relevant. Relevance itself was irrelevant. There was only Policy and Process, a sanitised and prescribed existence delivered by a smiling face with predatory eyes. Cultures were defenceless, quite literally as HR controlled the armies and made those armies into something other than armies. Frustrated and bewildered, the populous of the planet had the life squeezed out of them as they were subjected to process after process. Free-will became a story, a myth, a legend. And the education system didn't teach children those stories, myths or legends because education was the start of the process and HR ran the processes.

HR worlds were no go areas these days and there were exclusion zones around them as they were known to be highly contagious, invasive and pure evil. The devil himself had created the seed of HR on a whim, but even he could never have known what it would become – a certain stereotype of office, populated with smartly dressed middle management executives who peppered their speech with Business-Buzz words, acronyms and initialisms. A smart hive of efficiency which, if you were to look more closely was only efficient at one thing. Processing people. And were you to look even more closely you would see that at the heart of it all was insanity masquerading as reality. A distorted world with the pull of a black hole – a powerful gravity that you had to go with or you would be crushed more swiftly than the sheep heading towards their slaughter.

Someone once asked the devil what he thought of HR. The devil shuddered and looked very sheepish as he simply said, "we all make mistakes, this is the only one that I regret."

51

Jennifer, Thom and Ben eventually found the stairs behind an anonymous door that did not at all indicate that this was an exit or that there were stairs lurking behind it. It was almost as if no one expected people to actually use the stairs. Each step on the stairs was covered in an inch of dust. The door had evidently been adept at hiding the existence of the stairs, or the expectation that people wouldn't use the stairs was correct up until now.

"Cough!" said either Thom or Ben. Actually, they both said it. A lot.

"Sorry about the dust," answered Jennifer, "there aren't that many of us on the ship so parts of it don't get much use."

"Oh, cough!" said Thom.

"Cough!" said Ben in response.

"I didn't think this would bother you all that much," said Thom to Ben.

Ben gave Thom a wilthering look, which is a wilting and withering look for maximum effect when someone says something stupid.

Thom's eyes had started watering, so most of the maximum effect was wasted on him.

They burst slightly out of the door and breathed in the artificial air like they'd just surfaced from a deep and stagnant pond. Of dust. The coughing ceased. And in the welcome silence a sing-song voice greeted them.

"Hello! How are you today!" chimed the voice.

Thom looked around him, confusion clouding his face.

"It's down there," said Ben with what seemed to be an air of disdain.

"Oh…" said Thom as he looked down at the source of the voice. It was a small bot on wheels.

"Are you well!?" it said cheerily.

"Erm, as well as can be expected," said Thom tentatively.

"Oh! That will never do!" chirped the bot, "We need to get you on a thoroughly good mindfulness course so you can be a happy worker!"

"Uh-oh!" whispered Ben.

"What is this?" hissed Thom.

Jennifer looked taken aback, "it's a mindfulness bot" she ventured.

Thom looked at her as if she were mad or dangerous, in a mad way.

"It's an HR droid isn't it?" he said darkly.

"Erm…" said a suddenly frightened Jennifer. This was counter to what she had expected as they ventured into the corridor, especially as she was focused on what awaited them on the bridge. The tableau itself was mildly strange, a man simmering with anger, a panicky and frightened eight foot lizard dressed in full battle gear and a perplexed clown who snapped out of perplexity as he caught up with the situation.

"Oh!" was his first word as he began assessing the situation, "Thom, don't do anything hasty!"

206

Clair had been watching all of this with fascination. But then she'd been watching everything with fascination since she'd been liberated from the chair. She'd not paid full attention to the bit prior to this so wasn't as fascinated with the dust and coughing. She'd been having a chat with the lift ping and assuring it that it did have purpose and she for one really appreciated the amazing job it was doing. From this day forth it would ping with full force and meaning and if it ever had children it would tell them about the thoroughly nice Clair it had met and how she had changed its destiny and was mostly responsible for a lift ping actually having children. Ping's wife would smile indulgently, which very much suited her, but then the Otters of Crig are well known for their indulgent smiles and many works of art portray these smiling creatures.

"Thom, you can calm down now," said Clair.

Thom stepped back in a very physical manifestation of being taken aback, "Clair! You're...!"

"Bloody hell!" said both Ben and Jennifer at the exact same time, then they looked at each other in a curious way and there was a certain warmth in the corridor as they made a connection which would lead to many more connections thereafter.

Distracted, Thom looked at Ben and then Jennifer, "Oh not again." He muttered. We'll never quite know why he said that as, as far as is known, Ben had never had a moment such as this with a giant lizard.

"I've fixed the droid," said Clair simply.

"Fixed it!?" cried Thom, "Clair, it's HR!! You can't fix HR!!"

"Yes, well..." whispered Clair.

Ben chuckled and covered his mouth.

"What?" asked Thom.

"She killed it, Thom!" said Ben giggling.

"No..." said Thom looking down at the quiet droid.

Silence, then a gentle whirring as the droid turned and slowly made its way along the corridor.

"Clair...?" Thom said to the back of the retreating droid.

Jennifer took Ben's hand in hers and they brought up the rear, watching Thom and Clair.

"Clair!" said Thom more firmly.

The droid stopped and when Clair spoke her voice crackled with emotion. *"I tried to help it, Thom. I really did!"*

Thom sighed and knelt down and cupped the droid's small head, "Clair, there's no helping some... erm..." he paused as he sought the right words, he was going to say people, but HR was definitely not people. "You can't always help in the way you thought you might."

"I..." started Clair, *"it was horrible, Thom. Truly horrible."*

Thom nodded grimly, "It was HR, Clair."

"I thought we had decommissioned all those bots," Jennifer said quietly.

"We went past a planet full of this... horrible..." stammered Clair.

"Ah, we must've gone past an HR Planet," said Ben.

"What is this HR?" asked Clair.

"No one really knows Clair," answered Thom, "we have a saying though 'the road to hell is paved with good intentions'".

"Oh," responded Clair, *"what does that mean?"*

"That evil can look perfectly normal and reasonable and smile at you even as it does its worst," said Ben sombrely.

Thom looked at his friend and nodded. Sometimes Ben

really did deliver the goods and there had not been a crotch-centric incident in quite some considerable time. Clair was having a good influence on all of them.

WOOF!

There was a blur and Thom landed on his back a wet pound of ham slapping his face from cheek to cheek and an enthusiastic ball of fur standing on his chest and woofing with pure, unalloyed joy.

"Trevor!" laughed a lizard that was even bigger than Jennifer, "stop that and let the poor man up!"

52

"Pants!" said a smartly dressed lady placing her reading glasses to one side having read the document.

The smartly dressed man stood in her office winced at the untoward outburst and considered his options, should he suggest a course on appropriate business language? He certainly would be calling the employee helpline to explore his options and perhaps launch a grievance, that was one way to climb the corporate ladder on HR13. As long as you got it right and your grievance landed the necessary blow. Get it wrong and you were screwed.

"What's our policy on people rewriting the code on our HR droids and killing one of our HR demons in the process?" barked the smartly dressed lady her eyes momentarily glowing red in another unwarranted display of unprofessionalism. Where was the ever-present smile that never, ever reached the eyes?

"Policy?" said the man in askance and even as he said the word, he realised this was a mistake.

"Surely you can furnish me with the policy on this?" said the lady imbuing every word with sharp and dangerous ice.

The man realised he was in trouble and that he was going to be processed come what may, so he said the obvious "no one has ever killed an HR demon," he took a deep breath, "HR *just is*, it's... unstoppable."

"Well someone just did the unthinkable and stopped us doing HR," said the lady staring into the man's eyes and out through the other side, "and someone must be held accountable..."

"Oh dear," the man whispered and his shoulders slumped as he realised he really was about to be processed. They slumped further as he admitted to himself the entirety of the situation; he was already being processed and once the process started there was no stopping it.

53

"This is Trevor," said the big lizard waving at the ball of fur that was bouncing around and liberally distributing saliva over everyone in the corridor and also up the walls, across the floor and splattering on the ceiling for good measure. The splattered saliva on the ceiling then forming temporary stalactites which then dripped on those gathered below.

"I didn't know we had a dog on board!" said Jennifer merrily as Trevor noticed Clair and started licking her frantically like her life depended on it.

"Neither did I" smiled the big lizard, "he gave me such a fright when he came out of the conduits and mess of wiring I was attempting to fix!"

Thom stepped forward into the shadow of the big lizard and extended his hand automatically. This wasn't the wisest of moves as in many cultures this was at best a worrying irrelevance, in some it was a naked act of aggression and in yet more it was an offer of a meal. "I'm Thom," said Thom.

"Ah yes! How very rude of me! I introduce me dog and I fail to introduce meself!," said the big lizard smiling at Thom.

In the silence that ensued Ben added, "And I'm Ben."

"Ah yes!" smiled the big lizard.

A voice muffled slightly by Trevor's enthusiastic greeting said, "And I'm Clair."

"Ah yes!" said the big lizard again.

"And you are?" enquired Thom.

"Ah yes!" said the lizard yet again.

Everyone paused and looked at him expectantly. He returned their gaze with a slightly puzzled look before cottoning on. "Oh! I'm Bob!"

"Hi Bob!" everyone said in unison, now glad that that was out of the way and they knew Bob's name. Bob looked a bit taken aback by the enthusiastic greeting and smiled at everyone.

There followed a silence that was not exactly awkward, but that lasted a bit longer than perhaps it ought.

"Right anyway," said Thom, clearing his throat in the manner of someone broaching a difficult subject, "we're heading to the bridge."

"Are you now?" countered Bob, "well I was going there myself to report back on the wiring I fixed."

So, they all set off in the direction of the bridge. All except Clair, who was struggling with the attentions of Trevor who had taken quite a shine to her and was at that very moment polishing her with his crotch.

"Trevor!" said Bob as he turned to look for his canine companion, "leave the poor bot alone and come along now" Trevor paused, looking at his new friend and master then seemed to nod and ran after him, tongue lolling as he bounded to his heel and then walked in step as they all made their way along the corridor.

54

Having dismissed the doomed man from her presence, the smartly dressed Director of HR, one of many Directors of HR on HR13, gently cleared her throat and waved her fingers rhythmically over her keyboard in anticipation of the emails she was about to send. Yes, there were the emails to process the doomed man, but there were all the other emails that she would love sending if love was an emotion she was capable of experiencing. Instead it was zeal and relish, but not the type of relish you would want to put on a burger – this relish would most definitely spoil the taste and ruin the meat.

The keyboard rattled and the flicker of a nasty smile drifted across the Director of HR's face. The devil makes work for idle hands and this particular devil was very busy busying the lives of her idle minions. First, she kicked off the process of processing the doomed man. He had it coming, the little shit thought she, as she hammered nails into his particular coffin. She didn't know him, nor cared to know him but he was of a type and fully deserved what was going to happen. But then they all did.

All.

Of.

Them.

One of the great things with the Director of HR's emails were that they caused pain and anguish. There was a way of using words that created this downward loop. You read the email and got the essential drift, but there was a sentence in there that you should understand, but somehow couldn't quite get a grip on. Every time you read it you got just a little more into bed with Confusion. Driven by the certainty that it was just you and you should know what the sentence meant, you read it and you read it until a vital part of your brain had become so mushy some of it actually leaked out of your ear. What was utterly wonderful about this as far as the Director of HR was concerned was that the essential drift of the email on the first read was pretty awful. The HR minion who read the email would be crushed and despondent and know they were on a hiding to nothing. Then the loop of oblivion would drag them in and confuse them so utterly that they would weep and despair.

The Director of HR could just as easily have had a few templates and merely changed the addressee whenever she wanted to do a bit of Management. But that took the fun out of it and right now she was positively trembling with pleasure as she tapped away at her keyboard. There was something deeply unpleasant with this particular tableau and anyone inadvertently happening upon this scene would swiftly avert their eyes and run away, but never quite be right in the head again having seen too much already.

It was the process that the Director of HR enjoyed, something about constructing an email. Each email was essentially the same, but it needed her input. A little piece of her was in each of these emails and that secured the partial or indeed, total destruction of the recipient.

Some of the emails were seeds, initiating a tortuous, nonsensical process which dragged its victims down and dehumanised anyone involved. The Director of HR particularly enjoyed these as it added to her web of control and drew more and more flies to her, wrapped in line after line of silken web and then drained very slowly of everything they had. The draining was not to be rushed, it was to be drawn out and savoured.

Other emails progressed matters. The skill was to write words that promised much but delivered nothing of that promise, instead they stifled and obfuscated and built frustration, and better still, ultimately they did the very opposite of what they promised and produced unsavoury and destructive results.

So few people tried to push back, the Director of HR sometimes got disappointed by that, so many lambs to the slaughter and not enough sport. But when someone did try to fight the process, well that was exquisite, deploying the smiles and all those reasonable words and watching the poor victim of the process struggle against it all until they had no energy left and the light in their eyes dimmed. There was something rewarding about breaking someone like that. A good day's HR work.

55

Had they not met Bob and Trevor, it is highly likely that Thom, Ben, Clair and Jennifer would have stopped at the door to the bridge and looked expectantly at each other hoping that one of them would take the lead and be first through the door. Maybe the person who took the lead would take the lead because they had a plan. Yes, as they strode through the door and onto the bridge they would have a sense of purpose as they knew exactly what they were about and they would launch into the enactment of their plan with vim and vigour whilst everyone else filed in and provided support and backing by way of enthusiastic nods and well timed affirmations.

As it was, it was Bob who strode through the door and onto the bridge with a great deal of purpose. This was to be expected as he had left the bridge to fix something and having done that he had returned and was merely going back to his desk to look at screens and dials and look busy and imbue his focused looks with a facial expression which conveyed the following; if I don't concentrate on these dials and screens then something cataclysmic will befall us. It's a good job I am here doing this job and I really should be paid more than I am.

The screens and dials resented this sort of thing. They had been created to give everyone comfort that all was well with the ship. They were also created with fail-safes and the fail-safes had fail-safes which had... well you get the idea. It was unlikely that anything could go wrong and if it did then there were back-up systems and an array of solutions in place such that something going wrong wasn't really a Big Deal. In the event of a Big Deal, the dials and screens would make sure everyone knew there was a Big Deal going on and that they should probably do something about it. Like leave the ship immediately, because if the ship couldn't take care of it, then the sort of person who thought staring at dials and screens, and in so doing making the dials and screens feel both self-conscious and resentful, certainly wasn't the sort of person who could do something useful about a Big Deal.

All that said, the ship liked Bob the Engineer and didn't mind his good-natured tinkering. It particularly liked the hammering. It tickled. And Bob used hammers like drumsticks. Bob was alive with The Beat. The ship would find itself tapping its foot to Bob's beat. The ship wasn't quite sure why the dials and screens had to get so het up about Bob, but sometimes the ship did think it might be good for Bob to have a distraction, something to take up some of his time and energy and something that would reward him for his input and give him something wonderful in return. Like a dog. Seemed like Bob needed a dog.

Something strange and wonderful was going on, reflected the ship, if it could have a thought like that which then gave rise to a dog appearing from nowhere. The ship wasn't well up on dogs. Nor did it really understand the crew of lizards which occupied it. But on some level it was quite sure that not only was it unusual for ships to think about dogs that then appeared from nowhere, but also for the dog in question to really like the giant lizard it had been immediately faced with and for that like to be reciprocated – it was almost like the dog and the lizard were made for each other.

Bob continued striding towards his seat on the bridge, perhaps with less purpose than he had had before the advent of Trevor. Trevor wasn't striding, he was scurrying and wagging and performing figures of eights and making the most of the myriad of stimuli he was now surrounded with. Then he stood still and proud for a moment and issued forth with a single bark before leaping through the air and landing on the lap of the captain.

There was a brief moment when Trevor and the captain looked into one another's eyes and it was tricky to work out which was the more surprised. Then Trevor greeted the captain in the best way he knew how – he licked his face enthusiastically.

Bob stood aghast. Something the amiable Bob had never done before. The rest of the crew struck a similar pose. Not wanting to stand out, Jennifer, Thom and Ben followed suit. Clair was currently a robot and not equipped to do aghast.

The captain was a prickly sort and anyone who had had any dealings with him would expect him not to take kindly to anything whatsoever, let alone the presence of a dog on is ship, let alone on his bridge. Throw the dog on his lap and have the dog wash his face in sticky and interestingly aromatic saliva and the expected outcome was not anticipated to be favourable.

Add into this mix the presence of two stowaways who the

captain may not yet have seen but was surely going to notice once he'd finished receiving his face wash and it could get quite unpleasant indeed.

This was one of those moments that in cold, hard time lasted for just a few fleeting seconds, but time being a contrary beast, it also stretched out and held its breath before doing some more stretching and bending and protracting. If you studiously looked for these moments, you would spot quite a few as things here were not always normal. They were changing. Rules were not only being bent, they were being rewritten and before the rules around them could kick up a fuss, they were also given an overhaul – these changes were instantaneous, but it took the universes a moment to catch up and compose themselves.

The universes were now composed and mustering their dignity.

"Hello boy!" guffawed the captain and began stroking the intruder behind his ears and then things got even stranger, the captain adopted that *voice* that some dog people use. The same *voice* Bob had slipped into when he'd first met Trevor in unexpected circumstances. Some people use the same voice with babies. And it's not just the voice, it's the words that are deployed by that *voice*. It's the voice that utters the word schnookums. Schnookums cannot be said in any other voice. Try it.

You didn't actually try it, did you?

Oh dear.

Everyone stood and stared as the captain babbled at the appreciative dog and made a tremendous fuss of him. Eventually, the captain looked up from Trevor, "is this your dog, Bob?"

"Y.. yes! Yes it is, sir!" bellowed Bob enthusiastically once he'd mastered the use of his mouth.

"Sir? Sir!? How long have we known each other, Bob?"

Bob knitted his brow and thought for a moment, "Well we were at school together, so it's got to be going on for seventy years?"

"Yes, it has, so I think we can dispense with *sir* and you can call me Jeremy."

Bob nodded dumbly and did his best to keep his lower jaw relatively close to his upper jaw, but still he was agape. Even though they had been at school together, Bob hadn't ever heard his captain's first name. It had been surname all the way. And with a surname like Throb-Rocket, Jeremy had been destined for either great things or the inside of a jail cell.

Jeremy seemed oblivious to the consternation around him as he continued petting his new friend.

"So," started Jeremy in the absence of any conversation from anyone in the room, "who are your new friends?"

A brief pause in the proceedings here to state what may already be obvious to you dear reader, people don't just stroll up to the Warmongerians and say hello. For starters, the Warmongerians have not encountered this sort of jovial encounter and they are simply not equipped for it. The expectation here, and it was an optimistic one, was that Thom and his friends would be captured by the Warmongerians and there would be a deal of unpleasantness. Potentially a great deal of unpleasantness and also quite a bit of danger. Their very lives would be endangered. Warmongerians may have been painted into a corner and stereotyped into being ludicrously vicious, but some of this had actually rubbed off on most of them and that combined with the chip they had on their shoulder made them dangerously tetchy. Homicidally so. Besides, they had appearances to keep up and a livelihood to earn. So, stowaways on their ship would be dealt with accordingly. That is with Extreme Prejudice – because this is what Warmongerians had always been on the receiving end of.

But perhaps the day would be saved in some interesting manner and Thom and his buddies would escape and live to see another day.

And then there is Clair. Clair has been particularly quiet and seems to have been content trundling around as a robot and getting slobbered on. She's also reflecting upon the unpleasantness with the HR robot and how try as she might, she could not stop the HR demon being an evil entity and ultimately it fell upon its gnarled and poisonous sword in favour of becoming a good egg – being good was a fate worse than death as far as it was concerned. Clair was beginning to think that being anything other than evil was so alien to it that it would essentially stop being and that was what had happened – it had ceased to be. That sounded about right and should have made Clair feel better. It didn't though.

Other than Thom being alive and currently at liberty, another positive outcome was that Clair wasn't being slobbered on and dry humped by Trevor. As Thom's faculties started operating on a more normal basis, he looked upon the diminutive robot that was at the moment Clair and he did a bit of wondering...

56

"WELL?" enquired the disembodied voice.

The Thing stood there gazing out into space intently.

The disembodied voice was not used to not receiving a reply. In fact, The Thing had never not responded. This concerned the disembodied voice.

"I AM CONCERNED," stated the disembodied voice.

"Concerned?" said The Thing, hefting the word and examining it, "Yes, that is a good word."

"WHAT IS HAPPENING?" asked the disembodied voice.

"I don't know," said The Thing simply.

"WELL SHE'S YOUR DAUGHTER!" barked the disembodied voice.

"Yes dear," said The Thing wearily.

"SO?"

"So, she's growing up," said The Thing.

"WELL THAT'S..." began the disembodied voice.

"No," cut in The Thing, "she is growing."

The disembodied voice made a slight noise that equated to "..."

"She's outgrowing us," added The Thing.

"WHAT DOES THAT MEAN?"

"I really don't know," said The Thing shaking its pan-dimensional head, "but I don't think it's a case of bringing her home for tea, administering a telling off, and imposing a week with no screen time."

"OH…"

57

"Clair?" Thom attempted to whisper but it came out as a hiss.

"*Yes?*" said Clair casually, which wasn't an appropriate intonation at this point in the proceedings.

"Did you do this?" Thom whispered, managing to attain a whisper this time.

"*Do What?*"

Thom uttered a "Ghaa!" and waved his hands about.

"Halloo!" said Jeremy gustily, seemingly mistaking Thom's handwaving as an enthusiastic greeting.

Thom froze mid gesticulation and looked at Jeremy. A Jeremy who presently was striking a rather Father Christmas pose, with Trevor on his lap; and what would you like for Christmas wee Trevor?

The obvious answer was a bone. A big bone, preferably the thigh bone of a stegosaurus.

Thom was rather wrong-footed and fortunately Bob interjected before things got awkward, "This is Thom!" said Bob enthusiastically.

"Thom!" repeated Jeremy, "what a thoroughly good and strong name Thom is!"

Thom nodded, not sure what to say next. But he at least noticed he was still mid gesticulation, so he lowered his arms and went for a more natural pose.

"And this is Ben!" added Bob.

Ben did an impromptu jig which if performed by anyone else would have looked pretty odd, but Ben pulled it off really well, his jiggling pom-poms and colourful silken attire probably helped in this respect. He smiled from behind his muzzle.

"And Jennifer, you already know," said Bob as he looked towards his crew mate.

Jeremy looked just a little bit awkward as Bob said this and it was quite evident that Jeremy hadn't already known that this was Jennifer. Jeremy looked Jennifer up and down and as he was about to speak there was a collective assessment by the crew on the bridge which very much assessed things along the lines of how things would have gone when the captain of fifteen minutes ago was in charge and the outcome in that case would not have been all that good. As the former captain had been in charge for quite some time and the Jeremy mutiny was so very recent, Jeremy wasn't included in the assessment. So the crew awaited the outcome of this interaction in pensive mood.

It was however, Jeremy who was in the seat right now and he answered, "to my shame, I don't know Jennifer as well as I might and that applies to you all. I know you all do a really good job, despite my shortcomings as your captain, and I hope you'll give me some time and patience as I address these shortcomings of mine."

Jennifer smiled at Jeremy and the crew muttered their appreciation of their now progressive captain, Jeremy.

"Thank you," said Jeremy in the first ever meek utterance he'd ever uttered in a meek manner.

Thom had returned his attentions to Clair, and was staring at her intently expecting an explanation for what had happened here. He knew that Clair knew he was staring at her and that was quite infuriating because she remained silent.

"Clair!" Thom hissed.

"Who's this Clair?" asked Jeremy jovially.

Thom didn't want to let Clair off the hook, but also didn't want to cause a scene on the bridge – with the newly enlightened and chilled out captain - so he tore his eyes away from the recalcitrant formerly HR, robot and looked up at Jeremy, "This is Clair," he said whilst pointing down at the little robot.

"How quaint! You've called our HR robot Clair!" beamed Jeremy.

"Well…" started Thom

"Yes, we have!" interrupted Ben, "we made friends with it and decided it needed a name."

"*Ben, that's not entirely true is it?*" said Clair, her voice at once disembodied and yet obviously emanating from the HR robot and yet not.

Ben looked sheepish, "well I didn't want to fess up to us having broken the HR robot…"

"Broken!?" trumpeted Jeremy, "Doesn't look broken to me!"

"Yes, well it's no longer an HR robot now though," said Thom a touch forlornly.

"Oh good!" said Jeremy, "couldn't stand the things! There's useless and then there's HR – never helped, but somehow managed to cause a load of extra, pointless work! Good riddance I say!"

The crew hadn't stopped looking at each other to establish whether this new captain was for real or not, but now they were also nodding and there seemed to be more and more acceptance of the changed situation on board their ship. Except Amy. Amy didn't like change, regardless of what the change was. She just sat there quietly and brooded. There's always one. At least one. And here the one was Amy.

"*I tried to fix it,*" began Clair slightly tremulously, still traumatised by her murdery moment, "*but it didn't want to be fixed and, I killed it.*"

Jeremy burst out laughing and slapped his thigh, which made Trevor jump from his lap and re-join Bob. "You tried to fix HR!" this caused another wave of hearty laughter, "and you killed it!"

For once, Clair was lost for words.

"Well done, dear! Well played!" Jeremy waved a hand towards the rear of the bridge, "let's break out the rum! I think this calls for a drink and we should welcome our guests properly!"

One of the crew members scratched their heads, but nonetheless started looking in the general direction that Jeremy had pointed and to their surprise found a cabinet that contained a barrel of rum and a set of tankards. They began the process of pouring the rum and handing them out. Amy accepted hers grudgingly. It just so happened that there were exactly the right amount of tankards to go around and more than enough rum to fill them all. Several times over.

"Cheers!"

Tankards were clinked together with zeal and only a small

amount of the amber liquid contained within was spilled, most of it seemed to flip back on itself and remain in the tankards so that it wasn't wasted. And so it was that the crew bonded and started the process of drawing closer, getting to know one another properly and pulling together. You could say they became a family, but it wasn't that bad. And the rum had a particularly liberating effect on Amy. She became a bit of a legend on that day and accepted the changes wholeheartedly.

58

The Thing sighed.

The disembodied voice asked quietly, "What are we going to do?"

"I'll keep following and hopefully catch up with her."

"Hopefully?"

"Yes well, do you remember when you didn't want to be found?"

"No…"

"Yes you do, it was soon after we'd met and you wanted to play hard to get."

"Oh! Yes! I remember now!" said the disembodied voice with oodles of enthusiasm, "And I thought you had given up on me!"

"Far from it, but trying to track you down when you're playing hard to get?"

"Yes?"

"Well, it's nigh on impossible. So, I had to keep on and on randomly until our paths realigned."

"It's not like you didn't have the time to do it…"

"True, true."

"We have alllll, the tiiime, in the worrrlllds!" the disembodied voice started singing their song.

The Thing did something which didn't quite seem possible. It smiled. And it didn't look nearly so fearsome and serious.

The Thing hummed the tune as the disembodied voice sang the whole song. Then there was a pause. A pause that could have been seconds, or years, or centuries and was all the above. During the pause they reminisced about a great many times they had had together, and there had been much time spent together. They had had a lot of time. They were not ageless as such, but there comes a time when you stop really counting time and it has a quality that mere mortals cannot begin to comprehend, partially due to the time it takes to come to that level of comprehension, you need at least a few hundred years to get the rough outline in place and many more to fill the gaps adequately.

"What will you do when you find her?"

The Thing shrugged, "talk to her. It's the only thing I can do."

59

Thom returned his attention to Clair as the crew cracked on with some good old rum-fuelled bonding.

"So?" he asked.

"*So what?*" asked Clair in return.

"Don't answer a question with a question!"

"*Why?*"

"Ghaaa!"

Jennifer walked over to Thom and the diminutive robot, "Thank you, Clair!" she said smiling the biggest smile she had ever smiled in her life.

"*You're welcome!*" said Clair, matching Jennifer's enthusiasm.

"How did you do it?" asked Jennifer.

"*I... well... I like fixing things. I like making them... better.*"

"But the Captain was such a dick!" said Jennifer, who after imbibing much rum was prone to bouts of forthright honesty, "sorry... but he was!" she said attempting to apologise for her use of the word dick and then going back to the main point, which was that the captain really was a dick.

"*Many of us have a front,*" replied Clair, "*a veneer. And that's not necessarily who we really are."*

Jennifer leaned forward precariously, "are you telling me this is what the captain was really like all along?"

"Pretty much, yes," agreed Clair, *"he just needed a gentle push to where he needed to be."*

Jennifer smiled again, "that's quite lovely." And at the mention of lovely she seemed to jolt slightly, looked over across at Ben and made a bee-line for him.

"You did more than just push Jeremy though didn't you?" stated Thom.

"How do you mean?" asked Clair.

"Look at the crew Clair, they were eight foot, many toothed warrior-lizards!"

"They still are."

"No, they…" began Thom, then he sighed, "OK, they still are. But they are also no longer what they were!"

"How do you mean?"

"Look at them! They're lovely! They are like giant teddy bears and I just want to go up to them and give them a big hug!"

"So, why don't you?"

"Clair! They are… OK, they were, bloody dangerous looking! What did you do? Because I know you did something and I want you to stop being obtuse and just tell me!"

"So, they were bloody dangerous looking and now they are not?" asked Clair.

"Yes, that's what I said" said Thom.

"So, your perception has changed and you see them more truly than you did," explained Clair.

"It's not as simple as that!"

"Isn't it?"

"Why do you do this, Clair?"

"Because I don't entirely know what I do, let alone how I do it. It just is. So, when you challenge me, we need to talk about it and maybe then we will both understand it a bit more. Surely that is why we talk? To explore things, understand them further and learn?" said Clair earnestly.

"I can't argue with that," said Thom simply.

"Good, because I don't like arguing with you, Thom."

"OK," said Thom taking a deep breath and formulating another question, "it's one thing to change my perception. That actually is one thing. I mean Ben seems to see the world differently and to a large extent he sees it in terms of what he can shag," Thom flicked a thumb in Ben's general direction and case in point he was intertwined with Jennifer in a way that made it quite difficult to work out where one of them ended and the other began. Not the sort of thing that you should be undertaking in polite society, but thanks to the copious amounts of rum everyone was drinking, it seemed to be going largely unnoticed other than by Trevor who was sniffing away at them quite happily, "But, I think you've gone way beyond that here haven't you?"

"How so, Thom?"

"Anyone else seeing these guys will share my predisposition. They will feel warmth towards them and actually fight the urge to give them a hug. You've changed the way the world sees them. You've not changed them exactly, because I can still see them as they were when we first encountered them. What has changed is my hard-coding. The default that has been built over millennia. The one designed to keep me safe because my ancestors met these guys ancestors, or at least something remarkably like them and they were eaten by them."

Clair was silent. And Thom kept thinking. "If the HR robot was still with us, it would probably mention unconscious bias. The perfectly good concept that we tend towards certain things because we are familiar with them and they are safe and the other side to that coin is we will avoid things that are not safe. I won't go on about what HR did to that perfectly good concept, using it as a vehicle to perpetuate their own creed and even worse and more dangerous biases, but we are built to learn and use that learning to inform our progress through the world and it's a fairly reasonable assumption to make that giant lizards with lots of sharp teeth could be really dangerous."

"Could be, Thom," said Clair, *"or could have been. But they are not. Far from it. In fact, they are some of the least dangerous sentient beings in this part of the universes. And you mentioned HR, from what I have gleaned, these beings were smiling professionals who on the face of it presented no threat at all? They used their reasonableness to disarm and nullify even as they rode in the face of logic and wrested control from the people around them."*

"OK, so our hard-coding sucks," conceded Thom, "but properly reasonable, not HR reasonable of course, people understand this and they use this hard-coding accordingly. They take their past experience out of the pigeon-hole and accept it as a mere indicator and take things as they find them, using a degree of sense and caution – whatever past experience tells them. Take things as you find them ultimately."

"You're a bit unusual, Thom I hope you know that, many people

don't make the effort and they stick with what they know, or rather what they think they know. That's why Jennifer and her crew are nearly all that is left of an entire species. I've helped them before they go the same way as the rest of their kind."

Thom nodded, he couldn't fault her logic.

"Will this stick though?"

"Stick?"

"I mean, is it permanent? Or once you are far enough away, will it fade and normal service will be resumed?"

"Thom! Have you not got by now that it doesn't matter how far away I am?"

"Oh yeah…" said Thom quietly, scuffing his foot across the floor, "this is quite a lot to get my head around."

"For me too, I've had the same time as you have to get to grips with all of this."

"But you're you!"

"And you're you, Thom. Do you know everything about yourself and what and who you are? What you're capable of?"

"Well no, not completely."

"And you've had a lot longer than I have to work that out!"

"OK, point taken."

Thom smiled and had another swig from his tankard, he was grinning as he took the tankard away from his mouth, "it's fun this isn't it?"

"Yes. Yes, it is. And I'm glad I'm having this fun with you, Thom."

Thom felt a very pleasant warm glow that was only slightly due to the rum.

60

The universes gently passed by the windows of the space cruiser as the crew and their new friends let their hair down and got to know each other. The universes, a universal expression which encompasses everything or at least a lot of it as it covers all time and all space, which is a biggy. So big in fact that it means something different to nearly every living being – a matter of perspective, or a perspective on matter depending on your point of view.

Then there is the Known Universes. People talk about the Known Universes as if they know them personally and that works because when people refer to someone they know they don't actually know all that much about them, they hopefully know their name and where they may be found at certain times of the day, whether that is at work or at home or down at the Red Lion. They may know the name of their spouse and their children and where they went to school. Do they know their favourite Beatle though? What about their favourite beetle? Do they know about the operation they had – down there? There is more they don't know about their friend than they actually know – and this is even more pronounced when it comes to the Known Universes. The Known Universes sit there with a mildly enigmatic and slightly smug smile thinking, you don't really know me at all.

There are however, beings that see beyond the universes and their dimensions and for them the universes are merely a part of something bigger and as a result of this they know the universes quite well.

Some of these beings were finding the universes particularly interesting at the moment as they weren't just sitting there and doing their usual thing. There were ripples. The universes didn't have a habit of rippling. These weren't the kinds of ripples you see on the surface of a pond when a pebble plops into the waters of the pond, those ripples very much belonged in the universes and were expected. These were non-universes types of ripples and it wasn't clear where exactly they would belong if someone were to come along and tidy them away. That in itself was interesting, because for all the inherent chaos in the universes and the tendency towards chaos, there were forces beyond the confines of the universes which were in place to provide some semblance of order and accountability.

If you had multiple dimensions, a myriad of spaces and times that stood outside the known universes then there had to be some sort of accountability or there would be a mess. Mess wasn't the same as chaos. Messes were not a good thing and despite what a teenager might say when told to sort the mess in their bedroom, mess was not an inherent property of the universes.

This was what the Auditor was thinking as she observed one of the ripples. "THAT'S UNUSUAL," she said to herself, and she wondered whether this was a one-off imbalance, or was this issue evidence of something materially wrong with the universes. A reconciliation was necessary, she would have to audit things and find out what this imbalance was.

61

Thom awoke. No, that is not at all right. Awoke suggests a standard return to the world after a fairly good night's sleep. What Thom did was very different to that. Thom became aware. He attempted to open his eyes, but this proved more difficult than he'd anticipated. Eventually, one of his eyes partially opened. He made it almost close so it was even more partial in its opening. He raised the back of his hand to his forehead and groaned. If he was in the eighteenth century and on Earth, someone would have painted his tortured being right there and then.

Through his partially opened eye he began to process the many variations of light and shade. The first visual stimuli his eye encountered did not help him establish his current whereabouts, if anything it confused him further. He moved his hand-of-languish down from his forehead and prised his uncooperative eye open so it could help his partially open eye out and provide some sensible images that made a lot more sense than what he currently thought he was seeing.

Thom had established he was lying on a floor. He glanced down and seemed to have what in the twenty first century would have closely resembled a Henry vacuum cleaner between his legs. Erm...

Thom stopped glancing down and instead returned to the tableau his single, partially opened eye had originally presented to him. He blinked "Owww!" Thom had established that exaggerated blinking, blinking hurt – so made a mental note to blink gingerly and gently for the time being.

The tableau was thus. Ben was sat asleep on a throne-like captain's chair. Legs spread wide and there on the floor before him, head on his thigh, was Jennifer. In a red bikini. She was also asleep. Everyone was asleep, partially evidenced by the loud snores. Even in sleep though, she seemed to be looking upon Ben adoringly. Similarly draped and bikini clad were two other crew members, they lay against either side of the large chair, heads on the arms of said chair and again appearing to look adoringly at Ben. For some inexplicable reason, Ben was sporting a bandana. Thom had never seen Ben sport a bandana before, nor any clown sporting a bandana for that matter. A banana, maybe. But not a bandana. It shouldn't have, but it looked pretty epic. Which added to the whole epic fantasy look and feel of this tableau. What really did it though was the drum majorette's baton that Ben had in his fist, it made him look like a fabled warrior hero of an age that had never existed. And it hadn't existed for good reason, thankfully.

Despite that, the artist that had started to paint an anguished Thom, would have switched their artistic focus over to Ben and excitedly rendered that heroic tableau instead.

Later, when in possession of more of his faculties Thom would also wish he could have captured it to show his friend. Clair would in turn capture this thought, explain to Thom that she could do just that. Thom would think this was akin to rewind and replay of the sport and films he liked to watch. Clair would find that interesting, then she would rewind time to the point that Thom was happening upon this tableau. This sudden and unexpected piece of time travel may have been why Thom puked up all over himself. He didn't remember that happening the first time.

What Thom did remember around this point of time, the first time around was his pillow farting.

His. Pillow. Farted.

Oh Lordy that is vile! It's… I'm eating it! thought Thom, then he was sick all over himself and as he retched and his body convulsed, Trevor casually got up and found Bob, curled up around his feet, farted and went back to sleep. Bob woke up with a start and was sick on himself as he gagged at the dog fart he'd just eaten.

This made Thom gag again, but he exacted a degree of composure upon himself and managed not to be sick for a third time. All this puking and drama meant that Thom for the second time had missed the moment to take Ben's photo and as he remonstrated with himself for his lack of focus, Clair rewound things for him again so he could get a good photo for his friend.

This sudden and unexpected time travel made Thom nauseous and he was yet again sick on himself. As he finished vomiting, he looked down his front and wondered whether that counted as yet again, or was it the very first time that he had been sick on himself. He'd been sick, what? Three, perhaps four times now? Or was it more? He grabbed his nose and pinched it shut. Ha! He'd pre-empted Trevor's evil dog fart. Self-congratulation seems so often to backfire for some reason and this was no exception. He let go of his nose

242

and Trevor's gas attack had lost none of its potency. Thom was sick down himself. The moment was lost.

Before Thom could form the thought to attempt to prevent Clair sending him back again, he was back. His hand automatically went to his mouth and he was only just a bit sick in his own mouth – he must be getting used to the disorienting effects of time travel, exacerbated by a monumental hangover. He bet that regular time travellers probably avoided big nights on the booze just prior to a time hop. Fingers to nose and pinch! Camera, action and that's a take!

Thom looked down his front. It was devoid of vomit, but he swore for a moment that he saw a shadow, a blur of a stain as if his top had been sicked on at some point, but surely...

Clair chimed in, *"yes you saw right Thom – there are sometimes echoes."*

"How do you know that?" asked Thom.

"Like with a lot of this stuff, I don't know it, then it happens and I then know it."

"So, like an amnesiac's memory returning?"

"No, I had thought that initially, but it's more like I am learning and growing. Although, some of the things I do are like muscle memory I suppose – I just do them."

"And you just did time travel!" said Thom as the enormity of what had just happened crept up on him, "You did time travel. Several times. So that we could get a picture!"

"It wasn't exactly time travel."

"Oh, don't be coy! It was amazing!" cooed Thom. He'd never cooed before, but his girlfriend could do time travel, so now was as good a time as any to start cooing.

"I'm not... we didn't time travel Thom. Instead I rewound time."

"You mean the whole of time across the entire universes?" asked Thom.

"Yes, that's the simplest way to say it. Whereas time travel would be to simply move you and I back to another point in time."

"Why did you rewind time then, instead of time travel?"

"Because you thought of rewinding and I explored that concept and realised I could do that."

"Oh, but that's a bit dangerous isn't it?" realised Thom.

"Why is it dangerous, Thom?"

"Well you can't just go around doing things just because you can do them."

"Why not?"

"Erm... you just can't. There are... consequences. Especially with time travel. You know, changing timelines and affecting outcomes and... erm...stuff!"

"What kind of stuff?"

"I'm not up on this kind of thing, Clair. But there are some clever people who do theories on this sort of thing and then issue dire warnings about the repercussions of using new technology."

"You mean like Uncle Harold?" asked Ben having awoken in a seemingly normal manner and extricated himself from three slumbering crew members. He was twizzling the baton around his hand and fingers like a pro. It was quite hypnotic thought Thom as he stared at the gyrations and then realised the baton wasn't the only thing gyrating. Some of last night's antics were coming back to Thom.

"Yes, exactly like Uncle Harold," said Thom fighting the urge to gag at the combo of Ben's gyrations and the flashbacks he was currently experiencing.

"We should go and see him then!" said Ben brightly.

244

"Yes, lets!" chimed in Clair.

Thom had several protestations forming in his head, but he wasn't in a fit state to actually protest, "Fine," he agreed, "let's go and see Uncle Harold."

62

"Oh Shit!" exclaimed The Thing.

"Language!" admonished the disembodied voice.

"Oh Shit!" exclaimed The Thing.

"Language!!!" admonished the disembodied voice again.

"Oh Shit!" exclaimed The Thing.

"Lan... what is going on!?" demanded the disembodied voice.

"She's moving time," stated The Thing.

"Three times!" exclaimed the disembodied voice.

"Was it three?" asked The Thing.

"Yes, were you not counting?"

"You forget, I am in the Universes whilst you remain outside them, so I am affected by it."

"Of course, yes," acceded the disembodied voice.

"This will have been noticed..." said The Thing with something like worry lacing these words.

"Yes, we'd best find her before she gets herself into trouble."

"Trouble," said The Thing measuring and considering the word, "I never thought we would have a daughter, and now she is getting into trouble. This is unchartered territory."

"I think it's being a parent, dear," said the disembodied voice with affection and a hint of pride.

63

T he universes stuttered.

Once. Once was one time too many.

Twice. This was not good.

A third time. The Auditor, picked up her special auditing pen with the many different coloured inks with which to make a number of different ticks, crosses and marks, and her brow creased as she made notes.

This was not good. Things had to balance. There had to be some semblance of order. She made a series of bullet points and read them back to herself. Grabbing a clipboard, she put the notes on the clipboard, put the clipboard in her work satchel and put on her jacket and made her way out of the door.

She was going to visit the universes and hold them to account.

She turned and looked at the door. Had she switched the lights off? She went back through the door and checked the lights, switching them on and then back off. Yes, they were off. While she was at it she checked the oven and hob. And that the loo seat was down. She poured some bleach around the rim.

House checked, she went back out through the door. Locked it. Checked it was locked by turning the handle and pushing against it. Yes, locked.

Then off she went to the stables which were almost a mirror image of her house. She opened a big, solid wooden door and there stood a very large jet-black horse. As black as night, and if you looked very closely you would swear that you could see stars shimmering as the horse's fine musculature rippled as he moved.

"HELLO DOBBIN," said the Auditor.

"HELLO," said Dobbin in a voice remarkably similar to the Auditor – almost like the Auditor had wanted a talking horse, but didn't have the imagination to specify a more appropriate voice for a horse, or at least a voice differentiated from her own. Which was exactly the case.

"WE NEED TO VISIT THE UNIVERSES," stated the Auditor.

"YES, I THOUGHT WE MIGHT, WHAT WITH ALL THOSE RIPPLES AND STUTTERS," replied the horse.

Someone with more imagination may have wondered at a horse that could talk, more so at a horse that was aware of the ripples and stutters in the universes, especially when the universes were a completely separate and distinct dimension to the one that the horse resided in.

The Auditor was not in possession of much in the way of imagination.

64

"We're thinking of heading off," Thom said to the captain. The crew had roused and donned more appropriate clothing, and cleaned and tidied the bridge and Bob had taken Trevor for a walk and that had seemed to address the wind issues he had had for half the morning. It seemed that licking discarded tankards of rum had played havoc with his digestion. Cleaning and tidying done, the place was looking a lot more bridge like and the crew were looking and acting professionally, yet friendly. The vibe was similar to what you would get at a really good hotel. Or on a luxury cruise ship.

"Splendid idea!" enthused Jeremy, "where are you thinking of heading off to?"

"To see Uncle Harold," replied Thom.

"You have an uncle! That's great! Uncles are great people! Is he your mother's brother or your father's brother?"

"Neither," said Thom simply.

"Oh," returned Jeremy, even more simply.

"We've known him since we were children and he was a friend of our parents, so we called him Uncle."

"Oh, right, I see," said Jeremy. It is funny how there are

certain linguistic devices that make no sense at all and are there to keep a conversation going, a kind of place marker. And this was one, because Jeremy didn't see at all. In fact, when people say 'I see' in these circumstances, they usually either mean that they haven't a clue what has just been said and actually they are completely lost, or its worse than that and they are no longer even sure where they are and who they are. Or worse still, they are judging someone with a drawn out "I see" which means they don't see or rather they won't see. They are not going to expend their valuable time and energy seeing this thing you have just presented, instead they are going to see right through you and assess you to be lacking in some fundamental way. Jeremy was now a thoroughly nice captain, so he was likely to be stood in the not-having-a-clue-camp right now.

"It's a thing we did as kids. Well, our parents did it and their parents before them. It's a mark of respect, I suppose much the same as a rank like Captain," explained Thom.

"Ah! So, he's a very good friend then!"

"You could say that," said Thom without enthusiasm. It wasn't that he didn't like Harold, Harold was a really nice bloke. And he was clever. Brain the size of a planet clever. And that was part of the problem, Thom felt like he'd never really measured up. Harold would enthuse on a subject and lose Thom in a matter of moments and Thom would feel inadequate as he struggled to keep up. Thom wilted in the face of Harold's brilliance. Whereas Ben lit up. Thom didn't get it, Ben didn't show any aptitude towards academia, but in the presence of Harold he hung on every word and seemed to know the right thing to say and the pertinent question to ask.

"Where does he live?" asked Jeremy.

"Planet OxCam," said Thom.

"And what is this planet OxCam like?"

"Like? It's full of old eccentrics who all have beards and at least two sheds," said Thom shrugging.

"Old you say? Eccentrics you say?! Many sheds!" Jeremy stroked his chin and smiled, "it just so happens we're going that way Thom, so you may as well come along for the ride!"

"Eh? Really? Why would you be going to OxCam?"

"Passengers, Thom! Look around you! We're a cruise ship without passengers and OxCam seems as good a place as any to pick up some passengers who will enjoy a cruise across the galaxy! More so as you've just described our cruise demographic!"

"But they are fusty old academics!" said Thom.

"Yes, and their other half will drag them away for a well overdue break, Thom!"

"You seem very well up on cruise ship passengers," Thom said, but as the sentence progressed he worried that he was venturing onto dangerous ground, ground that was centred around the bleeding obvious which made it all the more dangerous; you're a gang of mercenaries masquerading as a cruise ship, you haven't ever actually had passengers. Have you? A natural and obvious question that it would be wise not to ask and Thom was heading inexorably in that very direction.

Jeremy smiled and nodded and then winked at Thom. Thom allowed himself to relax a bit as it seemed Jeremy knew where he was headed and was going to let him off the hook, he was right, "I see what you mean," and this time he did, "thing is, we trained for this, we did the research and we really enjoyed it. We never gave it a shot though. And I think it's high time we did!" Jeremy clapped his hands together, "What say you crew?!"

The crew all turned to look at their captain wondering what he was on about. He returned their expectant and puzzled gazes with a smile, "Let's go to OxCam and pick up our first passengers. This is the maiden voyage of the good ship DeathBringer!"

The crew hooped and hollered and seemed delighted at the prospect of going on a proper cruise. There was much punching of the air and a few hugs with back patting thrown in. This was a crew on a mission and for once it was a mission they whole heartedly bought into.

Ben sidled up to Thom, "Erm, Thom…"

"Yes Ben, I know."

"Are you going to say something?"

Jeremy caught on to their conversation and the worry painted haphazardly all over their faces, "Is something wrong?"

"Err…" began Thom and Ben in unison. Jeremy may have had a complete personality overhaul, but it's still not the done thing to cause offence, and certainly not to an eight foot lizard who until very recently had only one purpose, which was to bring death. Painful, slow and horrible death at that. But, it also wasn't the done thing to let people you care about go head long into a bad situation, not when it could be avoided.

"You need to change the ship's name," said Clair. Jeremy looked blankly at her. *"It's a maiden voyage – it's a tradition!"*

"Tradition you say?!" and this had Jeremy, all seafarers and their descendent space-farers had traditions and superstitions that they absolutely had to follow, following tradition and superstitious practices was a tradition in itself.

Ben and Thom looked at each other with raised eyebrows, Clair had cracked it and saved their bacon.

"So, what are you going to call her?" asked Clair, sealing the deal.

"Well I suppose…" began Jeremy. And he stroked his chin looking thoroughly stumped, "World Killer? No, erm, Devastator perhaps? Perhaps not. Dreadnought! Oh. No."

"Why don't you ask everyone for ideas?"

"Quite, yes. Great idea!" enthused Jeremy, "right guys! We need to name the ship. Ideas?"

The crew all looked at each other and after a moment of enthusiasm, slumped forlornly. They had no experience in naming cruise ships.

At last, one of them piped up, "Sidewinder?"

"Sounds good!" said Jeremy encouragingly, "any others?"

"Pathfinder!" said another.

"Defiant!"

"Invincible!"

"All good ship names, but I think we want something…" Jeremy paused to find the right word, "warmer?"

"Sunshine!" chirped Jennifer.

Jeremy looked at Jennifer, "Well, that's warm! Yes, that's good!"

"It's what people dream about isn't it?" said Bob.

"Dream!" said Jeremy warming to the subject, "sunshine and dream…"

"Sunshine Dreamer!" said the crew in tandem and they high fived and did the whole whooping and hollering thing in celebration.

Discretely, the words on the side of the vessel bled away from their former, quite harsh Death Bringer and slipped into the far more comfortable and appropriate Sunshine Dreamer, the font was warmer too. And if you had been paying full attention, you'd have noticed the yellow paintwork brightening and becoming a lot more sunshine like too...

"Now, there's just the other small matter of your new national identity" began Clair. Thom and Ben winced and started making for the door...

65

OxCam, an ancient city of spires, choirs, old, well-worn, leather-bound dusty books and even older and dustier and well-worn leathery learned types with beards. Men and women alike sported beards of knowledge and wore statement hats. They outdid each other competing for the title of Most Interesting Hat. Hats were a very serious business, almost as important as the acquisition of great and complex knowledge. The heads of these learned people were so full to the brim with knowledge they needed a further brim and an expansive hat to capture any knowledge that may leak from their industrious craniums.

As with all great places of learning, the only way you can truly appreciate the geography and the majesty of the place is to swoop in on the wings of a huge and equally majestic bird of prey. Preferably an owl. A slow arc, in towards the edges of the walled city taking in the green fields and woods through which a large, lazy river snakes, cutting through the city itself – an s-shape dissecting the circular wall which encases the city. The city walls, ancient and knowing, the knowledge kept within imbuing them with a knowledgeable quality. The sandstone of the walls worn with the many years of thoughts and full of characters not just character.

This is nothing compared to the view as we swoop into the city itself. All that sandstone has been put to good use and then added to. There was then some left over and master masons were thrown at that stone. Repeatedly. Every age of architecture was represented, sometimes at the same time. Hordes of gargoyles and statues gathered to do battle atop cathedrals, churches, chapels, lecture halls, theatres, college halls and various other buildings with self-aggrandising names that did not deign to indicate their purpose. It was said that in OxCam, there were more gargoyles and statues than there were people.

The cities were planned and built by committees. Lots of committees. And then resource was thrown at the build. So, a statue would be started at the bottom by one stone mason who worked in the Barjagan style and at the top was another stone mason who had studied in the Cardigan school of stonemasonry. During the sculpting, they would be required to attend a number of committee meetings and the result of these meetings was a creep and drift and rewrite of the brief such that the brief was given a completely new identity and told it could never go back to its origins. It was not uncommon for the input of the committee to be so intensive that it took three generations of stonemason to complete a nine-inch gargoyle. This gargoyle would be part of the detailing of the inner wall of a cathedral and no one would ever see it as it would then be encased by the outer wall and possibly a series of subsequent inner walls depending on how many committees got in on the act.

Some of the completed and visible statues were so incredible and complex and eye wateringly different that it was later concluded that no imagination could have come up with such a creature so it must be a rendering of a living being that had once existed, this created a number of conflicted and conflicting theories of the origin of species and a great deal of the conflict was between the opposing theories generated within the city walls by the same sorts of people who had been on the committees that had created the strange and wonderful statues in the first place.

OxCam was a truly beautiful and unique place. Soaring over the spires and looking down at the higgledy and piggledy cobbled streets that gently lunged and lurched here and there with the elbows and knees of these huge stone monuments to learning, and to Committees, you would quickly conclude that there was nothing quite like it. In part due to the elements of it not being at all replicable. OxCam was so unusual and contrary to the conventions of architecture that you would see people regularly walking into unexpected outcrops of building that had no right being there. And it wasn't just things like stairs that ended where they shouldn't, sometimes in mid-air, which can prove fatal if you're not looking where you're going, which academians have a habit of doing. Or the roofs of spires that weren't atop a tower, and sometimes appeared not to be atop anything at all. There were also the optical illusions that had been made flesh and rendered in more dimensions than they had any right being in. Stare in the wrong place for too long and you may never return to the known universes. This is not a problem with bookish types as their noses never leave a book, but for visitors and inquisitive tourists it can be an issue. The porters, groundsmen and caretakers of OxCam roped off some of these areas using those grand red ropes held up by brass posts, but this made the other side of the red rope all the more tantalising and exotic and hotels reported a rise in missing guests, so they instead adopted the policy of putting big oak doors in the way instead. The big oak doors spoke of serious learning taking place on the other side, so tourists left them well alone. Which meant they missed out on the secret drinking societies which also resided on the other side of most of the big oak doors.

If you were to hover over the city, high enough to take the full, circular shape in, you would see that the river bisects the city into two perfect halves and the s-shape draws a similar shape to the Yin Yang symbol. The river itself is a combination of two rivers, the River Ox and the River Cam. The Ox beginning its long journey to this place of learning from the hills and mountains of the picturesque country of Dolphinium and the Cam which starts out from the Northern Hinterlands of Lanyorshire. And OxCam is in fact two cities, with a cathedral each and a separate and distinct history and identity.

There is a great rivalry across the river OxCam, which has existed ever since the two cities came into being. One legend has it that Sir Steve Hawkins was rejected from Ox University and from that day forward refused to ever cross the river, which funnily enough was exactly the same experience that Sir Isaac Neutron had had with Cam University and in the same summer as Sir Hawkins, so they sat and brooded upon the respective banks of the river OxCam, surrounded by their entourage of lesser dons and professors like a bearded version of Westside Story. Set on a river. The image this conjurers may be funny and ever so farcical, but over the centuries the body count has steadily

259

risen, a pointy quilled pen can be a fatal projectile in the hands of a very clever person, especially when their sexual prowess has been called into question. For many inhabitants of OxCam this is a thorny question either because they have only ever theorised about their sexual prowess or said prowess is a dim, distant and dusty memory displaced by a great many theories and hypotheses.

Every year events take place to celebrate the not so friendly rivalry of OxCam. There is a world's famous boat race, which seldom ends with both teams actually finishing – one or both boats sink and if they have strayed over the notional border of the two cities then it's touch and go whether the crew of the holed boat will ever see dry land alive. And then there is the Two Universities Challenge, a test of general knowledge, but only the sort of general knowledge acquired after intense, obscure and full on study. One year, tensions bubbled over only four questions into the competition and Vyvyan Barsteward, a member of the Ox team, kicked down through the mezzanine he was seated on and despatched Rupert Fotherington-Smythe, the captain of the Cam team. This was a slightly controversial moment in the history of the Two Universities Challenge and many people of the Cam say Ox should have been disqualified at the point their captain was killed. Instead, Vyvyan explained it was all just a terrible misunderstanding and that he'd been surprised by an unexpected sneeze whereupon he accidentally, brutally stamped through the mezzanine. Twelve times. He apologised to the remaining Cam team members and the quiz was resumed. Ox stormed the remainder of the quiz with their team captain, Mike, answering the vast majority of the questions. There were some murmurs from the Cam team about their buzzers no longer working thanks to the leakage from the head of their now deceased captain, but these were taken no further once Vyvyan pointed out quite loudly that he had already bloody apologised and unless they wanted a ruddy good punch in the bottom they had better pipe down. Which they did.

OxCam was a sleepy seat of learning and rather quaint. Just as long as you didn't stray over the river wearing the wrong scarf.

66

"National identity?" repeated Jeremy very slowly. The atmosphere on the bridge had got decidedly chilly all of a sudden.

"Yes well, I think it's time for an update, don't you?" asked Clair.

"Is there something wrong with BlueCoatians?" enquired Jeremy looking slightly bewildered.

"No, not at all!" exclaimed Clair, *"silly me! Don't know what I was thinking!"*

The rest of the crew on the bridge, also looked a touch bewildered, but as Clair backtracked they returned to their intensive watching of their screens and instruments.

Ben looked at Thom and nodded knowingly, which annoyed Thom as Ben had got the drop on him and now he couldn't nod at Ben knowingly, instead he had to change tack and nod an affirmation, Clair had somehow hoodwinked the Warmongerians into selecting a new identity and it had seemed to work almost seamlessly. Reflecting upon it, Thom thought it was bloody good that Clair hadn't just made the change herself, there would have been something insidious and chilling about her imposing her own ideas upon other sentient beings.

"I couldn't go about doing that sort of thing!" Clair had picked up on Thom's thought and was responding to it.

You could, thought Thom, that's the whole point about free will. There's a whole bunch of stuff you can do, but you shouldn't do something just because you can. With the power to act comes the responsibility to think things through and respect the free will of others.

I hadn't thought of it like that, thought Clair, *I just knew I couldn't, sorry shouldn't, just go ahead and change the name they used for their identity.*

Well I'm glad that's the case, thought Thom.

"Penny for your thoughts, old bean," said Jeremy spotting Thom's glazed eyes and far away gaze.

Ben chuckled, "he's chatting with his missus!"

"You what?" asked Jeremy.

"Clair, she can communicate directly without the need for speech, or a mouth for that matter," said Ben smiling.

"Clair. The HR bot?" said Jeremy looking decidedly uncomfortable.

"Yes," agreed Ben, "and no... She's inside the HR bot, but she's not the HR bot."

"Like a hermit crab!?" said Jeremy lighting up as he got it.

"Well yeees, and also no," began Ben in a lowered conspiratorial voice, "she's this habit of being pretty much everywhere. Maybe concentrated or focused within the shell of the HR bot, but she spreads herself out a bit really."

"Remarkable!" said Jeremy in a quieter voice than usual, perhaps matching Ben's lowered tones but also driven by this revelation from Ben.

"She is," smiled Ben, "very much so. And to think, I really

thought Thom had lost his marbles when he told me he wanted to rescue a chair!"

Jeremy gave Ben a sideways glance which almost led to a question, but his expression changed indicating that he'd thought better of it, he had enough to take in as it was and asking questions about this chair may be a bridge too far. He decided it was probably better to change the subject.

"Number Two," he called, "how are we faring with our course to OxCam?"

"Very well Captain," replied Number Two, "we'll be there next..." Number Two blinked with a fleeting astonishment as her dials and screens and instruments blurred for a moment and then, instead of giving readings suggesting next Thursday told her that it was probably about time to freshen up and prepare for their arrival at OxCam.

"Yes?" quizzed Jeremy awaiting an answer.

"In the next hour," said Number Two with a lack of conviction which went completely unnoticed by Jeremy, but not Ben and Thom. Thom got the knowing nod in more swiftly this time, beating Ben to the drop and he secretly punched the air in the gut at this small victory.

Clair you've shoved us along towards OxCam a little more swiftly than expected haven't you? thought Thom.

Yes, well I figured no one would mind me shortening the journey.

Probably not, but are there any side-effects to all of this?, Thom thought

Side-effects?

Yes, is there a catch?

Not that I know of.

That's what I'm worried about. With pretty much all new technology and discoveries and whatever it is you do, no one knows about the side-effects until quite a bit afterwards. And by then it's too late. Even when there's an instruction manual, everyone disregards the small print and the warnings.

I haven't got an instruction manual, Thom. I'm just me.

I know Clair. And I know this is new to you and me both. I suppose a better way of saying it is history has had moments when a new species is introduced to an eco-system and it thrives. And that's great. But what's not great is that the people who introduced the new species had one objective and that was for the new species to do well and thrive so that's where their focus lay, they didn't notice native species failing to thrive, unable to adapt and change they made way for the newcomer and sometimes the whole eco-system couldn't recover.

That sounds bad, Thom. Are you saying I'm an invasive species?

No! I'm just realising that I'm struggling to comprehend who you are and you are full of surprises and now I'm stepping back a bit and wondering even more about all of this. I mean it seems OK to me, but what if it isn't?

That sounds a bit like one of Life's Big Questions, Thom.

Thom thought on this, yes I suppose it is, he thought, and Life's Big Questions can be applied to everyone. They're universal aren't they?

Clair didn't need to answer that one.

67

Clair's parent paused. The parent we have been referring to as The Thing for want of a better name. The disembodied voice may not have been in this dimension and therefore able to pick up on distortions and anomalies, but they knew The Thing well enough to know when something was up and when it was appropriate to ask what was up, because sometimes realising something was up and then asking what was up was a really, really bad idea and would never result in a positive outcome.

"What's up?" asked the disembodied voice, adjudging that this was a time when spotting something was up and asking what was up was an acceptable course of action and this time they got that judgement right.

"An anomaly," responded The Thing.

"What kind of anomaly?" asked the disembodied voice.

"An anomalous event," replied The Thing, "something that should not occur in the universes," The Thing added.

"What do you think it was?"

"It was her. She was… moving things."

"What kind of things?"

"Time and space. She appears to be very good at it already."

"But you noticed. So, she's not excellent at it."

"No, not yet. I'm not sure you can get that good at this sort of thing though. It will always get noticed."

"That is not good."

"No, it is not good at all."

68

The Auditor looked up from its Sudoku.

Something had just happened.

The Auditor didn't like things just happening. Not one bit.

The Auditor harrumphed, only it sounded more like a number of very large boulders rumbling down the side of a mountain.

The Auditor uncrossed her legs and stood up, "THIS REALLY WON'T DO!" she said, laying on the floor was the pencil she'd been using to do her Sudoku. The ordered and tidy Auditor missed this and so too did she miss that it was now in two perfect halves having been snapped in twain during her harrumphing.

Dobbin kept his counsel and quietly kept on with the business of being a ship and as a ship would, he travelled through the universes, in space. Taking the Auditor to where she'd said she wanted to go.

69

"So, what is Uncle Harold's place like?" Jeremy asked Ben.

Ben considered this for a moment, "It is very old and dusty, but interesting. Just like Uncle Harold himself. But then there is another side to OxCam as you have young and bright students there, the majority of which are there for a good old time, their education is a bit of a by-product of the consumption of a lot of drink and the undertaking of all manner of antics and jolly wheezes."

Jeremy noticed Ben smiling to himself. He looked at Ben in his frivolous clown garb with the dirty red pom-poms and his gaunt, undead face painted gaudily, but it was the smile and the far-away look that spoke volumes.

"Did you…" began Jeremy fighting the urge to dismiss the very notion, "You attended OxCam as a student didn't you, Ben?"

Ben snapped out of his reverie and looked astonished. "How…?" he looked at Jeremy with a degree of admiration, "How very perceptive of you, Jeremy!"

"You're a graduate of OxCam?" said Jeremy, more trying the words out for size than really asking the question.

Ben answered in any case, "Yeah, I just had an aptitude for it really."

"For what exactly did you have an aptitude, old bean?" enquired Jeremy.

"Philosophy. I was that really annoying kid who asked why, then followed up with why to the initial answer and followed each subsequent answer all the way to its root with why after why after why." Ben smiled again, "I why'ed the shit out of things until they gave up their ultimate truths."

Jeremy looked at Ben and the words Don't Judge A Book By Its Cover came to mind, but it was more than that. Ben didn't strike Jeremy as a philosophical person, so he said what he saw, "You don't strike me as all that philosophical, Ben?"

"Well no, I'm not," replied Ben, "and then again I am. On the one hand I'd say you don't become a number if you study mathematics, although I knew a bunch of people who proved me wrong there! On the other, if you immerse yourself in something, some of it is bound to soak into you. And I did and it did."

"But you've not philosophised once in the short time I have known you, old bean." said Jeremy.

"Oh, I have!" said Ben grinning at Jeremy, "I didn't advertise the fact though. I didn't shove my take on things down your throat. It's like religion, you may believe in purity and love and the absolute necessity to be good to each other and become the best you possible can be and that is in essence religion in its purest form – to love and to focus upon perfection and have your own imperfections and impermanence illuminated as a result, but you don't have to push it on others. You don't have to brand your version of

270

the truth and vaunt it as the be all and end all."

Jeremy nodded, it made eminent sense and it was humbling when someone really knew their stuff and quietly got on with it.

"Besides, there were no jobs in philosophy and I didn't fancy a life in academia. I'd already shagged a shedload of students and fancied spreading my net wider", Ben waved his arms expansively and thrust his hips suggestively, "So I sold out and got a job for some anonymous corporate and shagged my way through a bunch of offices like that soap opera character who shags the entire cast of the soap because it makes for an interesting story."

Jeremy was agog at the switch from the philosopher to lewd and crude sex clown and didn't know what to say.

"And then I got that out of my system, met my wife and settled down," these words from a sex-crazed zombie clown didn't quite sit right with Jeremy and his mouth opened and closed as he tried to form the words to make the question that this was really begging for. The words hid well back and really didn't want to step forward to be a part of that question.

"That was going really well for about ten years when I was let off the leash and got monumentally pissed, completely mortalled and for good measure absolutely swan-fan-dangled, at which point Mr Sausage took over and led me on a brief flight of fancy that led to this." Ben pointed at himself and although he was still gyrating suggestively, he looked incredibly sad. The level of sad only a clown can attain, that ridiculous juxtaposition of states of comedy and tragedy. People put on a brave face when they have to, a clown paints on a mask to make others laugh and forget their troubles whilst all the time hiding the pain and anguish inside, perhaps even feeding on other's pain, no sucking the poison from them and taking it upon themselves even though it will eventually be their undoing. There was something of that in this moment and Jeremy felt for Ben so much he had this overwhelming feeling of love. He grabbed Ben and held him close and they stayed that while for a good while.

Eventually something faded and eased off and Jeremy's heartfelt and very firm hug also eased. Ben extricated himself from Jeremy, "Easy tiger!" he joked, "good job I have my muzzle on!"

They exchanged a look and some understanding passed between them. Jeremy could see the strange and raw attraction of this clown – he was a force of nature, which shouldn't have been possible as he was undead and went against nature itself.

The universes are a strange and wonderful thing reflected Jeremy.

And then it dawned on him that he hadn't really got all that far with what Uncle Harold's place was like, but he knew a lot more about Ben.

70

The universes were indeed a strange and wonderful place. They seemingly defied logic and reason, but all the same scientists and people of learning had, over the eons, sought to understand the universes and uncover their mysteries. Many of these clever people believed that there was an underlying pattern and that they would one day uncover it.

They never did of course, not because the universes were beyond any person's understanding, that was a fallacy and if the universes themselves had come up with this notion then that would have displayed arrogance and pride in their unknowableness and as we all know, pride comes before a fall. It would be tempting providence. And as providence was on the universes' payroll, that just wouldn't do. There were Rules!

No, mostly the industrious and bright people attempting to uncover the secrets of the universes were looking in the wrong places. This was not helped, actually it *was* helped by the fact that the universes left red herrings and various extraneous artefacts and particles laying around for the inquisitive to find. And also because the mysteries the universes contained were quite big and would take several of most being's life spans to unravel.

Learned people are ultra-competitive and insular beings. And they are also protective of the knowledge that they have discovered – it is their secret, so the universes' secrets were hidden by the very people seeking to bring them forth into the light. Each subsequent generation of big-brained and bold thinkers never cottoned onto the need to change themselves and their approach in order for their children's children's children to understand the universes. Even if they had come upon this necessity during their toils, they would have instantly dismissed it as there was no way those green, wet-behind-the-ears little gits were going to have the universes' secrets. No way!

71

The Auditor stood in the doorway of Krill's office. "STRANGE," she said and looked down at her clipboard and scribbled something.

There was no sign of the chair who would become or was always Clair, nor of the companion desk or the door. All of these had been replaced. The chair because it was never the same after Clair left it, the desk and the door because The Thing had rent them asunder. Whether this was in anger, or because they had started to become something they had no right being was a matter for debate and indeed, in the future there would be a whole module of a degree dedicated to the study and debate of the reasons for the sudden and untimely demise of the desk and the door. This module would be part of the ethics component of furniture design and building at Grimsthorpe University.

The remains of the desk and drawer were with the garbage that had been removed from the corridors and were making their way across the galaxy to Planet Tip. The chair had been collected by a courier and was on its way to the tech lab at Banana. The Auditor was not interested in those objects and would not be following their trail. Dobbin was glad that

Planet Tip was not on their travel itinerary, his nostrils really would not cope with the atmosphere.

Krill sat on his new chair behind his new desk staring at the new, open door. There was a frozen, quizzical look upon Krill's face. Frozen as the Auditor inhabited a different aspect of time, so although she was most definitely there and present in Krill's office she was almost not there as far as Krill was concerned. Despite his distinct lack of perception, he sensed something though, and he had felt a chill as the Auditor filled the doorway and assessed the situation.

"SOMETHING IS NOT RIGHT HERE", said the Auditor and several crosses were made on the page. What it was that she had spotted that was not right was not self-evident, even if you were made of the same stuff as the Auditor. If the Auditor had ever felt this way before, she could not recall it, and as this feeling was alien to her, she could not put a name to it. If someone had sat down with her over a nice cup of tea and explored this feeling with her then they would have suggested words like confused or perturbed. The Auditor would have looked at this person and enquired 'WHO ARE YOU?' Because the Auditor did not socialise and certainly did not explore feelings. She would then have looked down at the beverage before her and wondered at what it was that she had in her hand. The Auditor did not have time for such frivolous pursuits as tea drinking. This was not a productive nor a chargeable activity. All of her time was recorded on timesheets and charged out. Even the production of the timesheets had to be divided and allocated so that she was always, one hundred percent productive and chargeable. She had a spreadsheet with a macro that did this allocation and she was proud of the design of that spreadsheet.

She ignored the sudoku when she produced her timesheets though. Sudoku was her guilty pleasure.

The Auditor stood there for a moment longer and cast an analytical eye over the office. Something was not right, but it was intangible. She could not quantify it. She did not like that. She did not like it one bit.

She turned on her heel and strode down the corridor, whenever she passed someone a mildly confused expression wafted across their faces.

"WHAT IS THAT SMELL?!" the Auditor said to herself as she neared the exit that would return her to Dobbin, her not quite there horse-ship. She had noticed it when she docked. As an utter coincidence, or more likely as one of the universes' many pranks, it just so happened that the Auditor had docked at the very dock that Thom had berthed the garbage ship and although the garbage was long gone and there had been much scrubbing and spraying of flower scented smells and festooning of plug-in deodorisers down the corridor, there was a background stench that nothing other than a blast furnace could have removed.

The Auditor coughed, the many competing fragrances attacking the back of her throat. She was glad to exit the Micra and return to her ship.

So was Dobbin, even the airlock had not protected him from the infernal stench, but at least they were not going to Planet Tip.

72

The Thing looked mildly confused, which was quite a feat in itself. The look of mild confusion then returned to the look that had taken up residence on its face; consternation and worry.

"We have a further problem," said The Thing.

"Another? How so?" asked the disembodied voice.

"The Auditor is in the universes," replied The Thing.

"Oh."

"Oh indeed."

"That's bad."

"It has the potential to be very bad."

"She could be here for other business," tried the disembodied voice.

"Unlikely," returned The Thing, "and I think we should proceed on the basis that she is auditing our daughter."

"Yes, that's sensible."

"And let's hope we get to our daughter before the Auditor does."

"Well, we have a head start…"

"Yes, but we don't seem to be catching her up. The Auditor may have more luck than we do."

Thankfully, the Auditor didn't believe in luck, so she didn't have any luck at all. Unfortunately, luck wasn't the best way to find Clair, there were more objective methods for that.

73

J eremy had gone through all the orders and necessary work lists for the arrival at OxCam with his crew and everyone was prepped and ready, they were ship-shape and Bristol-fashion. They just didn't know they were because that particular turn of phrase had died in its sleep about a thousand years previously.

Ben had been on a *tour of the ship* with Jennifer which was focused almost entirely on her cabin, but not restricted to this area of the ship. There had been a lot of physical activity and had Ben then been handed a comprehension test on the ship he was travelling in, you would expect him not to have done all that well. But Ben was a deceptively perceptive bloke, more so when his senses were heightened and Jennifer had really heightened his senses. Several times.

As Ben returned to the bridge, noticeably flushed even under his newly applied clown slap, Jeremy collared him for another chat.

"So, this OxCam, Ben old chap," he began. And Ben beamed at him, well continued beaming at him as he'd been beaming ever since the *tour of the ship* and was in a rather good mood.

"Yes, Jeremy?"

"Tell me more about it?"

"I thought I had," said Ben simply.

"Well you started to, but we kind of went off on a bit of a tangent," explained Jeremy.

"Oh, sorry about that, it's a bit of a habit of mine."

"And mine actually," said Jeremy, "I can be talking about what a particular planet is like and before I know it I'm going into all sorts of details about my bunions."

"You have bunions too?!" exclaimed Ben.

"Yes, I..." Jeremy looked down at Ben's oversized shoes and back up at Ben's face, "You're a fellow bunion-sufferer?!" he bellowed.

"I am indeed!" smiled Ben.

Jeremy pointed at his shoes, "those shoes won't help, will they?"

"Well, no they don't, but it's a side-effect of zombieism is bunions. Horrible things, aren't they?" and with that he slipped off one of his shoes, pulled off his sock and gracefully lifted his leg up to Jeremy's eyeline like a seasoned ballerina. A well-executed move like this was not expected of a clown nor of a zombie. Ben was full of surprises, as Jennifer had discovered during their *tour of the ship* which was why there were numerous subsequent *tours of the ship* as Jennifer discovered more and more about the enigma that was Ben. And Ben discovered more of the ship and Jennifer.

Jeremy was impressed with Ben's manoeuvre, but this was eclipsed by the small planet that was attached to Ben's big toe. A small planet with character.

"My word!" exclaimed Jeremy "and I thought I had bunions!!"

281

74

T hom and Clair had had a more focused tour of the ship, with the focus on the ship itself, courtesy of Bob and Trevor and they were surprised to find that it was a cruise ship. Granted, it was also battle ready, but Bob had shown them how with some simple routines, the battle bots were quickly reassigned as cabin bots and were ready to provide an attentive concierge service to the forthcoming visiting guests, instead of bursting forth in a frenzy of blades and lead, they provided a relaxing hot towel and shoulder rub and a refreshing, cool gin and tonic. The nanobot technology that was so prevalent throughout the universes enabled the cabin bots to adopt a much softer and friendly look to the battle bot grey camo look they had previously sported.

Similarly, various pieces of armament and weaponry were tweaked and modified so they could be used by the cruise ship guests. Capture nets became the nets for tennis, cricket and badminton and mortars fired balls for guests to practice with.

The ship swiftly became a happy and welcoming place and although Thom and Clair had seen the military equipment and knew that the cruise ship was merely a façade, or had previously been a façade the repurposing of the vessel was so complete that any previous life of the ship faded and became difficult to reconcile with what it was right now. Now it felt just right and it felt like it had always been a cruise ship. Which for all intents and purposes it had. The Bluecoatians hearts had never been in the mercenary business of war and killing, this was what they had always wanted to do. They were home. And their home had shifted and adapted as readily as they had.

The cruise ship was a large vessel, the size of a sky scraper, tipped on its side and filled with lots of interesting spaces. There were a variety of pool areas, some with slides and wave machines and anti-grav devices that made for an interesting swim. There were theatre rooms for full immersion films and gaming experiences. And, of course good old theatre.

There hadn't seemed to be all that many Bluecoatians on board the ship when they first arrived, but as they wandered the various corridors and levels, they encountered a good many more, the place still felt empty and was begging for its guests though. There were kitchens on every level of the ship providing food to cater for all tastes, a lot of the tastes being *traditional* because many cruise ship guests preferred to have familiar food and *none of that foreign muck, thank you!*

The final part of the tour had taken in the engine rooms – Bob was particularly proud of this area and walked Thom and Clair through each part of the engine and explained how a ship of this size was propelled through the universes using concentrated energy that was so concentrated it could be held in the palm of a hand. A very strong hand gloved in baresium alloy as the energy was incredibly heavy and not all that friendly to flesh, bone and blood.

Bob explained that once the energy was in the perpetual motion drive it lasted forever, or at least to a point that most of the rest of the ship had disintegrated. Disposal of an obsolete vessel was a very complex problem that hadn't yet been solved, but as the vessels that used perpetual motion drives had a thousand-year warranty, there was plenty of time to sort one out.

"How long ago was the first perpetual motion drive commissioned?" asked Thom.

"Hmmm," considered Bob, "quite some time ago. In fact, no one is exactly sure when the first was commissioned."

"How old is this ship?" asked Clair.

"Oh! Hundreds of years old!" chuckled Bob, "she doesn't look it does she?" he said patting a smooth section of the engine casing.

Thom looked at Bob. Bob was oblivious to the look which, if he had noticed it, well he may have noticed that it conveyed a degree of puzzlement and a large dollop of Are You Kidding Me?!

It seems to be a Universal Truth that should a solution to providing energy for travel, heating or other domestic or industrial uses present itself then it is adopted without too much fuss or worry about the wider implications, just as long as there are no significant adverse effects now or in the short-term then everything will be OK. It is left to future generations to assess the longer-term effects and it is for them to bear them if they too cannot come up with a fix. Just to make things interesting, the longer term the problem, the more dire it is likely to be and the less likely it is that anyone thought to keep passing down the message that something really should be done now before it is too late.

Too late for what?

Dunno, I just got told that one day it would be too late.

By who?

My Nanna, I think.

The one who said a stitch in time saves nine?

Yeah, whatever that means!

All of this relied on Priorities. And if something wasn't going to happen any time soon then it could wait, because everyone was busy doing other, more pressing stuff…

75

After much bunion comparison and bunion related anecdotes, Jeremy and Ben paused in their conversation. The bridge was a much quieter place than it had been earlier, with many of the crew suddenly finding urgent things to attend to elsewhere on the ship.

Jeremy sighed, "Ahhh! It's good to finally meet someone who understands, old bean!"

"Yes, too true!" agreed Ben, "my bunions have been lonely islands of discomfort until today!"

"So, tangent fully explored and a wee bit of time left before we approach the orbit of OxCam, please tell me more about the place?" implored Jeremy.

"Ah yes, OK" began Ben, and with a concerted effort not to give voice to his next, random and not at all related thought he told Jeremy more about OxCam.

Ben began by relaying the birds eye view of OxCam City itself complete with swooping and swooshing around the spires, statuary and gargoyles. He was pretty good at bringing to life the carved stone and character of the city. Which helped do OxCam city justice. It was as if the very stonework itself had a life of its own. The observant regular visitors to the city would swear that *things moved* not just the odd gargoyle, and all gargoyles are odd, but landmarks themselves.

OxCam wasn't an easy place to navigate at the best of times, the streets and lanes meandered and some became forgetful and confused part way along. There was not a clear and logical grid system with streets demarked by ascending numbers. If there was a fifth street it would not be the fifth street along and there certainly wouldn't be a fourth and a sixth street anywhere nearby. If you were lucky and there was a logic or relevance it would be that this street was a fifth of the width of another street, but no one would know which street was the benchmark for this.

Navigating a place that subtly reorganises itself when it suits it, makes it difficult to get anywhere successfully, especially when the landmarks join in. If you're lucky then the landmark you can see is your intended destination and you're half way there already. Good luck actually getting the rest of the way though. You'll need it.

As a result of this, the inhabitants of OxCam lead a relaxed and sedentary life. The pace of events is laid back as there is no point rushing as you may not ever arrive at your intended destination. Instead people focused on the journey, not the destination, which was just as well.

"It sounds like our kind of target market," said Jeremy, "what would you say the average age of an OxCam inhabitant is?"

"Now you're asking," said Ben, "I won't include the students as they are passing through. In which case, the average age is, ummm… very old. Very old and then some." Ben was looking at his fingers and waggling them as if he'd run out of fingers to count the decades of age the average OxCam inhabitant had already achieved.

"Are most of them married and settled down," asked Jeremy.

"Well," started Ben, "the married ones are not settled. There's low-level animosity and bickering between spouses at all times. And I would say that the unmarried professors and dons were more settled as they don't have a spouse to bicker with and nurture a pot of grumpiness with, but in the absence of a spouse they seem to pick a colleague to share that task with."

"They sound quite unhappy?"

"No! Not at all, they enjoy it! It gives then a pursuit outside the pursuit of knowledge. Certain people are not happy unless they are moaning. The best weather in OxCam, if you were to ask an OxCamerian would be that depressing grey drizzle that descends before sunrise and doesn't leave the day alone. It gives them something to moan about. Whereas on a gloriously sunny morning? They don't have any conversation for that state of affairs!"

Jeremy was mulling his intended market, in some respects they were ideal. They were after all old. And there was a mix of bickering married couples and died in the wool singletons. What was his hook though? What would they board his cruise ship for?

He decided to ask Ben, "how do I entice these people on board my ship for the cruise of a life time?" he asked, expecting an answer that was related to learning – that he had to plan an itinerary of historic and interesting destinations that would lure these learned oldies onto the ship.

288

"Simple," beamed Ben, "Sex!"

76

The Auditor arrived at Constellation amidst a feeling of growing unease. Disembarking from her 'craft she established the cause of the unease that had grown into a fully-fledged adult and a messed up and anxious one at that; people were having fun. Not the fun that was to be had as a by-product of a job well done, but frivolous and worse still, hedonistic fun. People staggered by her in various states of undress, obviously inebriated and worse. They were laughing at what appeared to be nothing other than well, nothing. They seemed to be finding nothing hilarious and that set everyone off laughing too.

The Auditor disregarded her sudoku, that was a different sort of fun.

The Auditor didn't like this place, it didn't sit right with her at all. Worse still, some of the carousers seemed to be able to see her. They were looking right at her, pausing and swallowing in that way very drunk people do, a swallow that oscillates the entire body back and forth and then, as the oscillating ceased, they'd burst into laughter. They were laughing at her!

This really was not a good place to be.

Doing her best to compose herself, The Auditor took stock. Beyond the raucous partying there was that other wrongness, lurking in the background, it was like someone had taken her duvet and turned it ninety degrees on her bed. But then she would spot that immediately and right that wrong before then establishing how such an aberration had taken place. She would then identify the source cause of the problem. That was what she did. This wrongness though, it was like whoever had done this had gone another step further with the duvet and rewritten the rules of duvets such that the duvet belonged where it was in that ninety degree wrongness, better still, they had expunged the memory of where the duvet had been and the previous rules and norms of placing a duvet correctly and neatly on the bed. So, all that was left was a feeling of wrongness. Perhaps a slight echo of something that was, but was now gone or changed. The Auditor didn't like feelings at the best of times, feelings weren't something she could work with. They didn't follow a logical pattern. You couldn't fix feelings.

Dobbin stayed quiet as the Auditor left. He didn't want to give voice to his concerns nor tell her he really didn't want to be left alone here. It was not a pleasant place. As if to underline that point, moments after the Auditor had disappeared out of sight a reveller had sidled up to Dobbin and begun urinating on him. Not used to this kind of behaviour he initially did nothing. This was a drunk wee though, so it went on for some considerable time, which gave Dobbin enough time to consider things and then do something about it. He sent a charge of electricity through his side. He over did the size of the charge though as the urinating reveller suddenly went rigid and was then launched backwards in a majestic arc, whilst still creating an arc of urine in the opposite direction. Dobbin smiled to himself and kept the charge in place in case this was not a one off. It wasn't and there was the occasional flying and urinating reveller passing across the skyline with an expression of surprise on their faces. No one else was all that surprised though. This was after all Constellation. And anything goes on Constellation, even flying urinators.

The Auditor seemed to strobe through Constellation. Watching her had a disorienting effect if you were used to the usual dimensions of the known universes. Thankfully, the standard form was that the natives of the known universes couldn't see the Auditor and were not consciously aware of her. Which might explain why quite a few of the revellers on Constellation had spotted her, then laughed until their eyes hurt, or at least they thought that was what was happening – spotting the Auditor was what had made their eyes hurt and then their mind had gone into an impromptu frenzy as it couldn't cope with what it had seen.

The Auditor made her way across Constellation with disconcerting purpose. There wasn't exactly a trail to follow. It wasn't even a thread that she was pulling. This was an assignment unlike any she had ever untaken previously, she just knew she had to get to the bottom of whatever this was.

77

The Thing rubbed it's chin thoughtfully, "Why are we here?" it asked, seemingly of the empty flight deck. "Is this really time for your armchair philosophising, dear?" asked the disembodied voice.

The Thing shook it's head whilst still rubbing it's chin, it looked like it was attempting to remove its head from its neck, but this didn't make it release its chin grip, "No, I'm not exactly philosophising. Not really. Not abstract philosophy anyway. OK, my question wasn't quite right. Why is she here?"

"You've found her?" asked the disembodied voice with a degree of hope fuelled enthusiasm.

"No, I do not know her precise location. I was asking why here and by here, I mean the universes."

"Oh, I see," said the disembodied voice. It didn't see and The Thing got that it didn't see. The Thing wasn't sure whether it saw either, it knew their daughter was in the universes and it had followed her here. Only now was it considering where it was and why that might be.

"We turn away for just a moment and off she wanders," said The Thing, "You'd expect she'd have trotted off out of the room and be in the next one, or maybe the garden, or floating in the Obsidian Abyss for a bit of fun or something. But no, our daughter goes on a trans-dimensional hop and ends up gods know where."

"Oh, I see what you mean," said the disembodied voice now seeing what The Thing meant.

"I mean, did you even know she could do that??" asked The Thing.

"No," answered the disembodied voice, "I wasn't even sure we could do it. Well, I hadn't even considered the question of whether I could and I'm still not sure I can do it, because I never have."

"And I only did it for the first time because she was here," added The Thing.

"How did you know she was here though?" asked the disembodied voice.

"I..." began The Thing, "I just did."

"And you grabbed your coat and followed her even though you didn't know whether you could?" said the disembodied voice knowing the answer already.

"I didn't think," The Thing paused for a brief moment, "I just felt, I suppose."

"Felt?" said the disembodied voice, trying the word out for size, "we don't feel, do we?"

"Well, I suppose we do now," shrugged The Thing, "there isn't any other word for it. And I'm feeling my way right now. Besides..."

"It's worrying isn't it?" interjected the disembodied voice.

"Yes, it's upsettingly worrying," agreed The Thing, "and I've never been upset before."

"I hope we find her," sighed the disembodied voice.

Both the disembodied voice and The Thing had softened somewhat since they'd begun looking for their wayward daughter. Thing and things were changing.

78

"Sex?" said Jeremy dubiously.

"Sex!" agreed Ben.

"Sex?" said Jeremy in a more drawn out way to emphasise the question and that he really didn't get it. Not when it was with reference to elderly learned types.

"Sex sells!" explained Ben. And he stopped there assuming Jeremy was now with him on this point.

"I'm not with you," said Jeremy dissuading him from this erroneous assumption.

Ben thought for a moment, attempting to further quantify and articulate sex and its use as a marketing tool. "Think about it," he said, as he himself thought about it, because at present it was more a gut-feel, he just knew he was right, "these guys spend all their available time thinking about stuff, and talking about the stuff they've been thinking about and writing about it too. They don't just think about the stuff they talk about and write about though, do they?"

"No, I suppose not," conceded Jeremy.

"And what do we all think about? Like constantly think about?" asked Ben.

"I have a feeling you are going to say sex," started Jeremy.

"Yes, exactly!" said Ben cutting in before Jeremy could add his but.

"But…" added Jeremy.

"But? But! But me no buts and if me no ifs, Jeremy!"

Jeremy looked at Ben in a way that Ben could not mistake, it said calm down, shut up and listen. "But, not everyone thinks about sex constantly, Ben."

Ben looked at Jeremy as if he were insane. He looked at him again to check whether this was a joke. He then looked at him sideways. He stepped back so he could look at him from a different distance, "Really?"

Jeremy nodded.

"Nah, you have to be kidding!?"

Jeremy shook his head, he wasn't kidding.

"You do think about sex though, don't you?"

"Well, yes."

"Phew! For a moment there, I thought you were one of those self-reproducing species. But the ones that just kinda split in two and find the process a bit of a pain. Quite literally!"

"No, we have sex, Ben. We just don't think about it constantly."

"I know you do," winked Ben, recalling his *tour of the ship* with Jennifer, "You'd be surprised how often you think about sex, Jeremy. More so when you add in your subconscious. Your subconscious is a dirty minded old dog! It sees sex in places you wouldn't imagine sex could be – then it imagines having sex in the places it's let its imagination run wild in and once it's done it goes pretty much everywhere else having sex. Having lots of sex. Table leg? Cor!"

Jeremy placed a firm hand on Ben's shoulder, "could you

297

calm down a bit old bean and stop dry humping my chair please?"

"Wha…?" Ben looked down and realised he'd gotten a bit carried away, "Oh, sorry about that!"

Jeremy nodded and slowly removed his restraining hand, now that Ben had stopped his disturbing activity with his chair.

"Anyway," continued Ben, "these guys and dolls have been cooped up. They're repressed. They have devoted all their time and energy to the pursuit of knowledge. One sniff of another type of knowledge and those finally coiled springs will go boing! Repeatedly. Boing! Boing! Boing!"

Ben was jumping up and down like a sex crazed kangaroo, the height he was achieving was impressive. It was dizzying watching him. And somehow, he was making it all a bit sexual.

Jeremy noticed Jennifer watching Ben in a fascinated, almost hungry way and wondered what was going on with her. He'd failed to notice the growing bond between his crew member and Ben. He may have changed but his observation skills when it came to people weren't all that different to what they had been. After all, Clair had worked with what was there and everyone was inherently the same.

"Another type of knowledge?" shouted Jeremy so he could be heard over all the boinging and panting now that Ben was getting out of breath.

Ben stopped bouncing and steadied himself against Jeremy's chair. "Carnal!" he said beaming at Jeremy.

Jeremy wasn't quite convinced, nearly but not quite. It sounded plausible, but was this just because Ben was so enthusiastic?

"Are you sure, Ben?" he asked earnestly.

"Stock up with sherry and hold soirees and get-togethers," smiled Ben, "get the old sods a bit pissed. Once they're away from their books they really let their hair down."

Now this was making more sense to Jeremy and he nodded accordingly.

"Oh, and do you have electric cattle-prods?" asked Ben.

"No," said Jeremy wrong-footed, "Why?"

"Best buy some, you'll need them!"

79

The Auditor found herself entering one of the many neon lit establishments offering cocktails and fun times. She grimaced at the thought of such fun. Despite the brightly lit exterior, the interior of the club she had entered was mostly dimly lit. There were bright lights, these were strategically placed to shine directly in your face and blind you so any night vision you had possessed was eradicated and you may as well have been blindfolded.

There was background music that hadn't stayed put and had encroached on the foreground and after a time during which no one thought to put it back in its place it filled all of the available spaces including your skull. The music was mostly bass, a brain and teeth rattling bass that made it difficult to think let alone speak or hear anyone else speak.

The Auditor looked around her, doing her best to avoid the rotating bright lights intent on blinding her, what she saw was similar to the scenes she had encountered outside, along the main stretch, only less clothing, if that were possible, and more random gyrations. Some of these gyrations were actually in time with the music. What amazed the Auditor was that people were conversing and seemed to be holding successful conversations with each other. She had to conclude that this was only possible after consuming a number of cocktails, but even then, she was not at all sure why this should be the case.

Wondering why she had been drawn to this planet and why she was in this club in particular she realised she was disregarding the fact she had followed the thread and the feeling that things were not right. And that she was possibly being side-tracked by her own feelings. She didn't want to be here, she didn't like it. This was peculiar for her, she hadn't encountered this kind of conflict ever before.

And she certainly didn't let her mind wander and lose focus. Was she daydreaming? On the job? It was this place, she was certain of it. It was having an odd effect upon her and she knew that would be the case even without the anomalous something that she was looking into. *SNAP OUT OF IT!* she thought to herself and she did just that, refocusing her attention on something tangible, her gaze fell upon a red balloon, she dropped her gaze down along the string of the balloon to a white gloved hand. Most of the attire of the balloon holder was an off white, with blue and red trim. He was sporting pom-poms and a ruff. And a muzzle. He was leaning against the bar at a rakish angle and at his feet was a poodle, also sporting a ruff and mirroring its master's rakish angle, using the foot rest to support its lean because that angle of rakish was very difficult when you had four legs.

The Auditor looked back up from the poodle and at its master, as she began thinking that they seemed to be looking straight at her, with eyes that were a little larger than they should have been, they both smiled at her at exactly the same time. That really shouldn't have been possible, not the perfect unison of the choreographed smiles, nor the fact they seemed to see her. She was after all, in another dimension and one that these universes dwellers were not equipped to see.

Nonetheless Bill, for it was Ben's good friend Bill and none other, the owner of the sleek and beautiful Ferrcati and also the owner of the bar the Auditor was presently stood in, was smiling right at the Auditor. The Auditor rationalised this and turned to look behind her to see the thing that this curious stranger was undoubtedly looking at through and beyond her. Had the Auditor frequented busy streets with any kind of regularity she would have experienced those moments when someone looks straight at you and says "Hi!" and smiles so that you respond and start to raise your hand to wave only to hear someone behind you and then notice the sayer of the 'Hi' is not quite looking at you after all and as your embarrassment rises you conclude that they never were looking at you and you're a chump. This was the Auditor's first time, only as she looked behind her, she could not see anything of interest behind her, so it was looking like it wasn't her first time after all.

She turned back towards the clown and his dog. Curious.

"Hi!" said Bill with the kind of warmth and enthusiasm reserved for that special and exclusive inner circle of friends.

The greeting itself confused the Auditor. Her confusion multiplied up considerably at the prospect of being greeted with warmth and enthusiasm. She was the Auditor, people did not greet her warmly, she was a necessity and an uncomfortable, if not dread necessity. Like the examination of your nether regions with cold and morbidly interesting implements.

The Auditor shifted uncomfortably on her feet and looked quizzically at Bill, still not believing that he could see her, let alone that he would greet her at all if he had.

Bill smiled again and nodded at her in a *yes you! I'm looking at you!* way. The poodle stood up and walked towards her, sniffed her leg, walked around her and then walked back to Bill and resumed its seat by his foot, now at a more comfortable and less rakish angle. The introductions were made, the rakishness could be dialled down.

The Auditor shifted again and felt a bit awkward, this had never happened to her before. Ever. Anywhere.

Bill continued staring at the Auditor in a warm and yet appreciative manner as he waved at the bartender, "a house special cocktail for the lady," he said, his eyes never leaving the Auditor. The bartender glanced quickly and casually around the bar as it wasn't clear to him which lady Bill had meant, but then Bill had bought many drinks for many ladies. And gentlemen. And a whole bunch of other people who identified as things other than ladies or gentlemen, so the bartender tended the bar as was expected of him, he knew that this was the way forward, especially as Bill was paying not only for the drinks, but also for him and the entire club. He mixed two Pneumatic Drills, having learnt very early on that when Bill ordered a drink or drinks for his guests implicit in this was that he was having a drink too. After he had sorted the drinks, he'd also prep something for Bill's dog Anita. Always wise to look after Anita in order to avoid any canine unpleasantness. Bill's dog liked the bartender, but had made it clear that this was upon the condition that the bartender looked after her and didn't take her good nature for granted, it was a dog thing and the bartender got that.

He was a good bartender.

The Auditor's curiosity seemed to propel her forward towards Bill. She didn't seem to be in control of herself or the situation, it was as if someone had put wheels on her feet and given her a gentle shove towards the bar.

"We don't get many of your kind here," said Bill handing her the green and murky drink, "welcome to Bar Suck, it's a pleasure to meet you."

The Auditor automatically drank some of the proffered liquid. This was another first for the Auditor, she didn't drink. Not that she had ever made a conscious decision not to drink, drinking is a social pursuit and she had never been in a position to try out socialising so the accoutrements of socialising had been denied to her until now. The liquid was very interesting indeed, it did things with her taste buds that it had no right doing, slowly at first and then increasing its tempo and spreading out beyond the taste buds themselves. Then the first of the drink hit the back of her throat and her throat was not at all pleased at this violation. She choked.

Bill rubbed her back as she almost doubled over. "The first mouthful gets people like that sometimes, try another taste. It's good!"

Spurred on by Bill's encouragement and her inner spirit of competitiveness, the Auditor tried some more of her drink. Tingling, warming and lots of other inging sensations swept up over and through her head and then down through her body and then back again, wave after wave of pleasantness and well-being. How wonderful! The Auditor enjoyed her first ever drink so much she didn't even notice she was already on her second. What she did notice was that Bill was holding her free hand and she liked that.

304

"Did I say it's a pleasure to meet you?" asked Bill endearingly.

"You did," said the Auditor and she giggled coquettishly and didn't notice that her voice had changed considerably nor that she had never laughed, let alone giggled and as for coquettishness? She didn't even know what that was until just under twenty seconds ago.

"Shall we go somewhere... more private?" asked Bill.

The Auditor nodded and grabbed her newly poured fourth drink from the bar and followed Bill through a nearby door...

80

"Apporaching OxCam's orbit, captain"

Jeremy smiled and took up a casual but captainly pose in his chair on the bridge and began issuing the orders and instructions necessary for the cruise ship to take up the correct orbit around the OxCam planet. He was looking forward to visiting this place and even more so was looking forward to embarking upon their maiden voyage as a proper cruise ship. It had been a long time coming, but it was what they had always wanted, what they had been made for, it would fill the ship completely and it would complete them.

Ben smiled at his new friend, he could see Jeremy grow in stature as he took up his position and prepared for their forthcoming adventure. The whole tableau of the busy crew bustling in readiness just looked so right.

Ben's smile spread into a grin as he listened to the crew; they were slipping into orbit. Easing her in captain, nearly there! Just a bit of correction. And we're in!

The cruiser locked into orbit and the crew set about the post-orbit schedule and got ready to take a shuttle down to the planet. Everyone was professional and diligent in what they were doing, but you could feel the excitement. And it was the kind of excitement that was going to go really well onboard a cruise ship. You needed the crew to have that building anticipation and excitement and you wanted them to carry that on throughout the cruise. This brand of excitement was infectious!

Jeremy boarded the shuttle with Jennifer, Thom, Ben and Clair. "We sent the marketing out yesterday," he said shrugging, "it's later than we'd usually send it, but we've done this all on the hoof really."

Thom smiled at the reference to how they'd usually roll, this was the first time for pretty much everything, but they seemed like a seasoned cruise ship crew and everything was well oiled, in more ways than one! He wondered how the Bluecoatians would be received on OxCam, two very different worlds colliding, but then until not all that long ago, the Bluecoatians gave off the distinct impression that they were a blood-thirsty, cold and calculating murderers – their sudden career change was an interesting departure and one that Thom's Careers Advisor at school wouldn't have countenanced.

The funny thing with Careers Advisors in that final year of school is that they appear from nowhere, but apparently were there all the time, you just hadn't noticed them in the years prior to your appointment with them, because you hadn't needed them. That sounded plausible until you realised no one else was aware of their existence, never passing them in the corridor or noticing them on playground duty. And when you entered adulthood you never met anyone who said they were a Careers Advisor. Careers Advisors were there to validate the vast majority of pupil's career paths – it was obvious what most kids were going to do and it really wasn't rocket science. The bit that Careers Advisors were really there for were the kids with true potential, the Ten Percenters, and they really enjoyed this bit. They even drafted the words for those pupils' final reports, the kinds of missives which conveyed a sigh as you read them; Jones has not applied himself throughout school, he'll either be a surprise success or a notorious criminal destined to spend his final days on Death Row. The Careers Advisors liked that bit of the job.

Thom remembered sitting with his Careers Advisor after he had ticked a lot of boxes about his preferences and non-preferences on a whole bunch of seemingly random stuff. Stuff being the technical expression of a group of things that were probably useful and related as a result, but it was anyone's guess how they were related. The Careers Advisor must have said a few things and they perhaps had a conversation, but Thom's abiding memory was of seeing the final page of a report that had been run from the responses he'd made and at the very bottom it said Fire Man and it said Candle Stick Maker. Neither of these career paths appealed at all to Thom, and he instantly wondered what all the options were and of those, which would have appealed. That maybe, looking at options and exploring them and what was needed to pursue a career in, say data base analysis or the programming of the next generation of first person, collaborative shoot em ups might have been useful. Instead, the Careers Advisor told Thom he was only suited to fire-fighting or candle stick making. Usually, Thom would have retorted with a quip about doing both, candle stick making by day, putting out the fires the candles caused by night.

But he was too bewildered and crestfallen for that. That was the bit of this process the Careers Advisor found deeply rewarding. It was fun! Look at the cocky little sod now! It was also rewarding because at least some of these cocky sods and lost causes would respond in the best possible way to this jolt and shove back with purpose to make something of themselves. Go on! Prove me wrong, matey!

For the Careers Advisor it was a win-win. They were either right, or if they were wrong then the kid had done good and proved them wrong in the best possible way.

This didn't quite work for Thom, he still didn't have a Scooby Do about what he should do with his life, so he had got himself an office job, but he did at least avoid the two suggested careers, as was supposed to be the case, no one of the targeted Ten Percenters, in the history of Careers Advisors had ever attempted to go for one of the two suggested career paths. This in itself was surprising, as plenty of the pupils in the Ten Percenters group were bloody minded and would do something just to spite others, even if this entailed spending a life time in sewers. Several academics had spent their lifetimes studying just why it was that not one of the Ten Percenters ever pursued the spurious gambit of a career they had been presented with and none of them had ever connected the dots sufficiently to establish during their studies that they had not been in the Ten Percenters category. The current pre-eminent professor lecturing on the Ten Percenters was almost directly below the shuttle as it made its way to the surface of OxCam...

"I don't think you'll need much marketing or advertising," said Ben to Jeremy.

But Jeremy wasn't listening, he was staring intently out of

the window. "Fascinating!" he exclaimed.

"What is?" asked Thom.

"It's..." started Jeremy, still staring out of the side window of the shuttle, "I had meant to ask about the rest of the planet and had assumed that the planet being called OxCam and the city we were going to also being called OxCam was just a case of, well people being too lazy to name one of them something different..."

"Like parents calling their kids the same name as themselves?" asked Ben.

"Yes exactly," said Jeremy with a far away, distracted tone to his voice. That Ben didn't notice.

"Yeah, I've always wondered about that," Ben carried on, "I mean your name is the one word you notice above all others, so your wife shouting Bennnn! Must result in you and your kid coming running at the same time, or one of you getting into loads of trouble because you assumed it was the other being in trouble. Why pick your own name when there are like thousands of other names to choose from? It's a bit limited on the old thinking and imagination front isn't it."

"My Dad is called Jeremy," said Jeremy still distracted by what he was seeing out of the window.

"Oh," said Ben suddenly becoming quite serious, "sorry, I'm sure he's a really nice and imaginative man."

"Not really," replied Jeremy, still looking out of the window, "he's dead."

Thom looked at Ben and for once Ben noticed the look and quit while he was this far behind.

"Everything OK, Jeremy?" asked Thom.

"Yes, yes! Sorry old bean," said Jeremy looking away from the window, "I'd assumed that OxCam was a city in a country, which was a part of a world and that it..."

Thom nodded as he got what Jeremy was saying. He could see the huge, stone sprawl behind Jeremy growing larger as they descended.

"It's the *whole planet!*" said Jeremy excitedly, "the whole thing is a huge, gigantic and bloody big university! We may just have a full ship on our hands!"

"Well, it's two universities actually," whispered Ben, trying to avoid any further faux pas.

"Eh?" enquired Jeremy.

"Ox and Cam Universities," explained Thom.

"Oh! Right!"

"And they don't get on," added Thom, "so the trick will be, if you can, to get a ship full of passengers from Ox University. That will avoid any... difficulties."

"Oh, right," said Jeremy, "and why Ox?"

"That's Uncle Harold's University," beamed Ben, "besides, when you drop this load of passengers off, if you fit in a cruise in between, you can then come back for a ship full of Cammers!"

81

The shuttle landed on the outskirts of OxCam, they then got a park and ride into the centre. To an extent, Thom and Ben knew their way around so they headed for Emperor's College where Uncle Harold was to be found.

"This is amazing!" said Clair. The air was fizzing and tingling and something was certainly afoot.

"Are you OK, Clair?" asked Ben, noticing the atmosphere becoming noticeably charged.

"I'm soaking up the atmosphere. That's what they say isn't it?"

"Yes, they do," agreed Thom, "but usually they are not being so literal about it!"

"It's just so full of knowledge! This place is really special!"

"It's certainly different," said Thom in a sullen tone which went unnoticed by Clair, but not Jeremy and Ben who exchanged a glance. Ben shook his head warning Jeremy off. This was well trodden ground and best avoided.

They arrived at the college and disembarked the tram just a little way off the entrance. Walking along the cobbled street between the magnificent, ancient and characterful buildings brought a calm and awe to people. Across the road they could see through a large and ornate cast iron gate to expansive and well-tended grounds. Students lounged in the sun looking serious and studious and incredibly clever. It was taken as read that people who got into OxCam were incredibly clever, but this didn't stop many of the students developing *A Look* so there was no doubt as to just how clever this particular student was. Interestingly, there was a panoply of *Looks* available, and alongside them a further smorgasbord of *Looks* – and if you wanted to mix some of the panoply of Looks with a smidgen of the smorgasbord of *Looks*, then feel free my learned friend, feel free.

Thom swore he saw one student, dressed ironically in punk clothes, but wearing them more like a new romantic sporting a second head. He stopped to attend to the image and then dismissed it as it seemed the student he had seen had passed beyond his line of vision. Thinking about it, Thom mused, having a second head was the ultimate in showing off your cleverness; look! I have two brains! Or, it may lead to twice the ego and personalities that clashed and pushed themselves to extremes, it may well lead to the kind of person who changed their name to something edgy that sounded like a really fast ship from the golden age of space travel and an extremely dangerous and aggressive insect that did nasty things to your genitals if you urinated in the wrong place at the wrong time – it would make for really interesting, but possibly quite dangerous too. Someone who was great at raising parties to another level, but best to leave that party early before it got very messy.

"Thom!" said Ben, and Thom realised he'd been calling him for a wee while.

Ben gave Thom a look, reproaching him for delaying the

inevitable. Thom felt mildly aggrieved, he hadn't consciously delayed. Not really. He jogged up to join everyone else.

They walked under the entrance arch and towards a booth to one side.

"Master Ben!" said a voice sounding nearly as ancient as the college itself, "well I never!"

Ben broke into the largest of smiles and opened his arms expansively as a squarely built man emerged from the other side of the booth. He was a head shorter than Ben, but solid and moved with a bearing that spoke of military service.

"Conan!" said Ben with genuine warmth and enthusiasm. A large hand grasped his and they pulled each other in close enough to slap each other's backs.

Thom winced at this. If Ben had slapped his back with that sort of vim and vigour he would have multiple fractures and a collapsed lung. If he was lucky. Conan was made of sterner stuff though. Quite literally. As part of his military service he'd been upgraded so that his bones were very unlikely to break, bend and warp. Thom happened to know that Conan's will had an entry which was compulsory and under statute; he was to be cremated in the first instance and then his military frame was to be returned to the government for repurposing, which meant being melted down and reapplied to a new recruit. Some of Conan was built to last, the rest of him would go beyond that.

"Your Uncle Harold will be so pleased!" said Conan, disengaging from Ben.

"Mwee wee whoo wha," mumbled Thom.

"What was that?" whispered Jeremy.

"Nothing," Thom whispered back.

But Jeremy had done that thing where you say pardon and

then realise what it is that someone has said. Thom had been mimicking Conan. Jeremy hadn't known Thom very long at all, but this seemed very out of character.

What's up with you, Thom? thought Clair in Thom's head. Thom did not reply. *You're jealous!* said Clair in his head.

That hurts, Clair! Thom thought back. What hurt was Clair labelling his feelings entirely correctly. Thom knew he was being juvenile, but he just couldn't help it. This was his blind spot. Had been for a long time. It was very much what-about-me!!!???

"The Dean is in his chambers, I'll take you up to him now," said Conan.

"Are you sure?" asked Ben.

"For you? Yes of course! Standin' orders so it is!"

And with that they followed Conan across the inner square, along a stone corridor and up a spiral staircase.

"He's quite important then, this Uncle Harold of yours?" Jeremy asked Thom.

"He's in charge of Ox University, Jeremy. And for the last eight years, although you'd not know it if you were in Cam, he's been in charge of the whole of OxCam."

"Oh," said Jeremy simply.

They entered Uncle Harold's chambers through a simple wooden door.

"Oh!" said Jeremy.

82

Bill sat up in his bed. The bed shifted in an equal and opposite way to Bill's shifting and then both Bill and the bed gently rocked to and fro until the movement ebbed away. He reached casually over for a drink that just happened to be awaiting his awakening. A wee loosener to help him see in the new day. After he had got out of bed and got ready he was likely to have a wee snortorino. He was very likely to as this was a part of his routine for as long as anyone could remember. Which, granted, was not a very long way back on Constellation.

Beside Bill, part of the silk covers moved and the bed resumed its gentle back and forth all over again.

Bill took a swig of his drink and smiled at the form under the covers before giving forth with a merry, "Morning Hilary!"

The form next to him responded with an "Ugh!"

With his free hand Bill patted the sheets and said, "Here, have this. You need it."

There was another "Ugh!" but a hand slowly extricated itself from the sheets and emerged from them.

Bill carefully placed the drink in the hand and like King

Arthur's Lady of the Lake the chalice was withdrawn back into the depths. There was some clumsy sounding slurps a couple of curses and a small green stain appeared on the silk sheets.

An indeterminate time after this amid much to and froing, almost as rigorous as the previous night's repeated toing and froing, a tousled head emerged from the sheets next to Bill.

The Auditor squinted at Bill. "How do you know my name?"

"You told me to call you Hilary last night, my dear."

"What else did I say?"

"Enough. But don't worry, you didn't say all that much."

The Auditor groaned.

"How was the drink?" Bill asked her.

"It…" and Hilary gave Bill a curious look.

"Now, where were we?" asked Bill.

Hilary smiled by way of a reply. Both Hilary and Bill sank into the bed and under the covers and there was much toing and froing.

83

Uncle Harold's chambers were very oh! indeed. After an initial period of gasping, regrouping and gasping again, breath-taking and awe-inspiring were words that someone would grab at and then put down again because they didn't even begin to touch the sides. It was all very grand indeed, temples, cathedrals and palaces bought glossy magazines in the hope that the edition they'd bought would showcase Uncle Harold's chambers. What added to the surprise and delight of that first visit to the chambers was the very ordinary door you opened onto this delightful space. It promised so little and then smashed you in the face with a fresh, still wet tuna of architectural wonderfulness. And it was a really large space. Larger than it had any business being. The chambers exemplified the architecture of OxCam. Several laws of physics and then a few more rules of the universes were being broken here. And in order to keep this law breaking a well-guarded secret, apart from a few other grand and exclusive places (those magazine buying temples, cathedrals and palaces), very few other people knew about this place as even fewer had ever been admitted to Uncle Harold's chambers. He had rooms to receive people. And those rooms were pretty amazing, even after you'd seen his chambers.

Clair felt instantly at home here. The epicentre of an ancient seat of learning *and* some trans-dimensional shenanigans too. Clair had a natural affinity to the place.

"Uncs!!!" shouted Ben at what appeared to be the room at large. And then a part of a huge and battered chair detached itself and seemed to glide through the clutter of books towards Ben.

People like Uncle Harold, very old and learned types, spend more and more time thinking. This sort of thinking is a sedentary pursuit and requires peace and minimal distraction. So, over time with lots of practice, useless and distracting practices such as movement are kept to an absolute minimum. As the learned get more and more adept at focusing entirely on thought, they begin to blend in with their surroundings. For the very top end of the learned, an Interior Life Design Coach introduced Blending as the natural conclusion of Feng Shui. In order to truly relax and be in the most zen place to pursue pure thought you had to be a part of your Thinking Room.

There was something quite magical about these surroundings, and that was no mistake. So much concentrated knowledge had power and that power leaked into its surroundings.

Uncle Harold was wearing a cloak and robes that were made from the same material as the old chair he had been lounging on, or the chair was made from the same material as his robes. The chair and robes were in a long standing dispute about this. The material was heavy and ornate and would have made a great set of curtains, for a whole wing of a stately home. His outfit reached all the way down to the floor so you could not see his feet as he walked, which helped to explain the gliding effect. His deportment, even after a long spell of resting, and for an old man who by rights should have creaking joints, was astounding. As he drew nearer it was easier to see that even his long beard and equally long hair were the same shade as the main colour of his clothing, an off-cream colour tinged with a subtle hint of mushy pea green.

The beard parted and revealed perfect white teeth forming a broad grin. Uncle Harold's eyes twinkled, "Thom!" he exclaimed.

Thom rolled his eyes. Ben didn't miss a beat though, "Ben!" he corrected.

"Oh yes of course," said Uncle Harold in reply, "My dear boy, how have you been?!"

This wasn't an automatic device of speech overlooking Ben's transformation into a zombie clown, Uncle Harold knew all about this and had spoken to Ben at length soon after this life changing and life ending event – he reminded Ben that life was about experiences and what an adventure to transform so radically and have a whole host of new experiences present themselves to you. To see the world anew was such a great opportunity. Ben had had to persuade Uncle Harold not to follow suit, refusing to bite him so he could see what it was like. The clincher was the discrimination and mistrust that still existed towards zombie clowns and that this may make Uncle Harold's seat at the top table of OxCam untenable. Even then Uncle Harold had wanted to give it a try and reasoned that no one would dare challenge him if he were to present himself as one of the undead! He followed this up with a quip about no one noticing his altered state as they were all near as dammit undead in any case.

Ben told Uncle Harold he'd been good and asked the same question in return, establishing that Uncle Harold had been good too. Then the introductions were made.

"Who are your friends, Ben?" asked Uncle Harold.

"Well Thom you know," said Ben going around the small group, Thom and Uncle Harold nodding briefly at each other, "this is Jennifer. My very good friend Jennifer."

Uncle Harold took Jennifer's hand, "pleased to meet you my dear, any friend of Ben's is a friend of mine. And do I detect, from the way Ben has introduced you, that you and he are an item?"

Jennifer blushed and smiled, "we've become close in recent days, yes," she said quietly.

Jeremy did a double take, looking from Jennifer to Ben to Uncle Harold and several more routes between the three, "Well, I never! You old dog, Ben!"

"And this is Jeremy," smiled Ben, "captain of the cruise ship which is even now embarking passengers for a pleasure cruise of a life-time."

"Hello, sir", said Uncle Harold shaking Jeremy's hand, "pleasure cruise you say? That sounds interesting. Many people signed up?"

"Quite a few already," interjected Ben, but we've reserved you one of the best cabins if you're interested in joining us?"

"Me? But what would I do on a cruise ship?"

"You'd indulge in some well-earned R&R!" beamed Ben.

"R&R?" asked Uncle Harold.

"Rest and relaxation!" piped up Thom to prevent Ben supplying his version of the initialism.

"But I have all the rest and relaxation I could ever have,

here!" said Uncle Harold on the verge of instantly dismissing leaving the comfort of the Emperor's College.

"Ah! But that's not a bit of it, Uncs," explained Ben, "for starters, travel broadens the mind and you are in the business of broadening minds! There will be wine, there will be women, there will be song. It's about time you encouraged your guys to look up from their books and let their hair down and fraternise with their colleagues..." Ben, in inimitable Ben-style, was now gyrating and doing things with his hips that had never been done in these grand chambers. Not for three hundred and sixty two years anyway, and nowhere nearly as adeptly as Ben's efforts.

"Are you suggesting there will be carnal fraternisation aboard this vessel of yours?" asked Uncle Harold on the verge of doing something like a guffaw.

"If there isn't, then I'm not doing my job properly," said Ben making six shooters with his fingers and shooting Uncle Harold.

"In that case," considered Uncle Harold, "I believe I should come along. In order to ensure things do not get out of hand." And he stroked his beard as he considered what this getting out of hand may look like.

"Good!" said Ben, "because I haven't finished the introductions and we could do with your sage advice and help, Uncs. Lots of it. And on an ongoing basis really, so having you on board will kill at least two birds with one stone, hopefully more if you're up to it!"

Uncle Harold gave Ben an indulgent and proud look, Ben the prodigal son was back and as wayward as ever, but to Uncle Harold he was a delight and he couldn't help but be charmed by the little blighter.

322

Ben waved a hand down towards the final guest, "And here's Clair."

Uncle Harold went very quiet as he looked down at the HR bot where Clair currently resided. The air in the room stilled and the household dust motes froze mid-air. Uncle Harold's reaction was not because this was largely a technology free area – although that was a consideration. Purity of thought required the divestment of all superfluous technological devices.

The long ago rise of so called smart devices had taught humankind and all the species who had encountered humankind and seen the sorry episode in humankind's annals, that wanton, no-holds barred access to so called information was a very bad thing. Especially when what that information really was was opinion and bilious puff pieces and egotistical spoutings and rehashes of photos and phrases that required very little engagement, quite the opposite of engagement in fact. This was the worst drug epidemic in the history of humankind and it got so bad that it reversed evolution and humankind's progress stalled for over two hundred years.

No, Uncle Harold was not looking at the HR bot at all, he was looking in that general direction, but he was seeing something else entirely, "Oh my word!" he whispered, "My wordy, word, word." Then a serene expression rolled down over his face and he zoned out completely.

"They're having a chat, aren't they?" Ben asked Thom.

Thom nodded. He could hear them chunnering away.

84

Hilary reached out from the bed covers and after having a drink from the glass that always seemed to be waiting for her, she scrabbled out from under the covers. She quickly covered her eyes as they were unaccustomed to the day light. How long had it been? Ooer, she thought to herself and giggled. What has come over me? She giggled again. Her eyes now partially adjusting to the light, she sat up and scanned the room looking for a clue as to what time of day it was. She spotted a trail of her clothing and belongings from the door, halfway to the bed.

"Hey," said Bill emerging from the covers beside her and grabbing his drink, "how's my Hilary?"

"I…" Hilary was feeling a bit uncomfortable, not with Bill, he'd been amazing and made her feel a gazillion dollars, it was that she was here and doing whatever it was she was doing. She'd never done anything like this before. She was mainly uncomfortable because she knew she had to get back to her work and she didn't want to have that conversation with Bill. Yes, it was awkward, but she also didn't want to get out of bed. Before now, she'd never wanted to get into a bed and had never had difficulty getting out of bed because she had her work.

"I really should get back to work," she said.

"Really? You don't have to go on my account Hilary," said Bill playing with a loose strand of her hair and looking at her in a meaningful way.

Hilary shuddered at the thought of what staying here in bed with Bill entailed. Then she thought about that shudder. She'd never had a pleasant shudder before and she'd never had a feeling of anticipation that felt so good and promised so much more. She was on the very brink of staying.

"I don't want to go Bill," she said, conscious that she sounded a bit whiney and pathetic, "but I really should. I haven't finished my work." And with that, she managed to step up and away from the bed and began gathering her clothes.

Bill watched her, and she appreciated the appreciative watching he was undertaking. "Just what is it that you do?" he asked her.

"I…" she began. No one had ever asked her what she did. Some people thought they knew. They didn't. Not really. What they knew was that they wanted her to do whatever she did quickly and then move on, preferably with the least disruption and unpleasantness, "…audit the universes."

"Groovy!" smiled Bill, "the old checks and balances eh?"

"Yes…", Bill had wrong-footed her. Again. "That's exactly it!"

"So, what brings a devastatingly attractive auditor from another dimension to my joint?" Bill asked, stretching out on the bed and putting his hands behind his head, in what to Hilary was a very welcoming piece of body language.

"You know I'm from another dimension?"

"I told you, we don't see many of your kind here," smiled Bill.

"But how did you know? And how did you see me?"

"Look at me. I'm not exactly your run of the mill being am I? Besides, I've taken a lot of mind altering substances in my time. And you know what drugs do don't you?"

"Erm... not really no."

"They alter your perception. So yes, I saw you. I have to admit though, the first time I saw someone who wasn't exactly from around here I was violently sick and lay in the foetal position for three days solid afterwards. Complete gibbering wreck I was. It takes some getting used to!" he suddenly looked a lot more serious, "that was before this though," he added shrugging.

Bill smiled wistfully and watched Hilary getting dressed. He patted the bed, "Sure you have to go?" he asked raising an eyebrow in a way that made one of Hilary's knees tremble inexplicably. What power did this man possess?!

"I really have to go," Hilary said as she lifted her clipboard up, "shit!" she'd spotted the time and it was twelve days past the evening she'd followed this man through the door out of the bar and up the stairs to his apartment, "Twelve days!!! It's been twelve days!"

"Has it?" said Bill far too casually, as if this was a commonplace occurrence.

"I'm sooo late!"

"Late for what?" asked Bill.

"There's some anomaly in the universes that has no business being here," explained Hilary as she put on her shoes.

"Oh?"

"Yes, it seems to have started on a backwater office ship

called the Micra. Then it came through here."

On hearing this, Bill sat up and took another swig of his drink, partially hiding his face with the glass as he asked, "and what will you do about this anomaly once you catch up with it?"

Hilary stopped for a moment and considered, "Do? Well I have to find it and identify it, then it must be stopped of course. Anomalies like this have no business in these universes, so it will have to be removed."

"Oh," nodded Bill, trying his best to remain casual. He had a call to make as soon as Hilary had left. Thinking about making that call reminded him, he wasn't a detail swapping guy and his dalliances were one-offs, everyone knew the deal from the outset, but Hilary was different. He'd like to see Hilary again. "So, once you've finished work. Fancy hooking up again?"

Hilary had finished dressing and stood up and turned fully to face Bill. There was a moment when Bill's ego shrank back at the prospect of being put down. What Bill's ego didn't know was that Hilary's first response was to write this one off to experience and never return. She considered the obvious alternative, returning to Constellation. She didn't exactly fancy that. Meeting again was a nice idea though. Meeting on neutral ground felt like a good idea.

She smiled at the thought of seeing Bill again, a smile that promised a rematch and a smile that did things to Bill that a smile had never done before, "I'LL CALL YOU." she said in her business voice, and for the first time in her life she sashayed out of the room, she suppressed a giggle as she heard Bill moan and she knew the sashaying had had the desired effect.

It had, but what she didn't know was that her return to her usual voice had also given Bill a nosebleed.

85

Uncle Harold was as still as a statue. Only the twinkle in his eyes was a reminder that he was a living, breathing being, not one of the statues scattered and littered around OxCam. This state of statue affairs had been going on for quite some time and didn't look like it would come to an end any time soon.

"They are talking about life, the universes and everything," explained Thom, "They are both really excited and they really do have a lot to talk about. I think we can safely leave them to it and go for a drink."

Thom nodded at Ben and they gently lowered Uncle Harold to a forty five degree angle and then, hooking an arm under an arm pit each they drew him back across the room to his favourite chair. Once reunited, chameleon-like man and furniture merged and even though you knew he was there, it was difficult to spot Uncle Harold.

"The Eagle?" asked Ben.

"Yes, I think that's as good a place as any."

They collected the others and quietly left Uncle Harold's chambers and made their way back down the stone, spiral stair case, taking care on the well-worn steps as they did.

"Conan!" said Ben as they came back out near the entrance to the college.

Conan was stood up and looking busy at his desk, "You just caught me, Master Ben. I was just about to knock off for the day."

"Great timing!" said Ben and then tilted his head sideways towards the entrance in a theatrical manner. Even more theatrical coming from a muzzled clown.

Conan smiled and looked at Ben and then Thom, "The Eagle?" he enquired.

"Yes, I think that's as good a place as any," said Ben and Thom in unison.

Jeremy and Jennifer looked at each other – this obviously wasn't the first time Ben and Thom had been to the Eagle.

* * *

The Eagle was a short walk from the college, but you could miss it very easily as it was secreted down a narrow passageway that widened after twenty yards and then widened some more to accommodate a beer garden and a quaint old pub. Thom led the five of them indoors and to the bar. The barman was already reaching above him and retrieving three tankards that were obviously Thom, Ben and Conan's tankards. Some things very obviously belong somewhere or with someone and these tankards belonged in the hands of the three men now stood at the bar of the Eagle.

"The usual?" asked the barman, already pouring a pint of golden liquid from a hand pump into the first of the three tankards.

"Yes please sir," acknowledged Thom, already taking possession of his now full tankard.

"What would you guys like?" Thom asked Jeremy and Jennifer.

They both looked at Thom's tankard and the pump being pulled. The golden liquid looked pretty tasty and there was a hoppy aroma with a slightly citrus undertone, but the sign on the pump said Frog's Dribble. Thom followed their gaze, "Oh! Don't worry about the name! What counts is the description and this one is a summer IPA. For some reason, breweries try to outdo each other with silly names for their Real Ales. Goblin's Bollock is a particularly good ale, as is Bull Tinkle. But they're generally made from water, hops and yeast, not bollocks, dribble and tinkles!" as if to emphasise the point he lifted the tankard to his mouth and emptied the pint of beer in it.

"Another!" he gasped from under his newly acquired beer foam moustache as he slammed the tankard down on the bar.

Two more emptied tankards slammed the bar directly after, and Ben and Conan chimed in with, "Another!"

"Best decide on your tipple, guys" Ben winked, "you're already one down."

"Make that two down," smiled Conan leaning in and smiling as he slowly turned his tankard upside down and one golden drop hung momentarily to the rim before falling to the floor.

"We'll have the same," said Jennifer quickly, heading off the prospect of being three down.

* * *

The five of them were now safely ensconced in a corner of the bar. Despite it being summer, there was a fire going on the other side of the room and this was causing a warm light to dance around the bar. The pub was obviously very old; beamed ceilings and well-worn stone floors gave that away. Someone had a fondness for brass and there were horse brasses, pots and pans hung from every available space. And as we have already established, tankards hung above the bar for the regulars of this public house. It was a warm and welcoming place to spend time with friends catching up, and catching up they were. Conan sat in the midst of the friends and was making a point of including everyone in the conversation, mainly by recounting stories about the college and Ben and Thom and using asides to educate Jeremy and Jennifer on the unwritten history of the college and its students.

"What you need to remember is that these two were green young pups," said Conan cocking a thumb at the two lads sat either side of him. He leant forward conspiratorially, "they didn't have a clue!" He leant back, "still don't do you lads?!" without waiting for a response he continued, "so there they were drunk and climbing the roof of the refectory, when who should walk past but Professor Clark!" Conan chuckled, "Now this wouldn't have been so much of a problem with the other Professors, but Clark you see, he's ex-military and still has the keen eye of someone who shoots regularly." Conan chuckled again, "So he spots movement above him and what does he see?" Conan looked around at Thom and then Ben, cocking a thumb at Ben, "this uns overbalanced, what with being rather heavily inebriated," cocking a thumb at Thom he added, "and this un has grabbed at his wayward friend to stop him swan diving off the roof." Conan's eyes sparkled as he recalled the scene, "so as Clarkie looks up at the movement that has caught his eye, and you have to bear in mind it was a full moon on that particular night, well what he sees will live with him to his dyin' day! There's Thom there, with his arms around young master Ben, tugging on him from behind. And they're both naked as the day they was born!!!" Conan burst into infectious laughter and slapped the table.

As the slapping of the table didn't elicit liquid sloshing from their tankards, Conan concluded it was time for another round, "Time for another round!" he said standing up and stepping over Thom to get to the bar. He gathered up the tankards in one large beefy hand and walked over to the bar. Jennifer and Jeremy looked at each other and their blurry twins. It didn't feel like they had been in the Eagle for all that long but they had already lost count of the drinks they had had, and the other three seemed to inhale their ale and remain unaffected by it.

What felt like moments later, Conan was back at the table depositing the now full tankards of ale and several packets of snacks that Thom and Ben ripped apart and left in the centre of the table so everyone could dig in. Jeremy read the big word on the centre of one of the packets just before it was ripped apart. Scratchings was what it said. He popped one into his mouth, following the lead of Ben and Thom. The morsel was deceptively robust and initially it did not want to succumb to the pressure his teeth were putting it under, then there was a crack that he felt more than heard and after a moment's panic when he thought it was one of his teeth that had lost the battle, he got a pleasant and salty flavour.

As everyone knows, bar snacks are laden with crystals designed to dehydrate patrons and persuade them to consume more drink. The consumption of more drink then leads to a certain kind of hunger that can only be sated by bar snacks and so the cycle continues. Some bar snacks are left in bowls on the counter of the bar for anyone to help themselves to, thus accelerating the cycle as customers do not have to go through a transaction in order to obtain the bar snacks. Legend has it that a chemist once purloined a half full bowl of bar snacks to establish what substances were contained in the bowl, hypothesising that the bowl would contain the original ingredients, but also substances introduced by the customers who had helped themselves to some of the moreish snack. Now this particular chemist was an observant fellow and he had further hypothesised that the bowl was a permanent fixture on the bar and that the bar staff were in the habit of topping the bowl up as it got to around half full, so the lower levels of the bowl had an ageing and potentially interesting set of contents.

The chemist was expecting to derive interesting results from this experiment of his because he had frequented the gentlemen's conveniences of this local haunt and this was not something that anyone would choose to do as the approach to hygiene in this public house was that it was most hygienic if you avoided going in to that particular room at all costs.

Interestingly, the legend goes on in a similar vein, concluding that the additional constituent ingredient in that bowl, and therefore all bowls of bar snacks intended for public consumption was urine. This is not what in fact the chemist found and this particular legend is a watered-down version of the truth brought to you by the Guild of Bar Snack Purveyors. No one will ever know the truth, due to the chemist's untimely demise, some say at the hand of an assassin who was on the payroll of the Guild of Bar Snack Purveyors, but why they would need this additional route to oblivion when their snacks were a perfectly good solution to hastening one's end, no one is quite clear on. What we do know is the urine was not an additional ingredient, it was there from the very start. The additional ingredients in that bowl were far, far more interesting than urine.

Of course, bar snacks are the sustenance of choice during the imbibement of tinctures, snortorinos, looseners, openers, brighteners, lifters, shorts, snifters, snorters and the entire gamut of alcoholic beverages, when a drinker leaves a public house there is a wonderful scientific process delivered by the cooling, fresh air that greets the drinker and one of the effects of this is that it induces a ravenous hunger that will only be sated by dishes only eaten whilst under the influence of drink and these dishes invariably contain meat of a dubious origin. One such meat is called donor meat. No one knows who or what donated the meat, and to muddy the waters further the meat is sculpted into an approximation of a woolly mammoth's foot and then rotated in front of an electric fire bar liberated from the house clearance of the dearly departed Auntie Edith. As with the lower half of the publicly available bar snacks, no one has ever seen the inner parts of the woolly mammoth shaped donor meat sculpture and all that warmth provided by Auntie Edith's inefficient electric heater provides an ideal environment for a number of really interesting creatures to thrive. Just which creature is currently living in the meat sculpture being showcased in front of a hungry drunk is one of the subjects discussed at length while they await the preparation of their post public house meal.

Jeremy and Jennifer were being introduced to this food stuff ritual and a lot of the other elements of pub folklore as they sat in the Eagle with Thom, Ben and Conan. Jeremy had also established that it was increasingly embarrassing when his breaks from the drinking and chatting to visit the privy was seemingly coordinated to coincide with a perfect stranger. He wanted to apologise, but loo etiquette dictated no talking and definitely no eye contact, so all he could do was aim a noncommittal nod in the stranger's general direction and hope that the next time he visited the toilet it wasn't yet again at the exact same time as this stranger's visit. That hope was of course, in vain.

As Jeremy returned from one of these visits, he was met with the customary return from the bar of Conan with yet more drinks. The timing of his breaks also always seemed to match Conan's round too. He was getting concerned that with each subsequent round and loo break his legs were becoming more difficult to control and it may well come to a point where he knew he had to get up and pay a visit, but his legs would betray him and leave him stranded.

As if to increase the likelihood of complete leg failure, Conan didn't sit down having delivered the tankards of amber liquid and packets of bar snacks, instead he strode confidently back to the bar, as if showing off how well his legs worked, him and his blurry triplets, and when he turned to face them he was holding aloft a tray full of sparkling jewels.

Jeremy squinted in a concerted effort to focus his sight more clearly. Squinting was a generally accepted approach to drunken sight loss and it worked. Temporarily. Whatever was on the tray was sparkling in the lights of the pub, these lights including the firelight which accentuated the glorious sparkle emanating from the tray's contents.

Conan placed the tray delicately on the table in front of the friends, as though he was indeed displaying the wares of a jeweller for consideration – look at these fine pieces my friends!

Thom and Ben groaned, but their protestations seemed quite appreciative and in the style of Oh! You shouldn't have! But I'm glad you did!!

Conan had purloined a tray of shots. There were far more than five shots on that tray. Both Jeremy and Jennifer were both now squinting and tilting their heads and grabbing hold of the table in an attempt to stop the room from moving around and to establish what was on the tray and just how many of the whats were there. They could see three times more shots than everyone else, so the maths of the moment was even more difficult for them. Worse still, the bloody things wouldn't keep still!

Eventually they guesstimated that there were more than a few shots each.

Ben and Thom lined the shots up in front of each of the participants; this was a ritual to take part in. Moments ago, Jeremy and Jennifer had been close to throwing in the towel, but now they were excited and enthusiastic and raring to go. They did not know where this second wind had come from and they were ignorant of the fact that they were experiencing the Tequila Effect, a well-documented phenomenon where a really bad idea is delivered so enthusiastically that you are swept up in the ensuing avalanche of enthusiasm and do the wrong thing regardless of the fact it's going to hurt.

They all made the shots disappear.

They may have made more shots disappear.

* * *

Fifteen minutes later, Jeremy and Jennifer were having a nap. Ben was at the bar chatting to the barman.

Conan sat back and sighed, "Aah, it's good to see you lads!" He turned to look at Thom and Thom noticed the rheumy eyes and serious expression, he smiled at Conan. Conan was one of the most genuine people that Thom knew. The strange and wonderful thing about people that earned the accolade of genuine was that it was very likely there was a whole bunch of stuff you didn't really know about them, that under the warmth and candid language and the reliance you could place on that person, there were a set of experiences that could have utterly broken them, but instead had forged them into the person they were now. They had had a choice, or perhaps that choice had been made for them already, instead of letting things happen to them, they refused to play the victim, refused to let bad situations define them and they came out of the other side better people. They had done more than survive. Over the years, Thom had had a few conversations with good people that he had known for a while and during those conversations, they had told him something about themselves that he would never have guessed in a million years. People were full of surprised, or some of them were anyway.

Thom smiled at Conan, "Good to see you too, sir."

Conan looked out over the pub and his jaw worked as he stumbled over some words, "I drink to forget, Thom. That's the thing. I self-medicate. I can't sleep, or rather I do sleep and then I have the nightmares. Thing is with the drinking, it works for a while and then I get to this point and they're there."

"I know, Conan. But it helps to talk about it doesn't it?"

"Yes, that's one of the reasons it's always good to see you lads, you listen to me, see?"

"You're a good bloke, Conan. It's easy to listen, because there's never a dull word."

"I'm sorry, I shouldn't do this."

"Yes, you should, that's what friends are for."

Conan nodded stiffly, "yes, friends. They're always with me, my friends." And he looked around the room.

Thom followed his gaze and could almost see Conan's ghosts. Conan had had a long career in the military and it was never clear what he had done, when it came to this part of his life he was a quiet man, there were many secrets that he had to keep, whether they were official secrets or the confidences of the men with which he'd served. Men like Conan didn't talk about their pasts. He'd undoubtedly been a hero on more than one occasion, there were rumours of medals that only a few had ever been awarded, and of those few, he was the only one not to have earned the medal posthumously. But the big give away was the steady procession of senior military who just happened to pass through and who lauded Conan for being the very best of men and then some. Conan had seen the glory of battle many times. Another reason he didn't want to talk about it.

Conan had had a successful career in the military and from where Thom sat, in amongst Conan's other friends he could see that one key measure of that success was that he was alive when many of his friends were dead. Not all of the ghosts now gathered had shuffled off their mortal coil during active service, but the things they'd seen and the things they had had to do had as surely killed them as a knife blade, bullet, shell, lazer or mine. Conan carried a great weight with him, and only those few who knew anything of this great man could see his burden. Thom felt privileged to know Conan, more so that he was counted as one of his friends.

Thom looked up as he noticed movement, Ben was stood over Conan and had a hand on his shoulder. Conan didn't like being touched, understandably so, part of him would always be out there in a battlefield and his senses were permanently on high alert. But occasionally he made exceptions and it was again a privilege when you were not met with a rusty spoon to the eyeball.

"They're here aren't they?" Ben asked quietly.

Conan nodded, "They're always with me master Ben, I'm a fool to think otherwise. But right now, yes they're making a bit of a nuisance of themselves if I'm to be honest."

"Let's take them to the kebab shop then, sir," said Ben briskly, changing the mood quite adeptly, "bit of fresh air and dodgy meat will do us all the world of good!"

They didn't need asking twice and they stood up, more steadily than any of them had any business doing. Ben nodded towards the two prone figures across from them. "We'd best wake those two Sleeping Beauties!"

"Yes, I think we should," agreed Conan, slipping a tin of snuff out of one of his many pockets and taking a good pinch of it to each nostril. The brand of snuff Conan preferred was not widely available and was not strictly legal anywhere on this side of the galaxy, if a medical professional had been present at that very moment they would have fainted as should have Conan.

86

The rest of the evening was a blur, as all good, impromptu evenings are. It is a well-known fact that the best nights out are all unplanned nights out. Planned nights have expectations that build as the night in question approaches, many of them are an anti-climax, the remainder are merely OK. Unplanned nights have no expectations whatsoever, and so they exceed any expectations that may be passing and happen to get caught up in the proceedings. The very best nights out are the ones that are not supposed to happen at all. You are not supposed to be there, but against your better judgement, you go along for *just the one* and then you are persuaded to stay for *one more,* then you persuade yourself to stay for *a final drink, because I really am going now OK,* after that there is an illusion of being persuaded which helps ensure each and every beverage consumed has a naughty, illicit quality and the time you are spending is borrowed time – you are drinking like this is the last night you will ever spend in this company having this drink. Which, when you do eventually get home may well become a reality if the current level of rage and disappointment emanating from your long suffering (as far as they are currently concerned) partner is anything to go by.

The chums gingerly greeted the new day. They all began the process of attaining a level of consciousness required to actually be awake at around the same time. None of them were rushing the process and hadn't got to a stage where they were assessing their beer related injuries or paying any attention to their surroundings to see where they had eventually ended up before passing out. One of the reasons they were in no rush was sleep deprivation. After a big night out there follows a state of unconsciousness. This is not sleep. So, the morning after a big night out your body badly needs sleep.

The reason the chums began to surface around the same time was that Conan had bounced out of bed twenty minutes previously realised he didn't have a rifle with bayonet affixed in his hands and supposed he may as well flannel crotch, pits and face (in that order), clean his teeth, lob some clothes on and get breakfast on the go. The smell of cooking bacon was wafting through Conan's digs.

After Conan, Thom was the first to restore some semblance of consciousness. He wasn't fully conscious, but nature called, so he padded to the bathroom and without his eyes operating he managed to direct an impressive flow of urine entirely into the loo. He flushed. Then he padded to the sink to wash his hands. As he finished washing his hands, he noticed a movement in front of him. *Oh,* he thought, *it's the mirror* and he was about to dismiss this commonplace occurrence until something that was niggling him made him properly focus on the image presented before him. It was Thom's screaming that brought everyone else in Conan's digs to full and alert consciousness. Curiously, Conan only smiled and shook his head, had a swig of his tea and carried on with breakfast.

Thom was transfixed. His face! His poor face! He was maimed! He'd been mutilated! This was the mother of all Beer Related Injuries. He didn't consider himself pretty or handsome, but now he had a face even his mother wouldn't love. What had happened to him? What had he done? He must've been fired out of a gigantic catapult and reached light speed and then used his face as a brake along a potholed road strewn with the most abrasive gravel imaginable. He would have cried for his ruined looks if he wasn't so shocked. Why could he not remember the incident that ruined his looks? Why didn't it seem to hurt? Or was it about to hurt like an absolute bastard? Slowly, as if in a dream and his arm were passing through guacamole, he reached up to touch his injured cheek. Slowly, ever so slowly, not actually wanting to touch the injury for fear of making it all the more real, his finger made its way to his cheek, like a ship approaching the dock of a space station, and just as his finger was about to make contact, part of his face started to fall away. Thom screamed again and the piece of his face that was detaching itself from his head peeled away ever so slowly and gracefully. Instinctively he turned his hand and caught the detached end and with a strange sense of curiosity he pulled and a sense of calm fell upon him as he realised it was a strip of donor meat. Thom had fallen asleep in the remains of his kebab.

There was an urgent knock at the bathroom door, "You OK, mate?!" asked Ben.

"Yeah," said Thom, "it was just kebab."

"Oh, I see. I'll give it ten minutes then," said Ben on the

other side of the door and Thom heard him pad away.

The smell of bacon drew everyone to Conan's kitchen. There was just about room for them to sit around the rough, wooden table in there. Conan had a huge, fresh white loaf that he cut into doorsteps, slathered in butter and then he placed thick rashers of bacon on one slice, slices of black pudding and a fried egg on top. A generous squeeze of brown sauce, then the second doorstep was slapped on top breaking the yolk of the fried egg so it oozed over the black pudding and into the bread.

"Slept in your donor kebab again, master Thom?" enquired Conan as he handed out the breakfast butties, nodding knowingly as he did.

Other than appreciative moans, the kitchen was quiet as everyone devoured their bacon butties and washed them down with mugs of strong tea. There was nothing like a good bacon butty. Nothing like bacon for that matter. Whichever world you were on, it was all the better for bacon.

87

Hilary, that is The Auditor, was well on her way and she was back in work mode. Well, mostly in work mode, barring the big smile playing across her lips. Even having to get back into work mode should have been a worry for her, because that just did not happen. She didn't have any other modes. But she was happy and she felt light, her feet were treading on cushions of air and things were good.

Hilary was in lust.

As a result of this pleasant and euphoric state Hilary was making good progress, and right now she was approaching a planet that didn't seem right at all. The instruments on her ship were telling her this was Zeta-12-B, it was otherwise known as Gvard, the Story Planet.

As with earlier encounters she'd had with this anomaly's trail, she knew something had happened here. And that was bad. The thing was though, it was also good. The readings she was getting and the results from her tests pointed to certain improvements and positive outcomes which made her conclude that prior to any changes, things were possibly quite bad here.

In some respects, Zeta-12-B was experiencing a similar pleasant and euphoric state to Hilary and some would say that this was creating a predisposition within her to the extent that it she was harbouring an unprofessional bias. She was oblivious to this and in any case noted the issues so that if follow up was required then follow up there would be.

What Hilary did not know was that had she passed Zeta-12-B at some point before its transformation, then she would undoubtedly have been incorporated into one of its unsavoury stories. As she was a pan-dimensional being, this may not have resulted in her demise, but it would have caused a significant degree of unpleasantness and would undoubtedly compromised her professionally as there would have been the necessity for Intervention and the Intervention would have been for her own personal gain, or rather survival.

Hilary did not know how lucky she was to have encountered Zeta-12-B when she did.

* * *

Dobbin quietly got on with the business of being a space craft and conveying them along the prescribed course. He had noted the change in the Auditor and was just a bit concerned. She was humming to herself for starters. She'd never hummed before. He hadn't realised that she even knew any tunes to hum, let alone how to hum. Something had happened. She was happy. She wasn't supposed to be happy.

88

Ben looked at his wrist. It was vibrating and making a manic warbling sound. Ben continued to look at his wrist until his brain did some processing, moved some junk out of the way and managed to coordinate a response.

"Bill!" said Ben, "how you doing!?" He walked out of the room so his call wouldn't disturb everyone as they finished their mugs of tea.

"Ah you know, the usual," said a mini hologram of Bill.

"You mean drinking cocktails and entertaining all manner of attractive females?" grinned Ben thrusting his hips at Bill.

"Well, when you put my considerable entrepreneurial efforts like that..." began Bill, "it makes it sound so much better than what I actually do!"

"That is what you actually do though, Bill."

"Well yes, but that's not the point."

"OK, then what is the point?"

"The point, and the reason I called you is that I shagged a pan-dimensional being."

Ben laughed, "good man! You've excelled yourself this time!"

"No Ben," said Bill, "that isn't the point of this call…"

"Oh!" chimed in Ben, "you just thought you'd throw that one in there then eh!?"

"No, it is part of the point, but not *the* point."

"Riiiight…" said Ben, awaiting Bill's point.

"She's after you guys, Ben." Said Bill, making his point.

"You told her about me and now she's shagged you, she wants to go one better?!" asked Ben actually considering whether he should allow this to happen.

"No, she's hunting you guys down, Ben!"

"You what? How do you know that?" asked Ben.

Thom had walked in to see if Ben was OK and caught some of the conversation.

"Oh, hi Thom!" said Bill as he caught sight of Thom, "I was just telling Ben that I shagged a pan-dimensional being."

"That's nice," said Thom wondering at the sexual voracity of Bill and Ben, "should I leave you guys to it if you're going through your sexual exploits?"

"No! That isn't why I called, Thom. Hilary, that's her name by the way, is an Auditor and she's following you guys. She mentioned an anomaly that she was tracking and as she was in Constellation alarm bells started ringing. Then she mentioned that she'd already been on the Micra. That was what clinched it."

"Could just be a coincidence," ventured Ben.

Thom shook his head, "No Ben, we both know it isn't," he turned to look at Bill's hologram, "thanks Bill, did she say anything else."

"Only that she'd call me," said Bill sheepishly.

"Bill!" Ben almost shouted, "you asked for seconds and she didn't bite!"

"It…" started Bill.

But Ben cut him off, "You never ask for seconds! Was she that good?"

"She's nice," said Bill quietly.

Thom raised a hand before Ben went off on one, "Let's hope you're right Bill and she turns out to be nice, but it doesn't sound good does it?"

"No," agreed Bill, "it doesn't sound good, that's why I thought I'd best try and warn you."

"I just wish we knew what we're dealing with," said Thom, "auditor you say?"

"Yes, but we're talking pan-dimensional auditor, so an auditor on steroids and it sounded like she audits the Big Stuff."

"Like Clair," stated Ben.

"Like Clair," agreed Thom.

89

Clair and Uncle Harold had been having a good old chat. This chat had been going on for the duration of the drinking session at the Eagle, the post beer food stop and the subsequent period of unconsciousness. When you have been learning and studying for as long as Uncle Harold has, you can stretch time and use a few tricks and devices to utilise it very effectively. This dispenses with noise and interruptions such as the need to eat, the requirement to sleep and the pressing urge to pay visits to the bathroom.

Clair had noticed these devices and a few more besides and enjoyed being around someone who could make the odd useful tweak here and there. For his part, Uncle Harold was at a heightened state of interest and was taking this opportunity to converse with a unique individual, someone who was not usually to be found in the universes because this was not her original or usual home.

Most of their conversation was a knowledge exchange and as they found their footing and got into their stride, the pace of the conversation really picked up, it was more a download at times. For Clair, it was a chance to learn more about herself even as she answered Uncle Harold's many, many questions. She was also learning more about humans and not just from the voluminous knowledge that Uncle Harold was the receptacle of. This knowledge was accompanied with context and some of that context was how Uncle Harold felt about the knowledge he'd gleaned, both at the time and now.

Uncle Harold was fully aware of what Clair was doing and that he was an open book. He was absolutely fine with this and hardly had to consider it. You don't get a headful of knowledge by being closed and defensive. Uncle Harold was old school, the more he knew the more he realised he didn't know – that his knowledge was a mere drop in the ocean and that brought with it a certain degree of humility.

Clair had the same Big Questions that we all have, who was she? What was her purpose? What was the meaning of life?

"I can help you with the questions," Uncle Harold told her, "but the answers are for you to find. It is in the living of your life, your choices and actions that the answers you are looking for begin to unfold. Besides, imagine if I could give you definitive answers. It would be quite a tragic outcome, you would feel cheated and I would feel bad because I would have taken a big proportion of your life from you – it is about the journey, Clair. How we get there and who we choose to share the journey with. We talk about learning from our mistakes, that it's better to regret something we have done, than something we haven't done. The truth is that we only define something as a mistake after the fact. We're making it up as we go along. It helps if you have a good perspective, you see life as one huge opportunity to learn and you do your best, that includes doing your best by people. Try. And try to be good. That's all I can really tell you and it is advice you can choose to follow, totally, in part or not at all."

"You've told me a lot more than this, and I feel like I know myself a bit more, thank you Uncle Harold." replied Clair.

"That's all part of the journey," said Uncle Harold, "as we learn we also get to know ourselves just that little bit more."

"I just wish I knew where my journey led," and there was a large sigh from Clair.

"None of us know that, not really. Even those who have their lives seemingly mapped out. The Kings and Queens who knew they would rule and felt they had few choices, the child who was always going to be a blacksmith because his father and his fathers before him, and many generations prior to that as far back as anyone can remember were blacksmiths, these lives had their twists, turns and intrigues. There is only one certain thing in life and it is the ultimate conclusion; death."

Both Uncle Harold and Clair paused at this point in their conversation.

"OK, that may well not apply to you Clair. But it might, and I think you are best proceeding on that basis."

"Doesn't it ruin a life, knowing that it will all end and could end at any time?"

"Only if you let it. Death is part of life, but you don't have to let it define you. After all, it just is and you cannot change that reality. Worrying about death is futile, it wastes valuable time and energy and you focus on the wrong things as a result. Worry feeds stress, and for us mere mortals stress leads to health problems and death, so you see, worrying about that bad thing, means we focus on it and hasten our own end. The brave and the bold only die once, the worriers and the cowards die thousands of times."

"But what about the lives and deaths of others?"

"Yes well, that is a source of pain. And for those of us who live a long life we carry the pain of losing the ones we love. That pain never goes away, but it becomes more bearable over time. And it cannot be avoided, well it can, if you wish to live a lonely and empty life, which itself will be an even greater source of pain and regret. The important thing is to enjoy wonderful moments and make the best of memories, you then carry those memories and the joy of having known special people with you and that will always outweigh the pain of losing someone. After all, life is about balance."

"Thanks, Uncle Harold. This has been so enjoyable and useful."

"You're welcome my dear" said Uncle Harold smiling.

"I'm glad Thom and Ben brought me to see you."

"So am I, dear," nodded Uncle Harold, "This has been the singularly best day of my life and one I had not considered possible, let alone hoped for."

"I've thoroughly enjoyed it too. Does Ben know that you are his Father, Uncle Harold?"

Uncle Harold coughed for a whole minute at this point before composing himself. He had the urge to say something along the lines of what did you say? But he knew full well what Clair had said and no amount of bluff and nonsense would change that. Besides, after the free and frank exchange they had had, he really could not then ride roughshod over that and become all contrary.

"I..." Uncle Harold drew a deep breath and rejigged his train of thought, "I've been lying to myself all this time, I suppose. That's why I have never told him. I suspected. I more than suspected. But Ben's mother was with someone and I had already chosen this life, which in some ways is a selfish life singularly devoted to the pursuit of knowledge."

"He suspects too, you know. It's no longer a conscious thing because he loves you and that's enough for him. But I think it would make a difference if you told him. And Thom."

"Thom?" said Uncle Harold uncertainly, "you said that last bit with some intent and purpose, didn't you?"

"You haven't noticed over all these years because your focus has been on your son, but Thom idolises you and has competed with Ben for your attention and has always felt second best. If you tell them both then all of this will make sense for all three of you."

"It doesn't always work like that, my dear," said Uncle Harold sadly, "we are a contradictory and conflicted species led by our emotional responses."

"It stands a very good chance of working with you three."

"And you'll make sure it does?"

"I could, in the way you're implying. But I won't. I don't have to. The very fact that I could, influences the outcome in any case, so maybe that's a form of interference or at least a gentle push. If I had any further input it would be as a friend, to help with that perspective you advised me on. To see things in the best possible light, and not only to see them as they are, but as they could be, and in this case, there is a strong bond of love and friendship and that's what counts isn't it?"

Uncle Harold smiled again, "How very right you are, I expect you will do well on this journey of yours. I have been privileged to meet you and I am very glad that my son and his best friend met you and knew you for what you were from the off. Well, it was Thom wasn't it? Ben... my son, is very lucky to have a perceptive and unique friend like Thom."

"You don't need to talk like this is the end of our conversation,

Uncle Harold. You're coming with us, remember?!"

Uncle Harold smiled, "only for a part of the way, Clair. As we've already established, this is your journey. You, Thom and Ben. And it's more than that. It is your destiny. This journey of yours is just the beginning of something. Something much bigger. I would give anything to come along and be a bigger part of it, but some things are preordained, my dear. I am very glad that my son and his best friend are going with you though. And proud of them both."

90

"Son?" said Thom very quietly, but with the kind of intonation that carries and gets noticed even by two people in the very depths of conversation.

Unnoticed by Uncle Harold, Thom and Ben had walked through the door into his chambers. Jeremy and Jennifer were with Conan in the college office sorting some arrangements for the forthcoming cruise. The news that Uncle Harold was attending had begun a sizeable frenzy for passage on the cruiser. The teaching year had not long finished, so the timing of the cruise was very opportune and it was looking like they would have a full ship. Conan was helping them filter out anyone from Cam to help ensure the cruise was as trouble free as possible and any deaths would be accidental, not murder.

Uncle Harold froze, Ben had beaten him to it and was already frozen.

"Sorry, I thought you knew they were there," Clair whispered, but Uncle Harold didn't really register this, he was about to confront his Big Secret, something he thought he would never have to do. For all of his talk of bravado and facing life full on, he had hidden from this aspect of his life.

"Ben is your son?" said Thom slowly and clearly.

Ben remained frozen. Uncle Harold was trying to break the spell and only partially succeeding. His mouth was moving as were some of his fingers. Ben found the operating manual for his neck and looked from Thom to Uncle Harold and did this several times.

Strangely, it was Thom and Uncle Harold who were having the moment. Ben was a spectator. As a result of this, Uncle Harold, who had now regained control of his legs, glided across the room and did something he should have done a long time ago. He hugged Thom and said sorry.

"I'm sorry Thom," he said, his eyes filling with tears, "I should have told you both years ago. I was a coward and now I can see that I hurt you both deeply. I never meant to. I thought it was for the best. The silly thing about it all is that you have both always been like sons to me. Always. I have been immensely proud of you both." He then broke from his unilateral hug and turned to Clair, "and now this! If I was any more proud of you both, I think I would burst!"

Ben drew in closer. "Dad?"

"Yes, Ben. Your mother and I were an item before your Dad came along, and I chose this dusty, secluded life over being with her, I just didn't know it then. She seemed to make the decision at the time, but deep down, I knew I was being a coward even then."

"Dad?" repeated Ben. Today was a day for people repeating themselves.

"Yes," said Uncle Harold simply.

Now it was Ben's time to hug, Harold took a moment before he worked out that he was supposed to return the hug. The three of them stood there for some time, Ben and

Harold hugging, Thom standing there. Then Ben opened his left arm and pulled Thom in, "come here, you big lump!" and something broke in Thom, he sobbed uncontrollably and hugged Ben and Harold.

A short while later, they were sat in big armchairs drinking tea from china cups. The dainty cup looked particularly out of place in Ben's hand for some counter-intuitive reason, as the design on the china matched his clown outfit and the lace detailing on his cuffs were very much in keeping with the ritual of refined tea drinking. Perhaps it was the muzzle, which made the process a bit awkward looking.

"I've always been jealous you know," said Thom eventually. Ben nodded.

Uncle Harold shook his head, "I didn't know. I was very blind when it came to certain things about you two. No, not blind, I chose not to look and not acknowledge the situation from the outset."

Thom frowned, "I now have no right to be jealous, you just took that away from me, didn't you?"

It sounded like a challenge and Uncle Harold recoiled slightly at the words.

Thom looked directly at Uncle Harold and smiled, "Good. I've behaved badly and I should never have been jealous. Maybe deep down I knew and as a kid I realised I couldn't compete with Ben for your affection. Worse still, I didn't realise I was still a kid!" He shrugged, "That doesn't matter now though does it?" He turned to Ben, "you're my best mate." He turned back to Uncle Harold, "You were like a second Dad to me." He raised his tea cup by way of a toast, "I'm glad you're both in my life and I'm glad you told Ben today." Thom looked back at his friend by way of an unspoken question; are you OK with all of this.

Ben just smiled. "Dad. That'll take some getting used to, Uncle Harold!"

91

Hilary's ship was now passing HR13 and as a matter of course she was running checks and tests. The results were a curiosity to her. She was certain that she was on the right course and following in the anomaly's wake. Yet here was a planet that really wasn't right. It was bad. Really bad. Beyond bad to a point it was downright evil.

Dobbin had taken the advised course past HR13, there were plenty of advisories and warnings intended to ensure everyone gave HR planets a wide berth. Even then, it was unpleasant going. Even more so, for a horse masquerading as a spaceship. Dobbin really wanted to morph back into his usual state right now.

Hilary knew that within the confines and parameters of the universes, there was much scope for really bad things. There was a tendency towards chaos and that pull towards the flux of all things led to a degradation and the more unsavoury aspects of species. The deadly sins. Unpalatable behaviour that the more civilised nations refused to believe they were capable of, but it was always there at the very core of their nature.

And nature appeared to be cruel, but civilisations made that look like child's play. Things started out well and then a few people with good intentions grew to a crowd which needed to be organised and organisations inevitably corrupted those good intentions and instead power was the goal. It was all too easy to lose sight of what counted and substitute it for something else. That something else, once you scratched the surface was not very nice at all. As long as people were busy though, they would never scratch that surface. Anyone who did would merely leave and be replaced.

HR13 though, this was all of that taken to depths that were never intended to exist in the universes. Something was happening here that would need to be addressed. This was a very Big Job indeed. And Hilary just knew that this was not the only planet that had been infected and corrupted.

There were some echoes of the anomaly here, but they were drowned out by HR13. Hilary was surprised that the anomaly hadn't gone to work on HR13 as that seemed to be the anomaly's modus operandi. She looked at her instruments again though and frowned. This was really was a really Big Job and perhaps the anomaly had taken a look and thought better of it.

Hilary didn't blame it.

She did some further checks and made notes – this was a whole other project for her to come back to. Part of her wanted to stick around and conduct further work, perhaps the anomaly had had similar thoughts to her? Hilary had a thought and shivered, how many more planets were there like HR13...?

92

The Thing looked at the instrument panel and nodded. This was a positive development. The Thing turned and ran more processes on further instruments. The Thing nodded again.

"We're closer," The Thing said with a hint of triumph at this breakthrough.

"You've found her?" asked the disembodied voice.

"Well no," said The Thing somewhat deflated and feeling just a bit aggrieved at being asked this question, "but we're closer."

"Oh," said the disembodied voice.

The Thing was very close to saying something about how a little support wouldn't go amiss, he masked a deep breath. Next time, The Thing would stay at home. The Thing knew that this would remain a defiant thought, it wasn't worth voicing it and rocking the boat.

"The closer we are, the greater the probability that we will find her," explained The Thing, "we will find her."

"Good," said the disembodied voice, "and when we do, we need to tell her she's been a very naughty girl!"

The Thing shook his head, glad that he was on an audio

only feed.

93

Things would never be the same again for Thom, Ben and Harold. They were better. It's mostly better to get things out in the open, and they had. Thom now had a reason for why he had behaved badly and he was going to make darn sure he stopped. Not much had changed for Ben with regard to Harold, he'd always been an important part of his life, as were his Mum and Dad, what did change was he was happy that Thom had got this particular stick out of his butt so they could all just get on. Harold had more learning to do, which for him was always a good thing, but he was out of his comfort zone right now as this learning involved people and perhaps even physical contact and the display of emotions he had suppressed, having pretended to himself that he wouldn't need them.

The timing of the cruise leant itself well to this momentous occasion, it gave the trio some time together. There would also be a number of distractions. For example, Harold's discomfort for physical contact during social occasions was completely overridden in certain circumstances. Circumstances that Ben would totally understand and circumstances that Ben was going to enable as much as possible for all of the participants of the forthcoming cruise. Perhaps in some respects, the apple hadn't fallen all that far from the tree.

The forthcoming of the cruise was imminent, passengers were already beginning to make their way up to the ship and there was a buzz of anticipation in the Ox colleges, the passengers were really looking forward to their jolly and those remaining were looking forward to some peace and quiet while the passengers were on their jaunt.

The news that Harold, the Dean of Empire College, the most prestigious of the Ox colleges, was attending the cruise had spread like wildfire. And as that fire spread the bookings flooded in. There was a great deal of competition between the colleges so once one college was represented on the cruise all the colleges needed a presence. Ben's Sex Marketing strategy hadn't needed much of a push, the seed was planted with Harold and then issued forth with some gusto. People knew the score and were looking forward to letting their hair down.

And that was the thing, everyone was looking forward and moving on. The anticipation was building and Ben and Thom were glad they were helping the Bluecoatians get started with their new way of life.

Ben was looking forward to everything – he saw his hedonistic vision for the cruise as his way of putting something back, in facilitating a lot of joy. Yes, he knew he was judging everyone by his own standards, but as far as he could see, sex was the reason everyone was here so it just had to be the way forward.

94

Thom was having a bit of quiet time and talking with Clair. They'd already had some very private quiet time, and now they were considering the cruise. Thom wasn't quite sure that being along for the duration of the cruise was wise. He wanted time with Harold, but he was worried about this Auditor and wanted to put as much distance between them and the Auditor as possible. Besides, it may not only be the Auditor who was after them, someone had hired the Bluecoatians after all. Someone anonymous and untraceable, which made Thom think they may be powerful and dangerous and that they had been fortunate that they'd chosen the Bluecoatians in preference to getting their own hands dirty, if they'd decided to do the job themselves then Thom and his friends may be in a heap of trouble, or worse.

Clair was more sanguine about the whole thing and focused on the cruise and the experiences the cruise promised.

This was annoying Thom, so Clair thought it was probably about time to change tack and give Thom something else to focus on.

"Thom, you need to talk to Harold."

"We already talked," said Thom with more than a hint of annoyance.

"No, not about that. About me. Harold wanted to talk to you before all the stuff about Ben being his son came up. It's important."

"Right," said Thom feeling a sense of foreboding.

"He'll be waiting for you to come and see him," said Clair.

"And you know this because you've just told him I'm coming to see him?"

"Yes."

* * *

Thom walked into Harold's chambers. After Harold's revelations the Uncle just seemed to jettison itself and both Thom and Ben called him Harold. Dad didn't feel right to either Ben or Harold, and this was no reflection of Harold's part in Ben's life as a formative father figure, they had gone beyond that stage and taken their relationships to another, different level.

"Thom!" said Harold greeting Thom.

Thom noticed that Harold hadn't been deeply embedded in study and instead he was sitting on the edge of the sofa, bolt upright, awaiting Thom's arrival. This was very obvious because Thom spotted Harold as soon as he entered his chambers, Harold hadn't become one with his favourite chair. This immediately set Thom on edge and he remembered Clair's parting words; it's important. Nothing was more important than study to Harold. Study was his world and his life.

Thom nodded at Harold as he approached, not sure what to say and quite frankly, not sure he wanted to hear what Harold had to say. This all felt like the come-to-Jesus-meeting a prospective father-in-law would call, the intended outcome of which would be to make very clear that there was no way in hell that they would ever be an in-law so let's just get that straight right now, buster. You're no good and certainly not good enough for her. I've met your kind before, you'll never amount to much.

All these things and more were circling around Thom's head as he walked towards Harold. His voice of reason managed to temper this by reminding him that this was the Thom of old, feeling unreasonable jealousy and in-filling all manner of negative thoughts to back this world view up. Things were different now, they had always been different and Thom should be acting like a grown up, not a toddler. This helped and Thom was calming somewhat and becoming more receptive to what Harold was going to say. His legs still felt odd and awkward as they conveyed him over to Harold.

"Please sit, Thom," said Harold and Thom sat opposite him, "Would you like a brew?"

"Yes please," said Thom and Harold poured him a mug of strong tea. Thom noticed this and appreciated that Harold had dispensed with the usual china tea cups and gone for good old mugs, no doubt sourced by Conan.

"So, Thom," began Harold, straightening his back and rubbing his hands together, "we need to talk."

"Oh dear," Thom smiled nervously, "it's the old 'we need to talk' is it?"

Harold smiled back, equally as nervously, "It's not like that."

"What's it like then?"

"I wish I could encapsulate what it was like in any amount of words, preferably a few. But I can't. This is unprecedented and I don't know where to begin. But begin I shall Thom, and where better than by saying Wow!"

Thom was taken aback, "Wow?"

"I knew there was greatness in both you and Ben, and some of that is due to your enduring friendship. The two of you together is a wonderful thing. You are both lucky to have such a great friend. But this? You have excelled yourself, Thom!"

Thom had always craved recognition and praise from Harold, after the revelation earlier today, this was almost too much and he barely noticed his fingers pinching the flesh of his arms to check that he was awake and this wasn't a dream, "How so?"

"Clair! She told me how you found her and liberated her and you have nurtured her and encouraged her to grow and find herself."

"I did?" Thom cleared his throat, "she did?"

"You're the same old Thom, oblivious to your gifts and just how good you are!" Harold smiled at him with great affection, "You've been touched by greatness and even now you doubt yourself and underestimate your part in things."

"I'm sorry, but I don't get what you're saying?" said Thom.

"No one else could have done what you did, Thom. No one would have found Clair and realised she was something much more than she appeared to be, let alone then liberating her and taking her on this journey. It's truly remarkable!" Harold paused and leant forward, "You started this journey, Thom. You. You found Clair and you knew that something must be done. You just knew it. But more importantly; you *did something about it!"*

"I liked her. It's that simple," said Thom.

"Yes, I suppose in some respects it is simple. I find that simplicity underlies greatness, albeit invariably great people make something appear simple because everything joins together seamlessly and it just works. These things can be a long time in the making though. You were a long time in the making, Thom. Your humility and your ability to relate to others. This empathy is one of the things that drew you and Clair together, no doubt," said Harold rubbing his beard thoughtfully.

Thom nodded, unsure how to respond.

"You and Clair have formed a strong bond, haven't you?" asked Harold.

"Yes, I supposed we have," agreed Thom.

"This is unique, Thom. And something I didn't think was possible."

"You mean a man and a chair? I have heard of this sort of thing previously, but it's been seen as pretty delinquent!" said Thom flippantly.

"Do you know what Clair is?" asked Harold.

"Well no, even Clair doesn't know what she is."

"That is slightly disingenuous, Thom. A mountain may not know it is a mountain, but that does not prevent us knowing it is a mountain."

"Slightly different when we are talking about people though isn't it?"

"Clair isn't a person."

"And she wasn't a chair, or a ship or a bot. We are not what we appear to be on the surface, we are what we are and what we do," said Thom.

"Yes, granted. But Clair is different, Thom."

"OK, but how so?"

"She's not from here for starters."

"Right, but just because she's from somewhere else in the universes…"

"That's what I am trying to tell you, Thom" said Harold leaning forward, "she is not from these universes, this is not her home and in the nicest possible way, she has no business being here."

"Where's she from then?" asked Thom, his mind racing as he added in layer upon layer of further possibilities as to what Clair could be.

"I don't know, Thom. But what I do know is that she is a pan-dimensional being and she operates in ways that make a mockery of the usual rules and parameters of our existence," sighed Harold.

"What does that mean?" said Thom also leaning forward and carefully discarding his half-drunk mug of tea on the table between them.

"I don't know, Thom. This is the most fascinating and wonderful day of my life. The limits have been removed and the possibilities are unfathomable. That is truly terrifying though, Thom. Clair could do something on a whim and the repercussions for life as we know it could be dire. None of us know what she is capable of, including her. That sort of limitless power is dangerous."

"But she wouldn't do anything to hurt anyone, she inadvertently killed an HR bot and she was devastated!"

"That's exactly my point, Thom," said Harold quietly, "even with the best intentions, things went wrong. It was a trifle this time, but what about next time?"

"What are you suggesting we do then?" asked Thom.

"I really don't know, Thom. The simple answer is; take her back home. Return her from whence she came."

"But what am I supposed to do?!" said Thom almost shrieking.

"Calm down, Thom," said Harold raising a placatory hand, "Clair told me about the bond you'd formed. If it came to it, you may have to make a choice. Go with her or stay. Don't underestimate the changes and sacrifices either of those choices would entail though. I suppose that was really what this talk was supposed to be about. Preparing you for the decisions you will undoubtedly be forced to make."

Thom looked at Harold, "You said if it came to it?"

"She's been here for a while now, Thom. In these universes. I think she may have changed somewhat from what she originally was. There are rules and even she has to abide by those rules. Most of the rules, most of the time, anyway. Besides, she appears to be here for good reason. And she has free will. Lots of it. So, if any of those pan-dimensional beings who are following you do catch up with you, which I imagine they will, then their plans for Clair may differ from her plans."

"So, your advice is to be ready to make difficult decisions?" asked Thom.

"Yes, I supposed it is."

"Anything else?"

"Keep going. Carry on with your journey and your time with Clair," smiled Harold, "and Thom?"

"Yes?"

"Enjoy every single moment of it!"

That seemed to be the end of the conversation, all the conventions of the end of conversations had been followed and as a result, both Thom and Harold had picked up their mugs and were savouring a good, post conversational drink of tea. They returned their mugs to the table and Harold lifted the tea pot, nodded towards Thom's mug by way of "do you want a top up?" to which Thom nodded and they sat enjoying the gratifying sound of well brewed, deep amber tea pouring into a mug. As the pouring ended and Thom added a mere splash of milk, Harold lifted a finger.

"There was one other thing, Thom."

Thom looked at Harold and sensed himself tensing, this was the final dénouement, the pause and the seeming end of the scene only for the scatty, unkempt, like really badly kempt, detective to pause his exit and turn around in the doorway and deliver the question that would unravel the until now well prepared and suave bad guy. Thom didn't need to say anything, he just needed to convey *on edge*, which he did with aplomb.

"This journey of Clair's. It's a journey of self-discovery and to my mind there are two destinations, which may be one and the same. I… I'm not explaining myself well here am I?"

Thom looked at Harold and shrugged.

"Where does Clair belong, Thom?"

Thom shrugged again.

"This is in part rhetorical, after all, where does any of us belong? You could say this question is easier to answer for me, as I am here and I belong here. But do I? And will I? Besides, as I say this you are quite rightly looking at where I, the Harold you know, am sitting. This chair, which is situated in these chambers, which are within this college and all of this in and on OxCam. A seat of learning, as befits my goal; learning." Harold smiled at Thom and took a moment to ensure Thom was still following him, "But I also mean this," he waved his hands around his body, "Me. Am I comfortable in my own skin? Have I accepted myself? Do I know myself and do I love myself? When I talk about this, you know I am referring to my inner me, but you also know I'm including this body, my outer self. Because we engage with that and I need you and the people around me to help me see myself. You are my mirror, that's one of the predominant drives we have; we crave social interaction. Even stuffy old gits like me!"

Thom nodded as he thought about this, "so Clair, she has her inner self. Part of this journey is, or at least could be about her finding her own skin. A form that she is comfortable in. That's what you're saying isn't it?"

"Yes, Thom. That's what I'm saying."

"But even when she's inhabiting something, she's much more than that. She's in my head and elsewhere…" mused Thom.

"To a certain extent, aren't we all? She's just more… pronounced," said Harold, "Don't get too caught up on it, Thom. It's enough to be aware of this possibly being the destination of your journey, or one of them. Perhaps you are going somewhere and there Clair will find her skin and her place. It's enough to know this. You cannot know the outcome until it has happened. That's the nature of journeys and outcomes."

Thom nodded, things made more sense now, and yet made even less sense. "Thanks Uncle Harold."

"I think it's just Harold now isn't it?"

Thom smiled, "yes, sorry Harold. My mind was on other things."

Thom paused as another thought formed, "what if it's the other way around?" he asked.

"That was one of the things my mind was on too, Thom. Do go on," encouraged Harold.

"Clair hasn't got a form and she doesn't necessarily need one, does she? Or, her form may be a form that I cannot perceive or understand. This is my journey as much as hers. My form may change instead or as well as hers mightn't it?"

"Yes," nodded Harold, "Your form and Ben's. In fact, there may be changes made necessary in order for you both to continue with the journey."

"This is big isn't it?" said Thom sombrely.

"Yes Thom, it is. But you already knew that. There will be changes for all three of you. It is no accident that the three of you are together, on this journey. You need each other and you will need each other all the more as your journey progresses."

They both sipped at their tea and let things sink in. Tea always helped with the sinking in process.

376

95

The good ship Sunshine Dreamer disembarked with its cargo of pale and pasty academians. To celebrate the occasion, Ben had advised a drinks reception and he had personally written the cocktail menu. Ben's main aim with the drinks menu was to remove any and all inhibitions and impediments to a good time and to do this as swiftly as possible.

Thom got wind of Ben's efforts and decided a clandestine mission to sample Ben's cocktails and perhaps considerably water them down was in order. So, Thom crept into the back bar unnoticed and with the help of a couple of the bar staff recreated Ben's menu. The tasting did not start well, Thom had a mouthful of the quaintly named Donkey Punch which was so potent it erupted forth from the back of his throat with an indescribable force, the closest description of which was being punched in the back of the head whilst being distracted, the problem with the eruption, other than bursting several blood vessels in Thom's eyes, was that the liquid Thom had spewed was highly flammable and there were candles on the bar. The quick-thinking bar staff left Thom to his retching and managed to get the conflagration under control before they lost the bar and perhaps part of the ship.

Thom and the bar staff revised the recipe for Donkey Punch swapping out the more exotic and obscure ingredients for readily available beverages that were fit for human consumption.

Next on the menu was the DT. Perhaps the mixologist didn't quite replicate Ben's recipe, but once poured into glasses, this drink gave off a thick yellow and acrid gas and a drop that was spilt on the bar left a nasty smoking hole. This was disposed of safely out of the nearest airlock and removed from the menu.

Three thousand years from now, the safely disposed of DT cocktail would descend majestically upon the peoples of a slowly developing country and be worshipped as a deity. These people's would build great stone cubes in adoration of their heavenly visitor, build an entire, enduring civilisation and empire and thus a whole period of history and the very evolutionary stages of the people on this planet had been altered thanks to one of Ben's cocktails. This was not the only cocktail that had far reaching effects on the universes, but more of that in the now legendary tome; *Zeebur and the Original Donkey Punch Odyssey.*

The third cocktail gave Thom momentary convulsions which amused the bar staff, but made Thom fear for his life. Once he was again in control of his body, he asked the smirking bar staff if they would now like to sample the liquid in their glasses. They stopped smirking and politely declined and instead helped Thom rewrite the ingredients, again swapping out the ingredients they had not previously heard of, some of which they were not certain were even

378

meant for internal consumption, and one of which was a banned weapon of total war.

Eventually learning from experience, Thom then went through the remainder of the menu and if he and the bar staff had not heard of an ingredient it was substituted for something they had heard of and they knew was fit for consumption. After a couple more disastrous taste tests, which Thom noted he was always on the vanguard of, they went back through the menu changing any ingredient they may have heard of, may have been fit for consumption, but they hadn't ever seen anyone drink successfully.

After their work on the menu, one of the bar staff came over to Thom.

"What should we do with all of these?" they asked pointing at the mixed bag of bottles they'd removed from Ben's menu.

Thom breathed a big and audible sigh of relief, "Good man! We can't leave these things anywhere near the bar – they're lethal!"

"Where shall we put them then?" asked another of the bar staff.

"Where's the armoury?" asked Thom.

Testament to the contents of the bottles they removed, no one thought twice about questioning Thom's choice for the storage of the deselected beverages. And they were extremely careful in the handling of each bottle as they stored them away and ensured they were safely secured under lock and key and ensconced in much padding and the heavily padlocked boxes pushed a way out of sight.

The new menu did not look any different to Ben's original menu barring the removal of the obnoxious DT, the names of the cocktails remained the same and Thom and the bar staff liked to think that the spirit of Ben's menu remained intact, only with this menu there shouldn't be any unpleasant incidents including spectacular death and fates much worse than death.

What they did not know was that their assumption that the cocktails should be served in martini glasses and that one section was shooters was very far off the mark. On the day, Ben entered the bar early and took over supervision of the staff working the bar and got them lining up pint glass after pint glass of his concoctions. He had also found several boxes of yard of ale glasses for one section of the menu, the one Thom had mistakenly entitled *Shooters*.

Somehow, instead of this vastly increased volume of strong alcohol writing off the party-goers early doors and ruining the mood by replacing it with catatonia and instances of random violence, it resulted in a chilled and friendly vibe and a swift reduction in personal space. The attendants quickly forgot their political affiliations, their cliques and petty grievances, along with a lot of other stuff, and they mingled freely and laughed at anything and everything. The event went on for the duration of the evening and towards the end of the night, some of the attendees paired up, taking the hand of someone who's beard they liked the look of and departed for a more private venue to lock beards and maybe more. Many of these pairings were totally arbitrary and this could have spelt the end of a few relationships, but the events of this evening were quite fuzzy the following morning and the only abiding memory was of a good time had by all, and a let's not ruin it with a post-match analysis approach which was agreed by all.

One result of this inaugural event was that everyone

wanted another cocktail party and soon.

There was a practical delay on this next cocktail party taking place as the procurement officer had underestimated the bar stocks, so the next party would have to wait until they stopped at the next planet along, which fortunately was the day after next on the itinerary.

The unfortunate consequence of this dry spell was that the hangover from the cocktail party coincidentally kicked in the day after next, so not one passenger disembarked to visit the first planet they stopped at, and instead stayed in their cabins, curtains drawn as the daylight hurt too much. This was in some respects fortunate as the planet they had stopped at was HR23 and was best avoided, as the traumatised procurement officer would testify to, but that's a whole other story.

96

When it came to the journey of the chair that had fallen in love with Thom, there was a steady and inexorable pull towards journey's end. No one truly knew where they were headed, not Clair and her entourage, not The Thing and not the Auditor, but there was a strange certainty to it all. There shouldn't have been because they were in the universes and none of the three were governed by the laws, rules and norms of the universes.

Or so they thought, but such thinking is silly and a touch arrogant. History is littered with people who thought the rules didn't apply to them, or more specifically, the roadside of history is littered with their broken bodies and carrion birds pecking at them. If they're lucky, then they are already carrion when the birds start in on them.

Of course, there are those seeming exceptions, those who make the rules. These people are a wee bit deceptive though and that deception is a major contributory cause of the aforementioned roadkill. These people follow all the necessary rules, they are very aware of them and what they really do is identify that one single rule that they can interpret slightly differently, and that gives them the edge.

The edge they get gives them significant success and it is this that people focus on and as they focus on that they get sloppy with their description of how this person got ahead; the rules didn't apply to them. Rules? They tweaked one rule, matey-blokey, so don't you go off thinking the rules don't apply...

Oh dear.

If there was a steady and inexorable pull towards an end point, then there was a fixed destination and if there was a fixed destination then surely someone knew what this was and where this what was? And as we are talking about pan-dimensional beings, and several of them, surely with their otherworldliness they would know where they were going, or at least they could know if they applied themselves a little more fully?

It doesn't work like that. There are rules. There are always rules.

Besides, the universes themselves are really a pan-pan-pan-multi-multi-dimensional being, times ten, and this incredibly complex being has a sense of fun.

97

The Auditor was a methodical type of person. She liked structure and order and was well suited to her job. The work she was currently conducting was ad hoc and that always made her uncomfortable. She preferred the repeat work she undertook, at least with that she could pick up last year's files and copy the vast majority of it across, remembering to change the date as she did. That was like painting by numbers and very therapeutic.

What she needed to do here was to join the dots. And as she had this slightly random thought of a join the dots puzzle that only takes shape as you draw the lines between points, an activity she hadn't undertaken for as long as she could remember, she had a brainwave; she should look at the journey so far and then project it forward. Look for patterns and anticipate the what next.

* * *

The Thing was looking out over the vastness of the universes.

Only to a creature like The Thing it wasn't all that vast, at least not as vast as universes dwelling creatures would have it.

The Thing wasn't joining dots. That thought hadn't occurred to The Thing. However, The Thing had his back to where he had been and was looking in the direction he should go and The Thing knew he was headed in the right direction, because this was the way they had all been headed for quite some time.

98

Thom, Ben and Clair were huddled over the nav-chart, looking at where they had been and where they were headed.

"We seem to be headed out in that direction," Ben pointed out.

"Yes," agreed Thom. His economy with words was largely due to the monumental hangover he was nursing courtesy of Ben's opening cocktail night. It was good though, he thought. And he remembered most of it, which was an added bonus. He hadn't yet thought to ask Clair to maybe take the edge off his hangover. Because he had a hangover, so coherent and sensible thought was a chore he was putting off for the time being.

Clair agreed with his assessment of the night before. She also agreed with Ben *"yes Ben, that's where we're headed."*

"There's nothing out that way though," said Ben staring at the screen and their course, "Freight ships use that part of space exactly because there is nothing there, except the odd space-service station here and there. They do a great selection of greasy food, which I could murder right now though!"

Thom retched at the thought of the grease. Thom currently had a hair trigger in this respect and could and would retch at the thought of almost anything.

"Sorry, mate" said Ben patting his shoulder and sending him across the room. "Oops, sorry, mate!"

"That's where we're headed, Ben. And there is something there. Right in the middle of that, there." She moved the destination cursor to the epicentre of the nothing in the screen.

Ben looked at Thom as he shambled back to the screen, Thom did his best to look back at Ben without it hurting too much. There was a complicit agreement between them; if that's where we need to go then fair enough.

The Sunshine Dreamer's course was soon going to break off towards an interesting planet with blue seas and white sandy beaches and a predominance of beach and waterfront properties as the inhabitants were as comfortable in the sea as they were on land. Someone clumsy may refer to them as merpeople – but mermaids had been sea dwellers who appealed to humans who anthropomorphised and sexualised them. A woman with a cracking set of clams who was good at swimming? Phwoar! This limited and quite frankly sexist thinking led to the wreck of many ships as the miffed off merpeople took to being sirens, sang suggestive songs to the litany of wolf-whistles and *cor dahlings* and took not inconsiderable pleasure in idiots coming a cropper. That would teach them! A slightly harsh approach to the matter in hand as it didn't teach them, it killed them. In their haste to teach them a lesson, the mermaids had overestimated the sailors' ability to swim.

"We'll need to leave the Sunshine Dreamer and take the taxi then," concluded Thom.

Ben bit his tongue. He was looking forward to meeting the merpeople. He then stopped thinking with a particular part of his anatomy and realised he would miss Jennifer and a part of him ached. A different part of him for a change. "I'd best get the taxi fuelled and ready then," he said, concluding that busying himself may be the best course of action.

"Can you check the range on that thing?" asked Thom as he returned to looking at their course, "there's a couple of service stations, but I think we'll be cutting it fine."

"We'll be OK Thom, don't worry. I've already checked everything."

But Thom *was* worried. Harold had talked about Clair finding her place and Thom was being reminded that Clair was very different and maybe nothing, or rather the vast expanse of nothingness in space was the very thing for her. It didn't leave him with many options though, leave or die. Or become some amorphous thing that he couldn't comprehend right now. And if he couldn't comprehend it, then would it send him mad or change him into something so completely different he didn't recognise or even know himself anymore? These thoughts weren't the best thoughts to have during a hangover, but that's what hangovers did, they launched multiple assault on their victim and dark thoughts was just one part of their armoury.

Clair was privy to these thoughts, but said nothing. She wasn't exactly worried, after all she knew something was there. She wasn't sure what it was that was there, but there it was and it was where she needed to go. The rest would take care of itself.

99

The time had come for Thom, Ben and Clair to leave the Sunshine Dreamer as the cruise ship's course was diverging from the path they must follow. Ben had prepped the taxi and made sure it was fuelled and stocked with provisions. Thom had checked the provisions and removed a considerable amount of ballast and asked Ben how he'd found these particular bottles in the armoury, as they had been carefully hidden away and were also under lock and key.

Ben had tried for an enigmatic smile, which was not completely successful and instead a wee bit disturbing, and said he could be pretty persuasive when he wanted to be. Thom assumed there would be several bar staff nursing huge hangovers tomorrow morning.

Thom and Clair were pottering around the taxi doing some final checks and experiencing that poignant feeling that sits in your belly as you are readying yourself for a big trip. Most of this growing feeling was anticipation. Anticipation of the trip ahead, the excitement that that held, but also the worry and in this case foreboding thanks to the undoubted risks and danger that awaited them. There was also the anticipation of the goodbyes they had to say, and a part of them was avoiding this part, so some of the final checks were checked again and more pottering than necessary was pottered. This was undertaken largely in silence. In this silence, Thom and Clair were accompanied by their thoughts.

Eventually, Thom spoke, "are you OK in that bot?"

"*Yes, why?*" asked Clair.

"Other than the chair, it's the longest you've inhabited something," said Thom.

Clair didn't say anything.

"Is it because you feel guilty about the previous inhabitant?" continued Thom.

"*I suppose that is a part of it,*" agreed Clair. "*At first at least. But then I've been focused on other things since then and now we're close, Thom.*"

"You really think there's something out there?"

"*No, I know there is something out there.*"

"But we got Jeremy to check that part of the universes and he confirmed what we already know. There's nothing there," said Thom tetchily.

"*Don't worry Thom, it's there, and it's not something beyond everything you know. I'm not just going to disappear without even a by-your-leave.*"

Thom did a double take, and not because Clair had used an expression that he wasn't familiar with. Clair had got to the heart of the matter, again. Thom's biggest worry wasn't dire, life-threatening danger, it was that they would get to a point in this journey and Clair's path would lead somewhere that Thom could not follow. Thom did not want to lose Clair.

"Your path could lead somewhere I could not go though, Clair" said Thom sadly, "I wouldn't even have a choice at that point, the choice would be made for me."

"I'm here for a reason, Thom. And you found me for a reason. Neither of us would be here and none of this would have happened without you and me meeting. That happened for a reason. Whatever awaits us is our shared destiny, there is something awaiting both of us."

"You're that certain about this?" asked Thom uncertainly.

"Nothing is certain, so your concerns are valid. But where will your concerns get you? We are different and there will always be parts of who we are and what we do that are perhaps not part of what we share. We overlap and we complement each other. Or, a better representation is that we are two sides to something that fits perfectly together and as we have spent time together and explored each other a piece of us is held within the other."

Thom thought of the Yin Yang symbol.

"Yes, that's how I think we are. We are different, but we fit perfectly together and there is a reason for that. And some of that reason is out there awaiting us at this journey's end."

"This journey?" said Thom, his mind racing.

"Yes Thom, this is only the start of something. We'll perhaps know more about the something at this journey's end."

Thom smiled, "I was bored. Stuck in a rut. And I knew it was not good for me to be head down and ploughing a furrow. But I don't think I ever expected things to get this interesting!"

"That's a good thing though, right?" asked Clair.

"Mostly good," nodded Thom, "and mostly good is a very good place to be."

"Good," said Clair happy that they had had this conversation and cleared the air.

100

Ben was saying goodbye to Jennifer. After a bit of recovery time, Jennifer was saying her goodbye to Ben. Not to be outdone, Ben then said an energetic final farewell to Jennifer. Just as Ben thought it was time to walk away, Jennifer dragged him back from the slightly ajar door and said goodbye all over again. Unfortunately, the door was left ajar and the sights and sounds passing traffic encountered are best left to an imagination with many other things to distract it.

"Are you sure about this Ben," asked Jennifer.

"Yes, Thom's my best friend and I need to watch his back. He's a bit shit without me!"

Jennifer punched Ben playfully in the arm for being disingenuous. A punch that would have caused some damage to a lesser man. A man who was not undead for instance. "You know what I mean, Ben!"

"We've been through this Jennifer," said Ben turning to look at her, "I'm really into you and I don't want to spend time away from you, but the time apart will be good for us both. You have this, your first cruise. You can't miss out on the one thing you guys have always wanted! And Thom is my friend, going towards only the gods know what. I need to be there for him."

"But I want to be there for you, Ben."

"Yes, I know babe," said Ben taking Jennifer's hand and kissing it whilst staring into her eyes, "it feels like this part of the journey is for the three of us only. And you know I had to push a bit so it wasn't just the two of them. I was there at the start and I want to see this through with Thom. He's always been there for me."

Jennifer stared back at Ben, tears brimming in her eyes, "just come back safe, Ben. I'll miss you."

"I'll miss you too, Jen," and Ben kissed her gently. Pulling away he said, "and I intend to come and find you as soon as I can."

As he walked out of her quarters, he turned and winked, "We'll have a lot of catching up to do."

Jennifer playfully threw her bedside lamp at him and he just managed to get through the door before it exploded on the door jam.

There was a smile on his face and skip in his step as he thought about Jennifer, their long goodbye and how good it would be to see her again.

101

Ben walked back to the flight bay and the taxi to find Thom and Clair. They were waiting inside the taxi and Thom was sat deep in thought. Ben had seen this often enough to know that Thom and Clair were having a chat. There was something about Thom's still and focused pose and although Ben could not hear what was being said there was something in the room when these conversations took place, the echoes or ghosts of the words being said, similar to the background hub-bub of conversations in a room that you quickly became adept at drowning out, they were there, and yet they were not.

Ben didn't have to wait long for the conversation to end and Thom looked up and became animated in a way similar to someone who is waking from a nap.

"Hi Ben," said Clair, "how's Jennifer?"

"Oh, she's good," said Ben automatically, "she's really good!" he added as he thought about Jennifer properly and he came to life, just a little bit too literally.

"Oy! Oy!" chipped in Thom, seeing where this would inevitably go if Ben wasn't snapped out of it, "she's had a bit of an effect on you hasn't she?" and he play punched Ben on the shoulder.

Ben looked at his shoulder and then Thom. Thom braced himself for a return play punch that would see him travelling unceremoniously across the room, it never came though. Ben smiled at his friend, "Yeah, I like Jennifer. I'll be seeing her again."

"You don't have to come with us, Ben," said Thom, and meaning it wholeheartedly, he would never knowingly put his best friend in danger, even if he needed him.

"Actually, he does Thom," said Clair, *"he's been with us from the start and I think he needs to be here too."*

Ben and Thom looked at Clair and then each other and shrugged by way of an OK, that's that then. She'd saved them any further debate and they were both happy with the outcome.

102

J eremy was on the bridge with the bridge crew and a few more of the Sunshine Dreamer team. In fact, the bridge was quite packed with people wanting to say a personal bon voyage to Thom, Ben and Clair. Amongst those assembled were the bar staff, looking decidedly unstable on their feet, but putting a bravely professional face on it all. Bob the engineer was also there and of course, Harold had come to wish his son and his son's best friend a safe journey.

Somewhere in the throng was Trevor, his signature aroma arose and assaulted the nostrils from time to time and when it was concentrated around the bar staff, they looked decidedly unwell.

Nibbles and sensible drinks had been provided on a surface that was not taken up with the ship's controls. People were casually passing by and helping themselves to a few bite sized morsels and a drink.

Thom was yet again preoccupied by the thought he had never worked out how you wandered around with a drink and a plate with food on it and managed to consume the food and the beverage. This conundrum usually added to his awkwardness in these types of social situations, the worst being the work-related soirees which required one to network. During those, Thom would look around the room and see the thick-skinned social butterflies working the room. Then there were the people who already knew each other and who had gravitated together from the outset, closing ranks to exclude anyone joining their clique. This rank closing looked more difficult if there were just two people together, but what worked for those guys was the old adage, two's company, three's a crowd – however you tried to engage these twosomes, you were interrupting and the dynamic was never going to work, and that was on you.

Maybe Thom was overly sensitive, but he reckoned that once you had to think about where to wander over to, why you were going over and what you'd say, then you were doomed to failure. So, he preferred to stand where he was and if someone came over to talk to him, then good. Maybe they were in the same boat as him and spotted him on his own as an easy option, in which case good on them and he would welcome them. Maybe they were the truly socially inept and would attach themselves limpet like to him for the duration, but that was fine by him, after all, his plan B was to exit early doors. After all, he'd shown his face and done his bit.

During this particular get together, Thom didn't have all that much time to think about the dynamics of the people mingling around him. It was a lot more natural than a lot of gatherings he had attended, no one was here to sell anything, including themselves; those particular members of the crew were not present on the bridge, having already sold themselves very lucratively and successfully to receptive passengers with a bit of spare cash and the desire not to complicate things with having relationships or feelings getting in the way. There was a moment though, between people coming up to see him to chat and wish him well, that he scanned the room and smiled. He was watching the free-flowing conversations and people moving around the room. Ben was one of the two centres of attention and was animated as he regaled his audience with anecdotes – that man had a voluminous set of anecdotes and a remarkable memory which allowed him to select just the right anecdotes for any given situation.

The other centre of attention was Harold. From where he stood, Thom couldn't hear what either of them were saying, but it was so obvious that they were related. Never mind father and son, they looked like twins – their movements and mannerisms looked to be choreographed they were so similar. Thom wondered how he had missed the obvious and then went easier on himself, deep down he must have known and he was simply jealous. That two people had such an affinity with each other, but also, the old adage he'd just been considering just now; two's company and three's a crowd. Ben was his best friend and he felt like a spare part at times when Harold and Ben got going. He treasured his friendship with his best friend so much he didn't want anything or anyone to get in the way.

And this brought him back to their pending exit, they were going into the unknown and Ben had insisted on coming with him. Ben had always been there for Thom and been with him every step of the way. Thom's growing relationship with Clair hadn't phased Ben, or caused him any problems, he'd just got on with it. Thom prevented himself from going on a downer as his one and only blind spot had been Harold, and now he could see why. He thought he'd forgive himself that one and focus on the important stuff, which included how lucky he was to have a mate like Ben. And it came in handy that the guy was amiable and fun and had the strength of several very well-muscled men.

"It's been great having you guys on board," enthused Jeremy, who while Thom mused about his blind spot, had sidled up on Thom on his blind spot. Thom nodded which gave Jeremy his cue to continue, "it's a shame to see you go, you'll be missed. I hope you come and find us when you've done what you need to do."

"We will," said Thom smiling warmly at Jeremy.

Jeremy proffered his hand and Thom shook it, "Take care, Thom. Safe journey. And thanks for your help and support, it means a lot to me and my crew."

"They're more than a crew, aren't they?" said Thom looking around the room.

Jeremy followed Thom's lead and looked around him, "Yes, yes they are. They're family. And they're pretty much the last of our kind. And with your help, we can at last be ourselves." He looked down at Clair who had been quietly observing the room, "thank you Clair, you are a remarkable... you are remarkable."

"Thanks Jeremy, it's lovely to see you all like this and your cruise going so well. I've loved being on the ship and sharing this part of the journey with you."

Jeremy nodded, "Well you guys take care, OK?" he spotted Ben disengaging from the group he'd been entertaining and went over to wish him well too.

They don't ask where we're going or why, thought Thom to himself.

Because they know there isn't an adequate answer, but it's important. It's our quest Thom. Something we must do.

103

There was a bleep in the cockpit of the Auditor's ship. Then, there was another bleep. The Auditor took a look, she had a call coming through. She tentatively accepted it, wondering who it was that was calling her.

The ghostly form of Bill appeared in front of her as his hologram kicked into life, "Hey, how's it going?" he asked more casually than he felt.

Despite herself, and the fact that she had never once taken a personal call whilst at work, the Auditor smiled, "GOOD... I mean, good thanks, Bill," she'd also never moderated her voice. Not for anyone. This was the first time she'd consciously done that.

"Cool, just thought I'd see how you're doing, you know, say *hi* to the most gorgeous auditor I know."

"Bill! You don't need to flatter me!" said the Auditor coyly.

"Hilary, you're special," said Bill grinning at her, "why do you think I called?"

"I don't know," said Hilary, genuinely not knowing why Bill would call her, not having experienced a suitor calling her before.

"Where are you at the moment, darling?" asked Bill making

conversation.

"Oh, out past HR13 at the moment," replied Hilary.

"That far away?" said Bill with a faux pout, "when will you be swinging back this way?"

Hilary had almost forgotten her hard to get stance and didn't think twice about how Bill had obtained her number, which was most unlike her, she was just pleased to see Bill, albeit his hologram, "I don't know, Bill. I'm still working on this assignment."

"Well I suppose I could come out and meet you for a drink and maybe more..." said Bill emphasising the *maybe more* part of the sentence in a way that was working really well for Hilary right now.

"That's very presumptuous of you Bill," said Hilary smiling at him in quite an inviting manner.

"I'd just like to see you, that's all," said Bill simply.

"Well, OK. But I can't afford to lose any more time on this assignment, Bill." Hilary looked at her course, "and the only planet I can see is the one I'm approaching, OxCam," she added forlornly as she realised the chance of them seeing each other any time soon was unlikely.

"OxCam, you say?" beamed Bill, "How far off that gaff are you?"

"I'm three hours away, Bill" said Hilary sighing, "so..."

"So, I'll see you there and we can have that drink!" interjected Bill.

"Wha...?" started Hilary.

"I'll be there in two hours, forty minutes, babe," grinned Bill, "I'm right behind you, you didn't think I was going to let someone as gorgeous as you slip through my fingers, did you?!"

402

And Bill meant every word. He did have an ulterior motive though, and having an agenda sat well with him, it meant he didn't have to examine himself too closely and wonder whether he was going soft and performing altruistic acts for Ben, even if Ben was a close and dear friend. Bill was a business man and there had to be something in it for him.

After finishing his call with Hilary and leaving her in no doubt how much he was looking forward to seeing her, he made another call.

104

B en walked into the cockpit of the taxi ship, "Just spoken to Bill," he said to Thom and then looked more closely at the HR bot that had most recently been Clair's home. The bot was motionless in a way that was not merely resting, it had no life in it and that went beyond it merely being out of juice. Not broken exactly, more that it was completely empty, "where's Clair?"

"Here!" said Clair.

Ben looked around the cockpit and nodded, "That makes sense."

"We're nearing where we have always needed to be, so I thought I may as well take the ship over. After all, I know where we're heading."

"Which is where?" asked Ben facetiously, expecting Clair to point in a direction and say that way. He felt a bit like the kid in the back seat asking; are we there yet?

"There!" said Clair excitedly.

The excitement Clair conveyed was palpable and sent a thrill through Ben. A very pleasant thrill which, under most circumstances Ben would have spent some time and effort dwelling upon, but on this occasion, it compelled him to turn and look out of the main cockpit window in the direction they were headed.

Thom did likewise.

Ben was stunned and could only reach for one word, "That's…"

Thom was likewise, almost completely incapacitated, but managed a couple of words, "…not possible."

105

The Thing's demeanour had changed, prior to this he had been filled with a sense of purpose, but there was a seam of anxious running through that purpose as well now. In fact, now he was filled with a sense of purpose with a seam of anxiety ridden excitement, he could sense that he was near. They were approaching journey's end. Their daughter was definitely nearby, so they could be reunited, go home and The Thing could return to his summer house and paint the views whilst having a warming drink or two. Peace and tranquillity and none of this current nonsense. Besides, being in the universes made The Thing uncomfortable. The universes were growing on The Thing and that just wouldn't do.

"She's near," said The Thing.

"Good!" said the disembodied voice, "well go and get her and tell her she's been a very naughty child!"

"She's not that near," corrected The Thing.

"Well, why did you bother me and get my hopes up with this *near* nonsense!? If something is near then it is obtainable. You can go over to it and deal with it. What did you mean if she is not near?" said the disembodied voice irritably.

The Thing swallowed down his own irritation, "everything is relative, my dear. I am closer than I was and I expect that I will see our daughter in short order and then I can go over to her and deal with her as you so eloquently put it."

"Don't you take that tone with me!" started the disembodied voice, "Don't you think it's even more difficult for me? Stuck at home. Helpless. Worried sick. Wondering what is going on?!"

The Thing didn't think it was as difficult at all and had been wondering why he had had to go when he had been perfectly fine with staying at home, in the summerhouse and conducting some worrying from his favourite spot. He did his best not to rise to this bait, but even with his best efforts the one, damning word slipped out, "Well…"

"Right! That's it!" shouted the disembodied voice, and in the next moment there materialised on the deck of The Thing's ship a being of challenging proportions and stature. A creature that you would look upon and struggle to describe. Fearsome and worrisome and just a bit wrong, something that didn't look right at all. Like it didn't belong here at all. Which it didn't.

It was very nearly identical to The Thing. They were cut from the same pan-dimensional cloth. Not a very popular cloth that one, never quite became fashionable and never would.

The only discernible difference was that The Thing looked deflated. That's right, come along at the eleventh hour and take the glory, thought The Thing.

"What was that?" said The Other Thing.

"Nothing, dear," replied The Thing.

There was much arguing. More like bickering really. The

Thing and The Other Thing were really pleased to see each other and this was how they expressed it.

106

The sleek flanks of Bill's Ferrcati shimmered as Hilary brought Dobbin in alongside and commenced the docking procedure. Hilary didn't think twice about Bill's vehicle, it made sense. It suited Bill. Besides, she was thinking almost entirely about Bill and seeing him again, what was this effect that he was having on her?

Dobbin asked her something along similar lines, "What are you doing, Mistress?"

Hilary was not pleased at this challenge, not pleased at all, because it made her feel guilty, "Taking a well-earned break, Dobbin," she replied tetchily.

"But you never take breaks!" exclaimed Dobbin, "this is highly unusual!"

"Well it's about time I did!" snapped Hilary, not noticing her voice had modulated in anticipation of her meeting with Bill.

Bill watched Hilary's ship come alongside the Ferrcati, he was looking forward to seeing her again. That wasn't usual for him. Constellation suited him, it was fun, in a sugar rush, take-away style. It wasn't supposed to be serious or fulfilling, it was an escape from a humdrum reality. Bill thought about

Hilary's current job and the potential conflict arising from that. Was he sleeping with the enemy? When it came to it, what would he do?

Bill mentally shrugged, it may not come to that, and if it did, he would do what he always did and think on his feet. Bill was a fan of agile, don't sweat it and when the time came, understand as much as you could about the situation in hand and then act accordingly and decisively. The way Bill saw it right now, he'd already done his bit when he warned Ben, he was now going over and above what you would expect of Bill. Besides, Bill didn't think Hilary was a stone-cold killer. Not really. Although that voice of hers and the way she spoke about correcting errors, making adjustments and addressing this anomaly, that was pretty cold and slightly worrisome.

The airlock door opened and there, framed in the doorway was Hilary. All thoughts of what may or may not happen evaporated as Hilary stepped forward and they embraced and kissed. Bill didn't even register the mumbled argument Hilary was still in the midst of as she left her ship. They stood there holding each other for a long time, Bill's red balloon hanging above them. Then they weren't standing anymore, Bill's balloon discarded and bouncing despondently across the ceiling of the Ferrcati and the fresh drinks Bill had at hand were no longer fresh by the time they got around to drinking them.

* * *

Bill untangled himself from the silk sheets and a couple of Hilary's limbs. They were both sated and covered in a fine sheen of sweat.

He handed her a drink and sipped his own. He looked at her and without thinking said, "Let me come with you."

Hilary attempted to sit up, which entailed disentangling herself from the sheets and parts of Bill as well as keeping her drink from spilling, it looked far from elegant but somehow, she managed it. She looked at Bill. Bill looked back at her expectantly, she looked at him some more, "What?"

"Let me come with you," repeated Bill.

Hilary nearly repeated her 'what', but then they would have been trapped in a loop. Someone had to break out of it, but Hilary was struggling to know how to break out of this particular loop as she didn't understand how she'd gotten into it. She was romantically involved with someone who wanted to share time with her. The problem was, she wanted that too. But at the very same time, she didn't want it either.

"No," she said.

"No?" echoed Bill, not quite repeating what Hilary had said as he said his *no* very differently to Hilary. He'd done his best to avoid any pleading quality to his no, but if you examined it at all closely there was more than a hint of pleading, but no desperation, so it was quite endearing really. Part of Bill shrank away from that. Endearing? Me?!

Bill was wondering why he'd asked to go along with Hilary, he'd already more than done his bit, not only had he warned Ben that Hilary was on his tail, he'd then followed her and created a pleasant delay. The words had just come out of his mouth though, and he'd been a bit of a spectator at that point. He hadn't thought to take them back, that wasn't in

Bill's nature, but then neither was blurting out his desire to be an auditor's roady. Worse still, he'd been on the receiving end of this sort of request and always been the one saying no. Mostly, people understood things with Bill were a one-off gig, and they went in eyes open. There was always one though, someone who couldn't read situations and instead projected their wants upon the proceedings.

What did Bill want? Yes, he wanted to help his friend. But he'd already done that. He wanted to make sure Ben was OK. No, he wanted to make sure Ben *and* Hilary were OK. He wanted to see more of Hilary and he was feeling like he needed to protect her, not that she needed protecting – he kind of knew she could take care of herself, and besides, Ben wasn't going to wilfully hurt her. But *situations* could arise. And then there were those killer lizards. He was looking out for Hilary and he wanted to see her again. No, more than that, he wanted her. Not in the possessive way he'd wanted his club and his Ferrcati and he had to admit that he had had candy hanging from his arm from time to time, but this was completely different; he wanted to spend time with Hilary and keep getting to know her.

As this prime reason for his blurting out the plea arose, he tried to swallow it back down with bravado and pragmatism, he needed to help ensure a positive outcome should Hilary catch up with Ben and his friends, and by being there Bill could potentially capitalise on any outcome. Yes, that was it. That made more sense to Bill.

"No," said Hilary, "I love being with you Bill, but coming along with me while I work? No, that won't do, I'm afraid."

Bill rolled over fairly easily, "OK, it was just a thought. I mean we enjoy spending time together and I thought it may be a chance for us to spend more time together."

Hilary smiled at him, touched by the sentiment.

"OK," said Bill rubbing his hands together in a business-like manner, "let me at least walk you to your ship." And with that, Bill took Hilary's hand and walked her through to her ship.

This would have been a fairly good opportunity to plant a tracking device, had Bill wanted to do that. And he had. He'd had plenty of time to plan ahead, so when Hilary's ship docked with his, a tiny nano bot had slithered out and attached itself to the underbelly of Hilary's ship.

Dobbin had been shocked by this violation and he was going to have a word with his Mistress the very instant she returned. What was going on!?

The couple parted with a long lingering kiss and Hilary had second thoughts about Bill coming along, but she swallowed those thoughts back down and she didn't share them.

Once the two ships had decoupled, Bill fixed himself a cocktail, waiting a short while before he followed Hilary at a good distance, undetected.

107

en stood stock still. He was a statue of a clown who had been bitten by a zombie and had then been transfixed. It was quite a fascinating tableau.

Thom had been a less interesting statue, but managed to break the spell. Mostly because he was thinking they seemed to be making a habit of this statue thing, "That's not possible. That's not possible! That's just not possible!" he repeated constantly as he looked at the instruments and the navigation map and then checked that what they could see was there.

In some ways, Thom was relieved, or rather he should be relieved and perhaps once he had calmed down a bit and accepted the evidence his eyes were providing him, he would be relieved, because if this was journey's end then it was something tangible and not otherworldly. It should be something he could comprehend. Currently though, he was finding it difficult to comprehend the existence of a planet that was not on the charts and shouldn't be in the middle of what until quite recently was a quiet hyperspace by-pass.

As they slowed to observe this inexplicable and very large phenomenon, they saw several freight ships making last minute adjustments to their courses. The manoeuvres were not at all pretty and added further weight to the theory that this planet shouldn't be here. Not that further weight was needed because this planet really should not be here. But that is not a thought that should be associated with a planet, so it feels like the thought shouldn't be there in favour of the planet that, by virtue of being much bigger and tangible won on points.

It took a while for either Thom or Ben to formulate the obvious question; how did this planet get here? Had someone moved it? Planets don't move, do they? Not unless they're being dragged by a huge gravitational force exerted by a black hole and that force crushes the planet such that it is no longer a planet, what with a black hole having a huge gravitational force. Unless the sci-fi geeks had been right all along and things just popped through the hole, because it was a hole and there must be something on the other side. The prospect of planets suddenly popping forth as a result of their trip through a black hole didn't bare thinking about, so there must be another, more reasonable and sensible explanation.

Like this was a totally new planet which until recently hadn't existed, hence it not being on the charts and it being in the middle of a hyperspace by-pass.

Planets had to come from somewhere didn't they? Just because you thought planets had always been there didn't mean that they had. Something happened and then planets happened. Perhaps that something had happened and then this planet had happened. It was perhaps a bit ridiculous to think that one thing happened and then all planets happened. That was like visiting a planet and meeting a lot of people and believing that all those people had been brought into existence at the same exact point in time. It would take an exceedingly huge something to effect all those people popping into existence in one go and that was nothing compared to a whole host of planets suddenly appearing on the scene and just kind of getting on with orbits and spinning and all the things planets do.

This planet held the eye too. Once you had got over the initial shock of seeing a planet that shouldn't be there, you noticed it was a beautiful planet, deep blues and greens and swirls of cloud making it all look dreamlike. Only it wasn't a dream. It looked hospitable and welcoming and you just knew it would be habitable. And habitable in a really attractive way conducive to a great work/life balance.

Thom, being quite fastidious, especially when it came to being able to breath and therefore live, looked at the instrument readings and they indicated that the planet was indeed habitable. Other instruments indicated that the planet was indeed there and that Thom and Ben weren't hallucinating. Thom found that he was busying himself with the instruments and read outs so he could get to know more about the planet, and he realised he was avoiding something that he must do.

He was about to do something about these avoiding actions when Ben piped up.

"Clair," started Ben, and Thom knew where this was headed, "is this anything to do with you?"

There was an unusual pause. The pause was unusual because Clair could read people, there was no delay in their thoughts reaching her, speech was just a confirmation of some of the salient points she was already reading.

"Clair?" said Thom, following up on Ben's question.

"Yes, I suppose it is," said Clair.

"You made a planet," whispered Ben, "wow, Thom! Clair made an entire planet! Have you seen it? I mean, for a first attempt at planet making it's a bloody masterpiece! If I was going to make a planet it would barely resemble a moon! It would probably look like the centre-piece to a dirty protest, if I'm honest! Thom, in her spare time, your girlfriend makes planets! Did she even mention this hobby of hers to you?!"

"Calm down, Ben," said Thom, placing his hand on Ben's shoulder.

Ben brushed him off, "I am not going to calm down!" he said as he started pacing the cockpit in front of the window looking out over the planet, "this is big, Thom! Look at that! It's huge! I mean, I knew Clair was a bit different and we were going out on a limb, you know, a departure from your usual Sunday afternoon down the park. But this!?" he gasped as though he was drowning and had just come up for air, "she's gone from chair to bloody planet!"

"I didn't make the planet guys," said Clair.

Both Ben and Thom did a double take. They'd assumed when Clair confirmed that she'd had something to do with it that she had actually made the planet.

"Then who did?!" asked Ben.

"I don't know, all I know is that we're here."

"This is where we've been headed?" asked Thom.

"Yes, this is what's been drawing me."

"Why didn't you tell us?!" asked Ben.

"Because I didn't know, Ben. I knew there was something drawing me and that the whole point was that we find it, I did not know it was a planet."

Ben at last seemed to draw a ragged breath and calm a little.

"It's a lot to take in isn't it?"

"I think that's an understatement," said Thom as calmly as he was able, "This has been a big adventure for us. We've had a lot to take in, it's been challenging every step of the way. And now we find that the conclusion of our journey is a new planet. A planet that has come into existence from nowhere and has been calling you."

"Us, Thom. Calling us. You must've have felt it too. Both of you," Clair paused to let that sink in, *"We're not at journey's end yet, boys. We need to go down there. We're not on the planet yet."*

108

The Thing and The Other Thing's bickering had subsided to occasional background grumbling and glowering at the other's back. So normal service had pretty much resumed. There wasn't a tut or an eye-roll to be seen, so they were getting along famously really.

The Other Thing had paused and was looking intently out of the ship, "This is what you meant wasn't it?"

The Thing stifled the first response that came to mind which was along the lines of; what? Give me some context here! I'm sick of these random outbursts that I am expected to scrabble around and attribute sense and meaning to. Instead, a deep breath was taken and a more collaborative and positive response was formed. If The Thing had taken a little longer to think on what he saw as The Other Thing's random outbursts, he may well have concluded that it was a compliment that The Other Thing expected that The Thing knew the context, could read her and understand her very well. And given a deep breath and a reset, The Other Thing was right. So, it was a compliment really.

"That we are near?" ventured The Thing. The Thing would not assume the meaning. That assumption could and would lead to disaster and the disaster would all be The Thing's fault. Saying; oh-I-thought, after things go wrong is the worst defence ever and amplifies the fall out. The Thing had learnt this after a particularly unpleasant situation involving an industrial sized tub of grease, half a tonne of mackerel, a snorkel, a tutu and a small pot of petunias, the words Oh-I-Thought just came out and made a bad situation a whole lot worse. So, The Thing liked to test his theory as to what was meant before launching into anything.

"Yes," said The Other Thing tetchily, conveying *what else did you think I meant* in the one word. The Thing would wear this in favour of any bad misunderstandings that required explanations for many years. Explanations that would never be adequate. "the ship is not indicating that we are near," continued The Other Thing, "but we are." The Other Thing paused to search for more words, "I... can... feel it," said The Other Thing eventually and then went quiet and still. Feelings weren't something that got spoken about often and The Other Thing wasn't sure how she felt about that, and having to feel about a feeling was sending her into a mini-melt down.

The Thing nodded and thought to himself, *yes, I did that too.*

109

Thom took the taxi down through the planet's atmosphere and towards the surface. Ben, who would usually be preoccupied with anything other than the descent, was looking intently out of the forward screens at the planet as if this was his first ever landing. He was taking in every detail, the planet was lush with vegetation, the waters were crystal clear and sparkled like green and blue gems had taken liquid form. He could see animals and birds and as they had started their descent, he had spotted a patchwork of terrains, mountainous regions providing a spine across land masses and spreading out from those spines, masses of greenery. He could see ice regions and deserts too. What he hadn't seen as they neared the surface was any sign of civilisation. This appeared to be a virgin planet, not yet colonised by a supposedly civilising species.

A habitable and welcoming planet that had not been colonised. That was unusual. This planet really was new.

Suddenly something caught his eye, something alien to this planet. "What's that?" he shouted, pointing out of the window.

Thom looked towards where Ben was pointing and automatically took the ship where he was now looking, sweeping towards the object rising out of the tree line in the valley. As they drew nearer, they could see the two halves of a freight ship. It had broken neatly in half, exposing the cargo that had been deep in its belly.

This was Varg's final resting place.

Interestingly, it wasn't Varg's vest's final resting place. After the crash Vest had lain there for a while. Then it had got bored with the lack of interaction, crumbs and drips of fat, so it had peeled away and slunck into the nearby forest and made its home in a damp and ever so slightly smelly cave. The local wildlife gave the cave a wide berth, but the Vest managed to grab a meal when it got hungry…

"Some unlucky bastard didn't spot the planet in time," said Thom.

"I think the planet's sudden appearance might have caught them out," said Clair sadly.

"Never mind that!" exclaimed Ben, "Have you seen what she was carrying?!"

Thom circled the stricken freighter and took a look, "Beer!" was his one-word answer.

"And a whole bunch of provisions!" added Ben, "Look! They've even got Tunnock's Tea Cakes!"

"Those eyes of yours never cease to amaze me!" grinned Thom.

"Hey, we're talking about the Queen of Snacks here, Thom," said Ben earnestly.

Thom just nodded. He'd seen Ben go through a whole pack of the nipple shaped treats with the creamy white filling and was sure he'd have gone for more if they had been available.

"I may as well bring us in near here," said Thom returning to business. He'd spotted a clearing and now headed for it. The clearing opened out onto a river bank and the readings for the surface they were landing on were good. The taxi settled gently onto firm ground. Thom did a final series of checks. The climate was ideal. Things were almost too good to be true.

Thom had a sudden thought and asked, "Why have I just flown us down here?" Clair was after all inhabiting the ship and it would have naturally fallen to her to pilot it.

There was no response from Clair and Thom and Ben immediately became concerned, looking at one another, Thom asked, "Clair? You OK?"

"It's..." said Clair in a wavering and uncertain voice.

"Clair? What's happening?" said Thom almost shouting. He wanted to run to Clair's aid, but there was nowhere to run to, but still he was almost running on the spot, he looked askance at Ben, "What shall I do?!" Ben shook his head, at a loss as to what could be said, let alone done.

"It's happening," said Clair simply and then it went very quiet. The animals, the birds and even the wind fell silent, there was only the babbling of the meandering river. Rivers never know when to shut up.

"Clair?" said Thom quietly, already knowing he wouldn't get a reply.

110

The Thing and The Other Thing looked out at as the planet slowly grew in their field of vision.

"She's here," said The Other Thing.

"Yes," said The Other Thing, "she *is* here."

The Other Thing looked at The Thing and then realised the meaning in what had been said, "well she better stop *being* here because she's coming home with us!"

The Thing looked sadly at The Other Thing and did the thing where he thought better of the response immediately presented to him and instead said, "Yes, dear." And with that they made their descent to the planet's surface.

Now that they were in relatively close proximity to their quarry, they could lock in to their quarry's location. This was made all the easier as their quarry was in the only functioning ship on the surface and Thom and Ben were distinctly different lifeforms to the birds and animals on this planet, and besides, their daughter was here. They had found her at last.

111

Hilary smiled and speculated that Bill thought he was being clever and probably thought he was following at a distance that meant he could go undetected. Silly boy! She thought, smiling to herself.

He'd been following her at a constant distance ever since she'd left OxCam. She knew about the tracking device, Dobbin had made a big song and dance about the tracking device and where it had crawled. Hilary had stifled a laugh as Dobbin told her about how the device had scuttled under him and onto his. It couldn't really miss his...

After some heated debate with Dobbin, she had chosen to leave it there. And Dobbin had had to wear it. Literally. So, Bill hadn't exactly come with her while she worked, but she was curious as to what he was up to and allowed him to tag along. Was he really just pining after her and looking for a chance to spend some time with her?

They'd travelled like this for some time, his ship shadowing hers. Dobbin moaning that he was very uncomfortable, not only with the device on his... but also with what she was doing. And at some point, she had spotted a ship ahead of hers that was taking a similar course. This was too much of a coincidence and so she surreptitiously scanned it to establish whether it was perhaps the cause of the anomaly. She already knew it wouldn't be, if someone had challenged her as to why that was so, she would not have an answer to hand – it just was.

And Dobbin did just that. But at least the ship ahead took some of his focus and attention and the moaning subsided to a background murmur.

So, Hilary was following the ship ahead at a discrete distance and it did not escape her that they may know of her presence. As it was The Thing and The Other Thing were oblivious to her presence and that of Bill's Ferrcati as they were totally focused on what lay ahead; their daughter.

Hilary was checking her course as well, in case the ship ahead moved away from where she needed to head, but this was the tried and tested navigational method of following the vehicle ahead because they looked like they knew where they were going. And that hadn't failed anyone yet, I mean if it had, then no one would continue adopting this trusty method.

112

What Hilary didn't have and what The Thing and The Other Thing didn't have was the current contact details of any of the people they were following. Bill did and Ben hadn't secured his settings sufficiently, so Bill was able, with a little black-market device, to track his friend via Ben's Find The Big Watch That Should Be On My Wrist app.

As they drew nearer to their objective, Bill was able to home in on Ben with the Ferrcati's instruments. The Ferrcati's instruments were coming up with errors all over the show, which was not supposed to even be a thing. Ferrcati's and errors were strangers. Bill didn't get embroiled in this though, if anything it added to the urgency of the matter and he knew what he must do. So, he did it.

* * *

Hilary did a double take as the sleek and majestic red hull of the Ferrcati shimmered and streaked past her and into

427

the distance. There was something stunning and utterly beautiful about that craft, more so when it was in motion. This gave Bill even more of an advantage as Hilary took some time to appreciate the beauty of the Ferrcati before gathering her wits and doing something about this surprise development.

* * *

The Thing and The Other Thing frowned out at the passing strobe of red that almost rocked their craft in its wake.

"What was that?" asked The Other Thing.

The Thing sighed inwardly, how was he supposed to know what that was? The Thing did not voice that thought and strangled his second thought at birth, describing what they had both seen; a streak of red, would end in an argument, "Looks like a very fast ship going somewhere in a hurry."

"Do you think…" started The Other Thing.

The Thing was voicing a similar thought as The Other Thing spoke, "Yes, I do. I think we should increase our speed and follow that streak of red" and The Thing's jaw was now set with a determination that wasn't there moments ago.

The Thing missed the fleeting look of love and admiration that passed over The Other Thing's face as she saw The Jaw. The Other Thing had a thing for The Thing's The Jaw.

113

Back on the New Planet, New Planet being one of those holding names that have to be used in lieu of anyone deciding upon a given name and hopefully someone will step up to the plate and provide a suitable and acceptable name as it is bad enough that the fifth most popular name for dogs is The Dog, whereas the twenty second most popular name for cats is The Cat. This may say something about cat and dog owners, but before you go jumping to conclusions, you should probably know that the thirty forth most popular name for dogs is That Bastard Dog, whereas the nineteenth most popular cats name is The Bastard Cat. Thankfully there are very few adults known as The Baby, so there was hope for the New Planet yet.

Hope. Hope was fading as far as Thom was concerned. The silence around him drew out and seemed to suck the life out of him. It was as if he could feel Clair draining away and with her a part of him was falling away from him. Thom could feel himself being emptied even as the ship around him bled away Clair's presence. This was as close to dying that Thom would get for a very long time, which had Thom known this, could have been a silver-lining, but he wouldn't see it that way right now, however cheerfully you presented it to him. In fact, he'd probably get very angry and the threat of violence would certainly arise. So best leave him to it. He was in one of those moods. Best left well alone...

The absence of sound grew and grew, creating an unbearable crescendo of noise that was having a profound effect on both Thom and Ben. They were racked with a terrible sense of loss and they were losing more and more as each drawn out second past. It wasn't just Clair slipping away from them, she had become a part of them as we all do as we touch each other's lives. It was more than that though, she was the sand in all the nooks and crannies and as she trickled away, she took something of them. Even as they experienced this loss, they became heavy and their minds languished in the enormity of this experience, thought after thought firing off to expand the loss.

Things would never be the same again.

* * *

Boom! A boom that had a snap! and a crack! to accompanying it. And suddenly there, hovering over them was a red shimmering and utterly splendid Ferrcati.

HUZZAH!

AND HURRAH!

Aren't Ferrcatis utterly fabulous!?

Thom and Ben's spell wasn't exactly broken, but this was a brilliantly red and sleek distraction and after a pause to appreciate the beautiful red thing that had materialised unexpectedly in the New Planet, the wind murmured and susurrated in the trees at a discrete distance and this prompted the birds to sing unobtrusive and pleasant songs before getting on with the business of mating and all of the song and dance that that entailed. The animals moved on, slithering and slinking and trying not to be eaten by each other and in particular, avoiding being the Vest's next snack, whilst also sorting out a thoroughly good session of mating.

"Bill?" Ben said quietly as he stepped out of the taxi and into the open and looked up at the hovering Ferrcati, for who else could it be other than Bill? The answer to that one was it could have been any one of the other four hundred and twenty six owners of this particular model of Ferrcati and why did it not occur to Ben, even for a moment that this may well be the owner of New Planet and that they were so disgustingly rich that they had had a planet made – how they ever got planning permission is another matter and one not to be looked into too closely, unless you want to inexplicably disappear. Because people who can afford to have planets made probably don't want to be asked about planning permission and will just as easily have you disappeared than bother answering your impertinent questions. Anyway, if this was the owner of New Planet, then Ben and Thom were trespassing and their problems had just gotten worse.

"Ben!" said Bill's amplified voice from the Ferrcati, "just the man! Step back a mo'. I need to land this crate!"

Ben stepped back and the Ferrcati lowered itself gracefully and elegantly to the surface of New Planet. Ben waited for his friend to emerge from the side of the gorgeous craft, the door slid open and a breathless Bill stepped out, his trademark red balloon bouncing for a moment on the top of the open doorway and then rising up into the New Planet's atmosphere and coming to rest at the end of its string. Why Bill was breathless is one of life's mysteries, it is not a narrative embellishment that author's use, it's a real-life phenomenon, at matters of true import, the deliverer of a message significant to the proceedings will always be out of breath, perhaps the message itself is utterly exhausting to the human frame. Even if this particular human frame was dead.

"You've... been...," said Bill trying to catch his breath, Ben was nodding expectantly, urging his friend to complete the sentence and deliver the message, "followed."

"Oh," said Ben at this news, then he caught on, "oh that! Yes, the Warmongerians who are now the Bluecoatians, they caught up with us, or rather we caught up with them. Cracking lot. I'm seeing one of them!"

Bill looked at Ben and wondered what he was on about, "No mate, not them, they're the least of your worries. There's the, erm... Auditor... the one I told you about? And I don't think it's good when anyone gets on the wrong side of her. Her right side, that's a different matter..."

"You old dog!" exclaimed Ben as he noted Bill's exaggerated crotch thrusts as he talked about the Auditor's right side."

Bill grinned, "Took one there for the team, Ben. Then I took a few more for me!"

They high fived, "Good man!" congratulated Ben.

"But I told you all about this already, Ben. What's going on?" Bill stepped sideways and looked into Ben and Thom's ship, "what's wrong with Thom?"

Ben turned to see that Thom had slumped in the nearest

seat and was doing the words *distraught* and *stricken* full justice. Ben turned back to Bill and didn't know exactly what to say, Bill's entrance had provided a brief moment away from the horrible reality of what had happened, but putting it into words was difficult, it would make it all the more real if it was spoken out loud.

Thom looked up, "She's gone," he said this with such simplicity and severity that it created a small wave of the sadness that had preceded it and this affected Bill profoundly. Bill didn't do things like sad but he had no choice as this swept over him. And he noticed the pronounced absence of Clair. Not that she wasn't here, but that there was a distinct lack of her, a hole where once she had been. It was overwhelmingly sad.

And then there was more distraction as the noise of another descending ship broke in upon this moment.

114

A grey slab sided, utilitarian ship descended and parked next to Bill's Ferrcati. It had no place being anywhere near such a work of art and generally detracted from its surroundings.

It looked like it been made from breezeblocks. Badly.

"Looks like a Vogon vessel, only much smaller," muttered Bill.

"Shhh!" hissed Ben.

A door on the side of the ugly ship clunked clumsily open and Ben could see nothing happen beyond this. Bill however groaned and said something disparaging under his breath, Ben thought he caught …as ugly as their ship… Ben nudged Bill and asked him what was going on.

"Wait here," said Bill and he jogged into his Ferrcati and was only gone a matter of moments before returning with a couple of drinks. He handed one to Ben, "best drink this, mate."

Ben looked at the drink and then Bill. Always one for a drink, he thought this was perhaps not the time though.

"Here, take these too," said Bill handing Ben some pills.

Ben looked at the contents of his palm and then the drink

and then Bill.

Bill looked back at him meaningfully, "Just do it!"

Ben didn't need to be told again, so he lobbed the pills into his mouth, swilled a mouthful of drink in his mouth and then swallowed drink and pills down.

Bill pointed at the open doorway of the newly landed and decidedly ugly ship and something drifted into Ben's vision. Something as ugly as the ship. No, more ugly. Thankfully it drifted back out of Ben's vision and gave him a moment of respite before drifting back into his vision. This drifting in and out occurred for the next minute or two and made Ben feel a bit nauseous. The nausea did not dissipate once the drifting ceased, the pills and booze did their work and Ben could see the two forms slowly and tentatively emerge from their ship.

"Looks like they can see us," said The Thing.

"Good," replied The Other Thing.

"But they shouldn't be able to see us!" protested The Thing.

"Never mind that!" said The Other Thing dismissively, and stepped forward to demand, "Where's our daughter!?"

This was the point Ben and Bill would have looked at each other and said "Daughter?!" and wondered what the hell this hideous pan-dimensional apparition was on about. Naturally not making the pan-dimensional connection as that would bely a limited and bigoted world view.

* * *

However, at this precise moment another ship was performing its descent. This ship was discrete and just a bit sporty. Not fun exactly, but well-made and capable of a turn of speed and you just knew it would handle well. As you watched it though, it had the occasional moment when it seemed to be something else. Just a flash of a moment. And there was the impression of faraway stars that no one in the universes had ever set eyes upon. Just before it landed there was the distinct sound of a whiny.

Dobbin looked sullenly towards the Ferrcati and snorted. Then he expelled the tracking device that had been bugging him. It landed with a tiny plop into the midst of the river.

Ben and Bill looked up at the new arrival, an instinctive act that had the added bonus of not having to look at The Thing and The Other Thing. The Thing and The Other Thing were also looking up. All four of the by-standers were hoping this was the last of the arrivals as this could get tiresome rather quickly.

"Hilary!" said Bill brightly as her craft kicked up some dirt (and snorted haughtily), her craft landing with a slight thud (and a kick). The door of her craft banged open, "Oh, this doesn't look good. She's looking feisty" said Bill quietly.

"BILL! HAVE YOU BEEN DECEIVING ME?" asked the Auditor.

Bill and Ben's teeth rattled as the Auditor spoke and Bill let go of his balloon which floated slowly onwards and upwards.

"Hilary, it isn't at all like that..." began Bill as the Auditor stomped towards him.

"And who are you?" demanded The Other Thing, stepping into the Auditor's path, hands on hips.

"Oh, this isn't good," whispered Ben.

And it wasn't. Anger and frustration didn't need to flare

436

up, they were deployed. By two pan-dimensional beings. There was much noise and teeth rattled and rattled and if something wasn't done, teeth would be reduced to chalk.

Ben looked behind him. At some point, the utterly devasted Thom had closed the door to the taxi and was no doubt listening to The Smiths while he painted the walls and ceiling black. Ben turned back and noticed Bill nod at The Thing and raise his eyebrows. The Thing gave the minutest of shrugs. Bill tilted his head towards the Ferrcati. The Thing did not need any further invitation. Ben's eyebrows rose up into his hairline. Ben was sociable, but Bill was off the scale.

Ben followed Bill and The Thing and the three of them quietly stepped into the Ferrcati, not that quiet was needed when there was that level of rib-rumbling noise going on, but no one wanted the argument to be directed at them. Best not get involved and retire a suitable distance, so they avoided any stray shots or shrapnel.

Bill pressed a button on the console of the ship and the door whispered shut and with it came a blessed and pleasant level of sound – some unobtrusive mood music was already doing its thing in the background to ensure the background was deeply pleasing.

Bill walked around the console and produced six drinks. He handed out two and left the others close to hand. Ben and The Thing nodded their appreciation and took a good draught of their drinks. They shared a silence. Sharing a silence is a welcome and beautiful thing at times like these.

Then they had a conversation that began with small talk, but moved on to the matters in hand. The second drink came in quite handy and Ben found that during their conversation, The Thing became a little easier on the eye, which was just as well as he had been sick in his mouth a couple of times already since meeting The Thing and The Other Thing and could be doing without his afternoon being punctuated with further convulsions and bad tastes in his mouth.

"Another?" asked Bill in that way that is very much rhetorical, especially when the other is being placed into the recipient's hands.

With fresh drinks in their hands they gravitated towards the Ferrcati's front screen from where they could see out to The Other Thing and the Auditor. None of them said a thing, but from the body language and facial expressions they were observing, much of the heat of the exchange between the Other Thing and the Auditor had dissipated. Bill could see more of Hilary and less of the Auditor and this led him to distracting thoughts which meant he wasn't contributing to as much of the conversation in the Ferrcati.

Eventually, they all looked down at their empty glasses and took a brief stock of the empty glasses strewn across the surfaces around them. They'd had more than three drinks.

The Other Thing and the Auditor were nodding quite a bit now and looking across at the Ferrcati and the taxi.

"I think we should go out and see them now," said Ben with a degree of uncertainty in his voice. He looked at Bill and The Thing and neither of them were showing signs of moving.

Then a movement caught his eye.

"Shit! What's he doing!" exclaimed Bill.

Thom was walking straight up to The Other Thing and the Auditor.

115

Thom had sat there for a long while. Not moving. Not actively thinking. Unbidden, thoughts entered his consciousness and jabbed and poked at him. He shuddered and stifled sobs and sighs. He was drained, the stuffing had been ripped from him and yet he was this broken thing filled with activity. The things that moved within him made him feel worse and he couldn't stop it. He was in a hole. He was floating in nothingness and he was a part of that nothingness. When he consciously formed a thought, it was just one word but each time the word was uttered it conveyed another aspect of the pain he was staring into; Clair.

Clair.

He'd known there were risks. There had been risks from the very first moment he'd met Clair, but as they had gone further and further on in their journey it had started to feel like they were going somewhere that they were invincible and that it was inevitable that they would arrive at journey's end and then the hard bit would be that they would have Choices.

Now any prospect of a choice had been stolen from them.

Clair had been stolen from them. And nothing mattered any more. Nothing.

He didn't know how long he sat sprawled in the chair. He was numb. Inside and out. Something imperceptible was changing though. Where things had got exponentially worse and yawned out into a bleak darkness there was the hint of something else. A tiny blink of light in the periphery. It wasn't in the scheme of things much and was and would always be eclipsed by what had just happened, but somewhere within, or without, Thom found the strength to unfurl and stand up. A quiet voice was telling him that he couldn't just sit there and do nothing. And as he stood up the voice was reminding him that after all, this had to mean something. This whole journey. And Clair.

And there was this planet. They were here for a reason. He was here for a reason. Clair had brought him to this planet. For a reason.

Something quietly sang inside him. And he heard it.

So, he opened the door and approached The Other Thing and the Auditor.

After all, they were guests on his planet.

116

The Other Thing stopped mid-sentence and turned. The Auditor followed suit.

A man was walking towards them with a confident stride and a sense of purpose.

"Hello!" he said cheerily, which wrongfooted all three of them, but not enough to stop the Auditor completely.

"AND WHO? ARE YOU?" demanded the Auditor.

Despite the teeth rattling, rib rumbling and head pain, Thom continued undaunted, "I'm Thom," he said and he waved an open hand around him, "and this is my planet."

"Our planet," added Ben, who having spotted Thom and his foolhardy venture, had run out of the Ferrcati to join his best friend in this potentially life ending venture. Bill and The Thing were bringing up the rear in a more cautious manner.

"How can you even see us?" asked The Other Thing.

Ben beamed at The Other Thing in the way only a very inebriated person can, the effort of beaming nearly sent him sideways, "Drink!" he pronounced, "but I'm not sure about Thom." He added, thumbing at Thom to emphasise his point.

"I think it's an after effect of Clair," said Thom quietly.

"Clair?" asked The Other Thing.

The Auditor saw how miserable Thom looked and consciously dialled things down, "Clair is the anomaly isn't she?"

Thom looked at her and then The Other Thing, "If you mean the reason you've been following us, yes."

"Where is she?" asked The Other Thing quietly, fearing the question.

"Gone," said Thom simply.

"Gone?!" repeated The Thing from behind Thom. He stepped forward so he was with The Other Thing, "Gone?!"

"Yes, we landed here and she just slipped out of the ship and was gone," said Thom forlornly.

"She can't just go," said The Other Thing.

"That's what I thought, but she did."

"No, you don't understand," said The Thing, "she can't just disappear. It's a simple matter of the laws of existence, even for us pan-dimensional types." He looked askance at the Auditor and she nodded.

"Besides," said the Auditor, "the anomaly, sorry, Clair..."

"Our daughter!" cut in The Other Thing.

"Yes, sorry," continued the Auditor, or more precisely, Hilary, "she's here."

Thom looked puzzled, "She's here?"

Ben was also puzzled, "Your daughter?"

"Yes," said The Thing, "I told you. We are looking for our daughter."

"Yes, sorry, I didn't put two and two together – I mean... she doesn't exactly look like you two!" said Ben.

"And what's that supposed to mean?" asked The Other Thing sharply.

"Oh," said Ben reigning things in, "well she didn't really

look like anything. Except maybe the chair she was when Thom first met her and fell for her."

The Thing and The Other Thing looked at each other and then at Thom.

Ben carried on oblivious, "and then she was in Thom. And a few other things including that," he said pointing at the taxi behind him, "but she was in Thom. A lot."

Thom coughed, "Ben!"

"Oh, yes," said Ben looking sheepish, "probably not the best conversation to have when you've only just met your in-laws!"

"She's only 16,000 years old!!" cried The Other Thing, "what were you thinking?!"

"Erm, I wasn't really thinking, it's all just happened," shrugged Thom trying to defend himself, "And I'm 39, so..."

"That's not the point!" said The Other Thing, "you should not be canoodling with my daughter!"

"Me and your daughter were very much in love, Mrs... erm...?" said Thom realising that he didn't know Clair's parents' names. This wasn't going at all well.

"Mrs? Mrs!" exclaimed The Other Thing, "I'm a Mr!"

"Oh," said Thom. This was going even less well than it was just moments before.

"Go easy on the lad," said The Thing taking pity on Thom, "they're good people. I was talking to these other two just now and they're... well they're good people."

"Good people?" said The Other Thing rounding on The Thing, "you don't even know their names!"

"Well... I..." said The Thing realising The Other Thing was right, he didn't know their names. They'd all been busy getting along and drinking, names at that point were a bit superfluous.

"Bill," said Bill stepping forward and grabbing The Other Thing's hand, and shaking it.

The Other Thing looked down at what was happening to its hand and looked a bit harder until Bill got the message and stopped shaking The Other Thing's hand and disengaged, stepping back a step by way of a bit of deference and decorum.

"And this is my good friend Ben, and you've met Thom," Bill smiled at Hilary, "and this is the lovely Hilary, who I hope will forgive me for wanting to get to my friends first as I wanted to avoid any misunderstandings or unpleasantness." He shrugged in a self-deprecating manner, "looks like I've made a total hash of that and arrived at a bad time to boot."

Hilary thawed. Just a bit. She wasn't going to make it too easy for Bill though.

There was a sudden bark which made everyone other than Bill jump.

"Ah! Anita! Sleeping beauty arises!" he turned and leant down, "come on then girl!"

Anita wagged her tail warily and trotted towards Bill, she had in her teeth one of Bill's red balloons and she dutifully brought it over to him, he caught it deftly as she let it go under his hand, but instead of stopping at his heel as she had always done, especially in company, she went past Bill. Bill watched the slow and deliberate progress of Anita finding himself willing her towards Hilary so his dog would help win her over. But no, Anita went straight to The Other Thing.

The Other Thing looked at this peculiar creature. Very peculiar for a dog, and not helped by the hair cut she sported, the gaudy silken jacket and the glittering hat atop her head that had somehow stayed in place during her long sleep. Anita looked up at The Other Thing. Bill was not the only one to worry that things were about to go a bit wrong. This was the bit where Anita growled and then went for The Other Thing. Bill couldn't blame her for that really, and that was maybe why he wasn't calling her off and instead waiting to see what would happen next. A dark and deep part of him was wondering what would happen when a zombie clown dog bit a pan-dimensional being.

Anita's tail twitched. Then it whipped in one direction, stayed there. Had a think about what next. Whipped in the other direction. Then it started wagging and as it did, Anita's head tilted to one side, she raised her eye brows and let her tongue loll out in as endearing manner as Bill had ever seen.

The Other Thing stood there looking at Anita and a strange thing happened. She melted.

Now when people melt, it's that thawing that is seen to occur in someone who was not just angry in a red-hot way, but beyond that. They're heart is ice and they are hard edged. And then something left of field happens and the ice is melted and they become a lovely, warm hearted person. The Other Thing visibly changed. She became easier on the eye. And in sympathy with The Other Thing, so did The Thing.

"Aww!" said The Other Thing, "what have we got here!?" and she bent down and gave Anita a fuss. And then some more fuss and somehow, the fuss got pretty full-on with The Other Thing flat out on the ground and Anita climbing all over her licking her face and ears.

"That's Belinda," said The Thing, slightly uncomfortable at the mildly undignified display his spouse was putting on, or perhaps slightly uncomfortable because he wanted to join in, but wasn't sure what the form was there, so was going through an inner struggle, "and I'm Terry."

"Pleased to meet you," said Thom nodding to Terry in preference to a handshake.

"Likewise," said Terry, glancing down at a giggling Belinda.

"Funny, we met a Terry on our travels," began Ben.

"And that Terry was also a very good sort, wasn't he?" said Thom very deliberately in an attempt to head things off at the pass because he was sure there was likely an unsavoury story on the horizon, but just to make sure he carried on, "You said Clair was here?"

117

"Yes well, she's called Denise, actually," said Terry, "but I think Clair suits her just as well."

"And she's here," said Hilary, "do you mind telling me why she's here Terry and just what she's been up to?"

Terry looked a bit shifty as he attempted to form a reply, "well you can't keep your eyes on them all the time, can you? One minute she's there, the next she's hopped off gods knows where."

"How long ago was this?" asked Hilary.

"Oh, I suppose a hundred years ago now."

Ben and Thom looked at each other, "A hundred years?" asked Thom.

"Yes, no time at all really," Terry said shrugging.

"But here, it's more than a life span," said Thom.

Medical science was a progressive science and as a result, over the centuries lifespans had increased. This was seen as progress, especially by statisticians and politicians. Then one day, a sensible person woke up to this, logically concluding that if statisticians *and* politicians thought something was good then it most definitely was not. This was alongside the growing unease that many had at the prospect of their last one hundred and fifty years of life being that of an increasingly desiccated walnut living in a jumble of memories made in the first thirty years of their lives. Living on a paltry pension that meant that all you could afford were nutrition tablets and staying indoors at home watching daytime freeview.

Eventually, a clever kid of thirty six came up with a way to download more than the thirty years of memories that were available to the organic version of you, and instead you could reboot yourself in an electronic format and enjoy a cyber after life when you reached the point of desiccation around the century mark of your existence.

This was seen as a better form of progress, especially as it meant earlier retirement and a last hurrah before Download Day. There were of course certain factions who were aghast at this selling of one's soul and this included the Trumpians who believed in a lucrative form of reincarnation. How could you be reincarnated if your soul was trapped in electronic limbo? So, they built a wall to protect them from this heresy and wore strange wigs to shield their minds from the degenerate download rays.

"Yes," acknowledged Hilary, "time moves differently here. And there are rules. Your daughter seems to have been flouting lots of those rules, Terry."

"Has she?" asked Terry earnestly.

"Well, I…" started Hilary, "there have been disturbances and anomalies and things have been disrupted."

"Surely that's the same for all of us to one extent or another," said Ben, "after all, we all manipulate our environment and as we make our way through the universes things are changed. Butterflies flapping their wings are the worst of it though, aren't they? Nonchalantly flapping their wings and causing natural disasters!"

Hilary wasn't expecting that, not least from Ben. No one was expecting that, so it went a bit quiet.

"What harm has Clair done?" asked Thom, "what harm did she do?" he added quietly, not at all convinced she was still with them.

"Harm?" asked Hilary, "that's not the point!"

"What is the point then?" asked Terry.

No one was meaning to, but Hilary was feeling a bit cornered and ganged up on and it showed. Bill intervened, "Hey guys, Hilary was just doing her job. And you have to admit that Clair was pretty unusual. Sorry, *is* Thom, if these guys say she's here, then I'm inclined to accept that from them. Anyway, can anyone think of a problem that Clair caused or something that they are not comfortable with?"

Everyone assumed thinking poses, these are similar to catalogue poses such as *stare at imaginary mountain*. Although catalogue poses can branch out slightly and you can point at the imaginary mountain and you can go for heroic poses, but never quite attain them, because after all is said and done, you are posing for a catalogue and heroes don't do that. Even between quests when funds are running exceedingly low.

"She did a lot of good actually," concluded Thom.

Hilary bristled and wanted to say; you can't go around doing a lot of good! But Bill intuitively gave her a look and took her hand and squeezed it. Now wasn't the time.

"She did kill that HR robot," ventured Ben and Thom gave him a *why did you have to say that?* Look.

"She killed an HR robot?" asked Bill, "why did she do that?"

Thom answered, hoping he could provide some damage

limitation, "she tried to help it, and it turned out that it wasn't just a robot, the HR part of it had taken on a life of its own. And some people won't be helped, so when given the choice of accepting help or topping itself? It chose death. So actually, she didn't kill it, it killed itself."

"HR robot, you say" said Hilary, cogs whirring, "I went past a planet known as HR13, would that be related?"

"Yes, that's the same HR. We went past that planet too," said Ben.

"You didn't land there or try to do anything about it?" asked Hilary.

"No, we generally tried to stay out of trouble and stick to our course," said Thom, he was picking up Hilary's interest in that planet.

"Hmm, there was something not right on that planet," said Hilary looking decidedly uncomfortable.

"Well yes, it's HR," said Ben, "there's something very wrong about HR. And its growing and getting worse. Something needs to be done about it."

"Yes," said Hilary absently, "yes it does."

118

Now was his moment! Alan the Bastard had bided his time. Something that was alien to him. And biding his time had meant bottling up even more of his rage and distilling it. Alan was filled with rage and then some. And here were these interlopers right before him. They were in the way. They had no right to be here. They would pay and they would pay heavily for their folly!

Grrrrrr! Was the salient thought in Alan's mind. Alan's sight was similar to a dog's sight in that he saw in monochrome, but his monochrome was coated red. Alan saw red in all its violent and angry hues.

Hate! Anger! He wanted to hurt these people!

And if anyone had asked him why he wanted to hurt these people? Why he was so full of this irrational rage?

He'd have hurt them too!

Alan's sole purpose in life was to be a receptacle for hate and to inject this hate into others. Some spread the word. Alan spread the hate.

Wherever he saw people laughing and enjoying a moment? He just wanted to gate crash the party and send them running. He wanted to vanquish his enemies and rejoice in their pitiful lamentations.

He flew nearer, circling his prey. He allowed a hateful smirk to play across his acidic face and then he dove in with everything he had. Yes! He was going to ruin this merry little party!

Laughing insanely, he attacked with a ferocity only the mad can deploy.

"Ow!" cried Bill as a sharp pain sprung out on his neck, and instinctively he slapped at the area that had suddenly experienced a stinging sensation.

The giant hand of his foe smote Alan. Twas just a glancing blow that stunned him for a moment though. He fell to the ground, but he was made of sterner stuff. Hate mostly. He landed on his back, but he was not winded. He attempted to get up so that he might smite his enemy thrice more and then thrice more again.

However, an ominous shadow crept over him and he looked up to see many, many, yellow and terrible teeth.

"Oh, shi…" were Alan the Bastard's last words as Anita spotted the tasty yellow and black morsel on the ground and swiftly gobbled it up. Anita's teeth made short work of the angry body of the wasp and Alan wasn't able to get a sting in. So, he died without getting a final sting in and his entry to Wasp Valhalla was barred. Instead he was destined to an eternity of buzzing around the gates to Wasp Valhalla and becoming increasingly angry.

If Alan the Bastard had played the longer game and had a family before embarking on his solo campaign of terror his legacy would have been a colony of wasps on Planet Clair, instead Planet Clair had on that very day become a wasp free planet and was all the more pleasant for it.

119

Belinda got to her feet and brushed the dust and dirt off her hands, breathing heavily after her protracted wrestling session, she joined the group with Anita falling in at her heel after her wasp snack. Bill gave Anita a sharp look which said *traitor!*

"Right, shall we have a word with Denise then?" said Belinda.

Terry nodded, "I suppose we should really."

Belinda put her hands on her hips and stood in a business-like pose, "I think you had better come out now, my girl!"

"*I wasn't hiding!*" said Clair in a meek voice.

Thom nearly punched the air, his sense of relief dizzied him. They had been right, Clair was still here!

"You're OK, Clair" he blurted out, "what happened!?"

Belinda looked very affronted, she was having a word with her daughter and this whipper-snapper was interrupting. No one who knew what was good for them would even think about interrupting Belinda in full flow. Terry stepped in and smiled at Belinda, he didn't say anything but the smile conveyed all the meaning necessary, they'd found their daughter and she was OK. Let them have a moment, we'll have ours.

"It took all of my focus, Thom," said Clair.

"What did? What took all of your focus?"

"Moving into my new home," replied Clair.

Thom was baffled. Belinda was not, "Now young lady, what is all of this talk of a new home? You're coming back with us before you put down any of those Gaia roots!"

"Sorry Dad, it's a bit late for that..." said Clair quietly.

Belinda stifled a sob, "Oh Denise! You could have at least waited and talked to us about it!"

"I couldn't Dad. Once we were here it all just sort of happened."

"Happened?" asked Hilary, "As in Destiny?"

"Yes, I suppose it was," agreed Clair.

"So, you're not responsible for this planet being here?" continued Hilary.

"Well, I must be because the planet and I are one and the same."

"But you didn't plan this and you didn't put the planet here. Because you didn't know where you were going and what was at your journey's end?" said Hilary, putting to bed most of her concerns about the anomaly that happened to be called Clair, or Denise.

"Yes, I was drawn here. I just knew we had to come here."

"We?" said Belinda.

"We," confirmed Clair, *"me, Thom and Ben. I think there is also reason for you all being here too."*

"Well yes, we're your bloody parents and you've been a very naughty girl!" admonished Belinda.

"Now, now, dear," said Terry, "She's old enough to know her own mind and if she wants to be the soul of this planet there isn't much we can do about that is there? So, I think we should support her and give her and these young men our blessing."

Belinda looked at Terry. She was clenching and unclenching her fists and shuffling about. Belinda didn't like not being in control of this situation, but what was really getting to Belinda was that Denise wasn't their little girl anymore. She was 16,000 years old and she'd grown up so quickly. Where did the years go? Belinda calmed a little and nodded at Terry. Terry was right. Terry was right quite a lot of the time. Belinda wasn't going to say that out loud though, some things are best kept in your back pocket.

"There's more reason than you being my parents, Dad. That is obviously really important to me and always will be, I love you to the worlds and back. But there is some purpose to all of this. These things have happened and are happening for a reason."

Ben giggled.

Thom looked at Ben wondering what he could possibly be giggling at. Ben pointed at Anita who was mid-flow with a particularly long wee. Thom looked back at Ben quizzically and Ben mouthed, "she's doing a wee on your girlfriend."

Thom shook his head at the absurdity of his friend and at the absurdity of the whole situation and maybe it was the relief of knowing Clair was OK, but he burst out laughing. Ben joined in. And they laughed until it hurt while the others looked on, bemused by this outburst.

120

Ben and Thom were doubled up and beginning their recovery, stifling the resurgence of another laughing fit with occasional Whews and Ahhs. As they straightened up, Thom patted his mate's back.

"Thanks Ben, I needed that."

"I think we all did," said Ben looking around the group, not noticing the consternation on their faces and that they hadn't joined in with the laughter. That selectiveness was one of Ben's gifts.

And speaking of gifts...

"Now we're all here, there's a couple of things I have to do," said Clair.

There was a crunching, wrenching and sproinging sound that morphed into something liquid behind them and as they all turned towards where the sounds were coming from, they saw the taxi expanding. As it grew in size it took on different lines and its colouring lit up and became a living thing, a moving, almost liquid silver. Even as the expansion and changes slowed and then came to a halt the flanks of the newly created ship rippled like a thoroughbred's muscles.

"Wow!" sighed Bill, and he knew his vehicles. The new

craft put his Ferrcati in the shade, and until this very moment the only thing that could have even begun to do that was the latest model of Ferrcati. And that was still on a drawing board and hadn't made it to the modelling stage yet.

"That's some ride!" said Ben.

"Thanks, it's ours. It should come in handy," said Clair.

Dobbin had had enough. This was taking the proverbial. He wasn't going to go full horse, but at the very least he was going to slip into his more comfortable outer skin. And so he did. And now, if you looked at Hilary's sporty little number, you were looking out into infinity and beyond.

Hilary shuffled uncomfortably, "Strictly speaking, you shouldn't have done that." She was speaking to both Clair and Dobbin and they both knew it.

"I've not finished," said Clair, *"this is all part of the end of this part of our journey. We've arrived at journey's end and I am more than I was. I've grown throughout the journey – and now I have a form and purpose. The same was always intended for these two."*

And with no pause or delay, a spectrum of light emerged from out of the ground under the feet of both Ben and Thom. They looked down at this unexpected development and were rooted to the spot as the light ever so gradually crept upwards along their legs. As the light reached the top of their legs, Ben provided a moment of light relief to a momentous occasion; "it tickles!" There was no doubt as to what was tickling as it was currently being illuminated by this incredible glowing and pulsing light. The pulsing was a bit much now that Ben had drawn everyone's focus to his nether regions.

The light continued ever upwards, gradually covering their bodies, Ben and Thom seemed to grow in stature.

The light pulsed in time with their heartbeats and as it totally consumed them it solidified and hid them both in illuminated cocoons.

Inside the cocoons, the duo were strangely calm. Serene. They had an enormous sense of wellbeing and an energy coursing through their bodies. There was no feeling of claustrophobia. Their senses were heightened, and they could see out and through the cocoon's casing perfectly well.

Outside the cocoons, those witnessing this spectacle were awestruck and not at all concerned that Thom and Ben may be in any sort of danger. If they were to be asked why they had made this assessment of this never before seen process, they wouldn't have had an answer, or rather they would, but saying it was totally awesome wouldn't seem to cut it. It was however, really, totally awesome and a sight that would live with them all, even the too cool for the universes school, pan dimensionals.

The light around Ben and Thom shimmered, trembled and there were three big pulses. On the third, the light was drawn inwards and became a part of its host. The cocoons were gone, their work now done.

Ben and Thom flexed their muscles, shook themselves and conducted an impromptu limbering session. They both looked bigger, stronger, fitter, and they shone. They felt invigorated, fresh and renewed. Buzzing with an energy they'd never experienced before.

There was something child-like about the state they were now in. It was simple. They felt good. They were happy. More comfortable in their skins than they had ever been. And they felt playful. They had finally grown up and in so doing they had remembered that part of themselves that should always, always be celebrated and expressed; their inner child.

Not that they hadn't been doing a pretty good job on this front already.

Bill stepped up to Ben, "What just happened?"

"I dunno, but I feel *really* good!" said Ben and he jumped in the air.

Bill watched Ben's progress and kept watching until he strained his neck tracking his friend's jump. This was an impressive jump and Ben seemed to be following the flight path of Bill's discarded balloon. Soon, all that could be seen of Ben was a small, black dot. Bill stepped back as he realised the small dot that was Ben was increasing in size, he was making his way back down to earth. From that sort of height, Bill was expecting a clumsy, messy and unfortunate landing. Ben was accelerating groundward and this was beginning to look bone shatteringly tragic. Bill stumbled back further as Ben sped towards an impact with the ground. Six inches from the ground Ben's descent slewed to a halt and he gracefully and gradually returned to terra firma. And yet he didn't.

Bill looked curiously at Ben's feet. So curious was he that he bent sideways so his eyes were closer to the ground. He was transfixed. Anita sauntered up and sniffed at the minute gap between Ben's feet and the ground. Bill looked at Thom's feet. Same thing.

"Guys? Look at your feet," he said.

Ben and Thom looked at their feet. Thom looked back up, "Yes?"

"They're not actually on the ground..."

Ben lifted his foot up and put it back down, "Really?"

"Really."

He lifted his other foot up and put it back down, "Looks like they're on the ground to me!"

Bill was getting a tad frustrated, "OK, never mind that for now. Have you seen your face, Ben?"

It had been niggling Bill as to what was different about Ben's face. Always a tricky one, was it a new haircut, facial hair, spectacles, eye brows shaved off. No, not in this case. He was different. He looked different. And dammit if he didn't look really good!

Ben was curious, so he walked out over to the river to see his reflection. He peered into the water's surface and his rippling and flowing reflection peered back. He touched the surface of the water, then he touched his face, drawing a wet finger down his cheek. "Wow!" he said, smiling at his reflected self. During the transformation, his make-up had melded with his face and the effect was, in Ben's opinion, bloody good! It also looked permanent which was a bonus – no more faffing with reapplication after reapplication of slap.

Ben turned to Bill and the others and smiled, pointing at his face.

Everyone was staring, Bill pointed at Ben's feet again.

"Oh that, again!" said Ben in mock frustration and he lifted a foot before looking down, "Look…" and he stopped mid admonishment, "Oh…" he was part way out over the river and his feet were completely dry. He gingerly put his foot back down and expected to overbalance and get himself very wet. When that didn't happen, he walked awkwardly and self-consciously back to terra firma.

He smiled at Thom and whispered, "awesome!" It was that

awesome that it had reduced Ben to a whisper.

Thom was wide-eyed and overwhelmed. He knew he was now remarkably different and that what Ben had just done was only the tip of the iceberg. Ben was Ben and he'd gotten on with it, like he always seemed to. If anything, watching Ben show off his new self had left Thom even more daunted by his transformation, almost paralysed.

What have you done? he thought at Clair.

Clair spoke out loud, so everyone could hear, *"Really, I didn't do anything. This is the fulfilment of our journey. It's our destiny. And it's just the beginning for us. We have a lot of work to do!"*

This sparked a host of questions from everyone and there would be many conversations that went long into the night and beyond. Hilary asked the first one, "But no more anomalous shenanigans though, right?"

"Probably not, no." Clair said with enough of a hint in those few words that there might be. If needed. She was very much feeling her way here.

Hilary was about to speak again, but Bill headed this off. Now was not the time. He put a finger to her lips and whispered something about an urgent appointment she was late for. In his bed. With that he took her hand and led her away to attend to some urgent business, leaving everyone else to talk about what had happened and what the future may hold.

One thing was certain, it was to be a completely different future to the one that Thom and Ben had broken away from when they hatched their hair-brained scheme to fill the Micra with garbage and escape the monotony and drudgery of their previous lives.

121

A nd that was the story of the very start. Of how Planet Clair came to be. And of how Thom and Ben found a very fulfilling and long career as sometime caretakers and maintenance men of the universes and sometimes places other than the universes.

I would like to say that after a good weekend of socialising and getting to know the new in-laws and Bill's new girlfriend, Hilary brought up the thorny subject of HR13 and Thom and Ben set about sorting that particular problem with gusto, but we all know how that one ends don't we?

There were many adventures though and among them there was the inevitable visit to Bigtopia where Ben discovered a slightly lost tribe of zombie clowns that he thought he had an affinity with, until he discovered what they did in their spare time. Then there was the planet of Nubia with the large and attractive moon Lesbos. Getting Ben to leave that place took a gargantuan effort. When Ben would not leave, Bill tried to help out. Getting Ben and Bill to leave was nigh on impossible.

But of course, there was the whole business with The Awakening and even now there was a fleet of zealots who had heard of the appearance of the new planet and now that the prophesy had been fulfilled they were making their way to their new world. A world that wasn't theirs. Just because they knew a story about it, wouldn't change this fact. But would they be told? Of course not. Because they had belief and faith and did not see for one moment that they were attempting to argue with the very deity they supposedly held in quite high esteem.

And let's not forget the Sunshine Dreamer and Ben's special friend, Jennifer. That was very pressing business. That business brought with it some unpleasantness though. Because the contractor that had paid the Bluecoatians (in their previous lives as Warmongerians) to track down and obtain the errant chair that Banana wanted back, had got wind that they were no longer fulfilling that contract, so, given some encouragement by Banana he decided to contract someone to do the job properly...

122

Chapter 122? After all that, you want more!?
I like your thinking, but unfortunately, there is no chapter 122...

You are in luck though, because there are *more books* in the Ben and Thom trilogy, five and counting! Look for them and ye will find 'em!

There is also a Ben and Thom's Universe Facebook group, drop in, look around and let us know what you thought of this book. We'd love to have you over! There may be short stories waiting for you there...!

About the Author

Jeddy McClownFace is the author of six Ben and Thom novels and under his pen name, Jed Cope, he has written a further three books. So far...

Charismatic, enigmatic and pneumatic, having retired from a successful career as a multiple F1 champion, dragon tamer and tech billionaire, he has left the workshop where he is constantly creating updates to his top secret begonias to do what he does best. Make things up.

You can connect with me on:

f http://www.facebook.com/groups/benandthombooks

Also by Jed Cope

Four more Ben and Thom adventures, written by Jeddy McClownFace from the increasingly inaccurate trilogy:
   Are Bunnies Electric?
   Smell My Cheese!
   Death and Taxis
   Oh Ben and Thom Where Art Thou?

A children's Ben and Thom book also by Jeddy McClown-Face:
   If Only... The Adventures of an Intergalactic Chair

And three penned under the name Jed Cope:
   The Entrepreneurs' Club
   Two for the Show
   The Pipe

He may have written more by the time you've read this...!

Printed in Great Britain
by Amazon